PRAISE FOR J

'Whatever you do, don't read this in the dark, or on your own . . .'
—Cara Hunter, author of *Close to Home*

'One of the most exciting, original thriller writers out there. I never miss one of his books'
—Simon Kernick

'Gripping from the start and full of surprises, this kept us up long after lights out'
—Isabelle Broom, *Heat*

'A compelling dark read that gets you thinking'
—*The Sun*

'Really clever concept and some great characters and twists. It's a real joy to read something totally original, smart and thought-provoking'
—Peter James, author of the Roy Grace series

'Wonderful concept, ridiculously entertaining . . . an absolute pleasure, the malevolence and impishness of a young Roald Dahl'
—T. A. Cotterell, author of *What Alice Knew*

'Fantastic . . . I can't remember the last time I was simultaneously this entertained and this disturbed'
—Hollie Overton, *Sunday Times* bestselling author of *Baby Doll*

'This will have you gripped'
—*Woman's Own*

HER

LAST

MOVE

ALSO BY JOHN MARRS

The One
When You Disappeared
Welcome to Wherever You Are
The Good Samaritan

HER LAST MOVE

JOHN MARRS

THOMAS & MERCER

Published by Thomas & Mercer, Seattle

www.apub.com

Amazon, the Amazon logo, and Thomas & Mercer are trademarks of Amazon.com, Inc., or its affiliates.

ISBN-13: 9781503948020
ISBN-10: 1503948021

Cover design by Tom Sanderson

Printed in the United States of America

For my dad, Charlie Marrs, Number 574

No man chooses evil because it is evil; he only mistakes
it for happiness, the good he seeks.

Mary Wollstonecraft

PROLOGUE

He craned his neck to look inside the tunnel's pitch-black entrance. He wasn't sure what he expected to see in the dark, but he narrowed his eyes regardless.

Next, he turned his head to look around the tube station platform. Floor-to-ceiling rectangular posters pasted on to the arched walls advertised exotic holidays on white sandy beaches. Another offered mattresses that promised to give him the best sleep of his life. He was so high on adrenaline that sleep was the last thing on his mind.

The clock on the overhead gantry told him the next tube would arrive in four minutes. It felt like a long time to be in an enclosed space, especially one that was crammed with so many people and so deep underground. His mouth was already parched and his skin began to prickle, so he put into practice the lessons he'd learned in the meditation classes he'd taken at a mindfulness centre in North London. The six-week course had cost him a small fortune, but it helped to prevent his muddled brain from thinking about everything at once and focus on the detail instead. It had also given him the tools to keep a lid on the pressure cooker of anger that was always so close to boiling over.

Hidden inside the binding strapped to his chest, his right hand was becoming numb. He wanted to remove it and stretch his fingers. It was unlikely anyone would notice what he was concealing; there were too many commuters minding their own business. But he had come this far without taking any unnecessary risks; he wasn't about to start taking them now.

According to Transport for London's website, engineers were working on routine track maintenance further along the District Line. As a result, there were fewer trains but the same number of passengers, making platforms busier than usual. He estimated commuters were five deep and spread out all the way along the platform. He'd overheard staff asking their ground-level colleagues through walkie-talkies to limit the numbers entering until the next tube arrived and carried away those already queuing. He would use the crowds to his advantage.

Glancing from side to side and satisfied he'd successfully blended in, his eyes returned to the man in front of him, the one he had followed from his house that afternoon. He was standing so near to Stefan Dumitru that he could feel the heat radiating from the man's sizable body. They had been in close proximity many times over the past few months, but never like this. Not even when he'd been inside Dumitru's home.

It was only now, while standing a hair's breadth away, that he could fully comprehend just how broad and muscular Dumitru was. He was at least sixteen, perhaps seventeen stone in weight, around six feet, four inches tall, and might well have been carved from granite. A mass of colourful tattoos began at his knuckles and crept up his arm, like ivy wrapping itself around a thick branch, until they reached his neck, stopping just shy of his square jaw. There would be no margin for error with this giant of a man, he thought. He would need to hit the angle and the timing perfectly for his plan to be successful.

Dumitru appeared restless, shuffling from foot to foot. Each time he moved his neck, the muscles across his shoulders rippled like the surface of a pond being skimmed by pebbles.

He looked towards the gantry again. The large yellow pixels spelled out three minutes remaining. With his free hand, he removed a tissue from his pocket and dabbed carefully at the beads of sweat forming under his hairline. He wasn't sure if it was the heatwave, claustrophobia or nervous anticipation that was making his skin burn now.

For much of the afternoon, he and Dumitru had never been more than a few metres apart. Even when Dumitru was shut away behind the front door of his two-storey Victorian home, his follower was waiting in a car outside, watching. The building had been converted and divided into two rental units. The watcher was struck by its poor maintenance. There was a long, vertical crack in the second-storey window, and the postage-stamp-sized front garden was littered with cigarette butts and empty cans of cheap lager.

While Dumitru wasn't house-proud, you could set your watch by him. At 5.20 p.m. promptly each afternoon, he'd slam the front door behind him. And, dressed in the same light, faded jeans and a T-shirt bearing the pinkish-white stains of the walls he plastered, he'd begin a brisk ten-minute walk to the tube. If he was downwind of Dumitru, sometimes he picked up a whiff of cheap aftershave or deodorant, both of which failed to mask the musky body odour too deeply imbedded in the fabric of his top to be washed out.

He'd learned Dumitru was employed to work on a million-pound renovation project in the heart of West London's Notting Hill. The home belonged to a former Britpop star, and according to the planning application he'd found, two new, super-sized basements had been excavated under an existing one to create an iceberg home. Now, in its final stages, Dumitru worked throughout the night – plastering, polishing and priming the walls.

Dumitru was both a stickler for time and a creature of habit, choosing the same position on the platform by the tunnel's entrance so that he could travel in the last carriage. His bulky frame and arrogant attitude led him to either push his way to the front or use his bulk and

3

menacing stare to intimidate commuters into parting like the Red Sea when they caught sight of him.

Two minutes, the gantry indicated, and his heart began to race.

He took a deep breath and caught another sour whiff of the man's body odour. The bitter taste lingered in the back of his throat. He felt more sweat trickling from between his shoulder blades, down his spine and stopping at the waistband of his underwear.

Suddenly Dumitru took a step back, perhaps sensing he was too close to the platform edge.

'That's my foot, idiot,' a man standing behind and a little to the left of him snapped.

Dumitru turned his head to glare at him, assuming the impact of his stature would be enough to end the confrontation. 'You call me idiot?' he replied in broken English.

But the injured party wasn't ready to back down. 'Yeah. Fuck off back home,' he sneered. Although the second man had brawn, he was considerably shorter than his counterpart. However, if either man believed their posturing might lead to a physical altercation, they'd have struggled. There was not enough room on the crowded platform to swing either a cat or a punch. Still, they continued.

'What did you say?' asked Dumitru as the clock counted down from two minutes to one. When the man didn't reply, Dumitru turned his head back and muttered in his native tongue.

Watching on, concerned, nerves threatened to take control of the man with Dumitru set in his sights. His legs began to tremble involuntarily, so he closed his eyes tightly and counted slowly from five down to one. It was now or never.

He removed his concealed right hand and held it low and out of sight. Then, with all his strength, he jabbed a syringe into Dumitru's left buttock, pushing the plunger in before removing it, all in a little over a second.

'*La dracu!*' yelled Dumitru, and heads turned towards him. He grabbed his buttock and rotated his whole body to square up to his assumed assailant, pushing other commuters into one another. Concern spread across the shorter man's face as he took in the size of his opponent.

'What you do to me?' Dumitru bellowed, to the other's confusion.

'What are you talking about?' came the response.

Then Dumitru pulled his arm back, ready to strike with his fist.

His actual assailant still had the needle hidden in the palm of his hand when the white headlights of the train in the far reaches of the tunnel caught his eye. He desperately hoped he'd got his calculations right. And when he saw that Dumitru was hesitating and had yet to lash out, he had his answer.

First, the man's deep-set eyes began to flicker, then his raised arm fell limply to his side. His head was the next to droop forward before he snapped it upright. As he felt himself begin to topple backwards, he moved his legs to try to steady himself. However, it had the opposite effect and propelled him even further in reverse.

The first Dumitru knew of the thirty-miles-per-hour approaching train wasn't the bright lights or the shrieking of metal against metal as the wheels clattered along the track. It was the impact of the driver's cabin colliding with his shoulder, pushing him forward and then dragging him under and into darkness. The train screeched to a halt, throwing the commuters inside around like rag dolls.

The man responsible for ending Stefan Dumitru's life remained frozen to the spot, and again used his mindfulness training to absorb everything from the moment. The sounds of piercing screams ripping through the air and high heels against concrete clattering up the staircase, the stench of rubber on hastily applied brakes – he drew from it all. He watched in awe as the public backed away, desperate to escape the stench of death before it attached to their clothes. He witnessed others run to Dumitru's aid, dropping to their hands and knees to look under the train for signs of life. There would be none. He was sure of that.

His teeth clamped down on the insides of his cheeks, biting hard to prevent his mouth from breaking into a victorious grin.

A rapidly deployed swarm of TfL staff suddenly appeared and fanned out, guiding him and those remaining towards the exit. Outside, staff pointed commuters in the direction of alternative tube lines and bus routes, but he knew where he was going next. First, he crossed the road, and then he gathered himself, closing his eyes and allowing the sun to catch his face while he took deep, cleansing breaths.

Dumitru was the first person he had ever killed. And while he wanted to replay each second of it over and over again while it was still fresh, he didn't have the luxury of time. Because in less than ninety minutes, he would be embarking upon his second murder.

CHAPTER 1

It wasn't the shrill noise of the tube train's brakes that first caught Becca's attention, it was the raised voices and screams.

She looked up from the game she was playing on her phone and turned towards the opposite end of the platform to see where the noise was coming from. A train was coming to a sudden halt, less than a quarter of the way along.

She yanked her in-ear headphones out, letting them drop to her shoulders, and watched as a tide of commuters pushed back from the edge of the platform.

Her instinct was to force her way through the throng of people and discover the cause of the commotion. But there were too many bodies holding her in place or pushing her backwards as they strived to reach the exit behind where she was standing. One man clipped her with his shoulder and pushed her head into the wall, forcing her jaw shut, and she nipped her tongue with her front teeth. She cursed him under her breath.

Trains didn't stop abruptly midway into a platform without good reason. The city had been no stranger to attacks in recent years, including some targeting the Underground. Every Londoner who relied on public transport knew they were a potential sitting duck, but took the risk regardless. Becca ran through the list of potential causes of the panic, but because of the lack of hysteria and the fact it appeared to be contained to one small area, she ruled out terrorism.

Instead, she assumed someone must have fallen on to the tracks. She remained standing where she was, and watched as Transport for London staff wearing red tabards over their blue uniforms jostled through the flow of people and towards the scene of the accident. Then she took her opportunity and followed the cleared path behind them.

She watched as some commuters to her right took the stairs two at a time to quickly exit the station. Those who remained ahead of her squinted at the base of the carriage, while others crouched and appeared to be shouting at something. Several ghouls had their mobile phones pointed towards it.

'Ladies and gentleman,' came a deep, male voice across the internal communications system. 'Owing to a passenger incident, this train will not be moving and we ask you to vacate the platform safely and as quickly as possible. Staff will be on hand to direct you towards the exit.'

Ahead, Becca spotted the driver leave his cabin and make his way along the platform, his head bobbing out of sight as he bent to look under the second carriage. When he reappeared, he held his hands over his face and Becca's suspicions were confirmed.

'Sorry, you can't go this way . . .' began a young woman in a TfL uniform. Becca flashed her police warrant card.

'Detective Sergeant Becca Vincent,' she said, and made for a group hunched around a carriage.

'What happened?' she asked, displaying her badge again.

'One under,' a staff member wearing a blue turban replied. His name badge read *Dev*.

'Someone's fallen under the train?'

He nodded. 'Soon as it happened, the driver contacted the line controller, who informed the station supervisor to evacuate.'

'Traction current off,' came a female voice from further along the platform. Several of her colleagues repeated it until everyone present was aware.

Becca stepped back a few paces to look under the train, but the victim was out of sight. All she spotted was a white upside-down trainer.

'Does it look like suicide?' she asked.

'Nobody saw him jump and someone said he'd been arguing with another man shortly before he was hit.'

'Are the witnesses still here?' she asked.

'No, I think they've gone.'

'Was the platform overcrowded? It looked busy to me.'

'We don't allow it to get overcrowded,' he replied defensively. 'There's a team upstairs who ensure numbers coming in at peak times are staggered.'

'Do people fall under trains very often?'

'Unfortunately so. There's one almost every day right across the network.'

Becca's attention was diverted towards a staff member lowering herself on to the tracks, and then crawling on her belly under the front of the train. She saw the back of a paramedic in a green uniform following behind.

'What are they doing?'

'Sometimes fallers roll into suicide pits – that's not what they were built for, they were dug to drain water away, but as a by-product they've also cut the number of deaths. But if we can't hear someone shout or scream for help, we'll need to go under to see if they're alive, even if it's just to reassure them an ambulance is on the way. I've known colleagues to lie across injured people to keep them from thrashing around while the current is turned back on and a carriage is moved.'

'I had no idea,' she replied.

'Not many people realise the lengths we go to. They're quite happy to call us all the names under the sun if a train's late though.'

They waited in silence, watching as the woman and paramedic disappeared completely. Becca's attention drifted towards the driver. He sat on the platform staircase, steam rising from a polystyrene cup he'd been given. He clenched it with both hands, but as a colleague tried to usher him away, he pulled his arm back, unable to tear himself from the gruesome scene. Becca felt for him. It was unlikely he could have done anything to avoid the collision, but she wagered that the guilt would be hard for him to shake. Guilt was something she had learned to live with. She hoped the driver could too.

Suddenly the sight of the female staff member emerging from beneath the train interrupted the uneasy quiet.

'He's gone,' she said, shaking her head and dusting black dirt from her hair and clothing. 'Almost decapitated by the looks of it. It ain't pleasant.'

A handful of figures identifying themselves as British Transport Police, along with two paramedics carrying a stretcher, made their way along the platform. One placed a comforting hand on the driver's shoulder and Becca suspected he'd be asked to take a mandatory drink-and-drugs test to clear him of any wrongdoing.

By the time she identified herself to a transport police officer and offered them the few facts she knew, the train had reversed along the tracks and the body been lifted on to the platform. Despite Becca's experience at many a bloody and fatal incident, she still wanted to avert her eyes. But a glint of something catching the overhead lights also caught her attention. She took a closer look and spotted the victim's shoulder and tattooed arm. He wore a chunky silver ring on his index finger. The tattoo extended to his hand and knuckles.

The design appeared to be devil-like, only with skin made of wood and horns protruding from white, wavy hair. Its face and eyes were red, and next to it was a yellow rose, the tips of its petals reaching down to his fingers.

His hand had gone back on itself, his wrist bone completely snapped. Becca shuddered at the thought of dying in such a violent, public way. More in hope than expectation, when her time came she wanted to fall asleep in the comfort of her own bed and just fail to wake up in the morning.

But if her job and her family life had taught her just one thing, it was that people very rarely got the end they wished for – or deserved.

CHAPTER 2

It wasn't unusual for Joe Russell to find the bus already packed to capacity by the time it arrived at his stop.

He squeezed his way on board, tapped his police-issue Oyster card on the electronic reader and stood in the aisle with one hand grasping an overhead strap. With the other, he chose a Spotify playlist he'd compiled of Ibiza dance classics, as the bus pulled away. A signal failure six stops into his tube journey meant he'd been forced to catch a bus. And two miles later, with the April sun glaring through the windows and directly on to his face, he was beginning to regret his decision not to wait for an emptier one. The air conditioning couldn't curtail the heat generated by sixty bodies on the lower deck of the Routemaster. As a result, he felt like a sardine crammed into a tin with the lid peeled back and left under a sunbed.

Strands of Joe's slicked-back, dark brown hair began to wilt and spring forward. He brushed them back into place but he was fighting a losing battle. In his headphones, a woman with a rich, soul singer's voice belted out a song over a thick electronic beat. He drummed his fingers against his thigh and hummed along to himself.

There were no official working hours to adhere to in his department, but it was accepted that the more of your own time you were willing to sacrifice, the greater your chances were of being recognised. Not that the powers that be ever admitted that their employees were expected to constantly go beyond the call of duty. But government austerity measures and personnel cutbacks had slashed numbers in the Metropolitan Police, so there was much reliance on the goodwill of staff.

Joe preferred to leave the office an hour or so after everyone else. The extra time gave him the opportunity to concentrate on some of his own, personal work. If any of his colleagues were lingering, he'd shut down various windows on his monitor rather than risk having them inquire as to what he was doing. An explanation would take too long and he preferred not to lie to the team he'd grown close to.

Joe didn't know how many of them – if any – were aware of his background. He hadn't brought up the subject, even with those he trusted the most. *Everyone has their secrets*, he reasoned.

The bus suddenly halted near High Holborn. Joe tilted his head and found a gap between the other passengers sharing the aisle, to see through the windscreen. He could just about make out a set of temporary traffic lights forty metres ahead. Half a dozen men in orange hi-vis jackets and chunky earmuffs operated pneumatic drills, digging up chunks of the road. Joe rolled his eyes. It wasn't going to be the easy journey home he'd hoped for.

Suddenly, a face caught his attention. It belonged to a man standing outside on a pedestrian island between the two lanes of traffic, waiting for a red light to turn green. Joe's eyebrows knitted and he squinted. He was sure he'd seen the man before, but was positive that it hadn't been in person. It must have been in a video or a photograph. However, he was unable to place where or why.

Possessing a photographic memory that never, ever forgot a face was both a blessing and a burden. For at least half his working week, Joe's job was to examine and memorise unfamiliar faces and mentally file their features away in his head. Then if they reappeared in person or were suspects in other crimes, he would, with luck, join the dots and identify them. And this was one person he was sure he'd stored some time back.

As the bus remained stationary he kept his eye on the suspect, unwilling to lose him until he could recall why he was so familiar. His gut instinct was that, because the man was memorable, he had likely done something illegal. But on occasion, familiar strangers turned out to be perfectly innocuous, like someone who'd served him in a shop a decade ago or who'd gone to the same school.

Joe's process of recollection differed from that of his colleagues. It was as if shutting his eyes tightly made his brain move faster. Once everything surrounding him had been replaced by darkness, barely two seconds passed before he had a name.

Alistair Brown. And he recalled why the man was wanted by the police.

Joe had to act fast. He pushed past everyone in the aisle with polite apologies until he reached the front of the bus.

'I need to get off,' he told the driver, his eyes still on the man outside.

'Not allowed, my friend,' she replied, safely ensconced behind her Perspex partition. 'Health and safety don't allow it.'

He flashed her his warrant card. 'Met,' he said, and the driver nodded.

'Have a nice day, officer,' she replied with a hint of sarcasm. The air in the bus's hydraulic system made a whooshing sound as the door opened.

Joe leaped out and hurried to the spot where he'd seen Brown. The man was no longer there. He looked in all directions until he saw his suspect had crossed the road and was walking towards a row of shops. So Joe began his pursuit.

If his memory served him correctly – and it usually did – Brown had been one of a group of white men accused of gang-raping an Asian teenage girl. They'd almost beaten her to death and then dumped her body by a canal in Camden four years earlier. By some miracle she had survived. Brown's four friends had been found guilty at trial and sentenced to eight years apiece. But Brown had evaded arrest, and despite a warrant being issued, he'd vanished. The photographs Joe remembered seeing him in had been culled from Brown's now-defunct Facebook profile.

Back then, his light brown hair had been crew-cut short, his face was clean-shaven and his frame skinny. This new version of Alistair Brown wore his hair dark and shoulder length. He had stubble, wore aviator-style sunglasses and had bulked up considerably. It was quite the transformation, but Joe had recognised others with even more radically altered appearances. However, before he called for backup – and for his own peace of mind – he had to get closer.

Brown crossed another junction and was making his way in the direction of Tottenham Court Road. He carried a rucksack over his shoulders, wore chunky on-ear headphones and was smartly dressed, as if he were just another man on his way home from work and not a suspected rapist lying low. Joe assumed he was now going by a different identity.

Joe remained around eight to ten metres behind his mark, until Brown reached a pedestrian crossing next to a flower seller's stand. Now they were almost shoulder to shoulder. As Brown texted on his mobile phone, Joe took the opportunity to turn his head and give him the once-over, then quickly looked away so as not to arouse suspicion. He would stake his career on having correctly identified him.

He allowed Brown to get further up the road before removing his own phone and calling his station's control room. While he might not be on duty, he could still legally arrest the suspect. But without equipment or backup, doing so wasn't an easy option.

When the call was answered, Joe identified who he was and who he'd been surveilling, to double-check whether Brown was still a wanted man. And once confirmed, Joe gave his location and requested assistance. In the background, he heard control dispatching the nearest available officers.

He was unsure what he'd done to arouse suspicion in his mark, but the self-preservation that had kept Brown out of sight for so long must have warned him that something was awry. He tore up the road without warning. 'Shit,' said Joe out loud and began to run after him, informing control of his new direction. Brown darted across four lanes of heavy traffic and weaved in and out of cars as Joe followed. Horns were blown at both men and Joe narrowly avoided being hit by a moped that skidded to a halt.

Brown took a sharp left and ran hell for leather down Charing Cross Road in the direction of Leicester Square. He was undoubtedly fit and was gaining a longer lead, while Joe was already breaking into a thick sweat. He needed to think fast and put himself in Brown's shoes. *Where would I go next if I was being pursued?* He assumed Brown was counting on the Leicester Square area being crammed with early-evening tourists and commuters. Brown was going to reach them before Joe and could easily lose himself in the throng.

He took a chance that Brown wouldn't want to risk using the Underground and becoming caught up at the ticket barriers of one of central London's busiest stations. If he were planning to stick to the roads and the crowds, Piccadilly Circus would be the next obvious location. From there, if Brown thought he had outrun his pursuer, he might make his way down to Lower Regent Street, then The Mall and finally the vast greenery of St James's Park.

It was a risk, but it was one Joe was going to take. With one hand trying to stop his satchel from slipping off his shoulder and the other holding his phone clamped to his ear, he breathlessly relayed his prediction to control and suggested where to direct backup. Then he left Charing Cross Road and turned a sharp right on to Shaftesbury Avenue, passing Soho and Chinatown and running all the way down the road until he saw the memorial fountain at Piccadilly Circus. If he'd known when leaving the office earlier that he'd be involved in a pursuit, he'd have worn the Nikes he kept under his desk and not clunky brogues.

Joe's calf and thigh muscles felt as if they were being stabbed by sharp, hot needles and his lungs were on fire. But he couldn't give up now. Instead, he kept his pace, his eyes scanning every person ahead of him, praying that his decision to take a diversion had been the right one.

Suddenly, further ahead, he spotted the only other figure running. At the same moment, Brown looked over his shoulder and, apparently sure he wasn't being followed, his pace slowed slightly as he made his way on to Lower Regent Street.

Just thirty metres separated them once Brown slowed down to a jog, and, coming in at a different angle, Joe took advantage of the suspect's complacency by using every ounce of energy left in his reserve tanks to reach him.

The first Brown realised he was still being pursued was when he heard the noise of Joe's leather-soled shoes smacking against the pavement. He turned quickly to find Joe in mid-air before being grabbed by the waist and pulled to the ground, where they both ended up in a tangled heap of limbs.

'Alistair Brown,' Joe panted, 'I'm arresting you . . .' His sentence stalled as he fought the urge to be sick.

At a few years younger than Joe, Brown had more strength left in him than the detective. So all Joe could do was keep his arms and legs wrapped around his suspect and hold on for dear life. Brown deliberately pushed his head backwards and caught Joe clean on the bridge of his nose. Joe heard it crack and felt a searing pain in the centre of his face and head. He yelled as blood trickled on to his lips and into his panting mouth. Still Joe continued to restrain Brown, and retaliated with a crafty elbow into Brown's Adam's apple that made him gasp for air.

Brown continued to thrash around like a fish in a net but was unable to escape. Then, just as Joe thought he couldn't hold on any longer, two uniformed officers appeared from nowhere. They grabbed Brown and dragged him to his feet, while Joe turned to his side and tried to catch his breath, wiping away blood from his mouth and chin.

'Alistair Brown, I'm arresting you on suspicion of rape,' he wheezed. 'You do not have to say anything but it may harm your defence if you do not mention . . .' He paused to cough and brought up a mouthful of vomit. He grimaced as he swallowed it back down again. ' . . . when questioned, something which you later rely on in court,' he continued. 'Anything you do say may be given in evidence.'

He didn't listen to Brown's protests or even watch as the man was handcuffed. Instead, he rose slowly to his feet, staggered towards the nearby metal railings, propped himself up against them and was sick over the pavement.

CHAPTER 3

DS Becca Vincent swiped the access card hanging from her neck through the wall-mounted reader and opened the double doors to the Metropolitan Police's Westminster-based Criminal Investigations Department.

Inside a less than spacious room were fifteen gunmetal-grey desks that hadn't been updated since the 1990s and were juxtaposed by modern, ergonomic chairs. On each desk were filing trays, some stacked six or seven high, like plastic stalagmites. In an ever-changing world with Clouds and invisible filing cabinets, Becca found there was something strangely comforting about being surrounded by old-fashioned paperwork. But she was less keen on the burgundy carpet tiles that seemed to stick to the soles of her shoes as she moved.

The CID chief's campaign to replace the computers – or at the very least, give them more regular software updates – had fallen on ears deafened by budget cuts. As a result, bulky tower cases reduced the legroom under each desk.

Twenty-four CID officers were based in this space, close to the former premises of New Scotland Yard before its move to Victoria Embankment. But the nature of the job meant they weren't always office-bound. Also, they were very rarely in attendance at the same time of day, so they shared their workstations. All except for Becca. Since joining the force eight years earlier, she'd grown used to keeping everything she needed to do her job within arm's reach. To her, it showed common sense and organisation. To everyone else, her desk was a mountain of mess that few wanted to share.

Try as she might, she was rarely the first person to reach work on a morning. Circumstances beyond her control, be they public transport or personal, often conspired against her and she'd frequently appear later than she'd intended. Today was the exception – the clock on the wall read 7.38 a.m. However, two colleagues were already there.

'What are you doing here so early?' she asked DI Nikhat Odedra. She noted the stubble on his usually clean-shaven cheeks, and his creased shirt and tie. The whites of his eyes that were highlighted by his dark complexion were pink, like he'd not slept. 'Have you just done the walk of shame straight from some poor girl's house to the office?'

'No such luck,' he replied, and ran his fingers through his short, spiky hair. 'I've been working all night. A body was found in a flat in Mile End just after ten and I was the DI on call. Because of other investigations, the murder team are assuming overall command but requested the borough team help.'

'What happened?'

'Neighbours thought the house had been broken into as the door had been left ajar for hours. A couple of community support officers were dispatched and found the body of a man inside.'

Becca was quietly glad she hadn't got the call to attend at that time of night. She was already treading on thin ice at home.

On a personal level, she liked Nikhat. He was witty and a team player and treated her with respect. But professionally, she was quietly envious of his accomplishments. He was still only twenty-seven and had sailed through his exams to rise up the ranks. Already, he was a position above her, and it'd taken him less time to get there. When she was in his presence, she couldn't help but wonder – if the cards had been dealt differently, she might not have been overlooked for promotion in favour of the new breed of high fliers and business graduates within the organisation. Maybe then she could have climbed another rung up the career ladder. Instead, she remained just below mid-table, watching as those who had joined the force after her moved beyond her reach with increasing regularity.

'What happened to the victim?' she asked.

'Well,' Nikhat replied, 'this is where it gets really interesting. He was found in his lounge with his hands, arms and legs tied together with thick tape and a towel over his face. He was tied to a weightlifting bench, his clothes were soaking wet, and by the looks of it, he'd been waterboarded.'

'Waterboarded?' Becca repeated. 'Isn't that how they torture prisoners in Guantanamo Bay? Orange jumpsuits and tied to planks of wood or something?'

Nikhat nodded and pointed towards his computer monitor. It contained images of hooded men lying at angles on the floor, with buckets of water being poured over their faces.

Becca read aloud. '"Waterboarding involves a liquid being poured over a cloth draped across a person's face – especially the mouth and nose – so it feels like they are drowning on dry land. It can cause an agonising death or can be repeated over and over again."' She screwed up her face. 'That's sadistic.'

'And get this, he wasn't killed with water, it was alcohol. And the killer wasn't in a hurry either, because we found seven empty bottles of vodka at the scene, so he must have taken his time.'

'It definitely sounds premeditated – and personal, too, since he wanted the victim to suffer. Any suspects in the frame yet?'

'No, we're trying to find out more about the victim first.'

'Have you got the photos back from forensics?'

'I was just about to start looking through them.'

As Nikhat clicked on his computer's email icon, Becca wheeled a chair towards his desk and studied the photos as they filled his screen. The first thing she noticed was that the victim's face appeared red and sore, like he'd been out in the sun too long. His eyes were open and blood vessels had burst in both. Across his cheeks were crimson- and scarlet-coloured, spidery veins. Behind his head, his dark hair was matted, and a rag remained in his mouth. He had tribal-style tattoos on both sides of a slim neck. They stopped just shy of his jaw but crawled down across his collarbone. He wore a stained vest, a pair of tracksuit bottoms and no socks or shoes. Suddenly, Becca caught a glimpse of something familiar.

'Are there any close-ups of his hands?' she asked. Nikhat scrolled through a selection of thumbnail-sized photos until he found two. 'I recognise that tattoo,' Becca said, looking at the reds, yellows and whites coming from the sinister devil design stretched out across the back of the victim's right hand. 'I saw exactly the same one last night. Some poor sod fell in front of a tube and he had an identical tattoo – and on the same hand.'

'Where did your guy live?'

'The transport police took over, but let me check.'

Two telephone calls later, she had her answer. 'Flat 2, 57 Dunslop—'

'Road, Mile End, E14 . . .' interrupted Nikhat.

'6NN,' they finished together.

Butterflies began to rise inside Becca's stomach. It was a feeling she only experienced when the potential for an interesting case made itself known. The glint in Nikhat's eyes mirrored her own.

'Two men living at the same address, with the same tattoo design on their hands, are both found dead hours apart but in different ways,' she summarised. 'This is far too unlikely to be a coincidence.'

'There's definitely one murder here, but maybe your guy killed mine, couldn't handle the guilt, then left the house and threw himself under the tube?'

'Mine's time of death was around 5.40 p.m. – what was yours?' Becca asked.

'He wore one of those activity trackers. The software showed erratic heart measurements in the lead-up to his death and then it suddenly stopped, suggesting he died around 7.50 p.m. But we don't have the results of the post-mortem yet.'

'That rubbishes murder-suicide then. Could one person have killed two people like that in quick succession, or are we looking at a pair of killers, or more?'

'It's possible it could have been two. One person would need to be highly organised.'

'One of the tube staff told me my man was overheard having an altercation on the platform with another guy shortly before he died.' Becca tried to play it cool but she was anxious to participate in the investigation. 'Do you have anyone working on this with you?'

'The PCSOs who found the body are doing door-to-door inquiries, and your mate Bryan Thompson is out there now trying to get an ID on my victim's body. You'll have to clear it with Webster though. She's assumed control.'

That might prove a challenge, thought Becca. There was no sisterly code when it came to Chief Superintendent Caroline Webster. She was firm but fair and professed to treat everyone equally, but Becca wasn't convinced. When it came to big cases, Becca often felt sidelined, like a hyena waiting for the lions to finish tearing apart a carcass so she could mop up their scraps. It frustrated the hell out of her.

But things would change only if she was proactive and fought her corner. And suddenly she was consumed by the need to make her mark. She didn't just want to work on this case, she absolutely had to be a part of it, and not just as support staff or carrying out admin work. She was going to prove to herself and those around her that she was every bit as good a detective as they were. The investigation had fallen into her lap, something that never happened.

And a feeling in her gut told her it had the potential to change everything.

CHAPTER 4

'Hello? Who is this?'

He used a tone that suggested he was unfamiliar with the caller's number. But the ringtone and photograph he'd assigned to her digits ensured he could recognise her call immediately.

'You know who it is,' she replied wearily.

'And you would be . . . ?' he teased.

His eyes scanned his colleagues in the open-plan office, then drifted towards the high street outside.

'It's your girlfriend, Zoe.'

'Can you narrow it down a bit? Which Zoe?'

'Why do you always pretend you have no idea who it is and then say that?' she moaned. 'It's becoming tiresome.'

'I like to keep you on your toes. I can't have you assuming you're the sole priority in my life.'

He was telling the truth about the role she played in his world, but he delivered it in such a way that she believed he was kidding.

Margaret, his manager, sat hunched over a celebrity magazine in the corner of the room, tucking into her second consecutive Twix bar and pretending not to listen in on his conversation. He allowed her to believe there was very little he did in that office which escaped her.

'Are you still coming around tonight, because I might be able to get away from work a bit earlier,' Zoe continued. 'Anna May owes me a couple of hours after I covered for her hangover last week.'

He pretended to leaf through his diary, but rustled the pages of the thick property section of the *Evening Standard* newspaper instead.

'Yes, I think I can do that.'

'Well, don't sound too eager.'

'I have a couple of after-hours appointments, so I'll make my way to yours when I'm done. Do you want me to bring takeout?'

'A Nando's chicken burger with medium sauce and sweet potato fries would be perfect. How did last night go, by the way?'

'Last night?' he replied, unsure what she was referring to. Then, for a split second, he panicked that she'd known all along where he was going and what he was doing. But that was impossible, he reasoned. You don't know in advance that your boyfriend is going to murder two people, then casually slip it into the conversation.

'Your new kitchen?' she continued. 'The appointment?'

'Ah yes,' he said. 'It's been a busy day and my mind went blank.'

He recalled how he'd informed her of his consultation with an interior designer from a kitchen installation company he was contracting. She was coming round to show him her final ideas. It was the latest project in an extensive line of renovation work for his apartment – an apartment that didn't exist. In truth, he'd spent much of the night on an adrenaline high, watching from a distance as the police and a forensics team went about their business in the house where he'd killed his second victim of the day.

'Yes, it went really well,' he said. 'I mentioned I wanted to swap the work surfaces from granite to Corian and change the steel sink for the porcelain option.'

'And am I ever going to actually get to see this mystery mega-flat of yours? We've been together for four months and I'm still waiting for an invitation.'

Four months, he thought, and bristled. *Why ever did I let it get this far?*

'Do you really want to be staying over at what is essentially a building site, with no running water and everything caked in dust?' he asked.

'Probably not, no.'

'As soon as it's in a half-decent state, you can spend as much time as you like there.'

'I'm going to hold you to that. Right, I should get back to work. I'll see you later. And be warned – you won't be getting much sleep tonight.'

When he realised he was absent-mindedly smiling, he stopped and reminded himself what Zoe really was to him. He logged out of his computer and called over to his manager. 'I'm going out to an appointment in Mile End. I'll be back mid-afternoon.'

'Okay,' Margaret replied. As he rose to his feet, her eyes scanned him from head to toe. The corners of her mouth rose and he recognised what she was hinting at. Every blind eye she turned to his disappearing acts came with a price attached. He would pay her back later.

He grabbed his keys, mobile phone, briefcase and suit jacket, but thought better of taking the latter. The office was comfortably air-conditioned – where he was heading would be quite the opposite.

CHAPTER 5

The more time Becca spent living and working in the capital, the more reasons she found to become frustrated by it.

They were the same irritations all Londoners complained about, like the extortionate price of properties and the volume of tourists slowing down even the shortest of walks. Now she'd found another reason to be irked – it was often impossible to navigate. Many owners of buildings didn't think to attach numbers to their properties or homes. Sometimes they affixed names, but often you could walk fifty metres before finding a number attached to a door or a wall, and then have to go back on yourself. It didn't help her mood that where she was going was likely to be a complete waste of her time.

Becca kept inside the shadows of the buildings along Finsbury Park, trying to escape the force of the sun's heat bouncing off the pavements. It was day five of an oppressive heatwave, and she was sick of it already. She was constantly slathering her fair skin in sunscreen; her hair felt dry and brittle and was begging for a decent conditioner. And a lack of sleep was making her irritable.

First thing that morning after comparing notes, she had requested to join DI Nikhat Odedra's inquiry into the tube and waterboarding deaths, despite the first victim not having been determined as murdered yet. The decision on who should be assigned to the case lay with Chief Superintendent Caroline Webster, and, as Becca had predicted, she'd been hesitant. Webster's office in CID was wall-to-wall glass and it reminded Becca of a large, Perspex cube. Webster sat behind an orderly desk containing two monitors, two phones and a keyboard, all neatly arranged in front of her. The room was also large enough to house eight chairs and a whiteboard, all of which were so pristine, they looked as if they had never been used. Becca wondered if Webster's home was as sterile.

'What stage are you at with the assaults around Old Billingsgate Market?' Webster had asked.

'Arrests have been made and the Crown Prosecution Service is reviewing the evidence. Sue Jenkins worked with me on it, so she can mop up anything else that comes along.'

'Has anyone actually been charged yet?'

'No. They're currently on police bail.' Webster's thin lips pursed as she stared at Becca, her face a picture of scepticism. However, Becca was determined not to let the opportunity slip through her fingers without putting up a fight. 'Look, ma'am, I really need this,' she said. 'I was the one to spot the link between the body under the train and the waterboard victim. It's been such a long time since I've been able to really sink my teeth into something. Let me show you what I'm capable of. I feel like I've got a vested interest in this one. Just give me a few days, and if you're not happy with my progress, then replace me.'

Webster held her fingers together like a steeple in front of her mouth. 'Okay,' she replied. 'As you know, I'm making Nikhat my senior investigating officer, so follow his lead. But I need you to be absolutely focused, Becca. If you're not, then I can't keep you on this.'

'Thank you,' Becca replied, and tried to contain her smile until she left Webster's office. She rejoined Nikhat and two other male CID colleagues who were gathered around his desk.

'Good timing,' Nikhat directed at her. 'Beccs, can you go to where Transport for London stores its CCTV footage? Get a better look at what happened when your man fell, and go back at least a couple of hours to see if anyone is lurking on the platform longer than necessary or if you spot any familiar faces. Check the entrance and exit footage too.'

'On it,' Becca replied enthusiastically. But quietly, she already felt a little disheartened. On past experience, she found sifting through recordings to be the most painstaking – and achingly boring – aspect of any investigation. Each one had to be viewed frame by frame and could take what felt like an eternity to complete. What Becca really wanted was to be out there at the crime scene of the second victim, taking statements from neighbours and piecing together his movements. Some officers hated house-to-house inquiries, and it was often left to uniforms lower down the ranks to do it. But Becca loved the challenge of trying to find a needle in a haystack.

'Oh,' added Nikhat. 'Top brass sent an email around a few days ago offering up the services of the super-recognisers. Perhaps give them a call, see if anyone's free to assist. Might speed things up.'

'The super-what?' Becca asked.

'Super-recognisers. The nickname for the Visual Images, Identifications and Detections Office. They're detectives with photographic memories for faces. They built up a unit around their abilities to recognise people.'

Becca narrowed her eyes. 'You're winding me up, aren't you?'

'No, they're for real. Sounds like bullshit to me, but what do I know?'

'Do these "super-recognisers" get to wear little superhero outfits too?'

'Ask them,' he replied. 'I'm sure they'll love you for suggesting it.'

'What next?' she muttered, rolling her eyes. 'A Ministry of Magic department?' She went back to her desk and searched the intranet for reassurance such a branch existed.

She turned to DS Bryan Thompson, who sat at a desk behind hers. He had been just as keen as her to be a part of the case. 'Bryan, what do you know about super-recognisers?'

He scratched his chin and shrugged. 'The powers that be stuck them out of the way in a former police building and left them to get on with it. From what I hear, they sit on their arses all day looking at photographs and trying to put faces to crimes, while we do the donkey work of actually going outside and chasing criminals.'

'Sounds about right,' Becca replied. 'It's funny how they manage to find the money to fund dumb ideas like that when the piggy bank is so empty that we're still using Windows 8.'

One telephone call later and Becca was en route. Eventually – and only after checking the postcode on Google Maps, retracing her steps, then twice passing it – she stumbled upon the address. She glared disapprovingly at the doorway, with its flaking painted walls and whiff of stale urine. A silver intercom was fixed to a wall, with four buzzers, none of which were labelled. So she pressed each one until she got an answer.

'Hello,' a male voice said through crackling static.

'Hi,' she replied. 'I'm looking for the VIIDO?'

'And you are?'

'DS Becca Vincent,' she replied. 'Here to see Joe Russell?' She displayed her warrant card to a tiny camera lens and drummed up a half-hearted smile. She usually felt a little nervous going into other departments. This one was going to be a waste of everyone's time.

The door unlocked and she pushed it open, making her way into an empty foyer. It had an art-deco feel to it, with its intricate glass lightshades, the swirling loops of black-metal stair railings, and the dark green marble flooring that hadn't seen a mop and bucket in an age. An 'Out of Order' sign taped to the lift door was faded, suggesting it had been there long enough to be bleached by the sun's rays.

Becca walked three flights up the narrow staircase, and as she became aware of the damp patches growing under her arms, she wished she'd worn a blouse made of a lighter material.

She stopped when she reached a corridor and a closed door. Muffled voices came from behind it. She paused, unsure of what and who would be greeting her inside.

CHAPTER 6

Becca was accustomed to working in messy offices, but this was something else.

As she opened the door, it was as if hundreds of pairs of eyes were coming at her from every square inch of space. Mugshots, CCTV stills and images of faces of all ages and ethnicities covered all four walls. The only spaces left empty were the windows and polystyrene ceiling tiles.

She looked around and counted seven actual people – four male and three female. Some turned from their computer monitors to peer at her, as if visitors were a rarity. It made her feel self-conscious.

Her eyes were directed towards one man in particular, oblivious to her presence and examining his reflection in a pair of mirrored sunglasses. He opened a pack of Band-Aids, tearing off ones already covering blisters on his heels and little toes. She found him strikingly handsome, almost pretty. His dark brown hair was swept back and held in place with a shiny gel that caught the light. His skin was pale, which made the purple and black bruises around his eyes stand out.

'Hello,' Becca began, hesitantly. He rose from a seat beside his desk and moved towards her, still barefoot, and introduced himself as DS Joe Russell. 'DS Vincent?' he asked, and held his hand out to shake hers. He gave her a broad smile and she nodded, then reverted to the behaviour of an awkward teenage girl, her face reddening, followed by a fear she was making her unprofessional interest in him obvious.

She noted that his rich, blue eyes – with long dark lashes she'd have killed for – didn't quite meet hers. Instead, he took in her whole face, pausing at her nose for a moment. She worried that something unsightly was protruding from her nostrils, so she sniffed. Joe glanced down at his hand, then her eyes again, and she realised she hadn't let go. She snatched her hand back.

'Come in, we don't bite,' he urged. His teeth were so perfectly aligned that if he had offered to bite, she might have let him.

'What happened to your face?' she asked.

'I was the wrong side of a headbutt during a foot chase. We nicked him in the end though, so no harm done. Well, just to my face and feet.'

'I thought you were all office-based, like support staff? I didn't know you went out into the field as well.'

Her question was greeted by a look of disappointment. 'So you said on the phone you needed our help?' Joe continued, and ushered her towards an empty chair by his desk. He sat down too, and slipped on his socks and shoes. Becca outlined the inquiry she and Nikhat were working on and recounted how she'd been at the tube station where Stefan Dumitru had died.

'And you want me to go through the CCTV footage with you?' he asked.

'Isn't that what you guys do – look at pictures of faces and see if you can recognise who's in them?'

'I'd like to think there's more to it than that,' Joe replied, sitting back in his seat and folding his arms.

Becca was savvy enough to know when she was riling someone, although it hadn't been her intention. *But really*, she thought, *how hard can their job be?* 'The intranet doesn't go into much detail about what you do,' she continued, 'but I got the impression this department was a bit of an experiment?'

A woman working at another terminal turned her head. 'We've been going for six years, so we're a bit more than just an "experiment", luv.'

'Because not everyone in the job is open-minded, it means we're not always understood by other departments,' said Joe. 'And that's their loss, because our clear-up rate is better than most. However, we don't then seek out the glory like others do to justify our presence. Being in CID, I'm sure that on a daily basis you're surrounded by people who put their egos ahead of everything else?'

Becca's hackles rose as the temperature between them dropped. She had worked hard and against the odds to get to where she was, and it had nothing to do with ego. And she didn't appreciate her colleagues being painted in a negative light.

'It must be difficult to justify yourself when nobody knows you exist,' she countered.

'You're right, the majority of people don't even know who we are. The moment they move us into New Scotland Yard is the moment we go above radar, and then we'll have to justify every single thing we do. And you can't do your job when you're being constantly scrutinised. So we're quite happy being here and left alone to do our thing. And we do it bloody well.'

'But you need to be held accountable for what you do, like the rest of us.'

'What we do isn't an exact science.'

'Is science even involved? Correct me if I'm wrong but you've just got good memories, right?'

'For faces, yes. Once we see you, we don't forget you.'

'Ever?'

'Well, it varies from person to person. But we were recruited from across various departments in the Met because our brains have an inbuilt facial recognition that's better than a computer.'

A man with grey hair and a yellow, nicotine-stained moustache emerged from behind his terminal. 'Take the London riots in 2011,' he began. 'I assume you remember them, or were you tucked safely away in your office watching it on the news?'

'I was in uniform and on the front line,' Becca replied. She recalled how she was just a year into the job when she was deployed to Tottenham Hale Retail Park. She and her team were expected to help break up the looting of shops following the police shooting of a man that had led to community tensions boiling over. During one of the many arrests she'd made over those four days, she ended up with a fractured wrist, a lost tooth and torn knee ligament.

'There were two hundred thousand hours of CCTV footage to sift through,' the grey-haired man continued. 'We generated five thousand images, and from them, we ID'd more than six hundred suspects. You name it, they were charged with it – everything from looting to arson and aggravated assault. Joe identified more than three hundred successful prosecutions alone. How many did CID spot?'

'I have no idea,' Becca shrugged.

'Seventeen,' he replied, and folded his arms. 'Check it out, it's on record.'

This is not going well, thought Becca. And she didn't like being ambushed. Their smugness annoyed her. She wouldn't give any of them the satisfaction of her being outwardly impressed by the statistic.

'You're welcome to sift through the tube footage on your own if you don't have faith in what we do,' Joe said, 'and I'm sure eventually you might find what you're looking for.'

Becca wanted to cut her nose off to spite her face, just to prove him wrong. But if they were as good as they claimed and his assistance meant she could rejoin her colleagues for real police work in half the time, then she would need to hold her tongue. And by now she was quietly curious to see first-hand how Joe worked.

'I've made us an appointment at the company that stores all TfL's digital footage,' she said. 'We'd best get going.'

'Sure,' Joe replied, and reached for his jacket and bag. 'Let's show you what a super-recogniser can do. Although I wish they'd picked a different nickname for us. Every time I call myself that it sounds like I should be wearing a superhero outfit.'

Becca smiled to herself, and wondered if there was a small chance they might be on the same wavelength after all.

CHAPTER 7

He leaned against the platform wall, grateful for the coolness of the tiles on his back. They permeated the fabric of his short-sleeved shirt and offered relief from the stifling heat. Once again, he used his mindfulness techniques to calm himself down and keep his claustrophobia at bay.

Each tube train powering through the tunnel and into the station brought with it a gust of air that felt just as soothing against his skin as the tiles. He wasn't yet ready to board another carriage though, not until he'd finished taking time out of his day to appreciate what he was accomplishing.

Less than twenty-four hours had passed since he'd closed the book on the lives of Stefan Dumitru and Darius Cheban. No more than three metres in front of him, he'd felled a giant with the smallest prick of a needle. Not that anyone waiting on the platform today would know. It was business as usual, and the only reference to the 'incident' was upstairs by the ticket barriers – a whiteboard with a photocopied police appeal for witnesses taped to it.

He hadn't had time to fully absorb Dumitru's death because it had been followed later that evening by a second kill. Two murders within two hours in two locations and in two entirely different ways – it was quite a feat, he decided, especially for a novice. His only regret was that he had no one to share it with.

There was no question in his mind that both men had got what they deserved. And even though it was still early days, a small part of him remained incredulous that he'd got away with it.

Neither Dumitru nor his cousin and flatmate, Cheban, had the slightest inkling he had been hiding within their shadows for the best part of a year. They hadn't noticed him following them by foot, tube, car or bus. They hadn't known he'd intercepted their post, applied for credit cards under their names or funded his lifestyle using their identities. Cheban hadn't even questioned him when he'd appeared on their doorstep with a clipboard, claiming to be the landlord's representative, there to carry out a spot inventory check.

Both men had been living on borrowed time, and it was time that he had lent them. And yesterday, he'd taken it back.

They had been partly responsible for his downfall. His thoughts briefly drifted back to a time when he could barely leave his hospital bed; when even the simplest task like washing his face or putting on freshly laundered clothes required a Herculean effort. Time was supposed to be a healer, and those charged with his recovery had kept reminding him it wouldn't always feel like this. He wanted to believe them, and had clung on to that hope by his fingertips until gradually he'd found another way to survive. The only way to fill the aching void that lay inside him was to hurt everyone who'd hurt him.

Initially, there had been doubt. He honestly didn't know if having their blood on his hands would be enough to rid him of his pain. But he had nothing to lose in finding out. His life as he knew it was already over – he was risking nothing, and he had everything to gain.

His eyes flicked towards the next train emerging from the tunnel and coming to a halt. The windows of the driver's cabin were too dark to see the face inside, and he wondered if it was the same driver who'd killed Dumitru. Probably not, he decided. He'd likely been moved to a different route, given mandatory leave or was undergoing counselling. He didn't doubt the man was reliving the moment of collision over and over again, because so was he. It was funny, he thought, they had both killed the same person but only one of them was laughing.

He closed his eyes and tried to remember if Dumitru's body had made a sound when he'd been struck. It'd all happened so fast that if it did, he hadn't registered the noise. All he recalled hearing was his own escalating heartbeat before the yelling and screaming of others began. He doubted Dumitru had made a noise. There was always a risk he could have survived the train's impact, but if that hadn't killed him, then the massive overdose of suxamethonium injected into him would have. After it paralysed his muscles, he'd have been dead in under a minute.

Cheban's death was different. There was none of the anxiety he'd felt killing Dumitru in a public place, where so much could have gone wrong. That murder had been methodical, detached and against the clock. He was far more in control of Cheban's destiny, and he'd given himself the time to fully relish watching him die.

He'd posed as a police officer to talk his way into Cheban's home, and from the moment he plunged the syringe deep into his neck, he'd been sure to give himself the time to enjoy the process from beginning to end. He had savoured taking full control of another man's life, from measuring just how much pain Cheban could bear through the haze of the sedative, to how long he should prolong the torture for. Then, thirty-five glorious minutes later and when Cheban was flat on his back, slowly asphyxiating, he'd felt so elated that he had to wipe away the tears cascading down his cheeks. Their actions might not have started all of this, but it was right he'd targeted them first. They were a warm-up before the big game began.

It wouldn't be long until his work was complete, he told himself. Two of the six names on his list were already dead, and his meticulous planning and organisational skills meant the rest would soon follow, one delicious murder by one.

Glancing at his watch, he noticed he had been standing on the platform for the best part of an hour, and he needed to return to the office soon. Margaret would only turn a blind eye to his flexible timekeeping for so long. Making his way into a carriage, he moved his hand up to the centre of his chest and traced the outline of the silver ring hanging from a thin chain under his shirt. He thought how much better the ring had looked on the finger it was meant for rather than around his neck. It was yet another reminder of why he was doing this.

He cocked his head when he spotted a woman exiting another carriage. She hovered on the platform, taking in everything around her. If he were someone who believed in fate, he might have considered it a coincidence their paths had crossed. But aside from love, he didn't believe in anything he couldn't see or physically touch. There were no coincidences in his world, only scenarios that he had carefully constructed. She was there because of him.

CHAPTER 8

Becca pinched at her eyes with her thumb and index finger. They were already sore from a lack of sleep and she didn't relish spending the rest of the afternoon staring at images on a monitor. She was long overdue an optician's appointment, but kept delaying it as she knew she'd be prescribed glasses. Only racy secretaries on television shows or hipsters could get away with wearing them and still look desirable. They made women like her, single and on the cusp of their thirties, appear frumpy.

Not that finding a man was high up – or even on – her list of priorities. She was constantly too exhausted to do anything but sleep by the time she climbed into bed at night. She'd yet to even buy batteries or remove the packaging from the treat she'd bought herself on the Ann Summers website. And she had no desire to start swiping an app left or right in the hope of finding Mister Perfect.

Joe was either completely ignorant or had forgotten he had company, as he barely said a word. Either way, it was irritating her. He remained thoroughly focused on the task in hand, searching for familiar faces on the monitors in the Barbican office where TfL outsourced the storage of its digital CCTV footage. Every moment of every day, cameras inside red buses, overland trains, tubes and on road lanes were stored on servers in this building.

Her eyes glanced towards the image on the monitor. 'Pause,' Joe said, and she pressed a button on the keyboard. 'That looks like Dumitru,' he continued, and pointed to a man with his back to the camera, intimidating his way through commuters to reach the front of the platform. Becca recognised the pinky-white T-shirt she'd seen in the graphic crime-scene photos.

'Now look at the people around him,' said Joe. 'If he's pushed, it'll be by someone within easy reach.'

They watched in silence as Dumitru became embroiled in an argument with a man standing behind him. Dumitru briefly faced the camera, then turned his back on the man. A moment later he turned around again, but this time, his body language was more aggressive.

'And you were on the platform and didn't see any of this?' Joe asked.

'I was busy checking my emails,' said Becca. It was better than admitting she'd been engrossed in a game of Candy Crush. 'Look, he's squaring up to him.'

But before a brawl could ensue, they watched as Dumitru's raised arm flopped to his side. Then he began to lose his balance and topple backwards. Even though they were both aware of the eventual outcome, Joe and Becca were still startled by the sudden appearance of the train. It caught Dumitru's shoulder as he fell, pushed him forward, and swept him under the carriage with the ease of a vacuum cleaner sucking up a grain of rice.

'Jesus,' whispered Becca. She'd witnessed the aftermath of deaths on film and in person, but never anyone actually being killed. But the nature of the job meant they very quickly became desensitised to Dumitru's demise as they rewound, paused and watched the footage over and over again.

Five cameras were affixed to the tube walls and the tunnel's roof, offering different perspectives. And each would need to be watched carefully, frame by frame. But a hungry Becca knew her concentration would lapse if she didn't eat soon.

'I'm going to grab a late lunch,' she said. 'Can I bring you something back?'

'Yes, thanks,' Joe muttered, but didn't request anything in particular. Becca shook her head and left, irked that she'd been saddled with someone so good-looking but so lacking in personality and banter. She wished she were back in CID.

She returned twenty minutes later with some eye drops from a pharmacy and a bulging carrier bag from Pret a Manger, from which she removed the food and two cold cans of lemonade. Joe had barely moved an inch in her absence, and didn't acknowledge her return. She tilted her head backwards and inserted two drops into each eye.

'How are you not blind from looking at the screen for so long?' she asked, and passed him a wholemeal wrap. Chicken and lettuce poked out from each end. Joe didn't examine what he was about to eat before he opened the cellophane and took a bite.

'If I've pushed it too far then I'll get a banging migraine that will knock me out for a couple of days. I try to be sensible.'

'But don't all the faces just blend into one? They're starting to do that for me.'

'It hasn't happened yet. I see something different in every single face I look at.'

Becca took too large a bite of her sandwich and felt mayonnaise drip on to her chin just as Joe finally turned his head towards her. She tried wiping it off with her fingers but ended up smearing it instead. She noticed him curtail his amusement.

He unlocked his phone and brought up a photograph of Stefan Dumitru that Nikhat had emailed. It had been taken from the criminal record database where Dumitru had a past conviction for assault.

'When you look at his face, what's the first thing you see?'

'His eyes.'

'That's what most people look at. However, people like me focus on the middle of the face and the nose. By doing that, we take in the whole of someone's face better and it sinks into our memory.'

'Can you train to be one of your lot?'

'No. It's something to do with two little bits on either side of our brains that become a hive of activity when we see a face or a photo. People like you can recognise up to twenty per cent of faces. For super-recognisers, it's closer to eighty per cent.'

'Now you're showing off.'

'If it's any consolation, the rest of my memory is pretty dire.'

As Becca listened to Joe talk, she couldn't fault the enthusiasm he showed for his job. She cast a sneaky look towards his wedding ring finger, and surprised herself at the level of satisfaction she felt when she noticed it was bare. It didn't mean there wasn't a long-term girlfriend, two-point-seven children and a Labrador waiting for him back at home though.

Two and a half hours passed before they reached their final piece of camera footage.

'Why are there mugshots all over your office walls?' Becca asked suddenly.

'We call them the "prolific unknowns". Over and over again they've been caught on camera committing the same type of crimes, but we've yet to get a positive ID on them.'

'I suppose super-recognisers must come with an expiry date though, don't they? Isn't this the kind of work facial recognition software was developed for? Even Facebook uses it. Surely that must be a lot quicker, and a better use of man hours?'

She caught him rolling his eyes. 'Yet another common misconception by people who believe too easily what they see in films or on TV,' Joe replied. 'Do you know how many people were positively ID'd by facial recognition software after the London riots? A grand total of one.'

'One,' Becca repeated, barely bothering to hide her disbelief. She wanted to add, 'Do you take me for a fool?' but resisted.

As the footage came to an end, she pushed her hunched shoulders back, making them click. The weight of the world was making its presence felt upon her frame.

'So we don't yet have any proof Dumitru was pushed,' said Becca, 'and I think we can rule out suicide unless he's a really good actor. It looks like he just . . . fell.'

'Unless you're at the gym 24/7, you don't get that muscular unless you're abusing steroids,' Joe replied. 'Perhaps his heart just gave out.'

Both sat quietly for a moment, neither trying particularly hard to mask their disappointment that the case wasn't as sinister as they'd hoped. Becca realised that by the time she returned to CID, there'd be enough detectives investigating Cheban's murder and she'd be competing for scraps from the table. She wondered if Joe was frustrated that he hadn't got to demonstrate his skills to a sceptic.

'Well, thanks for your help, anyway,' she said as they both rose to their feet and made their way out the door and along the corridor. 'Sorry if it's been a waste of your—' She was cut short by her phone ringing. Soon into the conversation, she stopped walking and tapped Joe's arm. 'Thanks, Nik.' She smiled and hung up.

'Nikhat's the SIO on the Cheban case,' she explained. 'He's got an old uni buddy who fast-tracked the toxicology reports. Both Cheban and Dumitru were drugged before they died. Cheban had enough Propofol in him to paralyse him, while Dumitru was given a massive overdose of something else. Nik says it was such a high quantity that he could only have had it in his system for a minute or so before it killed him.'

'Dumitru was on that platform for about four minutes,' said Joe. 'It must have been administered while he was there. We need to get as clear as possible images of the people surrounding him.'

Becca felt a renewed enthusiasm – her gut instinct about the case had been right. She was now at the centre of a double murder investigation.

They headed back to the viewing room they'd just left and, with the footage back on screen, hunched over the monitors to get a closer look at the three unidentified strangers nearest Dumitru.

A text message made Becca's phone vibrate. She looked at her screen and Joe appeared to notice her frown.

'Everything okay?'

'Yes,' she lied.

Thirty minutes later, Joe had printed out images of the three people. Going by build, Becca assumed the first to be male. Despite the soaring tube temperatures the evening of Dumitru's death, he was wearing a zipped-up hoodie that hid his face. Was he hiding himself deliberately? By the colour of his hands, he was likely Caucasian, and he wore no jewellery nor had any distinguishable features. After Dumitru vanished under the train, he hurried to help, even talking to the TfL staff, but once he walked out of shot, he appeared to vanish into the platform's blind spot.

The second was a woman with long, dark wavy hair and a baby in a sling pressed against her chest. The third was a balding man with tattooed arms arguing with Dumitru. Becca looked at Joe, who wore a satisfied smile.

'Him,' he said, pointing to the bald man on the screen.

'Who is he?'

'I can't give you a name yet. But he is familiar. You know that when almost any crime is committed in London, we'll look to see if it was caught on CCTV?'

'No, I only joined the job this morning,' Becca replied, with more than a hint of sarcasm.

'Sorry. There are a million CCTV cameras in London. So at a crime scene, we'll look through a nearby camera's footage, screen-grab the suspect's face and upload it to the Met's centralised forensic image database. It's had something like a hundred thousand idents – unidentified suspects – put on it in the last six years, and each has its own six-figure code which we then tag with metadata.'

'Metadata?'

'I forgot, you said you only joined the job this morning,' he replied wryly. 'Metadata are key words that have something to do with the crime or where it happened, or the suspect's appearance. That helps with future research – like now, for example. We know from the CCTV image that the man I recognise is white, male, aged around twenty-five to forty, bald, stocky and with a tattoo on his left arm. When I type in those details it cuts the search of one hundred thousand people down to a much more manageable number.'

'How much detail can you go into?'

'As much as we like. We use tags like "comb-over", "scars", "broken nose", "veneers", "acne", "bracelets", "rings", "necklaces", "lacking a finger", "missing teeth", "spider veins", et cetera. It never fails to surprise me, but many repeat offenders wear the same clothes to carry out their crimes. It's like they're putting on a work uniform. We'll tag images with things like "red bandana", "Superdry T-shirt", "white Converse trainers", et cetera. Then, when I get back to the office, I'll look at every picture that comes up of someone who fits the description of our man.'

'So how long will it take you?'

'I might strike lucky and get someone within a few minutes, or it might take a few hours. Once you start looking, it's kind of addictive. You don't want to stop until you've found your man.'

Becca was torn. While wanting to watch him work, time wasn't on her side. She glanced at her watch. It was approaching 5.30 p.m. Sometimes she wished she could work nine to five, not early until whenever she was done. But she knew that if she didn't set off for home soon, there would be repercussions.

'Well, don't work too late,' she said.

'Before you go, do you mind if I ask you for your number?'

The out-of-the-blue request made her stomach flutter. They hadn't got off to a great start and she knew she was a little rusty about the rules of attraction. But she hadn't picked up on any signs that he might be interested in her. 'Sure,' she replied.

'I'll text you later if I find him on the system,' Joe added.

'Of course,' Becca said, feeling foolish for believing it could have been for any other reason. She typed her number into his phone and noted the background picture, a dog lying on its back on a duvet cover, its legs pointing to the ceiling and its mouth open wide. It was almost smiling.

'Is he yours?' Becca asked.

'Yes, his name is Oscar,' Joe replied with pride. 'We got him when he was a puppy.'

'*We*,' she narrowly avoided repeating out loud. It meant he was attached.

'I kept him when my ex and I split up,' Joe continued, and for a moment, Becca's face lit up.

It was later that evening, as she sat in her lounge with the windows open and made the most of the cool breeze and a glass of white wine, that Joe's first text arrived. A mugshot was attached.

Becca, meet Nicky Penn, Joe wrote.

You found him! she replied immediately. *Is he one of your idents?*

You're picking up the lingo! No, but he has form for beating up an ex. Also got a suspended sentence for football hooliganism and was a member of the banned group Keep Britain White. But he's been clean for more than fifteen years.

You think these murders might be racially motivated?

Can't rule it out.

Becca called to update Nikhat, who decided that because of Penn's clean record since 2003, he should be treated as a witness rather than a suspect. Therefore it could wait until the next morning before he was paid a visit. When she texted Joe, he offered to join her.

Don't you have anything better to do? she typed.

I'd quite like to see this part through. x

His use of an 'x' made Becca wonder if he was flirting with her and she ventured a smile. What was it about Joe that kept making her feel like a giddy schoolgirl? They had little in common, and for most of the day they'd rubbed each other up the wrong way. Maybe it was purely physical. Perhaps she wouldn't need that Ann Summers purchase after all.

Get a grip, woman! she told herself. Then she promptly ignored that voice inside her and planned what she'd wear the next day. By the time midnight arrived, she'd coloured her hair, fake-tanned, shaved her legs for the first time in a month and ironed a blouse.

CHAPTER 9

He dipped his remaining slice of white toast into the poached egg yolk, then traced it through a spoonful of baked beans before lifting it towards his mouth.

Half a pork sausage and a strip of crisp bacon fat remained on his plate, but he was finished with his all-day breakfast. He had tasted better. He was famished, however, and beggars couldn't be choosers. Based on many visits to this pub, he knew that it was the most appealing choice on the menu. It was also one of the unhealthiest. Not that he cared. When his time was up, it wasn't going to be cholesterol that killed him.

He'd texted Margaret to tell her he was going home, after his appointments ran on longer than anticipated. His timekeeping didn't overly concern her, and as long as he hit the targets she set, he could come and go as he pleased. It wasn't like that for every member of staff though – he and Margaret shared a special arrangement and she never said no to him.

He'd first made advances towards her after last year's office summer barbecue. They'd drunkenly stumbled back to the office to pick up their bags and call taxis home. But within minutes, she was sprawled face down across his desk, paperwork swept to the floor as he thrust inside her. Margaret was a decade his senior, but had the ferocious sexual appetite of a woman half her age. The following day, he'd ignored his hangover and driven to the office just to replay the footage captured on the internal security camera. Then he made a copy of it and stored it in his Cloud. It would be the perfect leverage should he ever need her to do something for him that she was reluctant to.

He took in his reflection in the cutlery on the pub table. He'd transformed beyond belief since those shy, awkward, early teenage years when he was scrawny and pitted with acne, and a succession of hideous haircuts had made him invisible to either sex. For a man now in his late thirties, he was only just beginning to show physical signs of aging. A few fine lines had begun to frame his eyes, and there was a hint of grey in his blond curls. Perhaps there was one useful gene his useless mother had passed down to him after all.

Taking a sip from his mineral water, he used the straw to swirl the melting ice cubes around in an anticlockwise motion. Then he blew his nose and checked his handkerchief when he felt something solid fall out. It was a thick crust of blood, and he knew the cause of it. Amphetamines and high doses of caffeine hadn't worked half as well as cocaine in keeping him alert through the night. But there were consequences from its frequent use.

Noises from the play area in the pub's family section, close to where he'd chosen to sit, caught his attention. He turned his focus towards the Junior Jungle, where half a dozen excitable children squealed as they ascended net ropes and slid down small yellow slides into multicoloured ball pits.

'Careful!' he said out loud.

'Which one is yours?' came a woman's voice from behind. He turned to find an attractive brunette with an empty pushchair and a swollen, pregnant belly easing herself on to a wooden stool. She rubbed the base of her spine.

'The boy in the red *Fireman Sam* T-shirt,' he replied, and pointed to a child with white-blond hair, hopping eagerly from foot to foot like he was running on the spot. He waved at the boy as the mother tried to hold him steady and wipe food from the sides of his mouth. The child waved back and gave a big, toothy grin.

He adored watching them play together, mother and child utterly enraptured by one another. He loved children when they were that age; when their whole world was just the two people who had brought them into it. He never wanted that boy to grow up and see what he had seen as a child. Innocence was to be protected at all costs.

'He's a handsome little man,' the pregnant woman commented. He swelled with pride. 'That's my daughter, Izzy, on the slide with her father. He's on daddy duty this afternoon.'

'I'm taking a timeout before mine runs us ragged later,' he replied. 'Every other parent we know has kids who love an afternoon nap, but trying to get ours to settle for even half an hour is a nightmare.' He looked towards her stomach. 'How much longer do you have left?'

'Three and a half weeks. But Izzy was ten days late so I'm not holding my breath.'

He watched as the grinning boy took one last trip down the slide before his mum scooped him into her arms and tried to strap him into a pushchair. His response was to scream and kick his feet.

'That's my cue to go,' he said, and wiped his mouth with a napkin. 'On my way!'

'You're in for a fun journey home,' she responded, and gave him a knowing smile.

He lifted his briefcase from the floor and took a last sip from his straw. 'Good luck with the due date, I hope it all goes smoothly.'

'Thanks,' she replied.

'Hello!' he directed ahead of him. 'Aren't you forgetting something?' He rose to his feet, following the boy and his mother towards a set of double doors. 'You'd forget your head if it was loose.'

The woman turned to him, puzzled.

'Let me get the door for you,' he continued, and pushed it open. He placed his hand on the small of her back.

'Please don't touch me,' she snapped, and moved her body to create a barrier between him and her son.

His smile fell. 'I was just trying to be helpful,' he replied, then left them alone.

As he walked towards the exit, without warning his forehead felt like it was burning up and he became woozy. Collapsing to the floor became a distinct possibility. He didn't understand it – it felt like symptoms of his claustrophobia, but he was in an open space. He hurried outdoors into the fresh air and concentrated on his breathing until his heart began to decelerate and his skin cooled.

For a few beautiful moments, he had enjoyed playing the part of a family man, even if it was make-believe and he had no idea who the mother and child were. But the payback for allowing himself such gratification was the emptiness that followed, and the reality of knowing it was something he would never experience. Sometimes he craved it so much that it reached the point where it physically hurt. He could spend hours at a time, doubled up in agony and clutching at his abdomen, begging for the raw pain to dissolve. Eventually, he'd learned to channel the pain into revenge.

'Focus,' he said aloud, and gave his head a moment to clear. Then he moved it around in a circular motion and rubbed his cheeks with the palms of his hands.

In less than forty-eight hours from now, he would begin the next stage of his journey. And if all went according to plan, he could cross the third name from his list.

CHAPTER 10

Becca didn't feel comfortable and she couldn't put her finger on why.

The walk from her home to Angel tube station that morning had left her feeling peculiarly anxious and uneasy. It was like she was being watched, even though she knew how ridiculous that sounded. Nevertheless, on several occasions she found herself staring up and down the platform, then inside the tube carriage, to check if anyone was paying her undue attention.

She didn't mention her irrational concerns to Joe, as she knew they were precisely that. But as they met at their arranged location in Whitechapel before travelling the rest of the way together to their destination, she felt happier to have someone by her side.

Thirty minutes later and they were waiting inside a stuffy concierge building, as a man wearing a suit jacket with the word 'Security' emblazoned across the back scrolled through a computerised list of residents of the flats behind them. A plug-in air freshener and an electric fan were doing little to diffuse the staleness surrounding them.

'Have you done something different to your hair?' Joe asked.

'No,' Becca replied, suddenly embarrassed that the effort she'd made in her appearance had been noticed. However, they both knew that, when it came to appearances, she couldn't pull the wool over the eyes of a man with a photographic memory.

She distracted herself by reading from a wall poster. She learned that, before it had become Bow Quarter, the gated community had been home to the Bryant and May matchbox factory. When that closed, it lay derelict for years before becoming one of East London's first huge urban-renewal projects. Reopening in the 1990s, it was now home to 733 private apartments lived in by affluent owners and renters. Behind fifteen-foot-high black metal gates lay a sanctuary a world away from the hustle and bustle of the rest of London. She envied its residents.

'Flat sixteen, North West,' the security man said. 'I'll show you the way.'

'No, it's fine,' Joe replied and led the way into the grounds.

'Do you know where you're going?' Becca asked.

'I used to date someone who lived here,' he replied.

'Who dumped who?'

'I did, when I started enjoying access to the free gym and swimming pool more than the relationship.'

They walked along pebble paths, past immaculately trimmed lawns, flower beds and a pond generously stocked with colourful fish, until they reached a more modern building opposite the original factory. Becca pressed the buzzer for number sixteen. A female voice replied with a direct 'Yes?'

'DS Joe Russell and DS Becca Vincent, we're here to see Nicky Penn,' said Becca.

'He's not here,' she replied.

'We'd like to come up anyway, please.'

After a pause, the door unlocked and they walked up a flight of stairs and located the flat. The door opened to reveal a woman's partially hidden face.

'And you are?' asked Becca.

'Abigail Johnson,' she replied.

'Do you live here? Because there's no other name listed on the electoral roll . . .'

'It's my boyfriend's place.'

'And your boyfriend would be Nicky?'

Abigail nodded.

'May we come in?' Becca continued, adjusting her tone to something more sympathetic when she sensed Abigail's apprehension. 'We'll only take a few minutes of your time.'

Abigail nodded again, and they followed her along an entrance hall and into an open-plan sitting room and kitchen. Bright sunlight radiating through the open set of double doors overlooking the gardens showed Abigail's face clearly for the first time. The make-up she'd applied wasn't enough to cover up her bruised eye and cheek or her split lip. Judging by the swelling, the injuries were recent.

'I was attacked coming home from work,' she said, anticipating her visitor's next question. Her refusal to make eye contact suggested she wasn't being honest.

'Did you report it?' Joe asked.

'No point, I didn't see who did it.'

Becca wanted to press her further and to encourage her to admit to what had really happened, but she held herself back. It was unlikely Abigail had suffered so much bruising to her wrists, forearms and biceps simply from a mugging.

'What's this about?' Abigail asked, folding her arms. 'Nicky hasn't done anything wrong.'

Nobody in the room believed her.

'Can you tell us where he is, please?' asked Becca.

'At work. He's a security guard.'

'Can you tell us where he was late Monday afternoon?' asked Joe.

'Working.'

'Does he do regular hours?'

'No, he's on a zero-hours contract at the Onyx building. They tell him when they want him and he goes in.'

Joe thanked her and turned to leave. Before Becca followed, she removed a business card from her purse and handed it to her. Abigail read it aloud. '"Women's refuge centre",' she said. Below the wording was a telephone number.

'Keep this for when things get too dangerous for you to stay,' said Becca quietly. 'And believe me, one day that will happen. Don't leave it too late.'

Becca offered her a sympathetic smile and recognised familiar and undue shame in Abigail's eyes.

◆ ◆ ◆

It was hard not to miss the Onyx building when Joe and Becca reached the exit of Monument tube station.

A short walk across London Bridge, their destination was in close proximity to the Shard, the tallest building in the city. When the glaring sun was reflected by the Shard's 11,000 panes of glass, its rays seemed to vanish inside the semi-circular smoked-glass exterior of the seventy-seven-storey cylindrical Onyx.

Becca realised Joe hadn't generated one conversation since they'd left Abigail Johnson's flat, despite her best attempts to keep him talking. He appeared to pay everyone who passed them attention but not her. And while she was going to have to get used to the fact that was the way he operated, eventually frustration got the better of her. 'You're constantly looking around,' she said. 'Whether we're waiting for a tube or walking along the street, it's like it's your first day on earth and you've never seen a human being before.'

'Sorry, force of habit,' Joe replied.

'What do super-recognisers do when they're not looking at CCTV footage?'

'Most of us are scattered across different departments. You'll find a lot of SRs in front-line positions or leading Safer Neighbourhood Teams because we remember the faces of local troublemakers. We get out and about too – the Notting Hill Carnival, Gay Pride, or live gigs at venues like Hyde Park or Wembley. If there's a high footfall, we'll be there. And when we have some downtime, we'll be snapping.'

'And what's that?'

'We'll trawl through the forensic image database looking for familiar faces. If we think we've seen a face more than once, then we'll start coupling their crimes and joining them together. It's like a game of snap. And the more crimes we can link, the longer, in theory, they'll spend behind bars when we catch them. It's such a buzz when you get that snap.'

They entered the foyer of the Onyx; inside was equally dark and moody as its exterior, with oak flooring and tiled walls. Four large reception desks were manned by young women, all wearing identical smart blue jackets and make-up, their hair scooped back into tight ponytails. Across the foyer and behind waist-high reinforced glass barriers stood Nicky Penn. Joe spotted him immediately.

'There's our boy,' he said. Becca did little to disguise her growing disdain for the man they were about to meet.

Nicky Penn stood at no more than five feet, seven inches tall, but what he lacked in stature he compensated for with broad shoulders, as if he were wearing American football-style padding under his suit jacket. From forehead to crown he was bald, and what little hair remained was clipped short. He was clean-shaven, but his cheeks and forehead were pockmarked and his eyes beady and mistrustful.

When they introduced themselves to him, he ushered them into a back room and out of sight of his employers. It took just the one sideways glance from Penn for a younger man watching a football match on a mobile phone to rise to his feet and scuttle away.

'Whatever she's said, she's lying,' Penn began, pre-empting their conversation. Becca's head inched backwards at the stench of his stale coffee breath. 'She makes things up, she exaggerates.'

'What do you think we're here to talk to you about?' asked Becca.

'My girlfriend,' he replied, but as he said this he'd already realised he'd jumped to the wrong conclusion.

Becca removed a pocket notebook from her handbag. 'If we were here about the punchbag you call your girlfriend, what would you say?'

'That I'm a different man to what my record suggests,' he replied, and folded his arms defiantly. 'Turned my life around.'

'You were involved in an altercation with a man on a tube platform on Monday evening,' Joe said.

'Says who?'

'Says one of five CCTV cameras that have you arguing with him moments before he fell under a train.'

'Clumsy fuck stood on my foot, so I called him out.'

'And then what happened?'

'He mumbled something in foreign so I told him to fuck off back home. Brexit means Brexit, right? Then the muppet turned back around again and started on me.'

'To be honest, Nicky, you looked like you were about to shit your-self,' added Becca. 'Were you intimidated by the big man?'

Penn shot her the filthiest of looks but declined to respond.

'Did you have anything to do with his death, Nicky?' asked Joe.

'If you found me through them cameras then you know I didn't push him, or else you'd have arrested me by now.'

'You're a member of the Keep Britain White campaign, aren't you? Wouldn't that suggest you're not keen on foreigners?'

'That was a long time ago.'

'What happened to the man who fell?'

'He started grabbing the back of his leg and yelling at me. He was slurring his words and looked like he was losing his balance, like he had a stroke or something. Then he started falling backwards.'

'Did you try to stop him?' asked Becca.

'No, why would I?'

'Because that would be the decent thing to do.'

'Why did you think he was having a stroke?' said Joe.

'The way his face sank. His eye and cheek kind of drooped, like he was made of wax and was melting.'

Becca folded the cover over her notebook and put her pen away. As they exited the room, she waited until she reached the doorway to turn her head. 'By the way, tell Abigail I look forward to seeing her soon. I'm not sure when yet, I'll just drop in and surprise you both.'

As she and Joe retraced their steps through the foyer, she hoped that Penn loathed her as much as she loathed him. At the revolving doors, Joe slipped on his sunglasses and winced when they touched the swollen bridge of his broken nose.

'Still hurts?' she asked.

'Yep,' he replied. 'So what are you thinking? Is Nicky Penn our man?'

'No, he's a nasty piece of work but I don't think he's a killer.'

'So where does that leave us?'

'That leaves me with hours more CCTV footage to go through in the hope of tracing the other two people standing closest to Dumitru. If only I knew someone who was an expert in that sort of thing and who could help speed the process up.' She fluttered her eyelashes in a deliberately comic way.

'Come on then,' he sighed. 'Your place or mine?'

'Let's go to my office. I think I burned my bridges with your colleagues within the first five minutes of meeting them.'

'I wouldn't worry, they're a thick-skinned bunch.' Joe hesitated before he asked the next question. 'What was that all about with Nicky then? It was like you were almost . . . goading him.'

'I don't like bullies,' Becca replied sharply, but offered little else.

CHAPTER 11

Sleep evaded Becca for much of the night. No matter how much she chased it, Nicky Penn made sure to keep her awake.

Each time she drifted off, she dreamed he was looming over her bed, spitting and snarling like a feral animal. The muggy atmosphere in the room and the faintest of breezes coming through her open window were doing little to help guide her back into slumber. Eventually, frustrated with herself, she gave up and lay with her eyes open, staring at the ceiling.

She asked herself why she had allowed Penn to seep into her subconscious. It wasn't as if he was unique – she had come face to face with his kind many times over the years. But it was seeing his girlfriend's bruised face that reminded her so much of why she hated men like him. They were broken, and weren't content until they broke those trying to repair them.

It was just after 2 a.m. when Becca pushed away the thin sheet covering her body, opened her wardrobe and removed the shoebox hidden at the back under an old towel. Inside was a brown, cardboard-backed envelope. She switched on her bedside lamp and, one by one, studied the handful of photographs taken almost seven years earlier.

Had she not known the identity of the victim pictured, it would have been hard to determine their gender based on appearance alone. It was of a woman who had been badly beaten and battered to within an inch of her life. Her head was swollen to one and a half times its normal size, and the hair on the left-hand side was shaved where she'd been operated on to drain the fluid from her brain. Her face was a tapestry of black-and-blue bruising, dark stitches and red cuts and welts. Her eyelids were inflamed and sealed shut, and a white tube was affixed to her mouth with tape to enable her to breathe. Becca could still recall with such clarity the sound the respirator made, and the relentless *beep-beep-beep*ing of the heart monitor. They had all spent many days in that intensive-care unit, praying for a miracle that never arrived.

They were photographs she'd hoped she would never have to take, but there was something of an inevitability about them. In the back of her mind she had known that one day it was going to happen. Every now and again, when she doubted her choice of profession, she'd glance at those pictures and clarity would return.

Suddenly, a voice came from the open bedroom door behind her, startling her. Quickly, Becca stuffed the photographs back into the envelope and slid them under her bed and out of view.

'Mummy, I can't sleep,' began Maisie.

'What are you doing still awake, sweetie?' she asked, as her daughter climbed on to the bed. Becca joined her and Maisie curled up into a ball, her head resting on her mother's stomach.

'I had a bad dream about a big dog,' she said. 'It wanted to bite me and I got scared.'

'Don't worry, I won't let any big dog hurt you,' Becca soothed. 'I'll never let anything bad happen to my little girl.' Becca hated lying to Maisie. In her job, far too often she had witnessed bad things happening to good people. And promising to keep a six-year-old safe from the cruelty of the world was wishful thinking. But still she did it.

Maisie settled almost immediately, and purred as Becca stroked her hair. Gradually, her breathing became softer and softer as she drifted off to sleep. The little girl with the brown curls and the thumb often placed between her lips had been so excited to see her mummy when Becca had returned home from work yesterday evening.

Several times, Becca's mother, Helen, had texted her, asking what time she would be back. But Becca had been reluctant to give a time or leave the inquiry. She was too focused on playing her part in the murder investigation team, and she knew that CS Webster's eyes were on her. One slip-up, and she could be off the case.

By early evening, and when parental guilt had won out, Becca had left Joe at her desk examining footage to see where the two remaining witnesses were travelling to or from, and returned to her family. She didn't find it easy switching from detective to mum. She'd wanted to decompress with a long, soapy bath and a glass of red wine, but instead she was greeted by a daughter who refused to go to sleep until she'd been read three bedtime stories.

For much of the rest of the night Becca dozed without sinking into anything resembling a deep sleep. Eventually, she gave up and decided to get a head start on the day, and made Maisie's packed lunch for school. She put a basket-load of washing on, and after stacking the dishwasher, she opened the curtains in the hope of seeing a cloudy sky and a reprieve from the heat. But as the sun continued its ascent over the London skyline, there would be no such luck.

Becca squinted at a figure at the end of her street. From a distance, it looked like a man, and he appeared to be leaning against a set of black railings, his head turned in the direction of her row of houses. However, he was too far away for her to see his face. She couldn't put her finger on why, but something about his presence concerned her.

'When did you become such a domestic goddess?' her mother began.

'I couldn't sleep,' Becca replied, turning her head.

'Well, let's hope you can't sleep more often if this is the result.'

Helen pulled her dressing gown closed as she entered the kitchen, flicking on the kettle. Becca's gaze returned to the street, only now it was empty.

CHAPTER 12

He opened his mouth wide and stretched out his arms as the yawn left his body. It was the type that was so all-consuming, it left him light-headed. The cocaine he'd recently snorted from the top of a grubby toilet cistern might also have been to blame for the sudden dizziness, he couldn't be sure. But he'd been in desperate need of a pick-me-up.

Sitting at a table inside a greasy-spoon café, he stared outside at a Georgian-style, ashlar-stone building and the car park opposite. He had entered the eatery soon after it opened at daybreak. Behind him, a group of burly scaffolders in fluorescent yellow hi-vis vests and chunky-toed boots laughed raucously as one gave a detailed account of everything a prostitute had done to him in the red-light district of Amsterdam on a recent stag weekend. Apparently, it was better than anything his wife-to-be ever offered. She'd withdrawn from intimacy since the birth of their daughter several months earlier.

As he listened, his blood boiled at the bragging, and he fought the urge to grab the long aluminium spirit level lying by the workman's feet and smash him around his head. He loathed ingratitude and those who failed to understand how fortunate they were, especially when it came to people who loved them.

He took a sip of milky tea and continued to fix his gaze outside, contemplating how much longer he'd have to linger before the third name on his list came into view.

However, something about the scaffolder's bluster pricked his conscience, and an image of his girlfriend Zoe suddenly came to mind. In allowing her to believe they were a couple, he was being equally dishonest as the workman. What he and Zoe had was complex; it had begun as one thing but had developed into something completely different. And Zoe had no idea their dalliance had an expiration date, or that it was looming.

Rarely in his thirty-eight years had he fallen in love, and objects of his affection often barely knew he existed. Schoolboy crushes came and went but were never reciprocated. To his fellow pupils, it was as if he had been beige – a bland, boring colour that no one paid any attention to. He was neither liked nor disliked, loved nor loathed, popular nor unpopular. He was just . . . there.

When he reached his teenage years, he was no longer even noticed at home. By then, his mother had pledged her full commitment to booze, and was too drunk to bother to scratch, kick or assault him any more. He had interpreted her violence as a kind of warped affection, and when it was taken away from him, he had nothing.

When he'd thought of his future under that roof with her, all he saw was a lifetime of toxicity; of patterns repeating themselves; of wasted opportunities. He craved more than that. The best route out of there was to pass his GCSEs, go on to A levels and then leave London behind and start afresh as a new man at university. But further education didn't come cheap and it was unfortunate that his was the first year to have tuition fees inflicted upon it by the government. He couldn't expect a contribution from home. Any spare cash in the way of state benefits made its way straight from his mother's purse and into the cash register of the local pub or off-licence.

As a fifteen-year-old, he'd begun to earn pocket money by cutting the lawns and washing the cars of neighbours who felt sorry for the polite boy at number 65 with the intoxicated mother who hurled abuse at passing cars. And he'd learned to manipulate his personal circumstances by playing up to their pity. He'd purposely bruise his arms or neck – always visible places – and some would send him home with extra cash or packets of Hobnobs or Mr Kipling Cherry Bakewells that he'd hide upstairs in his room.

But it was Mr Reynolds who'd showed him where the real money was to be made. The grandfather-of-five paid him to wash his windows and rub down more than his paintwork. He'd slip him an extra five pounds each time he sat on the pensioner's lap and ground against his crotch. While it wasn't a pleasant experience listening to an old man ejaculate inside his own trousers, he did appreciate that someone had noticed him. And that attention was worth just as much as the folded notes that were tucked into his jeans pockets.

'It was tea rooms and lavs back in my day,' Mr Reynolds told him once. 'When we were demobbed after the war, that's where you'd go to pay for young male company. I'm sure it still goes on today. "Rent boys", they call them now . . . If a handsome lad like you ever wants to make a few extra quid, you could do a lot worse.'

It was all he could think about in the days that followed. Until finally he plucked up the courage to head into central London one Saturday evening and make his way towards a public toilet in Broadwick Street, Soho. Mr Reynolds had not been exaggerating. It took less than fifteen minutes of nervously hovering around the street level before someone made eye contact with him. He followed the stranger downstairs and into a cubicle and watched him masturbate for ten pounds.

Not all punters required an audience only; an equal number expected a helping hand, a willing mouth or more. But when it came down to it, it didn't matter what they wanted, what mattered was that what they wanted was him. They *chose* him.

He soon grew to learn what was expected of him and expanded his territory, rotating between more of London's public toilets, or those in department stores and saunas, and bars that turned a blind eye to his youthful appearance.

Over the next two and a half years he continued to make money from the desperate and the depraved. Some men he allowed to video him, others to take photographs, and some to recommend him to their friends or small groups, where he was passed around like a basket of breadsticks. His scrawny look appealed to an older clientele, and one even took a particular shine to him, becoming a friend and the closest thing he'd ever had to a male role model. He even assisted him with university application forms and helped him celebrate when one finally made him an offer. With enough money saved to pay for his first year, he secured a place at De Montfort University in Leicester.

In the run-up to his new life at college, it was time to leave the beige behind once and for all. When he wasn't selling himself or sitting by his mother's hospital bed watching her skin turn deeper shades of yellow, he was making the most of a membership to the council-run leisure centre gym and building himself a new body. Gone were the microwavable meals and fast food he'd been raised on, replaced with a regimented diet packed with vegetables and proteins. He traded his thick-lensed glasses for contacts, and began styling his hair and choosing clothes he saw other men of his age wearing.

Within months, he had transformed into a muscular, handsome young man. And once enrolled at university, the fresh, on-trend version of his former self was vibrant, engaged and sociable. He forced himself to join societies and political groups he didn't necessarily understand, and to take part in extra-curricular clubs. Occasionally, when money was tight, he'd return to London and make himself available to his old clients. But eventually, they were whittled down to just one.

And then, in his second term, Cally Lydon entered his life, and it was never the same again. They resided in the same halls of residence

– she one floor above him – within walking distance of the main campus. Cally was the most beautiful human being he'd ever been in proximity to, with her olive skin, green eyes, thick, auburn hair, and freckles that spread across her nose, cheeks and forehead. His love for her was so all-consuming and claustrophobic that sometimes he had to make an excuse to leave her side for a few minutes just to catch his breath.

His social circle merged with Cally's, and eventually they formed their own splinter group, comprising just the two of them. And he did everything in his power to make Cally's life as perfect as she'd made his. From cooking her dinner to helping her learn large chunks of scripted dialogue for her drama degree, and even cleaning her bathroom, no job was too big or too small for him. He burned her mixtape cassettes of their favourite songs, rented the rom-com videos that made her laugh and cry, and at night he'd walk her home from the student union bar where she worked part-time. She deserved the perfect boyfriend, so that's what he became.

The only tension between them came from his unease at how overtly friendly she was with customers at the bar. One night, he watched her from a table in the corner; she was flirty, smiling more at the opposite sex than at women. He didn't like it, and it was as if the walls and ceiling of the bar were closing in on him when he realised how effortlessly replaceable he was. With a click of her fingers, Cally would be able to muster up so much better. Eventually she was going to see him for what he really was – the bastard child of an abusive, alcoholic mother, and the beige schoolboy that not even social services had kept in their sights for long. He had leaped out of his seat and pushed his way through the strangers until he reached the street, gasping for air and craving space.

To her credit, on the many occasions he'd confessed his insecurities to Cally, she had offered him heartfelt reassurances that she was perfectly content with him and that no one else was going to turn her head. But she could have repeated the words a thousand times and he still would have struggled to believe her. Then, after months of trying to rid him of his self-doubt, Cally could take no more.

Even now, sitting in the café, he could clearly recall how deep his heart had sunk the afternoon she invited him to her room to discuss their future. There, she'd asked for a 'timeout' from their relationship, describing him as 'smothering' and 'too intense'. She needed to be on her own for a while 'to think'.

The following day, he responded by spending twelve months of his student loan on an engagement ring and asking her to marry him. He would never forget the look of dismay on her face.

'This is precisely what I mean,' she'd snapped. 'You don't give me any space, you're constantly there, all the time, telling me how much you love me. You're possessive and you're smothering me.'

'But we're in love,' he replied. 'People in relationships want to do things for each other, they want to spend time together.'

'Not like this, it isn't normal. We're young and we're at uni and this will be the only time in our lives we'll ever be this free.'

He offered to slow things down, but something about the way her eyes sank to the floor told him she had given up on them already.

In the aftermath of their break-up, he became introverted and moped around, missing lectures and not completing essays. He sent her flowers, left gifts by her door and 'accidentally' bumped into her in places he knew she'd be. And under the cover of darkness, he followed her, lurking outside the bar for hours at a time, watching her through the windows.

But it all came to a head when he let himself into her flat with the spare key he'd yet to return. He perched on the edge of her bed, flicking through a flipbook of photographs he'd given her of their months together. It dawned on him that maybe he'd read the signs incorrectly. If she'd kept that book, surely it meant she still cared? Could she simply be putting him to the test?

Suddenly, the door opened. Cally gasped when she saw him. It was only when it swung to the wall that he saw the man with his arm around her waist. He knew him as Danny, a student on the periphery of their circle of friends.

'What the hell are you doing in here?' she yelled.

'Waiting for you, I wanted to talk,' he muttered, glaring at her companion.

'You need to get out, this has gone too far.'

'Why's he here?'

'He's a friend, but that has nothing to do with you.'

He rose to his feet. 'This is why you ended it, isn't it? Because you've been seeing this arsehole.'

'Watch your mouth, mate,' Danny replied. His hand left Cally's body and he puffed out his chest.

'Just get out and leave me alone,' she said.

'You heard her, mate, give it up. She's not interested.'

'Fuck you, you clown,' he replied. 'I'm not your mate. And you have no idea what she's interested in.'

'If tonight's going to be anything like last night, then I have a pretty good idea,' Danny replied, and gave a mocking smile.

Danny barely had time to defend himself as his assailant flew across the room. He got the first punch in, square to Danny's jaw. But he didn't anticipate the strength of his adversary. Three quick successive jabs from Danny hit him in the face, eye and side of the head before he could retaliate.

'Stop it,' Cally shrieked. 'Get him out of here, Danny.'

He'd never felt a rage or rejection like it. Even when he was prepared to prove how much he loved her by fighting for her, Cally still chose someone else over him. Without hesitation, he raised his arm and hit her square in the mouth. He felt her two front teeth snap against his knuckles as she fell backwards to the floor. Danny took advantage of his distraction and wrestled him to the ground, repeatedly throwing punches at his face and torso.

He could recall very little about the rest of the night, or even the days that followed, only that the police briefly became involved, followed by the university. The expulsion board advised him that if he left immediately of his own accord, neither Cally nor Danny would press charges. He agreed, and by the end of the day and with his dream of a better life in tatters, he was on a coach travelling back to London. He hoped that, even now, all these years later, every time Cally glanced in the mirror and saw her scarred lip and veneered smile staring back at her, she'd remember how she had brought it on herself.

It was only when he met and fell in love with Audrey that he understood his relationship with Cally had been nothing more than a deep infatuation. What he and Audrey shared was like nothing he had ever experienced before – just the thought of her lit the touchpaper, and a hundred colourful fireworks exploded inside his heart . . .

'Can I top you up, hun?'

The unexpected approach from the waitress in the café made him jump. She held a steaming stainless-steel teapot in her hand.

'Yes, thank you,' he replied, and she began to pour. Then, outside, a figure caught his eye, walking towards the red-brick building he'd been watching. A backpack was slung over his shoulder, and by the colour of his trousers he was already in uniform. The third name on his list had arrived. Fishing his wallet from his pocket, he dropped a twenty-pound note on the table and left the waitress puzzled by his rapid departure and more-than-generous tip.

His research suggested that, on average, William Burgess arrived half an hour early for work, regardless of the time his shift began. From then onwards, it could be anything from five minutes to nine hours before Burgess left the building again. He would need to remain patient.

Making his way towards the car park, he hovered around the far end of it, partially obscured by one of the six stationary yellow, green and white vehicles. The CCTV cameras above him were out of action. It had taken him a day of online exploration to find the exact model and user guide so he could manually disable them without fear of electrocution.

He kept out of view of the pavement, hiding in a pre-planned spot by the medical waste bins for a full four hours until Burgess finally appeared, alone and fumbling with a set of car keys. Five feet, six inches tall and as thin as a rake, a less-prepared killer would have assumed he'd be easy to overpower. However, in two photographs on his Facebook profile, he'd spotted Burgess wearing white martial arts kit and holding a medal. He wagered it was likely his mark wouldn't go down without a fight. Failure to use a sedative on him would be foolish.

As Burgess approached, he looked puzzled then concerned by the stranger propping himself up against a bin, clutching the left-hand side of his chest and panting heavily.

'Can you help me?' he begged. Burgess hurried towards him just as he collapsed to the ground.

'What's happening, mate?' Burgess said calmly, dropping to his knees. 'Where are you feeling pain?' But before he could ask any more questions, the patient's arm raised and his fist collided with Burgess's neck. He thrust the needle in and pushed the plunger before his victim could swat it away.

Instinctively, Burgess yanked his head back, but the syringe was still embedded in his neck. When he pulled the needle from his flesh and registered what had just happened, his eyes opened saucer-wide and panic spread across his face. He rose to his feet to run, but his assailant raised both his legs and kicked out at Burgess, tipping him off balance and causing him to fall to the ground. Then he wrestled Burgess into submission, pinning his arms and legs until the fast-acting muscle relaxant worked its synthetic magic.

He removed the car keys from his victim's hand, pressed the unlock button on the fob and glanced around the car park to find which vehicle's headlights were flashing. He waited until a coach and two taxis passed before he grabbed a conscious but unreactive Burgess by his wrists, dragged him ten metres to the first responder's vehicle and bundled him across the back seat. Then he unplugged the shoreline from the mains that kept the computer system charged, and slipped the keys into the ignition. He ignored the TerraFix, the iPad-sized tablet in the centre console, as it automatically plotted the route that control was advising Burgess to take.

Instead, he programmed the small satnav perched on the dashboard for an address he already knew how to reach. Then he pulled the vehicle slowly out into the road and towards Burgess's final destination.

CHAPTER 13

'How come you get to take a car while I have to travel everywhere by public transport?' asked Becca.

Her eyes flitted around the Ford saloon; while it wasn't quite the height of luxury, it certainly beat a tube carriage crammed with a hundred sweaty commuters. She made the most of the space and stretched her legs out in the footwell, then turned up the air conditioning a notch just because she could.

'The guvnor told us to use it,' DS Bryan Thompson replied. He wound down the window and puffed on an e-cigarette, a fine cinnamon scent filling the car. He took drags in quick succession.

'I thought you'd given up vaping?'

'The missus thinks I have, so if you see her, don't tell her.'

Becca couldn't imagine Bryan keeping a secret from his wife, or from anyone for that matter, if his life depended on it. He was so transparent that his colleagues had nicknamed him 'Cling Film'. She had a lot of time for the seasoned detective – he'd been a close friend of her father's and had taken her under his wing when she first joined CID. He'd treated her like one of his own daughters, but in recent months she'd had her concerns about his health. He'd lost weight and a thin-set frame had aged him, giving him deep lines in his forehead. Becca wondered how she'd cope with raising four girls like he was, and the stresses that would bring. And she questioned how the pressure of the job would affect her when she reached his age.

'Did you hear Webster in the briefing earlier?' added Becca. 'I think she's frustrated that we're no further along, four days after the bodies were found.'

It wasn't just Becca who was feeling the strain of the investigation – the whole department was too. The CID branch had been separated into inquiry teams to investigate different aspects of the case. And as they'd sat around the table in the briefing room, each one updating the rest, Webster wasn't so much asking questions as firing them with the speed of a machine gun.

'I don't think the story in the *Evening Standard* helped,' added Bryan.

'I didn't read it. What did it say?'

'They reported that Dumitru and Cheban were cousins and that their deaths might be linked,' he continued. 'A reporter phoned Nikhat on a fishing expedition, trying to get us to say there was either a hit-man or a serial killer on the loose in London. It's a no-win situation, though. Say "no comment" and it sounds like we're hiding something. Say "there's no serial killer or hitman" and when they report our denials they still get to use those words and make it a story. Then later, if it turns out it's a Fred West or a Harold Shipman, it looks like we lied.'

'You don't think it *is* a serial killer though, do you?' Becca asked. 'I mean, I know they exist, but they're so rare, you're more likely to find one in *EastEnders* than on your own patch, aren't you?'

'No, it won't be a serial killer. It'll be someone with a vendetta against our Romanian friends. Nikhat told me just before we left that they both had criminal records back home for drug trafficking and they owed people a lot of money. That's what this case will be about, mark my words. They were probably keeping a low profile over here, but not low enough. Then someone got wind of their location, probably sent people over here to finish them off, then returned home the next day. We've got eyes and ears looking at the train, plane and ferry passenger lists.'

Becca stared through the windscreen as the heat radiating from the car bonnet and busy roads made the cars ahead shimmer. 'It's a shame, in a way,' she said. 'Serial killers are once-in-a career investigations. I'd love to come face to face with just one. Well, only after we'd nicked him.'

'What did you learn about this paramedic we're going to see?' he asked.

Becca removed a notebook from her bag and began flicking through the pages. 'He's the second of the three people nearest to Dumitru when he fell. His name is William Burgess, he's twenty-seven and lives a fifteen-minute walk from the station where Dumitru died. He's a first responder who just so happened to be on the platform and on his way to work at the time. He also helped out at the scene. He got in touch when he read about Dumitru's death being linked to the other murder.'

'Did you see him there at the time?'

'Only his legs as he crawled under the train. He'd taken his hoodie off in a platform blind spot and had his uniform on underneath. So it looked like two different people and we didn't make the link.'

'Is he still a suspect?'

'They all are until they prove they're not.'

'Spoken like a true copper.'

London's never-ending schedule of roadworks slowed them down for much of the journey. Becca wished the police could legally get from A to B by using the bus and taxi lanes, or that she could switch on the red and blue flashing lights affixed to the grille of the unmarked car and watch the vehicles in front of them part. Finally, they bypassed central London and arrived at the Turnham Green ambulance station in the west of the city.

A uniformed young woman invited them into the crew room and informed them Burgess was out on a call in a rapid-response vehicle. A computer revealed the number assigned to the vehicle he was driving. 'I thought he'd be back by now as it wasn't a serious trauma,' she said. 'Let me see what's holding him up.' She disappeared into another room.

Becca and Bryan waited on a threadbare sofa as a wall-mounted television played a home-auction show. She stared longingly at a picture-postcard thatched cottage in Cumbria and wondered if she and Maisie were ever destined to escape the capital for a new life in the country. But as much as it would suit her daughter, Becca would miss her career too much.

Almost fifteen minutes passed before an impatient Becca decided she'd had enough.

She knocked on the door the young woman had exited through and entered a room, with Bryan following closely behind. The woman and a female colleague who introduced herself as the office manager were staring at a large screen with the computerised version of an ordnance survey map of London that ambulance dispatchers used to plot and follow routes for specific vehicles and teams. She could see small ambulance-shaped icons tracking each vehicle's journey.

'We're having difficulties communicating with Will,' the office manager said anxiously. 'The ambulance that followed the call said he never arrived.'

'Which car is he in?' asked Becca, and the office manager pointed to a specific icon and zoomed in. The map revealed the street and building names.

'Have you tried calling him?' asked Becca.

'Yes, on his mobile, which is attached to his car, plus his base radio and his handheld radio. But he's not answering any of them. The vehicle's tracking device and the handheld radio tell us where he is, but it's nowhere near to where he's supposed to be.'

'Where is he now?'

'Acton Industrial Estate, which is four miles from here. His vehicle is stationary and in a cul-de-sac.'

Becca glanced at Bryan and raised her eyebrows. He responded with a nod, neither of them needing to put into words the ominous feeling that William Burgess's disappearance gave them both.

CHAPTER 14

Joe remained near to one of the glass entrances of the shopping centre, a coffee in one hand and his satchel over his shoulder.

The number of lunchtime shoppers was beginning to swell, and a high proportion of the faces passing him were office workers or school-children on lunch breaks.

He'd booked the day off on annual leave and headed for Euston station, where he caught an overland train thirty-five minutes north to Milton Keynes. Once there, a five-minute taxi ride followed before he was inside the 120,000-square-foot, air-conditioned retail centre and ready to begin.

An hour passed before he made up his mind to relocate from Midsummer Place, the section housing stores like H&M, Hollister and Topshop that appealed to a younger clientele. He walked the entire length of the building until he reached the John Lewis department store instead. There he'd find an older audience.

One by one, the strangers passing Joe were oblivious to his stare, but he glanced at every face he could, taking them all in and compar-ing them to just one person. Some were too old, some were too young, some had hair that was too dark and some he thought were likely too short in height.

The woman he was comparing them to shared his pale skin – almost translucent, his mother had once joked. But the trend for fake tan was making it impossible for the super-recogniser in him to guess the natural pigmentation lying underneath the surface.

Joe retained an unassuming, unthreatening air, keeping himself to himself, standing still, always looking away the moment anyone's eyes caught his so as not to spook them. He scanned each woman in the correct age bracket, trying to catch a glimpse of something familiar. He assumed her hamster cheeks had lost the puppy fat of youth, and he hoped that wherever she was, whatever she had been through, there had been happiness in her life and better childhood memories than he had.

He missed his sister Linzi like nothing else on earth.

Joe let out a sigh. If he didn't find her today, then he might the next time. He'd book another weekday off work soon, or perhaps – if he could get away with it – a Saturday, when the centre would be even busier. The thought of so many people contained in one place gave him better odds.

Joe was so lost in his own world that he forgot the coffee cup was still in his hand. When he finally took a sip from it, it was barely luke-warm. He dropped it into a bin and made his way towards a café to buy another, along with a toasted ham and cheese panini. He tapped his contactless card on the machine to pay, took a seat on a bench and began to eat his first meal since breakfast.

He took in the tall, evergreen foliage behind him, doggedly making its way upwards, past the triple-height windows and towards the glass ceiling. It was as if it refused to stop growing until it broke free. He too had determination and a goal, and it was to find her. But he knew that his time was running out.

CHAPTER 15

Becca and Bryan spoke very little on their journey, as the satnav led them to the address where William Burgess's Ford Focus was parked. It went unsaid by both that they were uneasy about what they might find. Although, to Becca's eyes, Bryan looked more anxious than her.

At the far end of one of several cul-de-sacs, the rear of the vehicle faced them. Becca was the first to leave their car and Bryan followed, looking around at their surroundings with an air of caution. The area was tired, rundown, completely vacant and made up of dozens of prefabricated buildings clad in corrugated iron. It reminded Becca of Indian slums she'd seen on television documentaries, but without the brightly coloured, overcrowded communities that gave them life. 'For Sale' and 'To Let' boards were optimistically nailed to the walls, and weeds grew from broken guttering and cracks in the concrete paths.

The detectives approached the stationary RRV from opposite angles, Becca flanking the driver's side, until they reached the rear doors. She noticed standard-issue red and green bags on the back seat, one containing typical first responder equipment and the other for cardiac arrests and major trauma. As they edged further forward, Becca spotted a green uniform reflected in the wing mirror. Someone was inside. Her breathing quickened.

She stretched her arm out to knock on the glass, but stood a little away from the door in case it suddenly sprang open. She looked to Bryan for approval before she proceeded. When there was no response they moved at exactly the same speed to their respective windows and peered inside.

Paramedic William Burgess was very clearly dead, his eye sockets empty and his eyeballs hanging from thin, red tendons and resting on his bloodied cheeks. His shredded fingertips jutted through holes in the broken glass screen of the TerraFix.

Bryan shook his head and took a step backwards, while Becca took deep breaths to regain her composure.

'You know what we were saying about this not being a serial killer case?' Becca asked. 'We might want to rethink that.'

CHAPTER 16

He awoke with a jolt.

Looking ahead and through the window, he saw a group of men and women, some dressed in uniforms or overalls, gathered around the RRV. Inside the perimeter of yellow crime-scene tape, camera flashes illuminated the early evening sky. And although he couldn't hear what was being said, there was much chatter and conversation spoken into mobile phones and police radios.

He wanted to know how long he'd been asleep for, but he couldn't take his eyes off the players. He imagined their positions on a chessboard and tried to decipher which piece was which in the game he was orchestrating. He wondered how they had decided to deploy them; whether it was the luck of the draw as to who was working what shift at the time of the call, or whether they'd realised how seriously his work should be taken and now they were bringing in more specialised investigators. A double murder wasn't an everyday occurrence; a triple murder with connections but no obvious motive was even more of a rarity. Especially now he'd included a member of the hallowed emergency services.

After killing William Burgess and manoeuvring his body into position, he'd made his way through a maze of alleyways towards the rear of the empty buildings that surrounded the scene of the crime. He'd climbed up a metal fire escape with several missing steps, and padlocked the door behind him. Once he reached the front of the building, he'd set up his chair and waited. But at some point, the mental and physical exertion of three kills in four days must have been too much and his brain shut down.

Now awake, he lit a cigarette. He knew he would keep smoking them, one after the other, until the pack was empty. That's how his mind operated – he was all or nothing. When there was a goal to achieve, he could become so ruthlessly single-minded that he wouldn't allow anything to stand in his way. It was the same with matters of the heart. When he loved someone, he truly loved them with every fibre of his being and he wouldn't let them go without a fight.

He tapped out a line of cocaine on to the windowsill and inhaled it in one swoop against the scene of the unfolding investigation. The paramedic's car began to slip out of view as the police forensics team erected a white tent above it. He'd left precious little evidence for them to preserve. Even though there was now not much for him to see, he remained where he was. It was enough for him just to be there.

Burgess had been his most ambitious kill of the three, and the second in broad daylight. But while Dumitru's had also been in the open, it was different. Perfect timing, a quick jab and it was all over. Burgess had been overpowered and then driven away to a second location. He could never inflict the same emotional trauma that Burgess had inflicted upon him, but the physical pain the paramedic had felt was close enough. To have been conscious but unable to prevent your eyes being gouged out must have been horrific, and no less than he deserved.

For the last three years he had felt like an empty well, drained and useless. But the satisfaction of each kill was slowly filling him up. He wasn't returning to the man he used to be, but becoming a new one. An empowered one. A man who was in control of not just his fate, but the fate of others too.

Suddenly, the phone he'd turned to silent vibrated in his pocket. He glanced at Zoe's number on the screen and waited until the call rang out rather than send it straight to voicemail. He'd speak to her in the morning when he could muster up the time and inclination.

Just as he was about to close his eyes again, a face he recognised appeared outside. He edged closer to the window, unable to take his eyes off it, every bit as fascinated by their movements as they were of his.

CHAPTER 17

It was almost midnight when Becca finally slipped her key into the lock and opened her front door. She glanced over her shoulder and scanned the dark street, looking for anything – or anyone – out of the ordinary. Once again, there was nothing to warrant her suspicions. In her job she often witnessed the dark side of human nature, and it was making her a mistrustful person away from work too.

Her mum was sitting at the table in the open-plan dining and living room, with a calculator, laptop, and dozens of envelopes and receipts spread out in front of her. Her glasses were perched on the end of her nose.

'I am so sorry, Mum,' Becca began. 'I know I promised I'd be back hours ago but it's been a hell of a day.'

'Because of that double murder case on the news?'

'Make it a triple.'

'What happened?'

'I'll tell you later. How's Maisie been today?'

'I had a meeting with Mrs Marshall and she says Maisie's thriving in the mainstream.'

Becca offered a grateful smile and felt immediately guilty that it was her mum having those meetings with Maisie's teacher and not her. But right now, Becca's work had to come first.

'When I was tucking her in, she asked if she could stay up so that she could see you when you came home. She misses you.'

'Why are you still up?' asked Becca, changing the subject.

'I think I've taken on too much.' Helen shook her head, defeated by the volume of paperwork. After her granddaughter's birth, she had rented out her home in Essex and moved in with Becca, then given up working full-time as a bookkeeper to help raise Maisie. But once Maisie began attending school, Helen had returned to work – only now it was from home – and had taken on the accounts of a dozen small businesses who couldn't afford the fees large accountancy firms charged.

Becca opened her mouth, then hesitated. 'Can I ask a favour?' she began, closing her eyes and awaiting the inevitable brusque response.

'To add to the thousands of others you already owe me? It's quite the tally.'

'I have a briefing at seven thirty that I can't be late for. Could you take Maisie to school for me?'

'Oh, Rebecca,' Helen sighed. 'I'd planned to get an early start on Maisie's costume tomorrow.' She pointed towards her sewing machine and some pastel pink fabric. Becca appeared puzzled. 'World Book Day, remember? Maisie gets to go as her favourite character and she's chosen Angelina Ballerina. You hadn't forgotten, had you?'

'No, of course not,' Becca replied, but it had completely left her mind. 'Please, Mum? You know I wouldn't ask if it wasn't important.'

'All right, but I need your help making her a tutu and I don't want to leave it until the last minute.'

Becca nodded, hanging her coat up on a wall hook and throwing her bag on to the sofa. She made her way into the kitchen, opened the cupboard door and removed a three-quarters-full bottle of white wine, filling two large glasses. She returned to the dining room and passed one to Helen. 'Am I a bad mum?' she asked.

'No, you're not, darling. But you do need to make more time for Maisie. You need to find a place for her in your life. She can't just be something you come home to at night. That's what you do with a cat.'

'I know, I know. In some respects, it was easier when she was a baby and we did everything for her. The older she gets, the more her personality comes through and the more I worry she needs more than I actually have to give.'

'That's motherhood for you. But you can't treat her any other way just because she has Down's syndrome.'

Even now, Becca still flinched at the words 'Down's syndrome'. She wondered if she'd ever get used to hearing them.

'I'll go and kiss her goodnight.'

As Becca made her way along the corridor and towards the staircase, she glanced at baby pictures of Maisie she'd had printed on to canvases. She stopped on the middle stair, and for the briefest of moments tried to imagine how Maisie might look if she was like every other little girl her age and not one with an extra chromosome. Guilt for such thoughts swiftly followed. Soon after Becca had come to terms with the diagnosis, she had vowed never to imagine 'what if?' and to accept her daughter as she was. But in moments of weakness, it was difficult not to wonder what might have been.

As Becca's workload increased, she had relied more and more on her mum to step in and fill the void she was leaving. As a result, the bond between grandmother and granddaughter had never been stronger, while Becca and Maisie's connection weakened. A vicious circle had begun. The more Becca felt like an abject failure as a parent, the more she threw herself into work and the larger the void became. Short of quitting the career she loved, Becca didn't know how to be all things to everyone.

Over time, she'd begun to justify her standoffishness by telling herself that once she got her career on track, it would have a knock-on effect and give her more confidence as a mum. However, deep down, she knew being a better detective meant working more hours and spending even less time with her daughter.

The tattoo on Becca's wrist caught her attention. It was on the underside – the name 'Maisie' inked in dark blue and a lower-case font. When she looked at it, her heart should have swelled. Instead, there was a disconnect.

Helen had been nothing short of brilliant, despite her own troubles, and Becca knew she wouldn't have been able to juggle motherhood and a full-time job without her. But Becca also missed being in a relationship, and coming home from work, snuggling up to someone on the sofa and sharing stories about their days. Deep down, she wanted a partner to watch TV shows with, to cook a Sunday lunch with all the trimmings for, or to enjoy spontaneous sex with in different rooms around the house. Momentarily, she wondered if Joe had someone to do all of those things with, then remembered she needed to message him before she went to bed.

She took another swig from the glass of wine she'd taken with her, then went into her daughter's bedroom, stroking Maisie's hair and leaning over to kiss her on her cheek. Maisie stirred. 'Mummy,' she mumbled, 'did you tell bad people off today?'

'Not today, sweetheart,' replied Becca. 'Perhaps tomorrow.'

'Will you tell Billy off, please? He makes fun of me.'

'Who's Billy?'

'He's a boy in my class. He says I'm retarded.'

Becca recoiled at the word, like someone had slapped her across the face. She had been prepared for the fact that once Maisie was at school, neither she nor Helen would be able to protect her from the harshness of the world. But it still hurt her to hear such cruelty. She made a mental note to report Billy to Maisie's teacher. 'Well, he's wrong,' she said firmly. 'And if he says it again I'll come to school and arrest him.'

'And then will you put him in jail with the other bad people?'

'Yes, sweetie.'

'Can I go to sleep with Flopsy? He's my favourite.'

Becca looked at the group of soft toys stacked on the chest of drawers and hesitated. She had no idea which one Maisie was referring to – another reminder of her parental inadequacies. She reached for a white, felt polar bear and put it by Maisie's side.

'No, silly, Flopsy is my rabbit.' Maisie yawned and Becca passed her the correct toy. She picked up her daughter's blue glasses from the side of her bed and cleaned the lenses with the sleeve of her shirt.

Becca remained perched on the side of the bed until Maisie drifted back to sleep. She tried to remind herself that nothing else mattered but being a mother to her child. But she struggled to believe it.

She hated herself for it, but she began to wonder if she would have loved her daughter more had she been Maisie's biological mother.

CHAPTER 18

Joe slipped his headphones over his ears and scrolled through the playlists on his phone he'd spent many an hour curating.

That evening, he was caught under a cloud of melancholia and wanted a collection that suited his frame of mind. Sigur Rós, Radiohead, Depeche Mode and Cigarettes After Sex would best reflect his mood, he decided. And as the opening xylophone bars of Radiohead's 'No Surprises' began, he sipped from a mug of tea and set to work.

As night fell, he was the only person left in VIIDO, having come in to play catch-up after his two-day absence spent assisting Becca and then in Milton Keynes. On his screen was the latest edition of *Caught on Camera*, the three-times-weekly Met-issued online bulletin that was uploaded with pictures of new idents linked to crimes. Joe clicked on each of them in turn, committing their faces to memory. Only when the faces became blurry did he take a break. His face was still sore from the headbutt he'd received. He'd never suffered a black eye before, and now he sported two. Colleagues often teased him for being the office 'pretty boy', and this gave him a temporary edgier appearance which he didn't mind. Any damage to his eyes was always going to be an immediate concern, but to his relief, it hadn't seemed to impede his vision.

The visit to Milton Keynes that afternoon had once again proved fruitless, and his rational side questioned why he'd expected it to be anything else. His sister Linzi was on his mind as he flicked though the photos, scanning each female face and trying to reconcile the gap between how he remembered her from when they were children and how she might appear now. Any photographs of her had long since vanished, but he didn't need them – they were stored inside his head with the same clarity as if he'd pored over them just that morning. But the odds of spotting her in the online bulletin or in a shopping centre twenty-six years after her sudden disappearance were infinitesimally small.

Joe's memory drifted back to when their mother had finally plucked up the courage to squirrel away enough money to leave her abusive, manipulative husband. After months of careful planning and covering all her tracks, an hour after he left for work, the removals van had arrived. It packed up all her and her children's belongings with military speed and precision.

By mid-afternoon, their home in Nottingham was an unwelcome memory and they were picking up the keys to their rental house in Milton Keynes.

They had been happy there for exactly three days.

Joe regularly scanned *Caught on Camera* in the hope of catching sight of Linzi. He knew that if she showed up it meant she hadn't made the best life choices, but he didn't care. He could help her. And at least it would prove she was still alive.

And when he could get away with it, he spent his free time standing alone in shopping centres in Milton Keynes, Nottingham and London, in case she'd gravitated towards one of those areas as an adult. But because faces could alter so much from child to grown-up, there was a chance they had passed one another without him recognising her, despite his photographic memory. It didn't stop him from trying.

The bulletin of idents came to an end and he closed the website's page. He returned to skimming through video images from a case he'd been assigned the previous week. There'd been a large-scale series of mobile phone thefts at music venues around the capital. Teams of pickpockets had been gaining access legitimately, and as revellers were distracted by the bands, they were unaware their phones were being swiped. Within half an hour he'd recognised two with criminal records and snapped three female idents. The accomplishment began to shift the dark cloud above him.

A text alert appeared on his screen from Becca.

Hiya, thought I'd let you know we found the paramedic. He worked at the Turnham Green Ambulance Service – note the past tense of the word 'worked'. We found his body this afternoon. We're officially now on the hunt for a three-times serial killer. Beccs.

Joe was pleased to hear from her again but felt a little disappointed that his involvement in the case was complete. As much as he loved his own department, CID's work was much more varied and exciting. And besides, he quite enjoyed spending time with Becca and proving her preconceived notion of super-recognisers wrong.

Thanks for letting me know, he typed. *Always around if you need anything else.*

He had moved from his desk to get ready to go home when Becca's speedy reply appeared.

Well, it's funny you say that . . . if you mean it, Nik would love to have you on board in a secondment? We still need to trace the woman with the baby. He's quite happy to call your guvnor to arrange?

See you tomorrow, Joe typed. And within the hour, he set to work.

CHAPTER 19

The team investigating the murders of Stefan Dumitru, Darius Cheban and now William Burgess had doubled in size overnight.

Since Becca and DS Thompson had discovered the paramedic's body, detectives from other departments had been drafted in to assist with the recently christened Operation Chamber. Now there were forty of them gathered around the table in the major incident room, and more in the space next door. The apprehension before the briefing was palpable.

The windows were wide open and a warm breeze made the vertical blinds rattle against the frames. Becca counted five faces she didn't recognise among the uniformed and plain-clothed officers. Many had worked through the night, while others, like her and Bryan, had got the time to return home and grab a few hours' sleep before returning to the station.

It was only when she'd reached the office that she realised she hadn't opened the door to Maisie's bedroom and kissed her sleeping daughter goodbye before she'd left that morning. She was angry with herself – it was something else to add to the ever-expanding list of her failings as a mother.

On a large whiteboard were photographs of all three victims, along-side their names, dates and times of death, appraisals of the crime scenes and suspected causes of death. A map of London was highlighted with a red marker to identify where they lived and where their bodies had been discovered.

As the meeting began, CS Webster and DI Nikhat Odedra sat at the front of the room, listening and making notes as, in turn, detectives updated everyone as to where they were in their particular part of the investigation. Three books of laminated colour photographs of each victim and crime scene were passed around.

Becca noted Webster's short, uneven, chewed fingernails, which were at odds with her otherwise immaculate appearance. Maybe that was her stress release. Becca's was a glass of Pinot Grigio.

As she listened to the updates, she was surer than ever that her instinct to talk herself on to the case had been the correct one. If she was failing in her parental duties, at least she could make up for it here.

She hadn't admitted to anyone, even Bryan, that finding William Burgess with his eyes hanging from their sockets had made her queasy, or that twice that night she'd awoken having dreamed about them. As they'd waited at the crime scene for backup and forensics to arrive, Bryan had appeared just as unnerved as she was.

The door opened quietly as Joe arrived. He and Becca greeted each other with a formal nod as he took a position at the rear of the room.

After everyone had been brought up to speed, the questions began.

'Do we think it's a serial killer?' an officer with whom Becca wasn't familiar asked.

'You know that I hate using that term because it trivialises the case,' Webster said. 'So I'd prefer it if we could refer to him for what he is – a killer. We are almost certain these cases are linked but there's no concrete reason for us to think he's a serial murderer.'

'Do we have any idea how a Romanian decorator and former drug dealer, his flatmate, and a paramedic with no form are linked?' asked someone else. 'Could Burgess have access to medication and been supplying them with drugs to sell?'

'I want a sub-team led by DI Boyce and DS Robson to take on that line of inquiry. There are a lot of gaps to fill, so I want every inch of their lives sifted through to see what they might have in common. They lived a fifteen-minute walk from each other, and the tube station. Is that just coincidence? Did they visit the same pubs, play for the same football team, learn to drive with the same instructor, have kids at the same school? I don't care how innocuous it may sound, right now the only thing we're certain of is that all three were unlawfully killed in different but equally brutal ways. We need to know why, and, more importantly, by whom.'

Webster pressed play on her laptop, and footage from Burgess's murder scene appeared on a screen on the wall. In a room full of seasoned detectives, who between them had seen it all, Becca noticed she wasn't the only squeamish one to avert her gaze when the camera focused in on the victim's hollowed eye sockets.

'See this mark on his neck where the bleeding starts?' Webster continued, pressing pause. 'We won't know until we get toxicology reports back in a couple of days, but it looks like a puncture wound. If it follows the pattern of Cheban, his murder will have been about the torture as much as the death itself. He'll have been heavily sedated but conscious when he died, and it won't have been swift.'

'What else has forensics found?' asked Bryan.

'There were no fingerprints found at either scene to link to a potential suspect,' added Nikhat. 'No hair traces, blood, saliva, semen, vomit or any kind of DNA. Also, there are no witnesses to date, or CCTV footage.'

Webster suddenly focused on Becca. 'DS Vincent, tell us more about the third suspect and witness to Dumitru's death.'

Becca froze like a rabbit caught in the headlights. There was no update, at least as far as she was aware. 'It's something we're still looking into . . .' she stuttered.

'I was under the impression she had been located?' Webster interjected. 'Is that no longer the case? If not, why not?'

Shit, thought Becca, and she suddenly wished she wasn't on Webster's radar at all.

Joe spoke. 'If you click on the red folder on your screen you'll see what was discovered this morning.' Webster obliged as Joe walked the team through the footage on screen. 'This traces witness number three to outside the tube station, where she appeared to hang around for a while after the evacuation. Then, using the bus lane cameras, we can see her walking back down Mile End Road, then Bancroft Road. Mile End Hospital cameras have her walking into Longnor Road and finally Bradwell Street. If you watch carefully, a camera outside a dry-cleaners shows where she ended up.'

Joe pointed to the left-hand side of the screen, and mother and child could just about be seen entering a block of flats and opening the door to a ground-floor residence.

Nikhat gave Joe an appreciative nod while Becca looked on, appalled at how he'd usurped her and used her case to better himself. It must have taken Joe much of the night to locate and sift through that footage, but she didn't participate with the praise. Trawling CCTV imagery wasn't a process she enjoyed, but neither was being humiliated by a colleague and made to look out of the loop.

'And is this woman lurking somewhere in that infamous memory bank of yours, DS Russell?' Becca hit back without bothering to disguise her caustic tone. By Joe's expression, it hadn't gone unnoticed.

'No, she's not.'

'I guess it'll take grass-roots detective work to find her then, rather than your "super-recogniser" skills.'

'There are two things which strike me as being a bit off about this,' Joe continued. 'If you saw a man fall under a train and die, the last thing you'd want to do is hang around when you're carrying a baby.

Surely your instinct would be to protect it and get away from there as quickly as possible?'

Everyone around him agreed.

'And look at all these images of her with the child. You can see the kid's arms and legs but they haven't moved.' He pointed at various screengrabs. 'Not when she's waiting for a tube, standing on the stairs, lurking around outside or walking to the flat. Not one of that child's limbs twitches.'

'That doesn't mean anything,' Becca dismissed. 'Babies can drop off to sleep anywhere or at any time.'

'Yes, but look at this.' Joe rewound the footage. As the woman turned her head to watch the ambulance arrive, she continued to walk but caught her child's leg on a lamp post. 'The baby didn't flinch, and she doesn't even try to comfort it.'

Becca didn't want to agree with Joe, but he was right. At that age, Maisie would have screamed blue murder.

'Beccs, do you want to go to the flat and see if you can find the mum and baby?' Nikhat asked, and she nodded her agreement. 'Then go back to the scene of William Burgess's death and view all the CCTV from neighbouring properties close to the ambulance station, like shops and offices. Do the same around the industrial estate. The killer picked a very specific place to drive the victim, to where he knew he wouldn't be disturbed, so he must have been there before to check it out. Take a couple of uniforms to help you. Tag along if you fancy it, Joe?'

'Does he really need to come?' Becca challenged. Nikhat cocked his head, apparently thrown by her reluctance. She quickly recognised how adversarial she sounded so she attempted to correct herself. 'I mean, I don't want to waste DS Russell's time if he's more use here.'

'Let's make the most of his Rain Man brain while we have him, shall we?' Nikhat said. 'We could do with a few more like him in CID.'

You've changed your tune, thought Becca, but decided it would do her no favours to mention it.

'So, we have three murders, all using different methods, potentially committed by one person who knows how to clean up after themselves,' continued Webster. 'What does that tell us?'

'That he's thought this through and is targeting each victim for a reason,' said Joe. 'None of these killings are spontaneous, and they've been meticulously planned. There's a chance it could be a cry for help; that he's trying to tell us why he's doing what he's doing within the manner of their deaths. But he gives mixed messages, because when you factor in that he's methodical and does his research – like learning how to knock out CCTV cameras at the ambulance station – that suggests he doesn't actually want to get caught. I think each killing is tailor-made for each victim, like he's teaching them a lesson – but for what purpose, we don't know. And even if the first two victims and number three didn't know each other, something definitely links them.'

'I agree,' said Webster, nodding, which irritated Becca even further. 'I also think what he's doing is personal. The victims haven't just been tortured, they've been tortured in very specific ways. Under a tube train, waterboarded with alcohol, removing someone's eyes then drilling holes and cramming their fingers through a tablet. It's carefully thought out, and it's brutal. And as this case is getting much attention inside and outside the Met, it'll come as no surprise to learn that all annual leave is cancelled until we nail him.'

As the briefing was dismissed, Joe followed a fuming Becca to her desk and then out of the building. Neither said a word to the other.

CHAPTER 20

He was glad he'd had the good sense to shower and clean himself up while he was still high, because the comedown was close to crippling.

Sitting in the driver's seat of the company pool car, he watched the girls in the office through the security bars of the rear window and took a few deep breaths. The aftermath of the previous day's attack had given him a high level of satisfaction he hadn't thought it was possible to reach. He had stayed awake long into the night, but doing so came at the expense of his cocaine stash. He'd used up every last gram of it, and the after-effects were like the onset of influenza. He wanted to curl up on the back seat and sleep until the headache, muscle pains and runny nose worked their way out of his body.

He'd promised himself he'd only ever use stimulants to help him function at night. But if he'd had any on his person now, he'd be using them to pick himself off the floor. His dealer wasn't answering his phone, and he didn't mix in the kind of circles where he could find a trustworthy replacement at the drop of a hat. He would have to ride it out for now.

Inside, after two strong coffees and with four paracetamols dissolving in his stomach, he took his desk near the shopfront window and pretended to focus on what was on his screen. Office work bored him rigid, and letting out rental properties neither interested nor excited him. The job wasn't challenging or intellectually rewarding, but it was a means to an end. For all intents and purposes, it allowed him to masquerade as an ordinary man with an ordinary life doing an ordinary job.

He called up an inventory on the computer's database. It had been carried out when the tenants of a furnished flat he'd rented out had moved in. He compared it to the forms filled in when they'd left. They appeared to have stolen all the spoons and light shades. It defied logic, he thought, because now they'd be paying for them out of their deposit, along with a ten per cent mark-up. Buying new from Ikea would have been more cost-effective. They'd seemed to him to be a respectable couple with decent references, and not the kind to steal pointless things. But he knew better than most that looks could be deceiving.

Sifting through his colleagues' online diaries, he made a note of the telephone numbers of potential customers who'd booked viewings of that particular flat, then erased their appointments. Later, and out of earshot, he'd call each one to cancel and then remove the property from the books for the rest of the week. If his colleagues asked, he'd blame an infestation of fleas in the carpets that required fumigation. The truth was, he'd need that flat for himself.

His eyes wandered to the front window and out into the high street, towards a group of teenage girls eating takeaway food. He yawned, and his reflection caught his eye. Absent-mindedly he was tugging at his right ear lobe, something he only did when he was anxious. It bore one of several physical scars from a lifetime of run-ins with his mother. When he was eleven years old, she'd smelled cigarette smoke on his breath and slapped his face until it was raw. Then, without warning, she'd grabbed at the silver hoop in his ear, deliberately tearing it out and splitting the lobe in two. It had never healed properly and had left a visible gap, half a centimetre in length. Later that weekend, she'd vanished without telling him where she was going or if she'd return, leaving him to fend for himself for nine days straight. He'd had no money to buy food, so in his desperate state he shoplifted a loaf of bread and a Twix from a local supermarket. But he'd been spotted and caught, and when the police couldn't find his mum, he'd been placed into foster care and sent to live with another family far away from London. He liked his foster mum, Sylvia, and her son, David, a lot. But when a girl called Laura joined them, the cuckoo in the nest wasted no time in trying to oust him. She'd even falsely accused him of pinning her down on a sofa and touching her inappropriately. And she'd encouraged David to attack him as punishment. Sylvia was forced to take Laura's side and had him moved to another foster family, before eventually he was shipped back to the capital. Once the mandatory monitoring from social services was complete, the hell at home had resumed.

Even now, the fear of separation from anyone he loved terrified him. However, he had become as transient as his mother.

His wages were average at best but his overheads were few. He could afford to live reasonably well, especially as he was of no fixed abode. Letting empty properties enabled him to move from empty location to location at a moment's notice, until a new tenant came along.

Sometimes it might mean a furnished flat for a week; on other occasions it was an office for anything up to a fortnight. He paid no rent and no utility bills, and if the gas, electricity or water had been switched off, he showered at one of London's public swimming pools. When he desired creature comforts, he'd stay at Zoe's flat.

He travelled light – one large suitcase and a holdall contained most of his worldly belongings, like his clothes, toiletries, laptop and a wireless hotspot router. It was shocking how many people still didn't affix passwords to their Wi-Fi. His furniture was a fold-up table and canvas chair. Each morning he packed up everything and returned it to the boot of his car, in case the property was to be unexpectedly viewed that day.

Often, he invented appointments and clients, or claimed a potential new landlord had sought out a valuation on a property that didn't exist, to get him out of the office. Then, every couple of hours, he'd phone in and touch base with his colleagues so they didn't question his whereabouts.

Much of that time away was spent following around the six names on his list. He knew that he was putting himself under undue pressure by allowing such a short space of time between kills. But the longer he left them, the more time he'd be giving the police to decipher what linked his victims. And if they could do that, it wouldn't be long before they worked out a pattern and thwarted its completion.

That was, of course, the last thing he wanted. He had put too much of himself into it to watch it fizzle out so quickly. Each person had made his list because of what they had done. They had played a role in making him the man he had become. They only had themselves to blame for creating a monster. And one by one, the monster was going to cause them more suffering than they could have ever imagined. He would end their lives in the same premature way that they had ended his.

Just two more deaths separated him from the final name on his list, and it was the one he was most anticipating. That person was the catalyst for everything that had followed; the blame lay squarely on their shoulders, so it was only right he worked through the others and perfected his skills before he targeted them. He felt like a hunter who, having started with smaller game, was gradually working up and up until he had the big game in the cross-hairs of his rifle. And how he would savour that kill. He would draw in and relish every second, from the stalking to the moment they breathed their last. Just the thought of that final confrontation stimulated him more than cocaine.

'Right, I'm off to show the Harpers around that semi in Parsons Green,' he directed to no one in particular. He shuffled some sheets of blank A4 paper lying on his desk for effect, and slipped them inside his briefcase.

'Have they still not found anywhere?' Margaret replied, tipping her head so her glasses slipped towards the end of her nose.

'No, they're the pickiest people I've ever dealt with.' The truth was they weren't, because the Harpers didn't exist.

As he drove, he tuned the car radio to a talk-show station. A presenter was discussing the early edition of the *Evening Standard*, with the headline story involving a serial killer stalking the city. Excitedly, he turned up the volume.

'Yesterday, police categorically denied they are looking for a serial killer,' began a voice with a cockney twang. 'However, we have it on good authority they are hunting for just one individual suspected of killing three people in the space of a few days. If that's not a serial killer, then what is? Tell us what you think.'

Briefly, he was tempted to get in touch, but held himself back. The very fact people were talking about him and taking him seriously was proof he was on the right path. But branding him a serial killer was lazy. *Serial killers and psychopaths murder out of compulsion*, he reminded himself. *They do it because they have no choice.* He killed with purpose. And eventually, everyone would understand why.

He listened for a little while longer until the subject of discussion changed. And by the time his car pulled up outside the parcel lockers, he noticed his cocaine comedown was beginning to ease.

One by one, he typed four codes into four doors, and opened them to find boxes of various sizes addressed to Stefan Dumitru. He had ordered them from online shops across Europe using a credit card he'd taken out in Dumitru's name. British firefighting equipment that had been replaced with more up-to-date versions was often sold and shipped abroad to fire services in less affluent countries. Now he was buying them back, for his own use.

Once the packages were in his car, he drove to a lock-up garage behind a row of terraced houses, carried them inside and checked that everything was accounted for in his inventory.

The ringing of his private mobile phone, the one that only two people had the number for, interrupted him. It wasn't Zoe, so it could only be one other person.

'What do you want?' he barked.

The conversation lasted less than a minute. By the time he hung up, he was rushing back towards his car.

CHAPTER 21

An awkward silence divided Becca and Joe as they walked up the path towards the ground-floor flat where the third potential witness to Dumitru's murder lived.

Becca hadn't tried to disguise that she was unhappy with something Joe had done, but for much of their shared tube journey to Mile End, he had still tried to make polite conversation. She had responded with monosyllabic answers. Just as Becca was about to push random buttons in the hope a resident would buzz them in, Joe paused.

'Okay, while I don't know you that well, I can tell that you're pissed off with me,' he began. 'Can we clear the air, please?'

Becca turned to face him, her lips pursed. 'There are two things you need to know about me, Joe. Firstly, I don't like being made to look like an idiot in front of my colleagues, and secondly, I don't like anyone thinking I can't do my job properly.'

'And what do either of those things have to do with me?'

'You've done them both.'

Joe folded his arms. 'How, exactly?'

'This is my investigation, I had to fight tooth and nail to get a place on it, and then you come along and in your first briefing, you're holding court like the bloody King of England telling everyone about the great work that you've done in tracking down whomever it is we're about to cold-call. So much for your department not being ego-driven.'

'Is that what you think happened?'

'It's what I know happened, I was there. Do you have any idea what it's like to be a female police officer and a single mum?'

'You have children?' he asked, surprised.

'I have a six-year-old daughter. Let me tell you what it's like. When you're a mum with no partner, you spend your life in competition with everyone else. You're in competition with families where both parents are present; you're competing with other mums who also hold down full-time jobs and make it look so effortless. You're competing with male colleagues who, even though they're not supposed to, have it so much easier than you. Then you're competing against yourself because you set career goals that you want to achieve but can't ever hope to reach, as you don't have the time to dedicate to your job. You're competing against the bastards in this world like Nicky Penn because they are the reason you joined the job and put yourself through all this crap – to make a difference. The one thing you shouldn't expect, however, is people who you thought had your back to compete against you. To have someone like you making me look like I'm not putting in the hours or pulling my weight, when I know I'm doing the best I can, makes me feel like total shit. That's what it's like to be in the police and be a single mum.'

Becca turned her head to face the door before pushing three random buzzers. Silence hung between them until Joe spoke.

'In the briefing, why do you think Webster came to you and asked about the woman we're about to see?'

Becca shrugged. 'I don't know.'

'Because I emailed her and Nik telling them we'd got an address. Note my use of the word "we". And I signed it from the both of us.'

'What?'

'I didn't tell them it was just me who tracked her down. And I blind cc'd you into the email to give you a heads-up.'

Becca hadn't opened her email that morning. She waited, red-faced, for the ground beneath her feet to open and swallow her whole, but the terra firma remained intact to shame her for longer. Eventually, the door unlocked and they made their way towards the flat they'd seen on camera. After ringing a bell, the door opened and they identified themselves to the woman they recognised from CCTV footage and asked for permission to enter.

It was obvious to Becca and Joe that the person standing in the gloom of the sparsely furnished sitting room was not genetically female.

'How can I help you?' she asked in a nervous, masculine tone. The curtains inside the room were almost completely closed, and the lack of light helped to soften her features.

However, Becca still noticed that her face was thick with make-up to try to disguise the shadow of stubble that was close to breaking through to the surface. Her eyebrows were too heavy and her lipstick too thick; the blue eyeshadow she'd painted on hadn't been used since the early 1980s. Becca wanted to wipe it all from her face and offer her a tutorial. Her dress clung in all the wrong places, and the clip-on earrings covered her lobes and gave her the appearance of a 1970s soap-opera barmaid.

'Can I ask your name?' asked Becca.

'Megan Bingham,' she replied, then hesitated. 'But I was born John.'

Becca made an immediate decision to call her by her name of choice. 'Well, Megan, we're here because we're investigating an accident involving a man who fell in front of a tube on Monday evening, which we believe you were a witness to?'

Megan nodded her head as the memory appeared to come back to life. 'It's something I won't forget in a hurry,' she said.

'Can you tell me from your perspective what you saw?' asked Joe.

Megan repeated the same story Nicky Penn had told them about the argument between him and Stefan Dumitru. 'The sound of the train's brakes screaming as it ground to a halt – they've been haunting me for days. I've not been able to get back on a tube since.'

'But you stayed on the platform for quite a while after the accident until the staff asked everyone to leave, didn't you?' said Joe.

'Did I?'

'Yes, then you waited for a moment outside too.'

'I think I must have been in shock,' Megan replied. She gently pulled at the fringe of her dark wig. 'I was hoping that maybe there was a chance he survived. Did he?'

'No, I'm afraid not. And it has since become a murder inquiry.'

'Oh gosh, really? But he just seemed to lose his footing and slip.'

'Do you remember the people you were standing next to? Did you see anyone acting suspiciously?'

'Not really. Why? Do you think one of them did it?' Megan's voice became more agitated. 'God, could it have been me under that carriage?'

'No, we think the victim was targeted.'

She didn't seem convinced. Becca decided their chat had been pointless and was ready to leave. 'Thank you, Megan, you've been very helpful,' she lied.

'Can I ask about the baby you were carrying?' Joe asked as they turned to leave. 'Whose is it?'

Megan couldn't quite meet his eye. 'He's not real,' she whispered. 'He's a doll.'

Even through the heavy make-up, Becca thought she noticed Megan's face redden. 'And why do you carry it?'

'Because my wife won't let me see our son any more.' She held one trembling hand with the other. 'I told her I was trans when Etienne was four months old. I know I should have faced up to it before we agreed to start a family, because it was completely unfair on her.'

'And she didn't take it well?'

'No, she ordered me to leave, cleared out our bank account and stopped me seeing him. Monday was only the second time I'd dared to go outside as Megan. I'll probably never get to see my little boy, and I thought taking the doll out with me might make me feel like a parent again. I couldn't push him in a stroller or people would think me mad, but if I held him close to me in a sling, people wouldn't see his face properly. Saying this out loud, I know how stupid it sounds. But I miss him so much.'

As Megan held her head in her hands, Joe was the first to move towards her and place his hand on her arm. When Becca watched him treat Megan with compassion, she knew she'd got him all wrong. He wasn't the kind of man to screw over a colleague.

'I know what it's like to lose people close to you,' Joe said, 'but you can never give up hope, okay?'

Megan nodded, mascara smeared across her wet cheeks.

The door closed behind them and they walked in silence towards Mile End tube station. Becca was desperate to ask who Joe was referring to, and wondered if it had hurt him as much as losing a loved one had damaged her.

CHAPTER 22

Becca and Joe stood side by side in front of the taped-off area surrounding the car park of Turnham Green ambulance station.

Television camera crews and a presenter she recognised from Sky News were reporting live from the scene. Becca had already guessed what would happen now the story was well and truly in the public domain. It would be both a help and a hindrance. It opened the floodgates for every person with a grudge against someone – a suspicious-looking neighbour or a peculiar relative – to light up the Met's switchboard with suggested names. Lessons had been learned from past mistakes, where leads marked less-than-credible had been ignored and then come back to bite the force where it hurt. So each call had to be logged and, where appropriate, investigated.

Forensic scientists were carrying out a fingertip search of the areas near to where William Burgess had been kidnapped and bundled into the back of his first responder's unit. Newspaper photographers took pictures from the pavement, while passers-by paused to gawp.

As it was Joe's first time there, he examined it from all angles, along with the surrounding buildings.

'Can we clear the air?' Becca asked suddenly, her conscience weighing heavily upon her.

'About what?' Joe replied.

'The briefing.'

'I don't recall what happened, can you remind me?' The cheeky glint in Joe's eyes made it clear he knew exactly what Becca was referring to. They crossed the road and made their way towards a row of shops.

'You know the gentlemanly thing to do would be to say "Forget about it",' she replied.

'Who told you I was a gentleman?'

She took a deep breath. 'Okay, if you need me to say the actual words, I'm sorry about earlier, I was being a cow.'

'Yeah, you were.' Becca wasn't expecting him to agree. 'Just for the record, I wasn't trying to get one over on you. I wouldn't try to get ahead of anyone at their expense.'

'I know, I was just being overly sensitive,' Becca said. 'Can we move past it?'

'I already have.'

They glanced up at the flats above a minimart and spotted a CCTV camera attached to a crumbling rendered wall.

'Shall I take the lead?' Becca asked.

'Of course. I wouldn't want you to think I was trying to take over your case, would I?' Becca shot him a glance. 'Joke!' he protested, and they entered the shop.

The external camera turned out to be a dummy, and inside, none of the minimart's five cameras pointed beyond the window. Regardless, Joe went through the footage looking for familiar faces among the shop's customers and putting new ones to memory. It was a similar situation at the other premises on the parade as, one by one, Becca and Joe sat in storerooms and offices, hunched over monitors, pausing, rewinding and fast-forwarding footage for hours at a time. And when 6 p.m. approached and they still hadn't turned up anything, Joe sensed Becca's frustration.

'Why doesn't facial recognition software work?' Becca asked. 'Surely it'd save us having to do all this.'

'There are lots of reasons,' Joe replied, without taking his eyes off the screen. 'Cameras are generally placed higher up on buildings to get a wider scope of an area, or so it feels less "Big Brother". And I mean Orwellian rather than the TV show.'

'I'm not entirely uneducated.'

'That means if an image of you is taken at an awkward angle or from too far away, it can distort your face. The computer then struggles when we ask it to compare that image to a mugshot already in the system. For the software to work perfectly, you have to be looking directly into the lens, like at passport control in an airport. Otherwise, it'll struggle when it comes to measuring the overall facial structure. And it can't take into account whether you're wearing make-up and if you've contoured it to highlight your bone structure, or how lighting behind or in front of you might change the way you look, or if you're hiding part of your face or pulling a stupid expression.'

'But they'll iron all that out eventually, won't they?'

'Probably one day, but not for at least another decade. And they'll always need a human to double-check it. No court in the land is ever going to convict someone solely on what artificial intelligence thinks is their face.'

After drawing a blank at an off-licence, florist and RSPCA charity shop, their final stop was an unkempt café, missing half its signage letters. Instead of reading *Tuck & Scoff*, it read *uck off*. Becca wondered if it was kept like that on purpose.

'Nah mate, no one's gonna rob this place so we don't bother with cameras,' scoffed a ruddy-cheeked cook behind the counter. The food stains smeared across his apron were many washes old.

'Have you seen anyone acting suspiciously outside?' asked Becca. 'Someone hovering around the ambulance car park, anyone parked nearby and sitting in their vehicle for long periods of time?'

'Is this to do with what happened over the road, to the ambulance bloke?' he replied. Joe nodded. 'We heard he had his eyes gouged out,' he continued. 'Is that right?'

Becca observed how his face seemed to light up at the gore factor. 'I can't confirm that, I'm afraid,' she replied, but offered him the subtlest of nods, like she was letting him in on a secret. She didn't see the harm in bending the rules if it helped to get someone onside. The cook seemed appreciative and his face scrunched up in thought.

'I can't think of anyone,' he replied.

'What about that bloke who suddenly started coming here? Always picks a table by the window?' asked a waitress who appeared from behind them. She replaced the cutlery in an empty pot with a loud clank.

'Was he acting suspiciously though?' the cook asked.

'Well, he's not our usual type of punter, is he? We get a lot of builders and scaffolders for the all-day breakfasts, but he don't dress like none of them. He looked, I dunno, normal, I guess. He's been getting here before dawn, sitting at that table by the window drinking tea for hours. Never orders food, no one ever joins him, he don't read a paper or play on his phone like everyone else. Just stares out of the window, like he's daydreaming.'

'Can you describe him?' asked Joe, and removed a notebook from his jacket.

'Average-looking, dark blond, wavy hair, dresses casual, sometimes wears glasses. I just fill up his tea mug and let him get on with it.'

'Any distinguishing features, like tattoos, jewellery, scars?'

'No – oh yeah, he has a scar on his earlobe, like it's been torn and didn't close up properly. He always leaves a good tip though.'

'Was he in yesterday?'

'Yeah, early on and left in a hurry.'

Joe pulled Becca aside. 'That fits in with the timeline of William Burgess's kidnap.'

'Is there anything in that description that rings any bells for idents you've seen?' she replied.

'No, it was too vague. But the earlobe scar interests me.'

On their return to Becca's office, she watched Joe using the waitress's description to compare to the metadata in the idents' database. Each time, he tweaked keywords and descriptions, but each time he drew a blank. By the time the clock on the wall reached 8 p.m., they were ready to call it a night.

'Do you want to come over to mine for some supper?' Joe asked suddenly.

Becca felt herself blush and dropped her head, pretending to look for something on the floor so that he couldn't see her cheeks.

'It'll give us the chance to go through what we've learned so far, before tomorrow's briefing,' he added.

'Yes, yes, of course,' she replied, and fought back the urge to break into a huge wide smile.

CHAPTER 23

'But why aren't you coming home?' asked Maisie in a whiny, sniffly voice. Becca immediately felt like the worst mother on earth.

'I'll be back later tonight when you're asleep, and I'll come and give you a big kiss. How does that sound?'

'And what will happen if the big dog comes back in my dreams and tries to bite me and you aren't here to stop it?'

'Well, Granny will make sure it won't get you, sweetie.'

'But I want *you*.'

'But you have Granny.'

'I want my mummy.'

Becca pulled the phone away from her ear as her daughter began to sob. She shook her head, feeling terrible for letting Maisie down again. Moments earlier, she had lied to her mum about her plans for the evening, claiming that because the case had escalated to a third murder, overtime was mandatory. While that wasn't entirely inaccurate, she omitted mentioning her work that night would only be with Joe, and that they'd be alone in his flat.

Even without that admission, Becca was familiar enough with Helen's telephone manner to know that putting work above Maisie was once again going down like a lead balloon.

'Here, tell your daughter yourself,' Helen had scolded before handing the phone to Maisie.

Five minutes later, and without making any headway in convincing the child that what Becca had to do was more important than reading a bedtime story, Helen hung up, but not before throwing Becca an acerbic 'well done' first.

This is your job, Becca told herself. *You have nothing to feel guilty for.* However, in her heart of hearts, she couldn't convince even herself of that, let alone her mum or her little girl.

She slipped into the fresh set of clothes she kept in her desk drawer for emergencies, then reapplied lipstick and eyeliner, sprayed some Jo Malone perfume on to her neck and behind her ears, and sucked on an extra-strong breath mint.

Before leaving, she briefed Nikhat of her and Joe's findings, and he informed her that a fast-tracked toxicology report revealed Burgess had been anaesthetised with Propofol, the same drug as Cheban. And he too had been alive when he was tortured and killed. Behind her steely facade, Becca shivered as she considered how it must have felt to be conscious but unable to prevent your eyes being torn from their sockets.

As she made her way across London and towards Joe's address, she reflected on how she had once vowed never to become involved with another work colleague after DCI Peter Addison. Maisie had been a year and half old when he asked Becca out for a drink, and she had delayed informing him her daughter had Down's syndrome. Part of her hadn't wanted to scare him off, and the rest was being stubborn. Why should Maisie's condition make any difference?

Two months after they began dating, she introduced her daughter to him with a picnic in Victoria Park. Peter didn't even attempt to disguise his disappointment that this ready-made family came with complications. So Becca ended their relationship the next day, and on the rare occasions they bumped into each other through work, their conversations were polite but brief. But she quietly resented him for making her feel like her child was not good enough. She was reluctant to admit it, but Peter's behaviour had brought to the surface buried fears that all potential partners would think like him.

However, something told her Joe was different. He possessed a strong but gentle quality, and it was rare to find both in a police officer – or just a man in general – at least in her experience. She wanted to know more about what made him tick.

Finally, she arrived at his building and lurked nervously by the entrance, patting out a stubborn crease in the front of her skirt before checking her make-up by reversing the camera lens on her phone. A moment after pressing the intercom button, the door unlocked and she climbed two sets of stairs to the third floor.

The three-storey block of flats in Wapping had begun life two centuries ago, as warehouses storing the cargo of ships that sailed up the River Thames before docking in the east of the capital. Becca assumed it must be a rental property, as a detective's salary wouldn't make a dent in the mortgage payments for a conversion development like this.

Outside the door of flat 11, she clutched her bottle of wine, hoping the Merlot she'd picked up en route at Tesco was the right colour for whatever it was they were about to eat. She'd spent fifteen pounds on it, around ten more than her usual brand.

'Play it cool,' she said quietly as she knocked on the door. 'Play it cool.'

Becca heard a dog bark, then footsteps coming down a set of stairs behind the door. She assumed the flat must be spread across two floors.

'Hi, you must be Beccs,' a man she didn't recognise began as he opened the door. He offered her his hand. 'I'm Matt, it's lovely to meet you,' he continued.

'You too,' she said. *Oh shit, I've misread it,* she thought. *He's invited his super-recogniser colleagues too.* 'Do you work with Joe?' she asked, unable to recall him from Joe's office.

Matt cocked his head to one side, like he was reading her. 'He didn't tell you he was married, did he?'

Becca's stomach sank as she shook her head. It was even worse than she thought – Joe's wife was upstairs. Becca was going to be the token singleton at a dinner party. Then an even worse scenario came to mind. *Oh fuck, please tell me Joe's not trying to matchmake me with one of his friends. Although Matt is quite fit . . .*

'And by the look on your face, he might have also neglected to mention he was married to a man?'

Becca smiled stiffly.

'And you thought he'd invited you round because . . .' He left the rest of the sentence blank to spare her blushes. Becca was grateful, but it didn't stop her face from reddening. Matt beckoned her into the hallway as a dog made its way down a wooden and metal staircase. Its bark had been deceptively loud for its small, wiry frame, but it appeared friendly.

'Oscar, right?' Becca asked.

'Yes. I like how his colleagues know the name of his dog but not his husband. Well, Becca . . . we can either spend the rest of the night tiptoeing around one another and feeling embarrassed, or we can crack open that bottle of wine you've bought and drink it while my idiot of a husband cooks us something delicious. Does that sound like a plan?'

Matt offered her a large, white-toothed grin that seemed to take up most of the lower portion of his face. His eyes were so green that she wondered if he was wearing contact lenses. Becca smiled back at him and felt her shoulders relax. He took her coat and led her up the stairs and into a spacious room.

'I honestly didn't have a clue he was married,' Becca said, almost apologetically. 'Some detective I am.'

'He never wears his ring, but I've learned not to take it personally.'

She took in her plush surroundings. The ceilings were high, the brickwork exposed and the cast-iron radiators chunky and painted a deep grey. A television twice the size of hers hung from a wall in front of two chesterfield sofas – one fabric and one made of dark brown leather. Behind them was a wooden dining table and six chairs. Next to them was a generously proportioned kitchen where Joe was cooking.

'Hey,' he smiled, stirring chunks of pink meat into a wok that sizzled and spat out tiny drops of hot oil. He flicked on the switch of an extractor fan to prevent the scent of aromatic spices spreading through the flat. 'Did you find us all right?'

'Yes, fine, thanks.'

'I should have asked – are you okay with Thai red curry? We've got some Quorn in the freezer if you're a veggie . . .'

'No, it smells lovely,' Becca replied, a little in awe of his home. Nothing was out of place, and it reminded her of the rooms on the covers of thick magazines that she saw on newsagents' shelves but never purchased.

Matt handed her a glass with a bowl wide enough to place her fist inside, and filled it up a third of the way from the bottle she'd brought.

'Well done for failing to inform Becca that I existed,' Matt directed towards Joe, only partly joking.

Joe arched his eyebrows. 'Oh, I just assumed you knew? Everyone else does, so I thought you did too.'

'You assumed wrongly again,' said Matt. Becca hoped he wouldn't bring to his partner's attention that she'd thought there was more on the menu than dinner. 'Shall we sit down while my socially inept husband finishes up?'

Matt pressed a button on a remote control, and instrumental tunes from a Balearic chill-out album spilled from speakers she couldn't see.

'Joseph's not really the mixing-business-with-pleasure kind of chap, so you're the first colleague of his I've actually met,' Matt continued. 'What's he like to work with?'

'You know I can hear you, don't you?' Joe replied.

'You were supposed to.'

'He seems very popular,' said Becca. 'And he's good at his job.'

'That bloody job. Do you have any idea what it's like dating some-one with a photographic memory for faces?'

'Dating?' interrupted Joe. 'We've been together six years and married for four. Why are you downgrading us?'

'In the hope that it irritates you.'

'It does.'

'Job done.'

Becca sensed the attraction between the couple. They shared the same playful sense of humour, and weren't afraid to make the other the butt of their joke. It was the kind of relationship she longed to have but had almost given up on, although preferably with a man who didn't like other men in the same way she did.

'You said "bloody job". Does Joe's memory impact your relation-ship?' she asked. 'I've seen the hours he works and he told me it can get a bit obsessive.'

Becca noticed them look at each other like she'd reminded them of a situation that was better left unspoken.

'Are you kidding?' Matt replied eventually. 'Shall I tell her about the time we missed our flight to Tenerife because you recognised one of our fellow passengers as being wanted for a post office robbery?' Matt looked to Becca. 'By the time he alerted the Luton Airport police and the guy was positively identified, we had to fly out the next day.'

'Oh, that's not fair,' Joe interjected. 'He had almost beaten someone to death.'

'How about the woman you nicked when we were out shopping for running shoes in Covent Garden? You made me join you in follow-ing her around for an hour and a half until backup arrived and she was carted away in a van.'

'She was one of London's most prolific shoplifters. We'd been after her for a year.'

'Becca, we couldn't even enjoy a night out with friends in Vauxhall without him spotting two lads who he'd seen on video in the London riots. He'd kept their faces in that super-brain of his for five years. And I hate to think about the amount of buses or trains we've left because he thinks he's seen someone else. Then there are TV programmes. He can even list everything else he's seen the background extras in by sight alone. But ask him to bring back a bag of salad from the supermarket on his way home from work and it's in one ear and out the other.'

'Yeah, my short-term memory is shocking,' Joe conceded.

'Joseph tells me you have a little girl. Have you got a photo of her?'

It had become Becca's default setting to hesitate before showing anyone who didn't know of her daughter's condition her picture. She opened an album on her phone and found an image of Maisie dressed in a Batman costume with the widest grin spread across her face.

'Oh my God,' Matt exclaimed, and Becca prepared herself for sympathetic looks and questions that she hated answering. Only they didn't arrive. 'I have never seen a child look so happy!' Matt continued, and took the phone over to Joe. 'Look at her.'

'Loving the costume,' Joe said. 'When I was her age I was convinced I was Thomas the Tank Engine.'

'I thought I was Ariel from *The Little Mermaid*,' Matt replied. 'It's no wonder that my coming out wasn't exactly front-page news for my parents.'

Becca watched Joe pouring the wok's contents into three bowls. She noticed him catch Matt's eye, and they gave each other a look that said, without words, how much they loved and appreciated the other person. Becca longed for someone to glance at her like that.

'Does everyone at work know you're gay, then?' she said as they sat at the dining table. The dog joined them, and lay by Becca's feet in the hope of catching a scrap of falling food.

'I've never made a secret of it, I just don't talk about my personal life that much. It'd be the same if I was straight.'

'Are they all okay with it? I know that officially there's no tolerance for homophobia in the job, but some of the older coppers . . .'

'Actually, you'd be surprised. They're the most open-minded because they've seen it all before and it doesn't bother them. Occasionally you'll get a snide comment that's wrapped up as a joke, but I laugh along with it and that disarms them when they realise they can't get a rise out of me. But I reckon it's the same in any job. Two generations from now and we won't even be having this conversation.'

'What about life as a single working mum?' asked Matt. 'That can't be easy with the hours you do?'

'It's not, but my mum lives with us and she's brilliant helping out with childcare, and I've got some friends who'll step in when I need them. It's important I show my daughter that I'm a strong woman, even when I don't feel like it.'

'What happened to her dad?'

'Matt!' said Joe sternly, and shot him a narrow-eyed glance. However, Becca didn't mind his directness.

'It's a long story.'

'And this is a big bottle of wine,' Matt replied.

'Please excuse my husband,' Joe said.

'It's okay, I don't mind.' Becca rested her fork by the side of her plate. 'Maisie isn't my biological daughter, I'm her aunt. Emma, my sister, is . . . was . . . her mum. She was killed by her partner.' Becca paused to take a long sip of wine. 'He'd abuse her mentally and physically, and I can't tell you how many times Mum, Dad and I tried to convince her to leave him. But he had some kind of hold over her and she wouldn't go. Then, when she got pregnant, it turned out it wasn't just one baby she was having – twins ran in his family. Emma was nearly seven months pregnant when she had a change of heart and packed her bags to leave him. But he retaliated by giving her worst beating of her life. By the time the police and ambulance arrived, he'd vanished and she'd gone into labour. But not before he'd kicked her so hard in the head that it caused a bleed in her brain. They performed an emergency caesarean and Maisie survived, but her brother – who didn't have Down's – died a day later. Emma followed him the next week.'

The table fell silent and Joe stared at his food. Matt put his hand on Joe's arm as if to reassure him of something. Becca was curious as to what.

'What happened to Emma's partner?' Joe asked.

'Damien Thorpe got four years for grievous bodily harm, but was released after three,' she said matter-of-factly. 'He's out there somewhere, probably doing the same thing to some other woman.'

Becca pulled out a silver locket from inside her top and opened it, showing the two thumbnail-sized photographs of her and her sister to Matt and Joe.

'You really look alike,' said Joe, which pleased her. Becca felt like she'd aged a decade since Emma's death. In that locket, she and her sister were forever caught in a moment of happiness.

'What do you enjoy about the job?' Matt asked. 'It seems to me you must only ever see the worst people doing the worst things.'

'Occasionally it seeps in and lingers. I end up dwelling on the victims who through no fault of their own have had their lives ruined. But I want to help the other Emmas out there who need someone like me to tell them there's hope. And then there are murder cases like this one that test every part of your skill set. I love working in a team because there's nothing like that feeling when one of you gets a break in a case and the rest of the pieces slot into place.'

'But that's not happened with the serial killer one yet though, right?'

'Not yet.'

'How common are serial killers?'

'There's no definitive number, but they estimate there are only around four operating in the country at any one time,' Joe replied.

'Is that all? I thought with the number of books and films about them, there'd be loads more.'

'What concerns me about this one is that he's going at quite a pace – three in four days,' added Joe, clearing the remaining sauce from his plate with some roti bread.

'And these are only the murders we know about,' said Becca. 'Webster has officers liaising with other forces for their ongoing investigations and cold cases, to find any similarities.'

Suddenly the sound of The Police's 'Every Breath You Take' came echoing up the staircase.

'Sorry, that's my phone,' said Becca, getting up to retrieve it. 'It might be Mum.'

As she made her way down the stairs, Becca wasn't sure if it was the two glasses of wine making her feel quite so relaxed, or the company. While dinner with Joe hadn't turned out to be anything like the evening she'd imagined, she was enjoying herself nonetheless.

By the time she'd answered her phone and reappeared back in the dining area, she had quickly sobered up.

'We need to go, Joe,' she said earnestly. 'They've just found a fourth body.'

CHAPTER 24

It was approaching 11 p.m. before Becca and Joe, both over the legal drink-drive limit, found a black cab to take them to the address of the most recent crime scene.

DS Bryan Thompson, who had called Becca to alert her to the murder in Vauxhall, waited for them further along the road of a new-build estate. The cordoned-off house was spread over three floors, and lights beamed brightly from each window.

'First east, then west, and now he's ventured south of the river,' Becca observed as Joe paid the taxi driver. 'He spreads himself out.'

'Do you think that's significant?'

'God only knows. My instinct tells me he's not local to anywhere he kills, and that he's a commuter. But he's spent time getting to know the areas well. He's followed his victims extensively but he's not a stalker.' She popped three breath mints into her mouth. 'Can you smell alcohol on me?' she asked, and blew into his face. Joe shook his head.

Much of the road was packed with marked police vehicles, and the pavement closest to the house was taped off. Nearby, a handful of police cars, two white forensics vans and two ambulances with their rear doors open sat idle.

Joe rubbed at his sore eyes and surveyed the street and the chaos that had descended upon what until two hours ago had likely been an ordinary neighbourhood. Some residents watched from their front gardens, others were huddled behind windows filming on mobile phones. He wondered what it must have been like to do his job without being recorded each time a stranger saw the flashing of a blue light. Nosy neighbours could be beneficial, though. They meant potential witnesses.

Elsewhere, uniformed PCs carried out door-to-door inquiries as others brandishing torches searched gardens, garages, drains and gutters. The road was illuminated by streetlights, car headlights and residents' homes, making it easier for Joe to scan faces, looking for familiarity.

'You're in for a treat tonight, ladies and gentlemen,' DS Nikhat Odedra directed at the puzzled duo. 'Wait until you see the victim.'

'Same suspect?'

'We're going on that assumption, because as far as we're aware there's only one person out there killing in such wildly varied ways. And this time, he's upped his game.'

'Who's the victim?'

'We think it's Garry Dawson, the homeowner. But his injuries are so severe, he's hard to identify.'

Becca and Joe looked at each other, both now expecting the worst.

'Who found him?' Joe asked.

'The wife when she came back from a day out with the kids. They're being kept away from the house and being looked after by a family liaison officer. Guess what Dawson did for a living?'

'Not another paramedic?' said Becca.

'No – close though. He's been a firefighter for eleven years.'

'That means there's a pattern to these last two kills then,' said Becca, nodding her head. 'What does he have against the emergency services?'

'No idea, but that's our strongest line of inquiry.' Nikhat pointed to a pile of sealed bags with plastic outfits inside. 'Suit up before you go in.'

The material rustled as Becca and Joe slipped the white overalls, gloves, masks and shoe covers over their own clothes. When they were clad from head to toe, they gave their names to the scene guard officer. Becca saw the doctor climbing into her car, the same one who had attended the Burgess crime scene.

'Even at this time of night, these are hot,' Becca exclaimed. 'It's like being wrapped in plastic and thrown into a sauna.'

'They must sweat so much weight off, so every cloud . . .' Joe replied.

They ducked under the yellow tape and trod only where their scenes of crime colleagues directed them. They were aware that the fewer the number of people at the location of a crime the better, to lessen the risk of compromising evidence. They avoided stepping beyond doorways as each room was processed and evidence gathered. A photographer took images of everything, no matter how unimport-ant it appeared. And a video camera operator recorded 360-degree footage of each room.

Outside the master bedroom, Becca nodded to DS Mike Ryan, the exhibits officer bagging and labelling everything pertinent and ensur-ing the chain of evidence wasn't cross-contaminated. Then CS Webster appeared in front of them. 'Has Thompson filled you in on what's hap-pened?' she asked without offering any pleasantries.

'Only on the victim's background, but not the details of his death.'

She moved to one side so Becca and Joe could take in the scene before them.

Garry Dawson was lying on his back, sprawled across the floor of the bedroom, positioned in a star shape. But so much damage had been inflicted upon him that neither Becca nor Joe knew what to focus their attention on first.

Joe's eyes were drawn to the horrific burns on his face and his hands. 'Acid?' he asked, and Webster nodded. Now he understood why Dawson hadn't been formally identified. Outer layers of flesh had been stripped, leaving catastrophic damage to his lips, nose, eyes and parts of his ears.

Then Joe noticed the gaps between the victim's hands, wrists, arms, shoulders, feet, ankles, shins, knees and thighs. He realised each had been removed and placed no more than a centimetre away from where it had once been attached. By the amount of blood soaked into the light beige carpet and sprayed across the geometric-patterned wallpaper, Dawson had likely been alive for at least part of his dismemberment. Finally, Joe took in his chest; it was split down the middle and open wide, his cracked ribs and torn skin kept prised apart by a large metal contraption.

'Jesus Christ,' he said. 'What the hell has he done?'

Becca shook her head and scanned the rest of the room. A lighting rig had been erected in the corner, but each of the bulbs had been smashed and glass shards jutted out from the carpet. A mattress was propped up against the wall and was smeared in dark patches.

'Blood,' said Mike, pre-empting her question. 'His body was discovered with the mattress on top of him.'

Mechanical equipment was strewn across the rest of the room. Joe recognised a defibrillator used to restart hearts, and other pieces resembling ordinary tools like pliers and cutters but on a larger scale.

'What is all this stuff?' Becca asked.

'From what we can ascertain, its basic equipment found on a fire engine,' Mike replied.

'He was murdered using his own equipment?'

'I doubt any of this was personal to him, or that he had it lying around at home. The hydraulic shears that were likely used to sever his limbs are for cutting metal and getting people out of vehicles. They're so powerful they slip through bone like a knife through butter. And the spreader keeping his chest open is used to force something like a car door open after a crash. Even the lighting rig is fire-service issue.'

'Perhaps if the killer had access to this equipment he might be in the service too, or an ex-colleague with a grudge,' Becca directed towards Joe.

'Because each death is so different, it feels like he's tailor-making them for each victim,' he replied.

'Mike, does any of this stuff have serial numbers attached so we can trace where they might have originated?'

'We'll be able to examine everything after it's been bagged up.'

Joe and Becca took one more look around before making their way downstairs. Joe examined photographs of the victim and his family in frames on the walls. Husband and wife on their wedding day; Dawson in full fire-service uniform with his young children; all four of them on a beach with Blackpool Tower in the background. He wondered how badly this would affect Dawson's children in later life. He knew how it felt to be robbed of your childhood without warning.

Nikhat left two uniformed officers he'd been talking to and approached Becca and Joe. A little further away, Bryan Thompson was standing alone, his eyes closed and his hands covering his mouth.

'Is he okay?' Becca asked Nikhat quietly.

'Yeah, for some reason this one has got to him.'

'He used to be unflappable. I think he's getting softer in his old age.'

'As immune as we think we are to these situations, sometimes it takes just one to remind us that we're all human. What do you think of what you saw in here?'

'He's really stepped it up a gear, hasn't he?' said Becca, as she and Joe removed their protective clothing. 'If he brought his own equipment with him then a neighbour must have seen him carrying it in. Anything from the door-to-door inquiries?'

'According to a fella at number 22, there was a van parked outside for an hour this afternoon. He saw a man wearing a baseball cap go in and out of the house three or four times carrying boxes, but didn't get a look at his face. We might know more later in the briefing.'

'There's no pattern in timings or locations,' said Joe, thinking aloud. 'Perhaps it has something to do with their jobs? Maybe we need to work out what profession he's going to target next. Any ideas?'

'Not a bloody clue,' said Becca, shaking her head. 'Fingers crossed it's not one of us.'

CHAPTER 25

From the opposite side of the road at the fourth murder scene, he watched carefully.

In the silence of an empty living room, he sat on a canvas chair, his foot rapidly tapping against the vinyl flooring as though he had St Vitus' dance. Despite lacking electricity, he didn't need to use his torch to navigate. The white and blue lights of the emergency services vehicles parked outside provided enough illumination for him to travel from room to room in the temporary accommodation.

By sheer good fortune, a month before the fireman's name had reached the top of his list, the two-bedroom semi-detached property he was now inside had been put on the rental market with his firm. It provided the perfect vantage point. Lady Luck was smiling on him. *It's a sign*, he'd told himself, although he wasn't the superstitious sort. *You're on the right path.*

He reached for a half-empty packet of Marlboro Lights lying on the floor and removed his fourth of the hour. As he raised it to his mouth he could still smell traces of petrol on his sleeve. He'd filled four cans and left them back in the lock-up garage he rented. Just to be on the safe side, he removed his hoodie, and as the cigarette crackled to life, he was reminded of the noise they'd made when his mother stubbed them out on his skin. It was never his arms or legs, where burn marks might be noticed by his teachers or social workers; there was always a degree of sobriety in her to ensure it was on his back or his bare buttocks. He took a deep drag and flicked ash to the side.

A brown, dying yucca plant left by the previous tenants drooped close to the fireplace. It was like one of the plants he'd kept on the windowsill in his bedroom when he was a boy. He'd deliberately stop watering them until the soil was bone dry and their leaves became brittle and began to shed. Only when they were on the edge of death would he give them the hydration and sunlight they craved, before repeating the process over and over again.

He'd worked his way up to insects and molluscs. He'd trap and starve woodlice and snails until they were completely lethargic, and then allow them to binge on decaying roots and leaves just to see how far he could go without killing them. And when they weren't enough to sate his curiosity, he'd turned his attention to the tortoiseshell cat next door. He kept her locked in his shed, giving her the bare minimum of water and no food for two weeks. Then, on the day he arrived to feed her, he opened the door to discover that overnight she had given birth to a litter of kittens. Only she'd been unable to feed them and they'd quickly died. She'd even begun to eat one of them. He had no doubt that, in similar circumstances, his mother would have done the same to him.

Behind him, his suitcase leaned against the wall and was zipped shut – he didn't want his clothes smelling of stale tobacco. On the floor were a rolled-out sleeping bag and a folded towel he'd be using as a pillow for the duration of his one-night stay. Underneath, and spread right across the flooring, was a polythene sheet to catch anything that might identify him, from a drop of saliva to an eyelash.

His part in tonight's performance was complete, but it wasn't the end of the story, and he suspected he'd be getting little sleep that night. He had discovered it was rarely an option in the aftermath of a kill.

He relished watching from the sidelines, fascinated by police procedure and how they made their way around a crime scene so efficiently and methodically, like worker ants building a nest. He imagined them inside, desperately seeking clues to his identity, moving in choreographed unity, completely unaware he was far too clever to reveal himself with careless mistakes. He hadn't dedicated two years to meticulous planning and research without giving careful consideration to absolutely anything and everything that might go wrong.

The death tally now stood at four. He took a moment to dwell on that number – he was more than halfway to the finishing line. Tonight, he would remain in the moment, and then he would make final preparations for his penultimate kill. He couldn't afford to hang around or to rest on his laurels.

His jaw clicked as a wide yawn caught him by surprise. A fresh supply of cocaine picked up en route to the fireman's house was keeping him alert, but made his brain at odds with his body. His muscles were still nagging from lugging heavy fire-service equipment from the van into the house and up two flights of stairs. Momentarily, he'd offered a grudging respect to the men and women who did that kind of work, day in, day out. Then he'd shaken his head and the empathy disappeared. *They need to know they're not untouchable*, he'd reminded himself.

He dropped his cigarette into a can and it sizzled when it came into contact with the flat Coke inside. The powerful acidic concoction he'd created from household cleaning products had made the same sound when he'd thrown it into the fireman's face as he answered the knock at the door. He'd sedated the other names on his list first before they'd had the chance to scream, so it was the first time he'd heard anyone react to the damage he was inflicting upon them. It was like a symphony to his ears. The sedation followed and he was able to overpower the enemy.

However, no amount of pain Garry Dawson suffered could make up for that which he had inflicted. His carelessness had been his undoing. Just days earlier, before Dumitru had been sucked under the wheels of the tube train, a tiny part of Dawson's killer had questioned whether he would have the stomach to handle torture. Now he had his answer. It was becoming second nature to him.

As with the others, he'd followed Dawson for months. There were times when he'd trailed Dawson and his family so closely that if he'd stretched his hand out, he could have stroked the daughter's hair. And the closer he got to the fireman, the more he despised him. He didn't deserve a family; he didn't deserve children who idolised him. He didn't deserve anyone to love him after what he'd done.

A black cab pulled up outside the cordoned-off section of the street and he squinted to see the new arrivals. It was *her* again. He rubbed his hands together and a smile crept across his face. Knowing that she was back, and how close she was, gave him a tingling sensation that ran up his spine and across his shoulders.

Using his phone's camera, he zoomed in to magnify her. Then, puffing on a fresh cigarette, he watched her slip on protective clothing and disappear into the crime scene. He tried to picture the expression on her face when she saw what he'd done to the fireman.

He hoped that at least a small part of her was fascinated and appreciated his hard work.

CHAPTER 26

'Have you seen anything yet?' asked Becca hopefully.

'Not yet, because the images are pretty grainy,' Joe replied, and moved the telephone to his other ear. 'It'd be easier if he hadn't stolen the van at night . . . daylight would've made things clearer.'

'I can see sod-all on my phone, even when I zoom in on his face.'

Joe kept his eyes on the images on the computer monitor. 'His cap is pulled down so it covers the top of his face, and the front of his hoodie has been yanked up to hide his mouth and nose. But I've had less to work on and still got a positive ID.'

'Is there something written on the cap?'

Joe further expanded the images and squinted. 'Looks like it's in French. I think it says Casino de la Forêt.'

Elsewhere in Operation Chamber's major incident room were at least a dozen other detectives, consumed by their own sections of the puzzle. The morning after Garry Dawson's murder, many more were still out in the field at his property, examining the surrounding area, continuing with house-to-house inquiries, and positioned in locations where passers-by might have seen something.

Across London, Becca was parking an unmarked police car on the Acton Industrial Estate, where she and DS Bryan Thompson had found

William Burgess's body. She took the phone off hands-free mode and cursed the heat as she left the comfort of her air-conditioned vehicle. Being allowed to sign out a car felt like a small victory in the battle to be taken seriously.

Becca and Joe had both received six images of a van, captured by automatic number-plate recognition cameras on a handful of roads as it was driven away from the premises of a local parcel-delivery company. It had been reported as stolen, and as the vehicle passed each camera the number plate had been read and automatically checked against a database of 'vehicles of interest'. When the signage on its side was mentioned by one of Dawson's neighbours to a PC during house-to-house inquiries, it was later confirmed as being the one that had been stolen. Joe desperately hoped he could identify the driver.

Earlier, he had told Becca how he'd once used his super-recogniser skills to identify a driver from ANPR photos whose car was involved in a hit-and-run with a pensioner. He'd recognised him from the Met's centralised forensic image database and linked him to a two-year-old burglary. It gave her hope he might be able to work his magic again.

She kept her phone to her ear and heard him pressing heavily on the keyboard and muttering under his breath as he tried various tricks and imaging software to improve the picture quality and pick up on any familiarities. But because each picture focused more on the registration plate than the person behind the wheel, it was difficult to see the suspect's face, especially as he was hiding so much of it.

'Bollocks,' Joe said eventually, defeated. 'All I can get is his nose and a tiny section of his right cheek. Let me email them to the rest of my department and see if they ring any bells. But don't hold your breath.'

'Your average crim wouldn't think to keep hiding his face on multiple different roads, would he?' Becca asked.

'No, why?'

'So he already knew exactly where the cameras were. He knew where to go, which roads to travel on and when to hide himself. He doesn't take unnecessary risks.'

'But he does when he unloads a van in broad daylight and carries equipment into the house of a man he's about to murder. It must have taken at least four trips from vehicle to bedroom to get it all in.'

'Do we have any idea where he got the equipment from?'

'The serial numbers say it's all old British fire-service-issue equipment from stations across the country that's been replaced with more up-to-date stuff. They sell the old stuff on to Eastern Europe. Then the stuff the Europeans don't want is sold online. We've got people looking at sites like eBay, Gumtree, Craigslist and Facebook Marketplace. Are you at the van yet?'

'Just arrived.'

The metal carcass of the burned-out stolen vehicle was hidden from view under a blue tarpaulin. It was being carefully lifted on to the back of a transporter to take back to the Met's forensic department for examination. Becca could just about make out the charred shell through the material when the sun was directly on it. They would be lucky to find any clues, as there was very little of it left. And the tyres had melted into puddles and would need to be scraped from the road.

'Why did he set fire to it in exactly the same place as he killed William Burgess?' asked Joe. 'Forensics must have only just left the scene when he rocked up.'

'Because he's playing with us?'

'Maybe it's an area he's familiar with?'

'Perhaps. Anyway, I'm going to have a look around to see if there's something staring us in the face that we've missed. Let me know if anything in that weird head of yours recognises him.'

'Will do.'

Becca hung up and turned to scan the dilapidated buildings surrounding her. Their corrugated iron roofs, rotten wooden window frames and boarded-up doors suggested they'd lain dormant for many years. Sun-bleached 'For Sale' and 'To Let' boards jutted out from the sides.

She stretched out her arms and moved her neck from side to side to ease the tension in her body as she walked towards a concrete forecourt and a row of buildings. She had arrived home long after her mum and Maisie had gone to bed, and was on her way to work before they'd awoken. She brushed aside her guilt once again, and promised herself she'd make up for her lack of presence when the case was over.

Becca pulled on the two door handles of the entrance to a vacant building. Both were locked. She peered through a cracked window, and saw roof debris on the floor inside and shards of daylight coming through gaps in the ceiling. Furniture remnants were scattered across patchy lino, and graffiti tags had been daubed on the walls.

She continued along the row until she reached the building closest to where Burgess's RRV had been found. The windows were reflective, making it difficult to see inside, but through a peeling corner she spotted footprints on the dusty floor. Curious, she walked around the side of the building, through broken fences and overgrown wasteland that police had already examined. Wooden pallets and metal oil drums lay in pieces across a weed-strewn car park. She realised the rear doors were all padlocked with the exception of one, up a first-floor fire escape.

She climbed the steps, pushed open the door and, using her pocket torch, explored her surroundings. There were a handful of rooms, all empty, and a mezzanine that looked on to the ground floor below. That space was also almost devoid of furniture, with the exception of empty plastic racks and a filing cabinet tipped on its side. Everything in the room was filthy, except for the window. Becca climbed down the stairs to take a closer look.

The window was covered in a mirrored film enabling her to see out but no one to see in. There was no dust on it at all, suggesting it was a recent addition. Behind her, an old plastic chair was placed dead centre, offering a perfect view of the murder site. There were more footprints around it – whoever had been sitting on the chair had been staring out the window, unseen but watching whatever was going on outside. And at the end of a cul-de-sac in this disused industrial estate, there was only one event that was worthy of any kind of attention.

'You've been here,' she said out loud. 'After you killed Burgess, you sat here watching us.'

◆　◆　◆

DI Nikhat Odedra and CS Caroline Webster were waiting for Becca at the scene of the fireman's murder while she raced across London as fast as Saturday morning traffic would allow.

Becca had telephoned Nikhat to explain what she'd found in the empty warehouse, then waited for two uniformed officers to secure the area before the scenes of crime team arrived. Once back in Vauxhall, she parked at the end of the police-secured road, squeezed past the news reporters and TV cameras, and hurried towards her colleagues. Webster, Nikhat and Bryan were standing in front of a long row of houses and flats, surrounded by unmarked white police vans. Becca guessed what – or who – they contained.

'Last night, and maybe even now, he's been watching us,' said Becca. 'He's planned this so thoroughly that he wants to watch each death through to the end; from the moment he sedates them until their bodies are taken away in the back of an ambulance.' She glanced at the houses around them. 'I bet you one of these windows has the same sort of mirrored film across it, so we can't see in but he can see out.'

Nikhat looked at his clipboard and scrolled through a list of names and addresses they'd compiled from door-to-door enquiries. 'Only two properties are unaccounted for,' he said. 'The neighbours of number 70 think they're away camping, and number 33 over there moved out a month ago.' He pointed to a property on the opposite side of the street, three doors away from the murder scene.

'He'll want to see everything that goes on, so he's going to find the best possible vantage point to do that,' Becca said. 'It's more likely he's in 33.'

Becca turned her head to view the house. It would afford the killer an almost-uninterrupted view from both upstairs and downstairs. Nikhat and Webster followed Becca to the larger of the two ground-floor windows, and she peered inside.

'They're reflective,' she said quietly. 'He's been here.'

All three officers backed away towards the road while Nikhat spoke into his police radio. The side doors of two vans promptly opened, and a dozen armed officers in body armour and clutching weapons spilled out on to the pavement. Four hurried to the rear of the property, and the others made their way to the sides of the windows and the front door. On Nikhat's command, one knocked heavily on the front door and identified himself as a police officer, then in a coordinated move with the officers at the back, they used a battering ram to break through the front and back doors and charged inside.

Becca's heart was racing twenty to the dozen, and she crossed her fingers and prayed that they would locate their suspect inside. After the longest two minutes of Becca's career, Webster finally received the all-clear to enter. It was empty.

In the living room, Becca recognised a similar set-up to that in the warehouse – a reflective film had been attached to the glass, and a seat, this time one made of canvas, had been placed by the window for a favourable view of the crime scene.

'Damn it,' Becca snapped in frustration, and hit the wall with her palm. 'I should've noticed it earlier.'

'Get a scenes of crime team back over here to search the house,' Webster demanded before clearing the area. 'Find out who owns the property and where they are right now.'

As they made their way back outside, Becca shook her head and then called Joe to fill him in on her near miss.

She had no idea that, among the news crews and crowds gathered further up the road, someone had set her in his sights.

CHAPTER 27

Her heavy snoring woke him up. Following her seventeen-hour shift and the three glasses of Merlot upon her return home, Zoe was out for the count.

Carrying her from the sofa and into the bedroom of her poky flat, he'd peeled her uniform from her body without her even stirring. Two, perhaps three, hours of sleep had passed before Zoe's heavy breathing developed into a full-on throaty grunt. He shook his head, slipped on his jogging bottoms and closed the bedroom door behind him.

Looking at his watch, he was shocked to discover it was now Sunday and that he had spent much of the last thirty-six hours dozing or sound asleep. He'd left the house opposite the fireman's home in a hurry, having planned to stay there for longer. That was, until he'd received the text message warning him of the female detective's theory that he was watching the aftermath of each murder scene. He'd underestimated her. Clearing up after himself, he escaped through the back door, opening the gate and disappearing into the next street along.

Having a police insider was proving highly beneficial.

Moving the empty wine glasses into the sink, he placed his laptop on the coffee table and opened up the Netflix app. He clicked on his favourites section, and the cover of the 1986 French movie *Betty Blue* appeared. Then he put on his wireless headphones and lay back on the sofa as it began to play.

He was only a boy when the film was released, so it wasn't on his radar until his university's Cinema Classics club showed it. Even now, the moment actress Béatrice Dalle appeared on the screen, the butterflies in his stomach rose en masse. It wasn't just her accent that reminded him of Audrey Moreau, it was her deep brown eyes, the slim gap between her two front teeth, and her raven-coloured hair.

He'd just celebrated his thirtieth birthday alone when he first set eyes on the love of his life. He was attending the wedding reception of his work colleagues Gabrielle and Luke when, in the pub garden at dusk, a string of bright lanterns illuminated Audrey in soft whites and creams. It was as if someone had pressed pause on a remote control, and everything else in the world stopped but the two of them. His heart fluttered and he willed himself not to pass out.

She must have been close to the six-feet-tall mark in her heels, a good two inches above him. Her hair was styled with a delicate wave, and her figure was more curvy than skinny. Her lips were ripe and he was overcome with the desire to know how they might feel pressed against his. She was in conversation with Gabrielle when Luke approached him, a bottle of import beer in one hand and a cigarette in the other.

'You having a good time, fella?' he bellowed louder than necessary over a song blaring from the speakers.

'Yes, it's been a really good night,' he lied. As a rule, he disliked weddings, but Luke was his manager at the building contractors he worked at. It wouldn't have painted him in a good light if he'd turned down the invitation. He was grateful, however, that the ceremony itself had been a family-only occasion and he'd just been asked to attend the evening celebrations. He'd been offered a plus-one but had gone alone.

He'd planned to sneak away after the hog roast while nobody was watching. That was, until he'd become fixated by Gabrielle's friend.

'Who's your new wife talking to?' he asked, barely able to take his eyes off her. She tucked her hair behind her ear then threw her head back and laughed at something Gabrielle said.

'That's why I'm here,' Luke continued. 'She's been asking about you.'

'Me?' he replied, disbelievingly. Compared to her, he was beige again.

'Her name's Audrey, she's Gabby's cousin from France.' Luke must have seen his face flash with disappointment. 'Don't worry, she lives here in London.'

'What was she saying about me?' he asked, and then stopped himself, fearing he might be coming across like an overenthusiastic schoolboy.

'She wanted to know who you were and how we knew you. I told her you were the office janitor. And that you were a total bellend who fucks around indiscriminately.'

It was as if his fists had a mind of their own and they clenched, as if he wanted to punch Luke for even making such a joke.

'Nah, I said you were single and that every Wednesday night I kicked your arse on the squash court. Come with me.'

Before he could protest, Luke grabbed his arm and pulled him in the direction of Gabrielle and Audrey. 'Just call me Mister Matchmaker,' he laughed as the two strangers came face to face. 'Now, if you'll excuse me, I'm going to whisk my beautiful new bride away on to the dancefloor.'

Throughout his life he had yo-yoed between shy, confident, insecure, self-assertive and controlling. Flirting had been an acquired skill, and he'd learned to effortlessly charm the women he met on dating websites into bed. However, in situations like this, where he had little control over his emotions, his claustrophobia made itself known. It was like the times when his mother used to lock him in the cupboard under the stairs – his insides felt like they were being wrung like a wet towel and his breathing became stifled. He felt nothing but awe for this beautiful stranger. It was love at first sight with his very own Béatrice Dalle. But when it came to conversation, he had no idea where to begin. Thankfully, she took the lead.

'My cousin tells me you work together here in London?' she asked. Her accent was gentle and melodic. He liked the way she pronounced the capital as 'Loon-dun'.

'Yes.' He smiled. She continued to stare at him, like she was hoping his response would be a full sentence rather a solitary word. But he was too tongue-tied to expand.

'I work at a nursery in Finsbury Park,' she said. 'Do you know the area?'

'Not very well, no.'

Another silence followed – he was going to lose her interest, he sensed it. Then he'd be kicking himself as he watched from the opposite side of the pub garden as she found someone more fluent in conversation to hold her attention. He waited for her to make her excuses and leave, only she didn't.

'How long have you been living over here?' he eventually mumbled.

'A year and a half now. When I was growing up, my family and I would spend our Christmases in London with Gabby's family and I fell in love with the city. What about you?'

'I grew up in the suburbs,' he replied. 'Then I moved back after uni.' He failed to mention university had lasted just a year.

Suddenly the music became louder and he could just about understand the muffled voice of the DJ urging everyone on to the dancefloor. Michael Jackson's 'Don't Stop 'Til You Get Enough' began to play and her eyes twinkled.

'I hope you dance better than you talk,' she teased, and took his hand in hers. It was warm and velvety. 'Come.'

As they moved among dozens of other bodies on the dancefloor, he saw only hers. He knew there was nothing he wouldn't have done to remain in that moment for the rest of his life.

'Why are you watching that bloody film again?'

He hadn't heard Zoe enter the room and her presence startled him. He rubbed his eyes and threw her a filthy look as the penultimate scene of *Betty Blue* played on his laptop. She had yanked him away from the woman he loved, even if Audrey was only in his daydreams.

'Honestly, I don't know how you can read subtitles, they hurt my eyes,' she moaned, and made her way into the kitchen. She removed a bottle of water from the fridge and swallowed two tablets. 'Aspirin,' she said without being prompted. 'It'll stop me getting a hangover in the morning. Now come to bed.'

He nodded, climbed unsteadily to his feet and took one last glance at Béatrice Dalle before closing the lid of his computer. He wished all it would take was the click of his trackpad to reanimate Audrey so easily.

He lay next to her until she sank into another deep sleep, then climbed out of bed and slipped into a smart shirt and a pair of trousers. After planting a lingering kiss on her lips and stroking her hair, he closed the door quietly behind him and left.

CHAPTER 28

The sun that had baked London's streets for ten days straight showed no signs of abating. And according to weather forecasters, it was just a few degrees centigrade away from being a record-breaker for April. Although it had been replaced with dusk by the time Becca stepped across the threshold of her house, the humidity made the air feel sticky and polluted. All day, she'd longed for a cool shower and a glass of wine.

She braced herself, and counted how long it had been since she'd last seen her mum or her daughter in the flesh and not just heard them on the phone. Lately she'd been arriving home after their bedtime and leaving before they woke. The last few days had blended in with one another, and she struggled to settle on a figure. It had been an uneventful day, catching up on paperwork and following leads that hadn't come to fruition.

Lately, Becca had pushed the two people closest to her furthest away into the back of her mind, telling herself that work was her priority right now. If she could re-establish her career and give herself a sense of purpose, then everything else, including motherhood, would slip into place. But trying to communicate that to Helen was going to be a challenge.

Before closing the door, Becca turned her head to look behind her. She was still unable to shake the sense that she was being followed. Perhaps the case was getting to her, she thought. The street behind her was empty, so she locked the door and put the chain on the hook.

'Mum?' she called out quietly, and made her way into the living room. Helen was on the sofa, her finger held to her lips to shush her daughter. Maisie was curled up asleep under a throw, her head on her grandmother's lap. A medical drama was playing on the television but the sound was muted. However, the dialogue was audible from Mrs Patel's TV next door. She was as deaf as a post and refused to wear a hearing aid.

'It's almost eight o'clock, why is Maisie still up?' Becca whispered. 'She should be in bed.'

She knew she'd said the wrong thing the moment the words tripped from her tongue. Her mum slowly slipped out from under Maisie and placed a cushion under her head. Becca followed Helen into the kitchen, where she closed the door with a quiet click.

'Don't you dare question why my granddaughter is up at this time when you haven't even seen her in almost three days,' Helen snapped. 'She's downstairs with me because she refused to go to bed until you saw her in her costume. Do you remember what day it was on Friday?'

Becca looked at her blankly. 'Of course you don't, even though it's been on the calendar you haven't bothered to check for a month. It was World Book Day.'

She closed her eyes and screwed up her face. 'Mum, I am so sorry . . .'

'I don't want to hear it. The school called me because Maisie was so upset that all the other parents had seen their children in their costumes but you hadn't. And when she started to cry, some of the other children started laughing at her.'

'Why didn't they ring me?'

'Precisely. I was their first port of call because I'm the one who picks her up every afternoon, who goes to meetings with her teachers to talk about her development, and who attends parents' evenings. And I do it all on my own. Why on earth would they call you? You never answer your bloody phone anyway. You're a virtual stranger to them, and the way you're going, you're going to be a virtual stranger to Maisie too.'

'That's not fair,' said Becca, taking offence. 'I've been putting my career on the backburner ever since she was born.'

'That's what you do when you're a parent! You put your child first! That's what I did with you and Emma.'

'That was thirty years ago, Mum. Things have moved on. Other mums now have full-time careers too. Why can't I do both?'

'Right now, you're not doing both; you're only doing one. You seem to forget you have a child with special needs.'

'Why can't she just be—' Becca blurted out, stopping herself just before she uttered the word she'd vowed never to say. But it was too late. Helen glared at her in a way that only a mother could, cutting her down to size.

'What, *normal*? Is that what you were going to say?'

'I'm sorry, I didn't mean that . . .'

'When we lost Emma and you were adamant you wanted to be Maisie's legal guardian, I said that you had to be prepared for what you were taking on. And that's why I gave up my life too, to move in with you and to help. But you're not keeping your end of the bargain. You're leaving it all to me and it's not fair.'

'It's been a rough few days, and everyone at work is feeling the pressure of such a high-profile case . . .'

'Rebecca, be honest with yourself, it's not just the last few days you've been distant. This has been going on for weeks – even months – now. What's going to happen when this case is over? There's going to be another one, then another one, and all the responsibility for Maisie is going to remain on my shoulders. I have a life too, but I'm constantly cancelling seeing my friends, I'm missing birthday meals and gym classes, because I'm a full-time mother.'

'But you get to work from home and do your own hours. You have no idea what it's like trying to keep up with everyone else in my department who doesn't have the commitments I do.'

'You think? I know full well because you tell me enough. "So and so has been given this case . . . So and so has been asked to work on that . . . Why aren't I trusted with something big?" Well, that little girl sleeping in the other room *is* something big, and she trusts you to look after her. And you're not, Rebecca. You're letting her down. If it were the other way around, Emma would be bending over backwards to help your daughter.'

At the second mention of the older sister she missed so badly, Becca felt an ache in her throat like she wanted to cry. She swallowed hard until it disappeared. Barely a year had separated them, and they'd been the best of friends before Damien Thorpe destroyed everything. If only Emma had reached out for help sooner, Maisie would still have her twin brother and her mum.

Helen took a bottle of red wine from the cupboard and poured herself a glass. She stood with her back to Becca, propping herself up against the draining board with her hands.

'I'm absolutely knackered all the time, Rebecca,' she said, turning. Her eyes were pinched with fatigue. 'Neither of us ever expected to be in this position. I should be retiring and you should be enjoying every minute of your career, or dating or thinking about having your own family. But the truth of the matter is that because of Thorpe and your father's selfishness, neither of us can have what we wish for. My granddaughter and your niece needs us both. And I can't do this on my own.'

Becca nodded, and couldn't hold her tears back any longer. They fell from her eyes and splashed against her blouse. Helen placed her arms around Becca, drawing her in towards her shoulder. They remained like that for a few moments until they were disturbed by the sound of the doorbell.

'It'll be for me,' said Helen, pulling a tissue from her pocket and wiping Becca's eyes.

'I'm sorry,' Becca replied, and Helen hugged her again then made her way to the front door. Becca followed her out of the kitchen, picking up a sleeping Maisie from the sofa and carrying her upstairs and into her bedroom. She looked so beautiful in her Angelina Ballerina costume, and it broke Becca's heart that she had hurt her daughter so much. They would both sleep in Becca's bed that night. But she knew that would not be enough to repair their disconnect.

As Becca headed back downstairs, she caught a glimpse of an attractive man in the hallway passing her mum a handful of bulging blue folders and a box. Before leaving, he smiled at Becca and gave her a wave. She smiled back at him. Something about him felt familiar, but she couldn't put her finger on why – she hoped she hadn't arrested him. She wondered what it would be like to have Joe's memory and to never forget a face.

'Who was that?' Becca asked as the front door closed.

'One of my clients.'

'That makes you sound like a prostitute.'

'Quite handsome, isn't he? I can put a word in for you if you like? He's not wearing a wedding ring . . .'

'Yes, that's just what I need, Mum – to juggle Maisie, a job and a boyfriend. Who is he, anyway?'

'He works for Smalley & Banks, they're an independent estate agent.'

'Okay,' replied Becca, nodding as she made her way to the kitchen to unscrew the cap from a fresh bottle of wine. Perhaps she should leave it to her mum to pick her dates, she thought. Then she wouldn't have gone dewy-eyed over a gay colleague. 'Thanks, Mum,' she added. 'Thank you for everything.'

'We're in this together,' Helen said. 'Don't forget, it's the three of us. We can get through it if I have your help.'

Becca's pained smile masked her misgivings.

CHAPTER 29

He waited until he heard Becca's front door close behind him before he allowed the broad smile he'd been holding back to spread across his face.

Now, lingering on the pavement for a moment, he held in his lungs a deep breath of the air he'd stolen from her house, keeping it inside until he could contain it no more. He'd expected Becca to be up to her eyes in the investigation and not at home. But as he'd spied her walking across the landing, his heart had thumped so fast it felt like it might burst from his ribcage.

That afternoon, Helen had emailed him, citing childcare problems for her inability to stop by his office this week to pick up the extra accounts paperwork she needed. She was clearly too old to have children young enough to need care, so he'd assumed she was referring to her grandchild. The opportunity to see inside her house was too good to miss. So even though it was late in the day on Sunday, he'd insisted on dropping them off to Helen personally so she could get a head start on the week. She'd gratefully accepted.

He'd only made it as far as the hallway, and he wished she'd invited him inside so that he could have had a better look round. A child's pink bike with a basket containing two plastic dolls had leaned against a radiator, a helmet on the newel post of the staircase. As he'd passed

Helen the requested files, he'd glanced further inside and into the living room. A laptop lay open on the table, surrounded by neatly stacked folders and paperwork. The sights and sounds of family homes often saddened him. Even if he had a house of his own, he would have no one to fill it with.

He climbed into the car he'd parked in a residents-only bay a hundred metres up the road, slipped the key into the ignition and turned it one click clockwise. He waited patiently for the air conditioning to kick in, then peeled back the plastic cover from a Marks & Spencer ploughman's sandwich and took a bite. He washed it down with a can of Pepsi and made a mental note to drive to Camden later to pick up more cocaine from the dealer who plied his wares from the kitchen of a Turkish restaurant. He couldn't risk running out again. The excitement of seeing Becca in her own environment would no doubt wear off, and he wanted to replicate the high later that night.

The fireman came to mind, and in particular his gruesome death. It had been necessary to escalate from violence to mutilation. He needed those investigating, like Helen's daughter, to appreciate the lengths he was going to in order to make the punishment fit the crime. Only when victims felt absolutely helpless and terrified would they understand why he was targeting them. They had to suffer like he had suffered, like those they had let down so badly had suffered.

What each of you have done to me, I will do to you.

He removed a hardboiled egg from a bag and peeled it. But as he glanced at its shape and his fingers touched its texture, it reminded him of the anaesthetised paramedic's eyes as he'd pulled them out. He placed it back in the bag.

Taking another swig from his canned drink, he touched his chest. Under his shirt he felt three penny-sized sores from where he'd misjudged the trajectory of the acid cocktail he'd thrown into the fireman's face. Some had splashed back on to him and burned through two layers of material before it reached his skin. At the time, his adrenaline was running too high for him to notice.

Before he left, curiosity made him scroll through Twitter to see what was being posted about his killings. He was delighted to see thousands of tweets about the murders, which had been trending. Some trolls said what he was doing was sick and depraved, but most posters had a morbid fascination as to his motives. They were desperate to know who might be next.

On his arrival back at Zoe's flat, he found a note she'd left informing him she was covering a sick colleague's shift and his eyes lit up. It left him alone to walk through how he was going to kill the fifth name on his list. This one concerned him. It would present him with more of a challenge than any of the others. He just needed the mettle to see it through.

CHAPTER 30

Telling lies didn't come easily to Joe, even innocuous little white ones. And lying to Matt was especially difficult. But sometimes he had no choice when he needed to follow his heart.

Today was one of those days. Matt was travelling to a Monday morning appointment at a client's house in Clerkenwell with a car crammed full of wallpaper and flooring samples – and, as far as he knew, Joe had an appointment at Moorfields Eye Hospital. But Joe had actually cancelled it a week earlier. Instead, he was spending the first two hours of his day in East London's Westfield Stratford, the country's third-largest shopping centre.

Having arrived home in the early hours of the morning, he wasn't expected to return to work until the afternoon. So he took the opportunity to hover in the vicinity of WHSmith and TK Maxx, studying the bone structure and appearance of each female face that passed him by.

Momentarily, Joe allowed himself to think about his mother and what she might be doing now. It had been three years since they'd last seen or spoken to each other, and he purposely hadn't forwarded her his address when he and Matt moved into their new flat. It was unlikely she'd ever just turn up on their doorstep unannounced, but he didn't want to risk it. He couldn't be bothered with another confrontation. In so readily accepting the death of one child, she had lost the other too.

Joe recalled the court transcripts he'd requested as an adult many years after the trial. He'd learned that his father, having returned home to discover his family had deserted him, got the name from a neighbour of the removals company from a logo on the side of their lorry. A young temp, who was new to the firm and hadn't been informed the customer had been guaranteed complete discretion, gave him their forwarding address without question.

Joe's father had set off at breakfast the next morning, then spent two days in his car, watching his estranged family's movements from afar. On the third day, when his wife and daughter returned from Linzi's school, they hadn't even set foot over the threshold before he'd knocked his wife out cold. By the time she regained consciousness, Linzi was gone and her mother was hysterical. A police blockade at junction 21 of the M1 forced his car to a halt that night, but he was alone. Linzi was nowhere to be found.

His clothes were forensically tested and traces of Linzi's blood found on them – a quantity substantial enough to suggest injury, but not enough to confirm a fatality. During three days of questioning, he refused point-blank to reveal what had happened to his daughter or where she was now. Even as the court sentenced him to serve fifteen years for murder based on circumstantial evidence alone, he wouldn't reveal her fate.

Over the years, Joe had made dozens of requests to visit his dad behind the bars of the various prisons he'd been rotated through. Each time, he'd been denied without an explanation. Joe assumed it was the only way his father could punish his traitorous son. Joe frequently wrote long, detailed letters to him, asking him, begging him and even hurling abuse at him – anything to gain a reaction or an answer. But in return he received nothing but silence. Upon his parole after serving a full tariff, his father had disappeared as quickly and quietly as Linzi. Not even the resources at Joe's fingertips could help find a trace of him.

In Westfield, Joe moved towards a vast soft play area for children, where parents stood watching their young ones, who screamed with delight as they threw themselves on bouncy castles and trampolines. Some ran around wearing superhero costumes and animal face-paint designs, while others sat at tables in plastic aprons getting more colours on their clothes than on the paper in front of them.

He remembered how much Linzi had enjoyed spending time in shopping centres when they were kids. It was a fantasy land of toys and clothes, fun and fast-food outlets. Although their father had given them no pocket money and their mother little cash for housekeeping, the three of them spent hours trying to stay away from the house for as long as possible. Together, they'd venture into the town centre and window-shop, dreaming of a time when they might be able to go further inside than the front door. Now, Joe held on to the hope that Linzi was alive and still frequented shopping centres – and that, one day, he might find her in one, going about her business.

Suddenly, the figure of a young woman caught his eye. She was of average height, in her late twenties, and had chestnut-brown hair and a stud in her nose. She held the hand of a little boy. He had light, mocha-coloured skin and sun-bleached blond-and-russet curly hair, and shared his mother's piercing blue eyes. It struck Joe immediately that the boy's mother was the spitting image of his own mum.

Joe's heart flipped as he moved to get a better look at them both. He rubbed at his eyes as though they might be deceiving him. The woman was browsing at a stand selling children's books. His mind raced as he tried to reconcile his memories of Linzi with how time might have aged her. He'd once asked a facial-composite-artist colleague of his to sketch an image of how Linzi might look now, based on photos of mother and daughter. The woman in front of them was almost identical to that drawing.

Could it really be her? With trembling legs, he walked a few, tentative steps towards her. Her nose was the same shape as his sister's, her ears stuck out at the same angle. He'd seen women with passing resemblances to Linzi many times, but none had ever been as strikingly close as this.

As he approached closer still, he examined the back of her hand for a scar. He'd accidentally caught it with the hook of their father's fishing rod. They'd been playing with it in the garden, and when attempting to cast off, the hook had gone deep into her skin and ripped it open like tissue paper. The incident resulted in their mum shouldering the blame, and all three were banished to their bedrooms for an entire weekend. However, he struggled to see this woman's hand properly as it was entwined with her son's.

Now just three metres apart, Joe's breathing became shorter and sharper – what was he going to do next? Of all the times he'd imagined a similar scenario, he'd never thought so far ahead as to plan his opening gambit. He couldn't just walk up to her and ask if she was his long-lost sister; it would sound ridiculous if he was wrong. But the more he took her in, the more convinced he became that it could be Linzi. He rubbed at his eyes again.

He took a deep breath. It was now or never. But suddenly, someone grabbed at his shoulder and spun him round. Joe's instinct was to pull his arm back and raise his fist. That was until he recognised his potential assailant as Matt, and he was as angry as Joe had ever seen him.

'You've started doing it again, haven't you?' his husband seethed. His eyes were narrow and his face was flaming red.

'What are, why are—' Joe stuttered, aghast.

'I know when you lie to me because you can't look me in the eye, or you start biting your bottom lip.'

Joe turned his head to see where his mark had gone. She was moving away. He was torn: desperate to hurry after her, but aware Matt was demanding answers.

'It's not the first time either, is it?' Matt continued. Joe shook his head sheepishly. 'At first I thought you were seeing someone else, but that'd be too out of character. Then I found four old train ticket receipts to Milton Keynes in the kitchen bin, so I guessed what you were doing. I followed you, hoping I was wrong. But you're looking for her again, aren't you?'

'I can explain . . .'

'I don't get it, Joseph. You know what happened last time. I don't want to see you go through all of that again. It's not fair on you and it's not fair on me.'

'I know, I know, and I'm sorry,' Joe replied anxiously. Everything Matt was saying was true, and since they'd got married he had made such an effort to put Linzi out of his mind. But she'd held firm. Each time a woman around her age and of similar looks appeared on *Caught on Camera*, her disappearance returned to haunt him.

And he didn't have long left to find her. His time was running out.

Even while being chastised by Matt, all Joe wanted to do was try to locate the woman he'd been following. Right at that moment, she was the only thing that mattered – more than his job, his health or his relationship. He craved the truth so badly, it was like a drug.

'You think that woman with the boy you've been watching is Linzi, don't you?'

'Yes . . . no . . . maybe, I don't know.' From the corner of his eye he saw mother and son moving further away until they were out of view. 'I have to talk to her.'

'And say what? "Are you the sister my dad kidnapped twenty-six years ago?" Do you know how ridiculous that sounds?'

'Please,' Joe begged. 'Please let me talk to her, just for a moment. I know it's crazy, but what else can I do?'

'You can move on. We both know Linzi isn't coming back.'

'I can't give up on her. I'm all she has left.'

'And I'm all *you* have left.'

Matt looked as if he was facing a losing battle, and took a step backwards. Joe paused for a moment, torn between his past and his present. Then he glanced at Matt apologetically, and left him. Joe dashed around the corner, frantically turning his head in all directions, looking for mother and child. But the woman had vanished from his life as quickly as she'd appeared.

'Damn it,' he said loudly, angry at both the woman who'd escaped him and Matt for interfering.

But by the time he had run back to the spot where he'd left Matt, his husband had also disappeared. Joe pinched at the corners of his eyes and shook his head. And he asked himself if he would ever be free of the memory of Linzi.

CHAPTER 31

Maisie sat cross-legged on the living room floor and used her dolls as drumsticks to batter the base of two saucepans.

Her grandmother ignored the clanking and sat at the table, making an early start on accounts and keying numbers into a spreadsheet. In the kitchen, Becca slipped four slices of brown bread into the toaster and poured orange juice from a carton into a glass.

'She's not the most genteel girl, is she?' said Becca when her mum joined her. They watched from the doorway as Maisie gleefully made as much noise as she could. 'I'm not sure who she gets that from – me or Emma.'

'A little from both of you, I think. You were always the less girlie one, though. When you were two and we thought we'd potty-trained you, you suddenly started peeing in the garden.'

'No I didn't!' Becca protested, while trying not to laugh.

'You bloody did! You told us that if the cat was allowed to wee outside, then so could you. You were bordering on feral. It was only when you pulled your knickers down, lost your balance and fell into the stinging nettles that you changed your mind.'

Becca shook her head, unable to recall the memory, but conceded it wasn't entirely unbelievable. She had always been wilful – 'stubborn' was a word frequently written in her school reports. The only person she would listen to was her father, but when she announced she planned to follow in his footsteps and join the police force, he had tried his best to talk her out of it. She didn't listen. Now, it disappointed and angered her that he hadn't seen his daughter leave the uniform behind and join CID.

She dropped a coffee capsule into the machine and pressed a button to heat the milk. She chose her words carefully before she spoke. 'Have you heard from Aunty Mary recently?'

Helen shook her head. 'No, why?'

'She sent me another email a couple of weeks back. There didn't seem any point in saying anything,' Becca continued. 'It was the same old rubbish we've read a hundred times before – Dad's still living with her and she's still trying to make us see that we're the ones in the wrong, and to give him another chance.' Helen nodded, and Becca hesitated before she asked her next question. 'Do you miss him, Mum?'

'I used to, but not any more, no.'

'Sometimes I struggle to remember what he was like before what happened to Emma,' Becca said. 'It's like what he became has overshadowed everything else.'

Helen nodded. 'I know.' The words snagged in her throat.

Becca carried plates and drinks into the living room and placed them on the dining table while Helen moved her paperwork and laptop. 'Maisie,' Becca called. 'Come and eat.' Becca spread peanut butter thickly across both slices of toast, just how Maisie liked it, and watched as her daughter devoured it. When she finished, Becca wiped the crumbs from around her mouth and glanced at the clock. She had already missed the first briefing of the morning and it made her feel jittery. Becca had come so far in the investigation that she didn't want to be relegated now, or thought of as unreliable. Given the choice, she'd rather have been at work for 7 a.m. than doing the school run.

Picking up her iPad and scanning the front pages of each national newspaper didn't help contain her anxiety. Every one of them carried the story of the serial killer's latest strike.

To prove to her mum the concerns she'd voiced a night earlier hadn't fallen on deaf ears, Becca had volunteered to take her place at school storytelling and help some of the children, like Maisie, who needed a little extra assistance with reading and writing.

Becca wanted to enjoy spending time with her daughter more than she did. It should have been a given that Maisie's happiness and development were more important than anything else, so why did she keep having to remind herself of it? What was wrong with her? She knew that making one breakfast and giving up one morning was not enough to reconnect mother and daughter. She was placing a Band-Aid over a broken bone.

She stared at the framed photograph on the wall of three generations of women in the Vincent family. Try as she might, she was struggling to be the person her mother and daughter needed her to be.

In her eight years in the police force, Becca had never worked on a case requiring as much manpower as Operation Chamber. Most of the time, her department was understaffed. Now, on her arrival at CID headquarters, she estimated the headcount to have risen to at least one hundred. Those people she didn't recognise were dwarfing the number of familiar faces. Becca assumed the overtime budget must have gone through the roof. It was funny how the power of the media and public attention could make money grow on trees when it had to.

It was 11.30 a.m. before she entered the major incident room, and she hoped the increasing numbers would work in her favour and that her absence had gone unnoticed. Almost immediately, she was grateful to learn there was to be an update in five minutes, which would get her back up to speed.

Becca squeezed inside and hovered at the rear of the meeting room, lurking behind some of the taller officers so she wouldn't have to make eye contact with CS Webster. The room was stuffy and had no working air conditioning. Even with open windows, the smell of Chinese takeaway consumed by those working nights hung thickly in the air.

Her attention was drawn to the door as Joe entered, carrying his bag. He appeared flustered and Becca hoped that he was late too. She couldn't see Nikhat or Bryan anywhere, though.

'Right,' Webster began. 'For those of you who have just joined us, another potential victim was discovered an hour ago. We're awaiting positive ID but it appears that a staff member at St Victoria Hospital in Angel has been murdered. DS Vincent, are you here yet?'

Shit, thought Becca. Her lateness hadn't gone unnoticed. She raised her hand.

'Can you meet DI Odedra and DS Thompson at the scene and see what you can find out about the victim? You proved in the cases of Burgess and Dawson that the killer likes to hang around and watch us at work afterwards. So, DS Russell, can you go too and see if there's anyone you recognise that you've seen at other crime scenes?'

'Can't we put the hospital on lockdown if he might still be there?' asked Becca.

'It's a logistical nightmare, and top brass has already said no.'

Webster looked pale and drawn, Becca thought, and she watched the chief superintendent grinding her teeth when others spoke. While they were all feeling the pressure, as the senior investigating officer the buck stopped with her. Webster would be taking the flak from above as to why there hadn't been any significant breaks in the case yet.

She continued for another ten minutes, making sure to pile the pressure on everyone. 'I don't have to tell you the shit storm we face unless we make some progress soon,' she said, her words frustrated and her tone weary. 'So far, all we have is a traffic-cam shot of an obscured face, and nothing of note from the crime scenes or properties he's been viewing us from. I need real progress and I need it soon.'

With the team dismissed, Becca was making her way towards Joe when Webster pulled her into her office.

'I'm sorry I was late,' Becca said first, in a pre-emptive strike.

'Let me be completely transparent with you,' Webster replied. 'When I first agreed to give you a key role in this investigation, I thought it might be too much for you. Not because I think you lack the skills or dedication, but because I know you've had to take time off in the past for family reasons. And I'm aware of the situation with your father too. But I need to be able to count on you. I have no doubt that raising any child – let alone a young one with special needs – is difficult, but then so is this job. Contrary to popular belief, I'm not a heartless bitch, but it wasn't that long ago that people like you and I were only ever thought of as mothers with badges, not police officers. We have come a long, long way, and I need to know that you can continue with no distractions.'

'I can and I will,' said Becca, nodding. But even she struggled to believe it.

CHAPTER 32

'You were late this morning,' Becca began as she and Joe approached the entrance of St Victoria Hospital's accident and emergency department.

'So were you. I spotted you up ahead from the tube station. Where were you?'

'Mummy issues. You?'

'Husband issues.'

'Bet it was your fault.'

'Why would you assume that?'

'When I was growing up, we used to have a Labrador called Lucy. The moment our backs were turned, she'd have her nose in the dustbins trying to dig out sweet wrappers and anything she wasn't allowed to eat. Each time we called her out on it, she'd look at us with the same hangdog expression you have now.'

'You don't look so chirpy yourself.'

'I just had a new arsehole ripped by Webster. Well, that's an exaggeration. She and the whole department have been pretty understanding in the past about Maisie's needs. But I promised to give this case my undivided attention and then I spend the first two hours of the morning reading *Shifty McGifty* and *The Pongwiffy* stories to a group of six-year-olds. Not quite Jane Tennison, am I?'

'You're more like Brenda Blethyn when she plays Vera, but with poorer taste in coats.'

'I keep making myself feel bad because I can't devote all the time I want to this case. Whereas you – you don't know how lucky you are, being a man in this job. When you're a woman, you've got so much more to prove.'

'Is it still that hard? Look at the success Webster's had. Plus the Met's chief is female, and other women have taken some of the top jobs.'

'Taken, as in taken from men?'

'That's not what I meant.'

'There's still a lot of sexism in the job, which you don't get. Granted, it's often the old-school coppers who'll make a comment about your arse or expect you to make them a cuppa, but it's still there. Although the public are a lot worse. I remember when I first started in uniform, and being called out to jobs and experiencing first-hand how disrespectful they can be. Half the time it's because of the uniform, and half the time it's because it's a woman wearing it and she's daring to tell a man how to behave. Then there's the job itself. We're expected to carry equipment designed for men that weighs a fifth of our bodyweight and to still run as fast as you lot, chasing suspects and jumping over fences like we're in the Grand bloody National.'

They paused as the deafening wail of an ambulance siren alerted them to the vehicle pulling up outside the doors of A & E. Inside, they were directed to a cordoned-off side room close to the waiting area. Patients sat craning their necks, trying to see what was going on, as behind a closed curtain, camera flashes illuminated the room.

They found Nikhat outside it, removing a mask and polythene hood.

'Same suspect?' Becca asked.

'As far as we can ascertain, it smacks of one of his attacks. But this time, the victim is female.'

'What's he done to her?'

'She's been strapped to a table with more than a hundred needles stuck in every visible vein.'

Becca shook her head. 'Do we know who she is yet?'

'Her colleagues tell us she's a twenty-eight-year-old nurse called Zoe Ellis.'

CHAPTER 33

He remained inside his stationary vehicle at the outer edge of the car park.

He was late. The temporary traffic lights, roadworks and traffic jam further along the street had been out of his control. He'd wanted to be there for 10.30 a.m., when the stereo sprang to life and began blasting out Roxy Music's 'Love is the Drug' on repeat. He had thought long and hard about his choice of song, and it seemed the most fitting.

Instead, he was forced to use his imagination to conjure up the image of Zoe's horrified colleagues the moment they found her mutilated body. He tapped two small mounds of cocaine on to the back of his hand and snorted them, one per nostril. Then he took a swig from a can of flat Pepsi to rid himself of the acrid taste trickling down the back of his throat, and swallowed two painkillers.

As he awaited the inevitable head rush, he stared into the distance at the building he was soon to enter, and thought back to Zoe. Her face, contorted in panic and terror when she realised who her boyfriend really was and what he was doing to her, would be seared into his memory for ever. She had loved him, and despite himself he had become fond of her; she brought out a side to him he'd thought he'd lost. But it had never been part of the plan for the hunter to feel anything for the hunted.

Twice after he'd started following her all those months ago, he'd found himself standing directly behind her in a queue inside Costa Coffee. He'd already learned she was a creature of habit and her breakfast order was always the same – a skinny latte and a gluten-free brownie to go.

Both times, they'd made eye contact and smiled at one another. He knew that he was breaking his own rules by emerging from the shadows, but she was a pretty girl with eyes that reminded him of Audrey's. Her hair was honey blonde and slicked back into a ponytail that hung to just below her shoulders. She wore very little make-up, only lipstick and eyeliner. Her skin was flawless, and to his surprise he'd had an urge to run his fingers across her cheeks. But he'd held himself back.

The third time in each other's presence, she spoke.

'Are you stalking me?' Zoe had asked as she turned, clutching her coffee and a paper bag. The question was playful rather than accusatory.

'I wasn't the first couple of times, but now I am,' he replied, flirting back. 'Would you like to join me?'

'I start my shift soon,' she replied, looking at her watch. 'But you can walk me to work if you like.' It was more of a statement than an invitation.

'What do you do?'

'I'm a nurse,' she replied, but he already knew that.

They made small talk as they walked, discussing where they were from, how they had come to live in London, where they hung out and about their careers. A stranger might be fooled into thinking she cared about her nursing job, but he knew differently. She was careless. The well-being and safety of her patients were worth no more to her than that of cattle to the staff of an abattoir. And by the time they'd reached the entrance to St Victoria Hospital, they'd made plans to see each other that night.

Meeting at a wine bar close to Zoe's flat, they'd sunk brightly coloured happy-hour cocktails until they were drunk. He stayed over at her place at her suggestion. Moments after stumbling through the front door, they were indulging in clumsy, spontaneous sex. Later, when she was still naked and in a post-coital slumber next to him, she draped her arm across his chest. Audrey had slept in exactly the same position, always needing to feel his skin against her, even unconsciously. And as much as Zoe was the enemy and he wanted to push it to one side, he hadn't realised how much he'd missed that feeling. So he left it where it was and drifted off into a warm, satisfied sleep.

He stayed at Zoe's flat the following night too, then much of the weekend, and a pattern emerged. Two weeknights he'd sleep over at hers, then again on Saturday evenings. The remaining days found him in empty properties on the letting agency's books. For all intents and purposes, they were a couple.

She was much more experimental than anyone he'd ever been intimate with, and he couldn't help but wonder if it was the *Fifty Shades of Grey* trilogy on her bookshelf that gave her such confidence and encouraged her to be more explorative. At the beginning, it had helped his arousal if he thought about Audrey and how it had felt making love to her. Then, as the weeks passed, he began losing himself in their moments together. That brought with it guilt, as if he were cheating on the woman he really wanted to be with. He would never find another Audrey – nor did he want to, and least of all in Zoe.

By now, the mixture of cocaine and codeine should have lifted his spirits, but instead he remained melancholic. He picked up the phone only two people had the number for, and scrolled through the texts. Hours earlier, he'd messaged Zoe from the unregistered, pay-as-you-go mobile phone, informing her that he had found the note she'd left for him, he couldn't sleep and that he was missing her. He used the aubergine and water-splash emojis, clearly spelling out what was on his mind. Knowing how much sex in unusual places excited her, he suggested he'd come to the hospital, where they could steal a private, intimate moment. In her first reply, she'd told him no and that she was 'too busy'. Then 'no' became an 'it'd be wrong' before developing into an 'okay, hurry up'. When he texted that he was already on the premises, she appeared at the door in under a minute.

Upon opening it, she'd been puzzled as to why he was dressed in white overalls. 'What are you wearing . . .' was all she could utter before he'd clamped his hand across her mouth and thrust the syringe into her neck, pushing the plunger part of the way and filling her veins with just enough sedative to render her immobile but conscious.

Zoe had mentioned the nurses used the room for occasional power naps between shifts. And on the days she wasn't working, he had wandered the hospital corridors unnoticed until he located it. Once inside, he'd opened the window no more than a couple of millimetres, enabling him access later, when required. If Zoe could get away with murder under that roof, then why couldn't he?

Once he was sure she was incapacitated, he'd glued the lock shut, stripped her down to her underwear and tied her to the bed. He turned up the dimmer switch on the light just enough to see what he was doing, and got to work.

He knew Zoe couldn't feel pain but was conscious of what was happening to her. He felt her eyes glaring at him, watching helplessly as he smoothly inserted the first needle into her forearm. He allowed a line of blood to trickle down her skin before he inserted the second.

With the exception of Dumitru, he had looked the others in the eye as he'd tortured and killed them, and he fed on their fear. But he couldn't bring himself to do that with Zoe. He was concerned that if he saw how petrified she was, he might not be able to go through with it. And as needles three, four and five followed, his feelings became ever more muddled. The satisfaction he'd elicited from the killing of others simply wasn't being replicated with Zoe. His need to punish her was being outweighed by his conscience.

He paused to show her a photograph on his phone, and explained why he was putting her through this. A flicker of recognition crossed her face before the penny dropped. And she wasn't the only one to shed a tear in that room.

Running his gloved fingers through her hair one last time, he made a snap decision to change his plan. He couldn't watch her suffer any longer. So he pushed the plunger of the first syringe still embedded in her neck the rest of the way until it emptied. There had been enough Propofol left inside to cause a cardiac arrest. Moments later, Zoe's eyes became the only ones he had palmed shut. Then, when he finished his work, he double-checked the stereo was lined up and ready to play at the required time and volume.

Turning to face her one last time, he'd thought he'd prepared himself for how it might feel watching her die. He'd been wrong. Killing Zoe felt altogether different from killing the others. There was no post-murder elation or satisfaction, no pride at striking another name from the list. Instead, he felt hollow; like the last piece of thread tying him to society had been severed. He was now completely alone.

He left the way he came, invisible in the darkness.

Hours later, it was time for him to return and watch the aftermath of his work. He exited the car and, assured there were no witnesses, took some deep, cleansing breaths. Bending his knees so that he was at the correct height, he placed his right shoulder between the car door and the doorframe. He counted down from five to one, and with the other hand, slammed the car door shut as hard as he could. The pain arrived a second later as the bone jumped out of its socket and pushed forward inside his body.

'Fuck!' he yelled, then sank his teeth into his biceps to stop himself from making any more noise. It was his mother who'd dislocated it the first time, hitting him across the shoulder with a cricket bat because he'd dared to leave it in the dining room. She'd also refused to take him to the hospital, so he'd gone alone and learned how to slot the bone back in place. However, today it would be someone else's job to do that. Clutching his arm and fighting back the urge to be sick, he walked until he reached the entrance to A & E.

He pulled his baseball cap down to hide his face, and two uniformed police officers standing guard pointed him in the direction of an alternative entrance, further away from the crime scene. He left a fictitious name and address at the front desk as the receptionist warned that because his injury was non-life-threatening, it might take longer to be treated. He didn't protest; it gave him more legitimate time to be there. He swallowed two more painkillers when the receptionist turned her back.

Passing the sick and the injured, he chose a seat away from everyone else and closest to the cordoned-off corridor where the police were gathered. But being inside a hospital brought back unexpected memories he didn't want to relive. Once, a place like this had been his last resort and he had begged them for help. But no matter what drug they pumped him with, it made no difference.

His position didn't offer him a perfect view, but the reflection given by a convex mirror and the internal windows gave him a good idea of what was going on. It was the next best thing to sitting behind a window in a house or on an industrial estate and watching their every move.

Suddenly, in the reflection of the windows, he spotted DS Becca Vincent coming around the corner and heading towards the murder scene. He pulled his cap down further, shrank into his seat and turned his head, watching her from the corner of his eye.

While she didn't look at him, someone following behind her did make eye contact. He'd never seen a face turn quite so pale, quite so quickly. He acknowledged them with a nod but they didn't reciprocate. Instead, they hurried away and out of sight.

CHAPTER 34

'How long had she worked here?' asked Joe.

DI Odedra consulted his notebook. 'Seven years,' he replied, and went on to explain why nurses used the room where Zoe Ellis's body had been discovered.

'What happened?' asked Becca.

'At 10.30 a.m. exactly, music started blasting from the room. When they couldn't open the door, maintenance had to break it open, and inside they found her, a portable stereo and a timer plugged into the socket. Again, because of the unusual nature of the kill, we're working to the theory that this is our suspect's fifth victim.'

'Is there a possibility it's a copycat?' asked Joe.

'Everything is a possibility right now.' Nikhat shrugged.

'Beccs, if you're going inside, I'll take a look around A & E and then check out the CCTV footage,' said Joe. 'He's managed to dodge everything but the ANPR cameras so far. Let's see if he's become complacent and made any mistakes.'

Becca made her way towards the doorway of the crime scene. Her eyes shifted around the room and settled on the body of Zoe Ellis, lying on a trolley. Her neck, arms, hands, waist, thighs and ankles were strapped to it with thick rope. She'd been stripped down to her underwear, but according to Nikhat there were no signs of sexual assault. The autopsy would offer confirmation of that, though. Becca's first thought was that – with so many syringes poking from her exposed flesh – Zoe resembled a kind of macabre modern-art installation. She was streaked in thin, dark-red lines where the blood had left her veins and trickled down her skin, pooling on the rubber mattress. Her eyes were closed.

'She's like a human pincushion, isn't she?' said Nikhat, and Becca nodded. 'We've counted one hundred of them. When you're done, can you talk to some of her colleagues and get a better picture of who she was?'

Two hours later, Becca was taking notes in a nurses' station behind the reception desk. She was part comforting, part interviewing a fourth colleague of Zoe's. Nurse Taja Khatri stood by an open window taking puffs on a cigarette.

'I know this hospital is smoke-free but I don't care,' she said defiantly, and Becca had no reason to disbelieve her. Taja brushed her eyes with the sleeve of her cardigan, her grief betraying her tough exterior. She explained how she'd been there as the door was broken open. 'I've seen some things in my time but I will never ever forget that,' she said quietly.

'Did anybody notice Zoe was missing?' Becca asked.

'No. She wasn't on the rota because she wasn't supposed to be working. Anna May called in sick and asked her to do her shift for her.'

'Can you tell me a bit more about Zoe? What type of woman was she?'

'I don't know what to say,' Taja replied, and swept her raven-black hair behind her ears. 'She's an ordinary girl, like the rest of us. She works hard, she's popular with the team and she likes a drink when she's off-duty.'

'What about a boyfriend? Is she dating?'

'There is a guy, but I don't think any of us have met him. She doesn't talk about him much. I got the impression it was more of a casual thing, nothing serious.'

'Has she ever mentioned a name?'

'If she did, I can't remember it.'

'Well, if it comes back to you, could you please give me a call?' Becca handed her a business card. 'One last thing. Is there any reason you can think of why someone might want to hurt Zoe? A former patient who might have been harassing her, or an ex who wouldn't leave her alone, anyone like that?'

'If there was, she didn't tell me.'

After informing Nikhat of the little she'd learned, Becca found Joe in the hospital's security department. It had been a week since they'd first started working together, but she had seen the back of him hunched over a keyboard so frequently, she was sure she'd be able to recognise his crown in a police line-up. She watched as he removed a small bottle of eye drops from his pocket and tilted his head back to insert them.

'I could do with those,' she said.

'Jesus!' he spluttered, sounding flustered as he quickly slipped them back into his pocket. 'Are you trying to scare me to death?'

'Can I borrow them?'

'Probably best not to, they're prescription.'

'What for?'

'Conjunctivitis,' he lied.

'Oh, okay. Have you done your super-recogniser thing and cracked the case?'

'Not yet,' he replied, unable to hide his disappointment. 'No stragglers, no one lurking suspiciously in the vicinity of the crime scene, no one entering it, only the victim at 3.49 a.m. And no one leaving it either. I've pieced together her movements from various cameras before she got there though.'

Joe rewound the footage until Becca saw Zoe on the edge of the screen checking on a patient in a ward. Moments later, she walked away, looked at her mobile phone and texted someone. She appeared to be smiling.

'Twice more she gets a message and texts, then she makes her way along two corridors and this is the last we see of her. Within six minutes of receiving that first text, she goes into the room where she's killed.' They watched uneasily as she closed the door behind her and vanished from view.

'She knew him,' said Becca, nodding, like she was agreeing with herself. 'She knew who he was and she knew that he was waiting for her in that room. She trusted him. He must have climbed through the window with the stereo, started texting her, telling her where he'd be.'

'And if he knew she was working that day, he's either a colleague, close friend or boyfriend. We need to get her phone number so we can find those texts.'

'The way the blood pooled around each syringe meant he'd inserted them post-mortem,' said Becca. 'Had she still been alive, blood would have been pumping around her body and more would have been released from the puncture wounds. The only reason to have killed her so soon rather than making her watch him torturing her was if he didn't want Zoe to suffer. He didn't offer his other victims the same mercy. I've got the address of the nurse whose shift Zoe took. It seems like a huge coincidence that the night she's ill, the colleague she asked to take her shift is murdered. Fancy joining me?'

CHAPTER 35

Although they could only see her partially hidden face peeking from behind the chained door, neither Joe nor Becca thought Anna May Chung looked unwell.

According to her colleagues, she'd been struck down by the norovirus a day earlier, causing her diarrhoea and vomiting. But Joe immediately noticed the remains of last night's make-up still on her face. Her deep red lipstick was faded, her foundation a little patchy, and one false eyelash had become unglued and was barely hanging on.

After identifying themselves, the door chain was removed, and judging by her outfit – comprising black skinny jeans, heels and an off-the-shoulder top – it was clear she had only recently returned home. She led them into a tiny, messy studio apartment.

'We'd like to ask you a few questions about last night,' Joe began. 'You were scheduled to work a shift, is that correct?'

'Yes.' She nodded.

'Your colleagues told us that you claimed to have the norovirus and wouldn't be in. You seem to have recovered remarkably quickly.'

'It's funny,' added Becca, 'because when I had it, it knocked me out for days. Not for a few hours. And isn't it just a winter thing?'

'It's contagious all year round,' Anna May replied, folding her arms. 'Mine turned out to be a stomach bug.'

'As a nurse, can't you tell the difference?' said Becca.

'What's this about, please? Why is the hospital sending the police to check up on me? I'm in the union. I know my rights.'

Becca glanced at Joe and then back to Anna May. 'I assume you've not been in contact with anyone you work with today?'

'No, my phone battery died. Why?'

'Zoe Ellis, the colleague you asked to cover you last night, was found dead.'

Anna May's jaw dropped. 'How . . . what happened?' she stuttered.

'She was killed at work in one of the old storage rooms your colleagues use to sleep in.'

Anna May shook her head, grabbed her phone from a charger and turned it on, unwilling to accept what they were telling her. As it sprang to life, beep after beep signified an influx of text messages and missed voicemails. Joe and Becca gave her a few moments to read some and to allow the news to sink in. Tears fell from her eyes.

'It's not my fault,' she sobbed. 'I only did what anyone would have done. No one would have turned down that money.'

'What money?' asked Joe.

'A man came to the flat a few days ago and asked me to phone in sick last night. He told me that if I swapped shifts with Zoe, he'd give me five thousand in cash as long as I didn't ask any questions.'

'Really,' said Becca, deadpan.

'Yes, I promise you! I thought he was a nutter at first, then he showed me the money – it was inside a plastic bag. He was insistent that it was only Zoe I swapped with.'

'Why?'

'I don't know.'

'Did you ask?'

'He said not to.'

'Didn't it strike you as strange?'

'Of course it did,' Anna May replied, wiping her eyes with her fingers. 'I was going to tell her . . . but look at this place. Nursing accommodation in London doesn't come cheap. You spend everything you earn on bills and rent. I can make five thousand pounds go a long way. So I said yes.'

As both Becca and Joe glanced around the cramped flat, their eyes were drawn to bulging shopping bags on the floor. Coco de Mer, Victoria Beckham and Burberry were all accounted for, among others.

'While your friend was being murdered last night, where were you?' Becca asked directly.

'Bar-hopping in Shoreditch with some friends,' she replied sheepishly.

'So there are people who can corroborate this?'

She nodded. 'I was with the same crowd all night.'

'Tell us more about the man with the money,' said Joe. 'What did he look like?'

'I don't know, just ordinary. I didn't look at him properly.'

Becca rolled her eyes. 'A man turns up on your doorstep with five thousand in cash and you don't give him a proper once-over? I don't buy that.'

'He was tall, quite good-looking, in his thirties . . .'

'What colour was his hair?' asked Joe.

'Dark blond or light brown, I think. It was hard to tell, he had a cap pulled down over his eyes. But his stubble looked dark blond.'

'What was on the cap?'

'Something foreign. Maybe French. I couldn't understand it. There was a scar on his earlobe, I'm sure. It was like a tear.'

Joe paused, then flicked through his notebook and turned to Becca. 'The waitress at the café opposite where the paramedic was taken said the man who used to sit there staring from the window had a split earlobe. Coincidence?'

'Paramedic?' said Anna May suddenly, putting two and two together. Her face paled. 'Was Zoe murdered by that serial killer everyone's talking about?'

'Investigations are ongoing,' Becca replied coldly, as she and Joe turned to leave.

'What did I do?' Anna May asked, then looked to them for reassurance that she was blameless. Although both could see how genuine her regret was, neither offered her any words of comfort.

'We're going to need to take for analysis what's left of the money he gave you,' Becca said. 'I've got some evidence bags in the boot of the car.'

'I've already spent it,' Anna May mumbled.

Becca shook her head. 'We'll be sending someone over to bring you to the station later today to make a full statement and pair you with a forensic composite artist to come up with a likeness. And I hope that every time you throw that Mulberry handbag over your shoulder or slip your feet into those Louboutins, you remember whose life paid for them.'

They could still hear her crying inside the flat as they made their way along the corridor.

'Stupid, stupid cow,' Becca muttered.

'A little harsh, perhaps?' asked Joe.

'Probably, but I really don't care. She sold her friend out for what? To spend a day living a life she couldn't possibly maintain.'

'Haven't you ever wanted to break free of your life, even for a day, and pretend to be someone else?'

Maisie's face sprang to mind so quickly that it startled Becca. She wished she could flick a switch and suddenly become the mother her daughter needed her to be – the one who could read books at school without keeping one eye on the clock, who could sew costumes, who could be there to pick her up when the end-of-day bell rang. But she couldn't be that woman and hold down the career she had longed for. So Becca shook her head until the guilt vanished. For now, at least.

'No,' she said. 'Too many people act first and think later. Then it's left to people like us to wipe up the mess they leave behind.'

Before Joe could ask her to elaborate, her phone rang. 'It's Nik,' she said, and answered. After several *yeses*, two *shits*, and a *no way*, she hung up.

'Zoe Ellis's flat was set alight this morning. From the speed it took hold, it's likely arson, and whoever torched it used a lot of accelerant.'

'The killer didn't want us finding any trace of him there,' said Joe. 'It's looking more and more likely to me that someone she was dating, and who'd spent time there, murdered her. Any news on her mobile phone? Any pictures of them together? Frequently called numbers?'

'It wasn't with her body. Either been turned off or destroyed. Nik's waiting for the call records to come in but he wants us back at the hospital.'

It took them fifteen minutes to get there, and neither Becca nor Joe noticed the car several vehicles behind, trailing them from Anna May's flat and into the hospital grounds.

'I'll meet you in there,' said Becca, closing the car door and staring at a text message from her mum, asking her to call home. As Joe walked on ahead, she held the phone to her chest and sighed. She knew what the right thing to do was, but still she delayed dialling. It couldn't be urgent, she reasoned; if Maisie was poorly, she was sure Helen would have telephoned, not texted. The latest murder and Webster's thinly veiled warning to keep her eye on the ball meant that unless it was an emergency, she couldn't allow any more distractions to come between her and the investigation, no matter what she had promised her mum. She would call her back later.

Becca returned her phone to her pocket and stood in the centre of the car park, where she had an unbroken 360-degree view of the grounds, the hospital and the neighbouring buildings. Clearly news of the nurse's murder had already broken, as ahead she spotted news vans, reporters and camera crews lining the road.

As she went to return the phone to her pocket, it slipped from her hands and fell to the ground. She cursed and reached to pick it up, hoping she hadn't cracked the screen. But as she returned to her feet, someone was behind her, blocking out the sun. She quickly raised her head to find the ominous shadow of a man above her.

CHAPTER 36

He held his breath as he watched her. She was so painfully close, he could smell the lavender extract in her conditioner, and the fumes from the nail polish she'd recently applied. She didn't have the slightest inkling that she wasn't alone and that he was so close. It aroused him.

Remaining where the light didn't reach and as upright as possible, it took all his effort not to move; his elevated mood at odds with his need to remain static. His thoughts veered in all manner of directions, like fireworks let off in the street by teenagers. It was a result of his most recent hit of cocaine and the freshly ingested painkillers dissolving in his stomach. One numbed the throbbing in his now-realigned shoulder joint, and the other overstimulated his brain to stave off his need for rest.

He fought hard to keep his breathing silent so as not to give away his position. As his eyes followed her movements, he became aware of just how much of his life he'd dedicated to watching people. From an early age, it was vital he could read his mother's body language so that he knew when to avoid her and when a beating was on its way. Then, before and during university, his reinvention came after studying what other young men wore, how they behaved and the subjects they discussed with their friends.

He'd also watched carefully the men who paid for his company. They came in all shapes, sizes and ages. Some wore wedding rings and the burden of shame; others seemed to delight in keeping secrets from their nearest and dearest. Some possessed dark souls and satisfied their cravings by causing him physical pain, but he always rose above it. None of them could hurt him like his mother had hurt him.

More recently, he'd studied the names on his list and grown to learn of their habits and routines. There was the paramedic who, having bitten off a fingernail, would retain it inside his mouth for hours. The fireman's head was turned by underage schoolgirls in uniform. The skinnier of the Romanians had frequently picked at the dark hairs sprouting from his ears, while his cousin always used the cubicle in a men's toilet then deliberately pissed on the seat. Zoe would watch TV while playing with the washing instruction label inside her T-shirt. Everyone had their quirks and compulsions, and he had noted them all.

She moved again, and he inhaled a faint trace of alcohol and couldn't determine if it was coming from her or the antibacterial handwash at the hospital. Or was it petrol? Some had splashed on his jeans as he'd doused Zoe's flat that morning, so he'd thrown his clothes into her bedroom and changed into a new set he kept in the one drawer she'd allowed him. Then he flicked the wheel of the cigarette lighter until a flame appeared, let it fall to the floor and closed the front door just as the fuel exploded into life.

Blood. He could suddenly taste blood. He moved his hand slowly and silently towards his face as it dripped from his nostrils. He wiped it away, spreading it across his lips just as she moved past him again. He watched as she dropped something on the floor, and as she bent down to pick it up, he was sure she would see him.

It was time to reveal himself, and as his body moved, it cast a menacing shadow over her.

CHAPTER 37

Becca had no time to reach into her handbag and grab her personal alarm. So, instinctively, she clenched her fist, ready to punch her assailant as hard as she could in the groin and then run.

She stopped, however, when their eyes met. She took in his thinner frame and his gaunt cheeks. In the five years since they'd last come face to face, he had visibly aged. His hairline had receded to his crown, and his once-sparkling eyes were milky. He was a haunted man.

'Dad,' she exclaimed, and rose to her feet. Her heart raced as she tried to regain some composure. 'You scared the shit out of me. What are you doing here?'

'I needed to talk to you.'

'Christ, couldn't you have just called instead of creeping up on me?'

'You've changed your number and you didn't reply to any of your aunty's emails.'

'I thought you were living in Sunderland?'

'I was. I still am. I got the train down to see you.'

'So you haven't got your driver's licence back then?'

'No,' he replied, hesitantly. 'Can we go for a coffee somewhere and talk?'

'I'm working.'

'I know you are.'

'How do you know?'

'I've been following you.'

'For how long?'

'A week or so.'

Becca rolled her eyes. 'I thought I was being paranoid.'

'I'm sorry. Fifteen minutes of your time, that's all I ask. And then I'll leave you alone if that's what you want.'

Becca considered his offer before nodding her agreement, albeit reluctantly. 'There's a Starbucks over the road,' she said, pointing.

The sun did little to thaw the frostiness Becca felt towards him. An awkward, silent walk followed before they placed their orders for tea and sat at a corner table away from the other customers. For the first few minutes, her father discussed his journey, the Travelodge where he'd been staying and his new life in Sunderland. Becca wouldn't meet his gaze.

'How's your mum?' he asked.

'She's okay.'

'Has she retired? Is she enjoying it?'

'She was, but because you were sacked for drink-driving rather than pensioned off, she had no choice but to go back to work.'

'Does she talk about me much?'

'No, not really. Neither of us do.'

A small part of Becca wanted to hurt him, because his behaviour had hurt their family. However, her animosity seemed to wash over him. Instead, he nodded, as if he'd rehearsed their conversation and these were answers he expected to hear.

'Are you going to ask about your granddaughter?' Becca said. 'Or are we still pretending she doesn't exist?'

'That's unfair. I've never denied her.'

'But you didn't accept her either.'

'You know how hard I found it looking at her and seeing . . . him.'

'Do you think that was easy on any of us? Because I tell you now, Dad, it wasn't. But you couldn't even be bothered to try. All you were concerned about was where the next bottle of whiskey was coming from.'

'I admit, that was the case back then, but not any more, I've changed.'

'Stop lying to yourself.' Becca shook her head. 'I can smell the booze on your breath and on your clothes.'

'I had a couple on my way here to take the edge off my nerves, that's all.'

'It's been five years, and even after all this time you still can't be honest. You can't face what life throws at you when you're sober.'

'And do you blame me?' he snapped. 'I was grieving my daughter and it didn't seem to hurt you or your mum like it hurt me. You were too busy with the baby. And when I needed your help, you turned your back on me.'

Becca slammed her fist down on the table. The tea mugs jumped and other customers turned their heads to locate the disturbance. 'Don't. You. Dare,' she seethed. 'How many times did I offer to go with you to Alcoholics Anonymous? We had a room booked at a rehab clinic for you, but instead you disappeared for days. We stood by you at your hearing before you lost your job and we did everything we could to try to help you but it was never enough.'

Becca could still picture her father in the hall of their family home, having returned from his last drinking bender before Helen ordered him out of her life. He had urinated and soiled himself, and his clothes were covered in vomit. He'd stood there, incoherent and steadying himself against the wall. Becca had called one of her father's colleagues – and their family friend – Bryan Thompson for help, and he'd eventually been persuaded to leave. It was the moment she lost the father she'd once adored.

'When your sister needed me the most, I couldn't save her,' he continued now, tears pooling in his faded eyes. 'It was my fault that she died.'

'No it wasn't,' Becca replied. 'None of us could have saved Emma. She was a grown woman who made the decision to stay with Thorpe, and by the time she was ready to leave it was too late. But it wasn't our fault she died, it was his. It was, however, your fault how you behaved afterwards. It was you who turned your back on us, not the other way around.'

Father and daughter paused to gather their thoughts. 'Can I see her?' he asked eventually.

'Who, Mum? That's her decision.'

'No – Maisie.'

Becca suddenly felt very protective of her daughter, and the strength of her maternal instinct took her by surprise. 'No,' she said adamantly. 'Mum and I have surrounded her with positivity, and God only knows it's been a struggle not to get angry or upset in front of her about what happened. Until you beat your demons, I can't let you anywhere near her. I'm sorry, Dad.'

As Becca rose to her feet, her father slumped back in his chair. She knew her words had finally hurt him, but she hadn't gained the satisfaction she'd hoped for. She wasn't aware she was crying until she could taste salt water on her lips. Then she left without turning back or saying goodbye.

CHAPTER 38

Margaret let out a shrill scream and fell backwards from her crouching position.

He wanted to laugh as she shuffled across the floor like a crab trying to get away from the figure in the shadows. She'd assumed she was alone until he moved from the darkness of the kitchenette and into the main light of the office.

'What the hell are you doing?' she snapped when she saw it was him. 'It's seven o'clock, you're not supposed to be here.'

'I'm sorry if I scared you,' he lied, then offered her his hand to help her up. She refused it. 'I've come to pick up some keys. I've got an early appointment tomorrow morning.'

'Where?' she asked in a tone that indicated she didn't believe him.

'Shoreditch High Street. It's the flat above the kebab shop.'

Margaret's eyes narrowed as she gave him the once-over, then she looked behind him at the half-open door of the safe that housed the rental property keys. She needed distracting.

'You look good,' he smiled, eyeing her up and down. 'It's been a while since you and I . . . well . . . you know . . . I'm sure I don't need to spell it out.'

Such flirtation usually resulted in her hands all over him and one of her breasts in his mouth. But, today, she looked uncomfortable in his presence. Only when he questioned it did he remember he had blood smeared across his mouth. That and the heat of the day, and the thick jumper he'd taken from his drawer at Zoe's flat, were making his brow bead with sweat.

'I was going to talk to you about the bookkeeper,' Margaret continued, changing the subject. 'I don't think she's going to work out for us. I've spoken to the area manager, and he wants us to go back to the old firm.'

'Rajesh said that?' he replied gruffly. 'Why? I negotiated a really good deal with her that saved us over a thousand pounds a quarter.'

'Well, they came back with another offer that bettered your friend. I'll be happy to give her a call and tell her myself, if it puts you in an awkward position?'

He let out an irritated puff of breath. 'So I've totally wasted my time then, is that what you're saying?'

'No, I'm grateful for your help. But as the office managers these decisions are ultimately mine and Rajesh's to make, and not yours.'

He bit down on his bottom lip and tried to keep a lid on his hair-trigger temper. He'd really wanted an excuse to go back to Helen's house, in the hopes of catching another glimpse of her detective daughter. But Margaret was ruining that.

'You're being an idiot,' he snapped, and shook his head.

'Pardon me? Who do you think you're talking to?' Margaret folded her arms. 'And while we're on the subject of your attitude, the girls have been complaining about the hours you keep and how I let you come and go as you please. It wouldn't be so bad if you were bringing in the revenue. But at the moment you're not, and I can't keep defending you. Your figures over the last quarter have nosedived. You need to sort yourself out.'

'It's the time of year,' he replied. 'You know what it's like – it's coming up for the summer, people are thinking about their holidays, not about moving house.'

'You don't need to explain the market to me. From now on, I want you to start filling in your online appointment diary so that we all know where you are when you're not in the office during working hours.'

His fists couldn't have been any tighter, but he lightened his clipped tone. 'Come on, Margaret,' he said, moving towards her. 'I thought we had an understanding? You and me . . . we have our own rules.' He let out a forced smile as he reached out his hand to touch her arm. Her response was to back away.

'That's in the past,' she replied coldly.

'It doesn't have to be,' he said, pushing himself further forward and grabbing her by the waist.

'No,' she continued, but he didn't listen, and nuzzled his face into her neck. He ran his fingers down her spine and across her buttocks. 'Stop it,' she continued, and squirmed. He held on tighter, pulling her closer to him, his hand trying to make its way down the tight waistband of her jeans.

Suddenly, she pushed hard against his other arm and he felt his collarbone move, sparking shooting pains across his shoulders. He winced.

'What is wrong with you?' she asked, backing further away to safety. 'Look at the state of you. Is that blood on your mouth? And your eyes . . . why are your pupils so wide?'

He responded with a slow nod, like it was all making sense. 'I get it,' he said. 'Patched things up with your husband, have you? Decided to start playing happy families with Mark and the kids instead of fucking me?'

'My personal circumstances have nothing to do with you.'

'They do when you're bent over my desk. Does Mark know about us? Is he aware that you beg me to cum on your face like a fat, desperate, middle-aged porn star? Do you suck his dick like I taught you to suck mine? Surely he must've noticed an improvement in your technique? Or is he too willing to get it over with, so you can put your clothes back on and hide those stretch marks and cellulite? Maybe he does what I do and pretends you're someone else . . .'

'Shut up!' Margaret yelled, her face flushed and cheeks puffed. 'You're disgusting!' She moved towards him and raised her hand to slap his face. He grabbed it and stopped her before she made physical contact. Her body trembled as his fingers dug so deep into her wrists that he could feel her tendons.

'Get out, get out!' Margaret yelled. 'I don't want to ever see you in here again.' He retaliated by laughing in her face. 'Go now, before I call the police!'

He released her, and as he made his way to the door, he kicked the papers she'd been picking up when he first surprised her, then turned his head.

'By the way,' he added. 'If Mark doesn't know about us, he will soon. I've been saving some of the security videos of us together in the office. I'm sure he'll be fascinated to see what his wife gets up to when she says she's working late.'

He gave her one last look as the door slammed behind him.

CHAPTER 39

All eyes were on Joe in the hope he might recognise Britain's most wanted man. To Becca, he appeared anxious and acutely aware of the pressure placed upon him.

He fixed all his attention on the two pictures compiled by composite artists, based on the separate witness descriptions from the café waitress and the nurse. But while there were similarities between the two faces, there were also wild variations. He shook his head, and the atmosphere in the room deflated. 'I'm sorry,' he muttered, shaking his head again.

'We've been using a police profiler to give us more of an idea of the kind of personality we're searching for,' CS Webster explained to the packed briefing. 'But this case is harder to profile than most because we're not looking for a traditional killer. His behaviour is contradictory. He's intelligent, cautious and organised – he leaves no fingerprints, footprints, fibres, hair, blood, semen, spit or sweat. There appears to be no obvious attempt to clean up crime scenes, which says he knows he's left no evidence and he's probably wearing protective clothing. Yet despite his prudence, he's taken a risk with three of his five murders by committing them in public. There's no sexual motive as far as we can ascertain, but he needs to dominate. By sedating them, he doesn't give his victims a fair chance. There is only ever going to be one outcome for them. He's there for a purpose, and that is to hurt and then kill. He displays elements of psychopathy and sadism, and wanting people to suffer plays a huge part in the torture before death. Perhaps he has been a victim of physical abuse, because he's not afraid to inflict it upon anyone else. He's a good timekeeper and doesn't get lost in the moment – he does what he needs to do and then leaves. But he does have a desire to absorb the aftermath of his crimes, perhaps to gain satisfaction or to relive them. It's likely that he wants to kill in a short space of time and in very different ways to confuse or wrong-foot us – the quicker the time period, the less time we have to put two and two together and identify him.'

Becca listened, albeit half-heartedly. The unexpected meeting with her father remained heavy on her mind and her conscience. Had she done the right thing in refusing to allow him back into their family? Was it really her decision to make? Perhaps if she hadn't smelled booze on him, the outcome might have been different. Or maybe if he'd been willing to admit his failings and acknowledge that he wasn't the only one who had suffered following Emma's death, she might have been more open to his request. But he wasn't. And she didn't want Maisie tainted by a past that wasn't her fault.

It was only as she made her way home, no longer with the feeling she was being followed, that she remembered Helen had texted that afternoon, asking her to call. She cursed her terrible memory for failing to do so. Then she recalled failing to contact Maisie's teacher after a fellow pupil had called her 'retarded'. Becca tried telling herself that a fifth murder in eight days and her estranged father's sudden reappearance were good enough reasons to have forgotten. At least it was better than admitting that, once again, she'd put herself and her career above her daughter's needs.

But since seeing her dad earlier, Becca had felt something inside her beginning to shift. She was mirroring his behaviour – a parent putting their own needs above their child's and being too stubborn to admit it. And she didn't like how horrible it was making her feel.

Hanging her bag over the banister, she kicked off her shoes and silently padded up the staircase in the darkened hallway. She opened Maisie's door and saw her fast asleep, surrounded by stuffed toys. Helen arranged them like that when Maisie was feeling particularly anxious. Becca leaned over the bed and smoothed out Maisie's duvet, kissing her gently on the cheek. It was enough to stir Maisie and her eyelids fluttered open.

'Granny?' she muttered.

'No, it's Mummy.'

'I want Granny.'

'She's asleep, sweetie. You can see her in the morning.' Becca stroked her daughter's hair and took in the scent of strawberry bubble bath.

'I love Granny.'

'So do I. And do you love me?'

'No, because you don't live here any more.'

Becca paused. 'What do you mean? Of course I live here.'

'Then why don't I see you?'

As Maisie's eyes closed and she fell back to sleep, Becca didn't know how to reply.

She needs me, Becca realised. *She needs me and I'm failing her*. But instead of just feeling her usual levels of guilt for letting down Maisie, this time she added shame into the mix. Her daughter wasn't asking for much, just her mummy to be there for her. And Becca couldn't even give her that.

Suddenly, it was like her daughter's words had lit a fire inside her. The only thing stopping Maisie from being her priority above every-thing and everyone else was her. And she needed to make that change soon, before it was too late. She made a decision – once the inves-tigation was complete, there would be no more working late nights or impossible hours, no more guilty conscience and no more making herself feel lousy. Her job would never love her back, but the little girl at home would – if Becca allowed her to. While she'd told herself the same thing many times before, this time it felt different. This time, she truly meant it.

Back downstairs, Becca's first stop was the cupboard for a glass of wine. Her second was for two aspirin from a drawer in the living room. Then she threw herself on the sofa and allowed her legs to dangle over the arm, and began to plan how to tell Nik and Webster that she wanted to reduce her hours once the killer was caught.

'You're back then.' Helen's stern voice came from the doorway and startled Becca. A few drops of wine spilled from the glass on to the carpet. She sat up and dabbed at the damp patch with a tissue.

'I'm sorry,' Becca replied as her mum joined her. Even in the dimly lit room, she could sense the disapproval written across Helen's face.

'I guess I was daft for thinking we might have turned a corner this morning.'

'Please, Mum, not tonight.'

'Why, because you don't want to hear the truth?'

'No, because in the last twelve hours, I've had to deal with a dead nurse, a psychopath who nobody can remember well enough to draw an accurate picture of, and to top it off, Dad turning up out of the blue.'

Helen hesitated. 'Your father?' she asked.

'Yes,' Becca replied. 'He's back in London.'

'What did he want?'

'I had hoped that it'd be to say sorry, but it wasn't. It was the same old "Woe is me, why don't you understand me?" bullshit.'

'Oh.' Helen let out a long breath. She pulled the cord of her dressing gown tighter and joined Becca on the sofa. Helen took two large sips from her daughter's glass.

'The other day, you asked me if I missed him and I said not any more,' she said. 'I lied. I do miss him.'

Her confession came as a surprise. 'Do you want to see him again?'

Helen shook her head. 'No. It's the David Vincent I married that I miss, not the man he became. He left me alone to grieve for our daughter.'

'I was here too.'

'I know, but that's different. Me and your dad, we made you, we made Emma. Only someone you created a life with can understand what it means to watch as it's taken away. But instead of helping each other through the worst days, he changed and ran away, and I can never forgive him for that. I don't hate him, in fact I have no feelings for him whatsoever. He's a complete stranger to me. And I have no wish to see a stranger.'

'He asked to see Maisie.' As she said her daughter's name, Becca realised she was tracing the name on her tattooed wrist.

'What did you tell him?'

'That he couldn't.'

Helen nodded her approval.

'How has she been today?'

'When she got home from school, all she wanted was you. You could have spoken to her on the phone for just a couple of minutes, Rebecca. It wouldn't have taken long. It is difficult trying to put a positive spin on the fact she isn't at the top of her mum's priority list right now.'

'Things are going to change, honestly. Please don't make me feel any worse than I do already.'

'Darling, I'm not trying to. But as I told you yesterday, we can't go on like this indefinitely.'

'Just give me until the end of this case. Then we'll sit down and re-evaluate everything. This is all I can focus on right now. I can't let it go.'

But something inside her was already doing just that.

CHAPTER 40

When he stared in the car's rear-view mirror, he saw that the blue veins on either side of his temples had risen to the surface. And when he shut his eyes tightly, he felt them pulsate like they were ready to burst.

It was all he could do to stop himself from driving back to the office and showing Margaret who really lay underneath the mask he wore. He felt himself becoming more enraged. What right did she have to treat him like that? He couldn't be used by her, then tossed aside like a piece of rubbish just because she'd developed a conscience about a family she hadn't given two shits about when she was fucking him. Who the hell was she to reject him? Her, a middle-aged waste of space, telling him that their grubby little relationship was over? No, he thought, he was done with women telling him when they'd grown tired of him. They needed to start playing by his rules, not the other way round. He badly wanted to pin her to the office floor, wrap his hands around her throat and throttle her, listening to her gasp her last desperate breaths, her limbs flailing uselessly by her sides as she tried to push him off.

The only thing stopping him from teaching Margaret a lesson was that hurting her was too risky. The success of his murders to date had been down to his meticulous planning. He couldn't allow a spontaneous death to undo all his good work. Besides, killing someone with his bare hands and no anaesthetic or tools would be too personal. And he was saving such intimacy for the last name on his list. Later, when he'd reached his destination, he'd message Margaret's husband and her daughter on Facebook with footage he'd filmed of their extracurricular activities – and that would do for now.

Pressing down hard on the car's accelerator, he tore through a second set of amber traffic lights, blowing his horn at other motorists who were content to bumble along at the legal speed limit.

Margaret's brush-off brought back familiar feelings of rejection, from his mother. Now, try as he might, he couldn't get her face out of his head. He could recall the stench from her decaying body when he'd found it the first Christmas he returned home from university. She lay sprawled on her back on the kitchen lino, bloated, putrid and clutching a bottle of cheap cider. He'd left her there, taken the remainder of her disability allowance from her purse and used it to pay for a three-night stay at a Holiday Inn.

A call from the police some two weeks later had informed him she'd been found by neighbours complaining of the stench. He didn't organise or attend her funeral; he left that job to the council. He hadn't owed her anything. At one time – and despite the horrific things she had done to him – she'd had a son who loved her unconditionally. Instead of being grateful for that, it seemed to make her hate him even more. So she'd gradually chipped away at him until he looked for love from anywhere else but her. Now, he felt nothing but contempt for people who didn't appreciate what they had.

Finally, he reached a set of traffic lights he couldn't beat. As he pulled up behind another vehicle, he used the opportunity to take one more hit of cocaine from the back of his hand. It was larger than the others, and pain travelled up his nose with the speed of a bullet and came to rest in the centre of his brain.

Hurry the fuck up, he thought, waiting for the red lights to turn. He knew that in his heightened state he was a danger to himself, that if he was allowed to remain in public – angry and high – he could make a mistake and see all his good work go to ruin. Yet he couldn't control himself. If he could just harness his rage towards Margaret, towards Cally, towards his mother, towards every woman who had treated him so appallingly, and reach the property where he'd be lying low for the next few days, then he could regroup.

The lights switched to green and he slammed the car into gear. However, the Fiat 500 in front of him had still not accelerated. He blew his horn yet again, long and hard, but the vehicle didn't budge. What the hell were they playing at?

Incensed, he threw open his door and made his way towards the driver, banging his fists on the window.

'What are you doing?' he screamed. 'Why aren't you fucking moving?'

The driver was female, which infuriated him further, and in his irrational condition, she represented every woman who had got in his way or destroyed his plans. All except for Audrey. She had made him a better man.

He grabbed the door handle. It was locked. 'Open it now,' he growled. Instead, she gripped the steering wheel with one hand and kept twisting the keys in the ignition with the other. 'Don't ignore me,' he continued, 'or I'm going to smash this fucking window and drag you out.'

He meant every word of it until she turned her head to look at her tormentor and he realised that she was just a frightened teenager. Suddenly her vehicle burst into life and she sped away. But the lights had returned to red and she drove into the path of a white delivery van.

Stopping in his tracks, he was momentarily paralysed by the noise of metal crunching into metal, breaking glass, and the smells of spilled radiator fluid and rubber against asphalt. Many times he'd pored over photographs of crash sites and closed his eyes, trying to imagine the noises, the screams for help, and the panic. If he could feel those moments, then perhaps he could understand. But now that it was real and he was caught in the middle of it, it didn't sit comfortably with him.

He quickly came to his senses, jumped back into his car, carried out a heavy-handed three-point turn, mounted the kerb and tore away in search of another route to his destination. His breathing was fast and he turned the radio on to take his mind off what he had just put that girl through. The station was playing 'Rock DJ' by Robbie Williams, a song he remembered hearing frequently during his student union days. He had danced to it with Cally. No, he corrected himself, he hadn't, he'd danced to it with Audrey. Or had he been with Cally when he first heard it? He wasn't sure.

Not so long ago, he'd remembered everything with clarity – sometimes too much clarity. It was key to making his operation run like clockwork. Not so much lately. Now he was in the midst of his plan and the pressure was on. But faces were becoming blurred and memories muddled. Even the ones he treasured, the ones he cherry-picked to bring glimmers of light to his darkest days, were becoming buried beneath the horrors he'd inflicted on other people.

He made himself think of Audrey again. She was the only person who could calm him down when he felt like this. He needed to be close to her, he needed to see her again. He took a diversion from his planned route, and within ten minutes he was parked outside her flat in Shepherd's Bush. Along the side of the building was her front window. The lights were turned off and the curtains open – she wasn't in, and the hollowness opened up in his stomach again. He pulled his phone from the side pocket of the car door and scrolled through the dozens of photographs he had stored on it, focusing on an album of pictures they'd taken on a weekend in Brighton.

Staring at her – her jeans rolled up and knee-deep in the water, leaning against a wooden prop under the pier – he was reminded that he'd never fallen so deeply in love with anyone as he had with her. Instantly, he began to relax.

After meeting, that beautiful, magical night at Luke and Gabrielle's wedding reception, they'd swapped numbers, and every night that followed they'd spent in each other's company. She made him wait three weeks before she invited him into her bed, and he had been happy to remain patient. He'd had liaisons with women since Cally, but they had been purely for sexual gratification and had meant no more to him than a polite handshake with a client. But Audrey was different, and even in the bedroom they were more compatible than anyone he'd slept with before.

Audrey lit up a room the moment she entered it, and he'd watch as both sexes gravitated towards her. Not since the early days of his reinvention at university had he enjoyed such a social life as he did with her and her many friends and acquaintances. But all the while, he kept his eye on her girlfriends' men. He knew how their brains worked, and he wouldn't allow her head to be turned by anyone else.

He recalled their first summer together in France. For a fortnight every year, Audrey, her sister Christine, her brother-in-law Baptiste and their three children descended upon the Loire Valley and holidayed in the private French chateau her parents rented annually. Everyone's days were spent in or around the swimming pool, visiting vineyards, basking in the sun or exploring nearby rustic villages and towns.

Audrey shared a close relationship with her family, something he had no experience of. He'd not known his father, and his mother had taken with her to the grave the names of his half-brothers and sisters that she'd put in the care of social services over the years. Often, she'd remind him he was the chosen child, and that he should be grateful she'd kept him and not given him up like the others. But he would much rather have had their lives than the one she had forced upon him.

One evening, Audrey had volunteered to babysit for her nieces and nephew, allowing everyone else the opportunity to enjoy a meal at a local fish restaurant without the demands of three under-six-year-olds. He hadn't been accustomed to babysitting, so it was a baptism of fire, and he learned that their bath time was a wet, messy affair for all involved. But he'd savoured every minute of it. He desperately wanted to start his own family and to have a son of his own. He could make up for every mistake and act of cruelty his mother had inflicted upon him with his own flesh and blood. But when he plucked up the courage to raise the subject, Audrey dismissed it.

'We've not been together long enough for that,' she said. 'Half the children in my classroom have parents who are not together. Call me old-fashioned, but I want a child to be raised by both parents, not two who live apart.'

'You make it sound like you don't think we'll last,' he replied, saddened.

'I'm just a realist. You never know what might happen in the future.'

'I understand,' he'd told her, but he hadn't understood. And, over time, the insecurities that destroyed his relationship with Cally began to rise to the surface once again with his new love. He couldn't contemplate any kind of existence without Audrey. He was scared to lose her, scared to be alone, and scared that if nobody loved him, he'd end up like his mother.

On the pavement outside, a traffic warden approached and signalled him to move his car away from the double yellow lines he was parked on. He drove until he reached a car park behind a modern multistorey block of flats. Then, when he was inside the partially furnished accommodation on the eighth floor, he sank into his canvas chair by the Juliet balcony and surveyed the North London night sky. It wasn't long before he heard his belly rumbling and the acid gurgling, like his stomach was trying to consume itself. He had to eat, and he cursed himself for not thinking to pick up some food on his way there.

Twenty minutes later, and pulling the brim of his baseball cap down over his face, he removed a basket from the dispenser by the supermarket's sliding doors and made himself aware of the positioning of the security cameras, careful not to face any of them. His earlier recollection of Audrey in her native France reminded him how she'd broadened his horizons when it came to new cuisine. It gave him a craving for breads, cheeses and meats, so he walked the empty aisles, filling his basket with a Roquefort, an Epoisses and a Brie de Meaux, then cured meats, a terrine and three different flavoured pâtés. But as he walked towards the breads, he came to a sudden halt.

Standing by the sliding doors was a little boy, no more than a toddler, wearing Spider-Man pyjamas and slippers. Dropping his basket with a clatter to the floor, he closed his eyes and held them shut before opening them again, as if sleep deprivation was causing him to hallucinate. It wasn't.

He turned his head quickly to look around the shop floor, expecting to find a worried adult hurrying towards the child. But the boy was alone. As far as he could tell, it was just the two of them. The child didn't appear scared and he remained motionless, a plastic beaker in one hand and his thumb between his lips. Their eyes fixed upon one another's, until finally he moved towards the boy. He bent down so they were at the same level.

'Hello,' he said gently, and raised his hand to offer a static wave. 'What's your name? I'm Dominic.'

He repeated it to himself: *Dominic*.

Zoe, Margaret, his colleagues in the office, they had all called him by the name of his assumed identity, John Bingham, which he'd used for his National Insurance number and bank account. It had been so long since he'd stripped himself of this fake identity that it felt peculiar to hear his name again.

Dominic hadn't realised how much he was shaking until he brought his arm down to his side. He reached out his hand towards the boy, who eyed him warily. Then the child reciprocated with his own hand.

As he stood, the sensor opened the sliding doors and Dominic and the boy disappeared into the night and out of view.

CHAPTER 41

'Hey, buddy,' Joe said as Oscar stood up on his hind legs and pawed at his master's trousers.

Joe knelt so that Oscar could excitedly lick his neck and cheek. He rubbed the fur on the dog's belly and closed the front door behind him. At least he could be sure someone in the flat was happy to see him.

Oscar ran into the bedroom, picked up a rope toy he'd left hidden by the chest of drawers and dropped it at Joe's feet in the hope he'd play tug. 'Give me a few minutes, let me go and see Matt first,' he responded, and the dog obliged, like he understood Joe had more pressing matters to attend to.

Joe paused and rubbed his nagging eyes, preparing himself for the confrontation ahead. In working late and sifting through more hospital CCTV footage, he'd avoided returning home for as long as possible. It had come at a cost – his vision was blurry and he'd had to use double the dose of prescription eye drops just to focus properly.

The stairs felt steeper than he remembered as he made his way up to Matt, sitting in silence at the dining table. Laid out in front of him were fabrics, paint swatches, and dimensions scribbled inside a notebook. BBC News 24 was playing on the wall-mounted television but the sound was muted.

'Hello,' Joe began, and leaned over to kiss Matt on the crown of his head. 'How's your day been?'

'Busy,' Matt replied, about as coolly as Joe had expected.

'Is that why you didn't pick up when I phoned?'

'Partly. I've just been watching your boss in a TV press conference talking about the case. I assume you're still on it? Because I don't really know what's going on in your life right now, do I?'

'Can we talk about this morning?'

Joe took a seat at the opposite side of the table, as Matt removed his glasses and folded his arms. Matt's stare held Joe's. 'Look at your eyes,' he said. 'They're red-raw. You're struggling to see me properly, aren't you?'

'I'm sorry,' he replied. 'I really am.'

'And I believe that you are. But why, when you swore to me you wouldn't do it again, did I find you in the middle of a shopping centre looking for your sister?'

'I don't know.'

'That's not a good enough answer. Try again.'

Joe shook his head and went to pinch the bridge of his nose, but it was still swollen from his fracture. 'I went there because I don't want to give up on her. And I don't know if I can live the rest of my life without knowing what my dad did with her.'

'You're not a fantasist, you're a realist, and you must know that Linzi can't still be alive. It's been far too long. The chances of you finding her are infinitesimally small, and in your heart of hearts you must be aware of that?'

'I know, I know,' Joe said. But while there was no body, there was hope, and the word 'miracle' existed for a reason. Until he had absolute, definitive proof she was dead, he could not rest.

'Do I need to remind you of the last time you put yourself through this? It was right after your diagnosis.'

'This is different.'

'How?'

Joe opened his mouth, but he was stuck for a reply. Both were aware Joe had gone back on his word after promising he wouldn't become fixated on trying to find Linzi again. Now, he struggled to pinpoint the moment when his sister's niggling voice in the back of his head had grown too loud to ignore.

'It became an obsession for you,' continued Matt. 'It ended up being the only thing you could think about. It reached the stage where you couldn't sleep, because when you closed your eyes, all you could see were the images you stared at each day on your computer, hoping one might be her. It was like an addiction and it almost broke you. It almost broke us. You were signed off work for two months with nervous exhaustion. And God only knows what damage it did to you physically. You've been warned what's going to happen, and you're doing nothing to help yourself.'

Joe didn't say anything, his head hung in shame. Searching for Linzi had escalated from a yearning to a compulsion he'd lost control over. It became the only thing that mattered. Much of that time three years ago was either a blur, or snatches of memories.

'Have you told your therapist what you've been doing?'

'No,' Joe replied.

'Do you think you should?'

'I haven't been going.'

'What? You swore to me you were seeing her.'

'I did, for a while, but then I cancelled my appointments.'

'When?'

'Two months ago.'

'Why?'

'Because I knew she'd think the same as you and she wouldn't approve.'

'If your own husband and the person you pay to climb into that head of yours and rewire it think it's a terrible idea, what does that tell you?'

Joe nodded. 'But it is different this time.'

'I've heard that before but you can never explain how!'

'Because I have it under control.'

'Where have you been going every Wednesday night then, since you've lied about going for counselling?'

'I've been staying late at work.'

'And trying to find Linzi online again?'

'Sometimes.'

When Joe ran out of images to examine on the *Caught on Camera* bulletin, he'd flick through random Facebook and Twitter profiles looking for her instead.

'I think I need to contact your mum. Maybe she can try to knock some sense into you.'

'No!' Joe replied abruptly. 'She made her choice, now she can live with it.'

'She made the choice to get on with her life, how can you resent her for that?'

'Because she gave up on her daughter! How can a mother do that?'

'What was the alternative? Live in a state of limbo for the rest of her life?'

'But she replaced Linzi, she replaced both of us when she started another family with him.'

'His name is Len, he's your stepfather, he's a good man and together they've got two daughters you won't acknowledge and barely know.'

'I don't want to know them, they've got nothing to do with me.'

'Oh, grow up, Joseph!' Matt replied, exasperated. 'You sound like a sulky little kid who's being forced to share his mum. You're a grown man. You need to stop punishing other people just because you don't approve of their choices. She hasn't forgotten Linzi, I bet not a day goes past when she doesn't think about her, or you for that matter. But if she hadn't allowed herself to move on, she'd be trapped in a moment twenty-six years ago, and it's not fair for you to expect her to.'

Joe lifted his head to look at Matt for the first time since sitting down. While Matt wasn't shy when it came to issuing home truths, his stern expression took Joe aback.

Matt placed his hand on Joe's arm. 'I'm telling you this because I love you,' he said firmly. 'This has to stop. There's nothing I want more than for you to find your sister, but it's not going to happen. The next five or ten years are going to be hard enough for us to negotiate, we both know that. But I'll be right by your side helping you through the transition when the time comes. However, it's not fair on me that by stressing yourself out, you're bringing it closer than it needs to be. For your sake, for our sake, please make an appointment to see your therapist and promise me you won't do this again.'

Joe nodded. 'I promise,' he replied. However, he knew that even with the best will in the world, he could not guarantee such a thing.

CHAPTER 42

'Oh, look who's back to lower the tone,' mocked one of Joe's colleagues as he entered the VIIDO. 'Everybody, can I have your attention please. The prodigal son has returned.'

The rest of Joe's workmates turned their heads and let out light-hearted, mocking groans.

'Sorry, I didn't mean to wake you during office hours, Bruce,' Joe replied, and draped a jacket over the back of his chair. 'I notice my desk has come in useful in my absence?' Empty cans of carbonated drinks and a dozen empty mugs containing cold tea and coffee were scattered across the surface.

'It's never seen so much use,' Bruce replied. 'We thought you might need a little washing-up to keep you busy when you came back from playing with the big boys. How's the hunt for the serial killer?'

'We don't reckon he's a serial killer.'

'*We?* Your feet are firmly planted under the table with CID, aren't they?'

'They're an all right bunch actually,' Joe replied, stacking mugs on a tray to carry to the kitchen. 'There's a shitload of pressure on them to get results, especially with all the media attention the case is getting.'

'Has your eagle eye been of any use to them yet?'

'A little, but I've not made as much impact as I'd have liked. If nothing else, they now understand more about what we do here.'

The door opened, and he waved at DS Tracy Fenton. 'Who let this twat back in?' she asked, with good humour. 'You back to stay or is this just a flying visit?'

'I'm here to download some files,' he replied, turning his computer on and inputting his password. He didn't mention they were related to the disappearance of his sister.

'While you're here, can I pick your brains – or what passes for brains in that pretty little skull of yours?' she asked. 'There's an ongoing missing persons case in West London. Little boy, Evan Williams, two and a half years old. Wakes up sometime between 9.30 p.m. and midnight yesterday; parents don't hear him go downstairs or let himself out of the house. He walks half a mile to the supermarket in his pyjamas, goes inside and then leaves holding the hand of a stranger a few minutes later. Hasn't been seen since.'

Joe shuddered. 'So he's been missing, what, about seventeen hours now?'

Tracy nodded, then snapped a chocolate bar in two and offered him half. He declined. 'The major incident room is reviewing footage of the car park. But they want us to take a look at images of the suspect and compare him to any of the known paedophiles on the system.'

Joe followed her to her desk, where Tracy showed him the footage of Evan Williams walking past a set of traffic lights. No one appeared to be following him, either on foot or by car.

Two cameras in the supermarket car park revealed Evan approaching the bright lights of the entrance. Then, a much clearer image of the toddler in his Spider-Man pyjamas could be seen. He stopped and waited for the sliding doors to open before he entered, then stood still. From the foyer camera, Joe spotted an adult carrying a basket approaching the child and remaining opposite him for a moment, before kneeling down to his height. The man's face was obscured by a cap. Then, moments later and hand in hand, the little boy walked off with the stranger.

An image of Joe's sister jumped into his head, and of how she might have appeared had cameras captured her last moments as she was led away into the night. A lump developed in his throat until he coughed it away.

'We have prints from the shopping basket and food packaging, but no matches. I've cleaned up the pictures as best we can,' continued Tracy, and she clicked through a series of images taken inside the supermarket. In each one, the man held his head low, his face obscured by his cap.

Joe's eyes lit up, then he let out a sharp breath.

'What does that mean?' asked Tracy.

'Give me a minute,' he muttered, and leaned forward to concentrate on each of the images. He absorbed every identifying marker, from the suspect's height to the length of his arms, the stubble just about visible on his neck, and the pattern into which it had grown. But it was his baseball cap that really caught his eye, and in particular the use of a swirling font on the front. 'Do you have any clearer images of what that says?' Joe asked, pointing to the words.

Tracy took control of the mouse and opened another folder, housing a clearer image. 'Casino de la Forêt,' Joe read. He turned to look at her, wide-eyed. 'It's him, it's the same bloke,' he said.

'What same bloke?'

'Our suspect wears exactly the same cap.'

Within five minutes of emailing Nikhat, a folder appeared in his inbox which Joe double-clicked. He scanned a dozen photographs until he found the ones he wanted. By now, other members of the team were gathered around Tracy's desk.

'Look at this,' Joe said, and enlarged pictures of the man who'd stolen the van used to drive to fireman Garry Dawson's house. 'ANPRs picked this up. See what he's wearing on his head? It's the same cap. Surely that can't be a coincidence. Bruce, do me a favour, log on to

Amazon, eBay and ASOS and see if this brand is something you can buy easily online or on the high street.'

As Bruce went back to his computer, Joe took another close look at the shady figure on the screen.

'I can't find anything on any of those sites,' said Bruce after a few minutes.

Joe logged on to the forensic image database and typed in 'Casino de la Forêt'. Of the photos of thousands of suspects, the only match was the ANPR-camera picture of his killer.

'I'll contact whoever's in charge of the Evan Williams major incident room and let them know our thoughts while we look more into the cap's origins,' said Tracy. 'Joe, you contact your people and let them know. If it's the same guy, that's bloody good work, mate.'

Joe nodded, then called Becca to fill her in on what he had pieced together.

'Jesus, this is huge,' she exclaimed. 'Does Webster know about it yet?'

'No, I thought you might want to tell her.'

Becca sounded taken aback. 'Thank you.'

'What really concerns me is how off-kilter this case has suddenly become,' Joe said. 'Abducting that boy doesn't fit into anything we know about the killer.'

'But what do we know about him? Only what was in the profiler's report, and they aren't always right, are they?'

'Okay, but why has a man who seemingly has no hesitation in torturing people to death in carefully orchestrated scenarios suddenly snatched a toddler he finds in a supermarket? It's too opportunistic to fit in with his MO.'

'Do you think he's a paedophile too?'

'No. If he was, he'd have just grabbed that boy the moment he looked around and realised his parents weren't coming. The way he bent down to Evan Williams's level and held out his hand to him tells me he has a soft spot for children. Something about that little boy has knocked him off course, and I have a gut feeling it's going to be his downfall.'

CHAPTER 43

Dominic stared at the sad-eyed boy. The child's lips were dry and flaky from his tears and runny nose, and from where he'd been wiping them with the sleeve of his pyjama top.

The boy was sitting in the corner of the lounge, his bottom flat on the floor and his knees drawn up close to his chest. His arms were wrapped tightly around them. The only word he'd uttered since they'd returned from the supermarket was 'Mummy', over and over again. Dominic had tried to make Etienne understand that it was just the two of them now. But the child stubbornly refused to accept it. Dominic was at his wits' end.

'I'm not going to hurt you, I promise,' he pleaded. 'I promise you, Daddy would never hurt you.' He'd been repeating the same thing again and again, but it wouldn't sink in. He could only hope that, eventually, it might.

Dominic hesitated, and sniffed at an acrid odour he recognised as urine. The boy had peed himself again. He shook his head and resigned himself to it not being an easy transition. Just because father and son had been reunited didn't mean every piece of the jigsaw was going to slot into place right away.

He saw their reunion as a miracle; Etienne was a gift from a God he'd long stopped believing existed. He was a sign, a reward even, for sticking to his plan and following it through to the letter. It was the only way to explain how their paths had crossed. Etienne had somehow recognised his father and had sought him out.

But then God had started testing Dominic again, because back at the apartment Etienne had quickly become agitated by his unfamiliar surroundings. Twice now, in a matter of hours, he'd wet himself, and Dominic was forced to strip the trembling child of his damp pyjamas and rinse them out in the bath. Then he bathed him, apologising for the cold water and for forgetting to put the immersion heater on, and for making the freezing boy tremble. He wrapped Etienne in a towel and hugged him tightly, scared that if he let go, he'd vanish from his life as quickly as he arrived. Dominic couldn't understand why his son wasn't reciprocating.

It wasn't until the early hours of the morning that Etienne finally gave in to sleep. His head began to fall forward, then snapped backwards and his arms twitched. Eventually, his eyes closed and he whimpered his last for the night. Dominic carried the unconscious child and laid him down on the floor with a coat for a blanket. He stroked Etienne's velvety-soft blond hair and traced his mouth with his thumb. He wasn't sure from whom he'd inherited the dimples in his cheeks.

'You know I couldn't believe it when I found out I had a son,' Dominic whispered as he recalled the proudest moment of his life. 'Your mummy didn't think we were ready for a family, but sometimes surprises occur and they turn out to be the best thing that could have happened. When she got pregnant, I could feel you inside me too. I hope you never find out for yourself that sometimes misunderstandings can get in the way of good intentions . . .' His voice trailed off. 'Anyway, now here we are, and we've got our second chance.'

He brushed away his tears, then curled up against Etienne. Their chests rose and fell together, and Dominic slept more deeply than he had in months.

◆ ◆ ◆

When Dominic awoke the second morning after finding Etienne, there was no one by his side. He panicked and sat bolt upright, terrified it had all been a dream. He scoured the room and was relieved to find Etienne in the corner the boy seemed to favour. Once again, his knees were drawn in tightly to his chest as he quietly pined for his missing mummy.

Perhaps a picnic in Mile End Park might cheer him up and help them bond, Dominic thought. The flat contained very little in the way of food, so he locked the boy inside alone and headed out to stock up on bread, crisps, chocolate bars and sugar-free cans of drink from the corner shop. But as he made his way towards the shopkeeper's till, a row of newspapers stacked on a shelf forced him to do a double take. Every front page contained images of him, his face obscured by his cap and Etienne. *Serial killer kidnaps toddler*, read *The Sun*. *Missing child – police fear the worst*, the *Daily Express* reported. *Killer abducts child, 2*, said the *Daily Star*.

He couldn't make sense of the headlines – why were they accusing him of kidnapping his own son? Why were they mixing up Etienne with a boy called Evan Williams? It was typical of the tabloids to jump to the wrong conclusions or simply to lie, but the broadsheets too? He read a quote in *The Guardian* from a chief superintendent called Caroline Webster and quickly realised she was the one responsible for spreading lies about him. He hazarded a guess why – she was no closer to finding out who Dominic was or why he had killed five people. So she was deflecting from her failings by trying to blame him for something he hadn't done.

The word 'abduction' angered him. To Dominic, it suggested the taking away of someone by force. The images the police had released of the reunion of father and son showed to the world it was nothing of the sort. The boy had offered him his hand and left willingly with his parent. How on earth could any right-minded person think that was taking someone away by force?

He hurried to pay for the food in the corner shop and then ran back to the flat, firing up his laptop and playing a video clip on BBC News 24 confirming the search for Etienne. Dominic's anger soared as he watched. 'What is wrong with them?' he yelled, directing his voice to the only person inside the room with him. Evan pushed his back further into the wall. 'You're my son, you're not a stranger! They're making this sound far worse than it is!'

He picked up his phone and dialled one of the only two saved numbers. After four rings, it was answered.

'Why the fuck didn't you tell me they had my picture!' he yelled.

'I haven't had the chance,' the nervous voice replied. 'They don't have a full name or a clear photograph yet.'

'What do you mean, *yet*?'

'I don't mean yet, I just—'

'I swear to God, if I don't get to finish this, I'm taking you down with me. You're my eyes and ears, and if you don't want the world knowing what kind of cunt you really are, you'll do your job.'

Dominic ended the call and slammed his phone down on the kitchen counter. Etienne appeared anxious again. Apart from the difficult first night, the boy had been emotionless, as if he'd retreated into the safety of himself. Dominic was familiar with the move. Like Etienne, when he felt threatened, Dominic knew how to blend into his environment and cause as little fuss as possible. He had done it many times during his mother's frequent drunken, violent outbursts. She could bruise his body and hit him with a garden rake as often as she wanted, and his body could remain under her control. But his imagination would never be hers. Inside, he'd be living with the father he had never met or seen a photograph of. That faceless man would be reading him stories, teaching him how to ride a bike, playing football with him and helping him with school projects.

Out of Etienne's line of vision, Dominic racked up two lines of cocaine on the bathroom sink and snorted them without pausing to level them out or cut up the lumps.

What if they're right? a voice in the back of his head whispered. *What if you're the one who's in the wrong and the little boy isn't Etienne? You hadn't seen him in the flesh until two days ago.*

Dominic hesitated. He wasn't used to questioning himself. But as the stress of his kills and now Etienne being unresponsive towards his own flesh and blood escalated, he worried that he was losing his grip on his sanity.

He reached for his laptop, searching for a particular folder. There he located two photographs he'd found on the Facebook profile of Audrey's friend Lucienne. They'd been the only images he'd ever seen of his son, and he calculated Etienne must have been five months old. They had been taken at a child's birthday party, and while everyone was gathered around the little girl blowing out the solitary candle on a cake, Audrey was standing in the background with their son in her arms. A day later, and they were the only two pictures from the album to have been removed – at Audrey's request, he assumed. But he'd already saved them.

Examining the photographs carefully and comparing them with the child in the room, it was only now that he could see the difference in their eye colour. The five-month-old Etienne's eyes were blue; the boy in the room's eyes were brown. Their skin tone was also different: Etienne's was more Mediterranean, while this child was pale.

Dominic's heart sank. He had been so blinded by his desire to be a father that he had made the child who he wanted him to be. Pulling his cap from his head, he threw it to the floor, then ran the kitchen tap and splashed his face with cold water to bring his rising temperature down. He opened the window to allow cool air inside the stuffy apartment. Reflected behind him, he could see the boy staring at him.

Remaining with his back to Evan Williams, Dominic's short, sharp intakes of breath gradually made way for longer, deeper ones until eventually he calmed. Then he returned to his laptop and continued to watch more news bulletins, until he found one featuring the boy's distraught parents. They were at a police press conference, sitting behind a table flanked by uniformed officers and in front of a backdrop of posters emblazoned with telephone numbers and images of the child.

He pressed the pause button and looked carefully. He knew what their loss felt like. But he didn't feel empathy towards them, only disgust. They were ungrateful, and hadn't cherished what they'd got. If they had done their job properly, their son wouldn't have been standing alone in a supermarket late at night. If he were Evan's father, his boy would have been cuddled up in bed with a dozen soft toys under his duvet.

Evan's mum and dad didn't deserve a child, because they hadn't protected him like they were supposed to. It was too late to be snivelling into tissues and dabbing at their eyes and throwing the blame at Dominic's door for their loss.

There had been two reasons why the child had suddenly appeared in his life. The first was to remind him of why this had all begun. The second was to give him the focus he needed to complete the task at hand. And once the boy learned there was nothing to be afraid of, perhaps the two could embark on a journey of their own, regardless of the fact they were not related. Maybe they could form an understanding, a friendship of sorts. The name Evan sounded a lot like Etienne, especially when spoken quickly. It might not be too long before the boy became used to it. It would likely be a slow process, but they would have all the time in the world.

You're fooling yourself, the voice in his head said. *He has no place in your plan.*

Dominic stopped allowing his imagination to run away with him. The voice was right. He was kidding himself. It was too late for anyone to grow to love him. And after the sixth and final kill, he had somewhere he needed to be. It was a place that he couldn't take anyone else to, especially a little boy.

Despite his young age, Evan appeared to sense a dip in the room temperature as his captor held him firm in his stare. And as Dominic made his way towards the boy, the child wet himself again.

CHAPTER 44

Becca could barely keep her eyes open as she and Joe made their way upstairs and into the staff canteen.

She headed towards the seating area, slumping down on a chair, her forehead resting on an arm she stretched across the table. Joe made for the self-service station and returned with a tray containing two deflated croissants and two mugs of coffee. He slid the plate in her direction and she poked at a croissant with a knife. The hot beverage followed. 'Three sugars, no milk, right?'

Becca nodded her thanks and yawned. She sipped her coffee then scowled at it. 'Just because the Met is one of the oldest forces in the world does not mean the coffee has to be too.' She removed a compact mirror from her handbag and used it as she applied lipstick. 'I just want to sleep for a week. I could barely stay awake for the first briefing.'

What Becca didn't tell Joe – because she didn't want to admit it to herself – was that the more she worked, the less fulfilment it was giving her. What was spurring her on through the long days of the investigation was not the satisfaction of seeing the killer brought to justice, it was the free time she would gain and use to get to know her daughter again. Soon into the investigation, she had imagined how it might feel to be the one who cracked the case. Now she didn't care who it was, just as long as it happened soon.

'I kept thinking about that missing boy all night and why our suspect might have taken him,' said Joe, stirring his drink absent-mindedly.

'So did I. Every time I saw the CCTV footage on the news of him being led away, I kept thinking back to the 1990s and the images of little James Bulger being taken out of the shopping centre by those two children before they killed him. I was only a kid when he died and my mum tells me after that she never took her eyes off me when we went out, even for a second. Then I start putting myself in Evan's parents' shoes, wondering how the hell I'd cope if that happened to Maisie. She's so trusting of people.' Chills spread across Becca's chest and back.

'I don't think you'd ever forgive yourself.'

'Good spot by you though, on noticing the words written on the suspect's baseball cap,' Becca added. 'What's the update on that?'

'Nikhat told me the French casino says its souvenirs aren't sold by third parties, so either our man bought it on the premises or he was given it as a gift. It's possible he might have a link with France.'

'You are aware that you're Mister Golden Bollocks in CID, aren't you?' Becca said, changing the subject. 'After linking our suspect with Evan's abduction, they couldn't praise you enough in the early-morning briefing.' Joe blushed and Becca noticed. 'Aw, I've made you go red, haven't I?' she teased, and reached out to pinch one of his cheeks. 'The super-recogniser's gone all shy!'

'Hands off, or I'll have you done for sexual harassment.'

'Chance would be a fine thing,' said Becca. 'I'd be flattered to even be considered as a sexual predator these days. Do you know how long it's been since I—'

'No, no, no!' Joe interrupted, and thrust the palm of his hand towards her. 'Why do all straight women think that gay men want to hear about their sex lives? Newsflash, we don't.'

'Newsflash, nobody has used the word "newsflash" since the nineties.'

A text message lit up the display of Becca's phone. 'It's from Bryan,' she said, and began to read. 'Oh, this is interesting. Cameras in the supermarket captured part of the car's registration plate. And here's your link – it's a Mercedes that's registered to a French national, Audrey Moreau. They have a last known address for her in London, and Bryan reckons the car was also involved in some road rage incident. The driver of the other vehicle ended up hospitalised.'

'Before or after Evan Williams was abducted?'

'Before, but on the same day.'

Joe's brow furrowed. 'Something happened that really knocked him off course, didn't it? He's gone from being organised to erratic within a heartbeat. But I suppose we're not dealing with an ordinary mind here, are we?'

'Audrey Moreau . . .' repeated Becca slowly. 'Why does her name ring a bell?' Joe shrugged. 'Do you want to go and see her, while I visit the driver at the hospital?'

'Sure,' Joe replied.

'Be careful though.'

'Of what?'

'That you don't smack your big golden bollocks against the canteen door on your way out.'

◆ ◆ ◆

An hour later, and Joe was making himself comfortable in the patio area of a compact garden in Balham, while a middle-aged woman poured him a cup of tea from a ceramic pot.

The morning sun caught the silver in Pamela Nicholson's hair, which reminded him of fine threads from a spider's web. Even though her garden was only a few metres in length and width, Joe envied it.

He loved his flat, but with no balcony or access to outdoor open space, sometimes he'd take the dog out for a walk just because he needed to feel air on his face.

On discovering Audrey had moved out some years earlier, he knocked on neighbours' doors to see if they remembered her or held a forwarding address. Pamela lived in the basement flat of the three-storey terrace building, and recalled Audrey.

'I don't know how much I can really tell you,' Pamela began as Joe took notes. 'I wouldn't say we were good friends, but I knew her well enough to chat to if we passed each other on the path or on our way to the bus stop. She seemed like a nice girl . . . and with such a beautiful accent.'

'How long did she live here?'

'Perhaps six or seven months? Shortly after she moved in, so did her boyfriend, although I didn't see him very much as he used to leave for work early and didn't come home until late. Then, one morning, she knocked on my door to tell me she was moving away. She gave me a hug and I didn't see or hear from her again. I got the impression she didn't want him to find her, especially after all that funny business.'

'Funny business?' Joe repeated.

'The ceiling and walls were much thinner then, they've been sound-proofed since, but it wasn't difficult to hear them arguing.'

'Do you have any reason to think the relationship was abusive?'

'I didn't hear them fight physically, but that's not to say it didn't happen. I just remember in her last few days, there being lots of yelling.'

Joe looked at his notes. 'You mentioned you got the impression that Audrey didn't want her partner to find her. Why do you think that?'

'I asked her if he was leaving too and she shook her head. Then she begged me not to tell anyone I'd seen her. Later that night, I had to call the police because of the noise going on up there. I live on my own and I was frightened. When officers turned up, I crept up behind them, and when the door opened, it looked like he'd ransacked his own home. There were drawers and papers all over the floor. He told them he was looking for something, then they went inside with him and shut the door. The next day he asked me if Audrey had given me a forwarding address. I told him I didn't have one and he glared at me like I was lying. Even if she had, I wouldn't have offered it up. There was something about his eyes I didn't like. She and the baby were better off without him.'

'The baby?' Joe asked, glancing up from his notebook. 'Audrey had a child?'

Pamela smiled. 'When she said goodbye, her coat was open and it was clear she was pregnant. I didn't get the chance to ask her about it because she left in such a hurry.'

'Did she ever confide in you or talk to you about the problems she and her partner had?'

Pamela removed a long, thin cigarette from a leather case, lit it with a disposable lighter and took a deep drag.

'Do you live in London?' she asked, and Joe nodded. 'Then you know what kind of city this is. People keep themselves to themselves, not like in the old days. Community spirit seemed to die when they let all the immigrants in and gave them free houses.'

Against his instinct, Joe let her comment pass. 'What can you tell me about her partner?'

'Not much, really. I only saw him on a handful of occasions.'

'Was he French too?' Pamela shook her head. 'Do you remember his name?' She thought for a moment. 'Something beginning with a D . . . David or Donny or something like that. No, Dominic. That was it – Dominic. I don't think I ever knew his surname.'

'Before I leave, could I ask you if the man in either of these photofits resembles him?'

She slipped on the glasses hanging around her neck. 'We are talking a few years ago now, but from what I remember, the one on the left does resemble him. I remember the scar on his earlobe, like a tear. Quite unusual.'

'Thank you, Mrs Nicholson.'

'You're welcome. He's done something very bad, hasn't he?'

'I'm afraid I'm not at liberty to say.'

'Whatever he's done, I hope you get him. I don't know why, but sometimes you can just tell when a person has a dark soul. His was the darkest I've met in a long time.'

CHAPTER 45

Becca perched on a plastic seat by Chloe Bayfield's bedside at the Royal London Hospital. She shuffled her buttocks from left to right, trying to find a comfortable position.

While the weeping girl was comforted by her mother, Becca took in her surroundings. Like many people, there was so much Becca hated about hospitals. The sound of noisy, repetitive, beeping machines and the clanking of wheels as trolleys were pushed around; the stench of bland food lingering in the air and the antiseptic that battled to over-power it. She cursed the tropical climates of wards and the deafening snores of sleeping patients. Everything around her brought back awful memories of the days she and her parents had spent at her sister's bed-side, none of them wanting to be the first to let go. Instead, they had delayed the moment the equipment keeping her alive was switched off until her two-month-premature daughter left the incubator and was placed on her biological mother's chest for the first and last time.

They had all silently prayed the CT and MRI brain scans would reveal a miracle and that somewhere deep inside Emma, she was cling-ing on to life. But there was no recorded activity at all.

Becca had been the first family member to hold her niece. She remembered how the newborn felt on her skin and how she'd never wanted to let go of her. She'd prayed that tiny, fragile child would accept her and not realise the arms carrying her did not belong to the body that had given her life.

Her father's reappearance had ignited something inside her. Amid the noise and the bluster, all Becca now wanted was to feel her baby girl like she had back then. She had been forced to let go of Emma, and she didn't want to do the same with Maisie. She missed being a mum.

Becca glanced at the teenager in the hospital bed; she was the polar opposite of her bulky, tattooed mother. Chloe was skinny and fragile, and injured from the impact of her car accident. The right side of her body had taken the brunt – her arm was fractured and set in a cast, and her leg was also in plaster and suspended mid-air by a metal contraption. Her eyes were red, and an almost-empty box of tissues sat on the top of a bedside cabinet, surrounded by Get Well Soon cards.

Her mother, the type of woman Becca's father would have described as 'rough as arseholes' based on appearance alone, was perched on the side of Chloe's bed, her fury directed towards the man who had done this to her child.

Again, Becca thought of Maisie. Those days after her birth, she had felt just as protective as Chloe's mother was now. And more long-buried memories came to the surface, of how the smell of the sister she had lost came through every pore of the child's skin. Then, to her shame, she remembered how she had been blindsided by Maisie's Down's syndrome diagnosis later on. She had reacted by pulling away from her, frightened of a baby with extra needs who'd require extra patience because she was an extra-special person.

While she'd continued to love her daughter, they had never regained the closeness they'd shared the first month after her arrival in the world. Becca had begun to believe she wasn't good enough for her daughter, and slowly but surely she'd come to rely on Helen to be everything for that child – a mother, father, grandmother, grandfather and aunt. Helen took her to appointments for all the required therapies – occupational, speech and play – and for her evaluations and doctor's appointments. Maisie's preparation for a mainstream school had been down to Helen's hard work, not Becca's.

Becca cleared her throat and her head and got back to work. 'So, let me just go back over your version of events, Chloe. You passed your driving test a week ago, and on the day of this incident, you were on your way to work when you stalled your car at the traffic lights. You kept turning the ignition over but it wouldn't start. Then the vehicle behind you, a red one, began blowing its horn at you.'

Chloe nodded, and her mum gripped her hand tighter. 'He just came out of nowhere,' Chloe said. 'He started banging on the window and then on the windscreen, calling me horrible names and telling me he wanted to kill me. I kept turning and turning the key but nothing was happening and I was crying because I was so scared.'

Tears gathered in the girl's eyes once more, and her mum brought her daughter's hand close to her face to kiss it.

'Eventually I started the car and put my foot down. I was so frightened I didn't even notice the traffic lights had turned back to red. And that's when I was hit by a van coming in the other direction.'

'When you catch that bastard, I'll rip his bloody face off for what he's done,' her mother threatened. 'And I know other people who'd like to get their hands on him too.'

Becca made a note to ask forensics to visit the garage where the car had been towed, to check for fingerprints on the door handle or palm prints on the windows. She suspected they'd match any found on the supermarket basket.

'Is the man who did this in either of these photographs?' asked Becca, passing her two e-fits.

'He might be, I'm not sure,' Chloe replied. 'When I saw how evil his eyes were I just wanted to get away.'

'That's okay,' Becca replied, and hoped that Joe was having more luck in getting a positive identity. She had a feeling that, after the next briefing, they'd be spending much of the day going through traffic-camera footage of the accident and surrounding areas.

'Has he done this before then?' Mrs Bayfield asked. 'If you've got drawings of him, he must have.'

'It's a line of inquiry we're looking into,' Becca replied vaguely. She saw no benefit in scaring the teenager any further by informing her about just how close she'd come to falling prey to a five-times murderer.

'The dashcam recorded it all, do you want to see what's on it?' Chloe's mother added hopefully.

'I'm sorry?' replied Becca.

'The insurance company made her have one installed as she's a new driver. It keeps her premium down.'

Becca felt her pulse beginning to race. 'Is the camera still in the car?'

'No, it's here in my handbag.' Chloe's mother pulled out a brown padded envelope and handed it to Becca. 'I was going to post it to the insurers on my way home.'

'Has anybody else seen what's on here?'

'Only her stepdad. He picked it up from the garage this morning and downloaded it just to make sure we had another copy in case it got lost in the post. He reckons you can see that animal as right as rain.'

'Thank you so much for this, it could be a big help.'

Becca hurried through the maze of hospital corridors, trying to contain her excitement. She was keen to learn what the footage contained. It might be the break in the case they so desperately needed. But as she thought about the recognition it might bring her personally, she felt nothing.

It wasn't praise she needed right now, it was Maisie.

Days earlier she had told Joe that, as a woman in the police force, every day was a battle. But it wasn't until now that she'd considered the battle Maisie was fighting. She had fought to survive a difficult, premature birth, she had fought to learn and develop as quickly as her friends, and now she was fighting for her mother's love and attention. The latter was a battle she had been losing.

But not any more.

There and then, Becca vowed to redirect all the effort and attention she put into her career into her daughter instead. And, importantly, she wasn't going to wait until the case was over. When she returned home that night, everything was going to change. She had never been more clear about anything in her life.

Suddenly, her phone started to ring. It was Helen.

'Hi, I was just thinking about you,' Becca began.

'I need you to come home.' Becca knew immediately from her mother's tone that all was not well.

'What's happened?'

'Maisie keeps being sick and I need your help.' In the background she could hear her daughter sobbing. Immediately, Becca felt alarmed. 'She has a temperature and she's crying for you.'

Becca squeezed the padded envelope containing the dashcam camera. 'Mum, I need to drop something really, really important off to forensics,' she said. 'It's on my way home anyway, and then I'll be straight back within the hour. I've made up my mind to take some time off, starting from today. And I mean real time, not just a weekend or a day here and there. Things are going to be different from the moment I get home, I promise.'

'I love you,' Helen replied and hung up. Becca could have sworn she'd heard her mother crying too.

Becca allowed the corners of her mouth to curl and she offered a huge smile to no one but herself. In hearing how upset her daughter was, she felt the tug of maternal heartstrings that she hadn't thought were still attached. She'd email her apologies to Nikhat, then inform Webster of her decision to step down from the investigation and request an immediate sabbatical for personal reasons. There were plenty of others who would snap at the chance to step up and continue her work. Becca had different priorities. This was her second chance to be the mum she'd never believed she could be.

CHAPTER 46

Four times in half an hour, Joe hit the redial button, but on each occasion his call ended with Becca's voicemail.

The fifth attempt was made as their colleagues began assembling inside the major incident room for the afternoon briefing. Moments earlier, he'd received a text from Becca explaining what was inside the package she'd left with forensics and that she wouldn't be attending the update. Then Nikhat informed him Becca had something personal to do, and Joe assumed it concerned her daughter. It must be serious if it meant missing out on the dashcam evidence, he thought.

Joe was one of the last officers to enter the room, and positioned himself close to the door in the event he needed to leave and answer Becca's call back. Even before CS Webster entered, the anticipation in those gathered was palpable. It had been two days since the last body had been discovered, and all were silently hoping that the next one wouldn't be little Evan Williams.

Joe reasoned that killing the toddler wouldn't fit the pattern of murders to date. The suspect couldn't have engineered finding him alone in the supermarket. It must have been a dreadful coincidence that their paths had crossed. But why not leave him; what had compelled the man the former neighbour had identified as Dominic to actually take the child away? As far as Joe was aware, this was his first spontaneous act since his killings began. If he wasn't a paedophile, then seeing that boy must have brought to the surface a trace of humanity still left inside him. Was it something to do with Audrey Moreau's pregnancy? Had it triggered a memory he wanted to relive?

He checked his phone again just as Webster began to speak. His CID secondment had been brief, but he could recognise the toll the pressure was taking on her. Her skin was pale, as if she hadn't been outside in the sun in days.

'It goes without saying, the safe return of Evan is our utmost priority,' she began. 'As soon as we get the images from the—' However, she wasn't able to finish her sentence because, as if on cue, the door opened and a member of the forensics team entered. 'Speak of the devil,' she said. 'Any chance of some good news?'

The room fell silent as a bearded man handed over an inch-thick pile of photocopied images. 'We've got him,' he said. 'As clear as day.'

Restrained excitement engulfed the room as each detective waited to glimpse, for the first time, the face of the man who had come to dominate their every working hour. Hi-resolution colour images were passed from person to person – three facial shots taken through a car windscreen and at different angles.

'When are we going to the media with these?' a voice asked.

'Not straight away,' said Webster. 'I don't want to alert him that we have a positive ID and have him go to ground.'

Joe was aware that facial images could be distorted depending on the angle a camera was fixed or the type of lens inside it. But these photocopies couldn't have been any clearer if a portrait photographer had taken them.

A pilot light in his brain exploded into life as he got to work. First, he registered the face as a whole. Then, he concentrated his attention on the length and width of the suspect's nose, followed by the shape of his eyes, how far they were apart and how deeply they were set. Then he took in the jawline, and the height of his cheekbones and eyebrows. He also noted the scar on his earlobe that hadn't been visible in the previous grainy images. It was only then that he could be sure.

Joe recognised the killer.

But where from? He closed his eyes and blanked out the chatter in the room, searching his memory's lifetime of faces for where their paths might have crossed. Within a handful of seconds, he'd found a match. They had met in person, and only days earlier.

'I know him,' Joe said, shaking his head. 'I know his face.' A hush descended across the room as all eyes were directed towards him. 'Beccs and I went to his house.'

CHAPTER 47

Joe hurried from the crowded briefing room and towards Becca's desk. He poured the contents of his satchel across it, frantically searching for his notebook. Webster, Nikhat and Bryan followed, moments after they brought the meeting to a premature halt.

'Where do you recognise him from, Joe?' Bryan asked eagerly. 'Who is he?'

'*He* was a *she* when we met,' Joe replied, locating his book. He flipped through it as he spoke. 'She was one of the three suspects we identified, who'd been standing at the tube platform next to Stefan Dumitru when he was drugged. Beccs and I tracked her down, and it was obvious straight away that she wasn't genetically a woman, but living as one. *Megan Bingham,*' he read from his notes, 'that's what she called herself, but she told us she was born John Bingham. And that's the person captured by the dashboard cam, only without the hairpiece and make-up. It took me a few seconds to recognise her because make-up and contouring can change the angles of a face. But not when you look into them as closely as I do.'

'So is his name John – or Dominic, as his old neighbour called him?' asked Nikhat.

'We should look into both. But Dominic is what he was going by three years ago, before all this started, so it's likely to be that.'

He scribbled down Megan Bingham's address and passed it to Nikhat, who – accompanied by Bryan – disappeared from the room to deploy a team to target the flat. A dull ache behind Joe's eyes was beginning to make itself known. *Please, not now*, he thought to himself, and was glad he wasn't asked to join them.

In a few minutes, a van containing armed officers in body armour would be deployed in the event an attempted arrest escalated into a violent stand-off. From a different station, a plain-clothed hostage negotiator would also be en route, in case Evan Williams was still inside the sparsely furnished property.

Joe was angry at himself for accepting Megan Bingham at face value and for offering her empathy and respect for her struggle to live as her authentic self, when he and Becca were actually being conned. For much of his life, Joe's family circumstances – and, to a lesser degree, his sexuality – had made him feel like an outsider, and he'd made an assumption that Megan was the same. More fool him. If he and Becca could have prevented the murders of Garry Dawson and Zoe Ellis, he would never forgive himself. Something niggled him, though – why had Dominic been wearing women's clothing when he and Becca visited the flat? Was he really trans, or had he been expecting them?

He considered calling Becca again and leaving a voicemail to inform her of the case's latest twist, then talked himself out of it. There was nothing to be gained in both of them being angry. Now was not the time for what-ifs.

Armed with the knowledge of exactly what Dominic looked like, he used Becca's computer to search through some of the 100,000 images on the centralised forensic image database to see if he had form. He doubted a normal person could suddenly wake up one morning and decide to coordinate a murder spree without having fallen foul of the law in the past. But with no surname, it was going to be a struggle.

He hunched over the keyboard, staring at Dominic's dashcam photographs and typing keywords into the search function. He rubbed at his sore eyes, and this time he concentrated on the suspect's blond curly hair poking out from beneath the familiar French baseball cap. He inputted metadata, including Dominic's slightly crooked nose, alongside the typical descriptions like his eye colour, cheekbones, square jaw and dimpled chin. Seventy-four suggested matches appeared, but none were of him.

A different approach was required, but if he didn't look away from the monitor soon, he feared he might pass out. The ache behind his eyes was now marching across his forehead and towards his temples. A combination of stress and tension was manifesting itself as a migraine. Based on past attacks, unless he took his medication soon, he would be lucky to have thirty minutes before it swallowed him whole. Even then, he might have left it too late. A migraine was like a time bomb, and he needed to delay its detonation for as long as possible before it rendered him useless. He swallowed four of the tablets the doctor had prescribed, two more than he was supposed to take, and washed them down with three cups of water from a dispenser to help speed up their dissolving.

Blinking hard to clear his muddied eyes, he had settled back into the chair when he heard Nikhat's voice across the room.

'Joe, could you get someone to find out what you can about Audrey Moreau please, mate?'

'On it,' he replied, then asked one of the office support staff to assist.

Joe then began assembling into order the fragments of what he knew about Dominic's life that he'd gleaned from 'Megan'. He double-checked his notebook and spotted he'd scribbled the word 'Etienne'. He recalled it being the name Megan had given the doll she'd carried and tried to pass off as a child. It was too unusual a name to have simply been plucked from the air without forethought. Could that have been the name Audrey Moreau had given their baby?

If she and Dominic hadn't reconciled and their relationship remained hostile, she might not have used his name on the birth certificate. Joe completed the relevant searches regardless, but no child's birth had been registered in the UK with that Christian name and surname in the given timeframe. Perhaps Audrey had moved back to France to have her baby? If the search for 'Audrey' came back with nothing, he might have to request help from his European counterparts at Interpol, but that would take time.

The light of the monitor continued to pierce Joe's eyes, so he turned the brightness down.

CID's office manager approached him, breaking his train of thought. She held a pink Post-it note in her hand. 'Joe, someone's been trying to get hold of Beccs for the last couple of hours,' she began, 'but she's not picking up her phone. Would you be able to call him back? He says it's important.'

'Sure,' Joe replied, and took the paper containing DC Nigel Morris's name and a telephone number. He was about to pick up the desk phone when he was interrupted by a call to his mobile. It was a number he didn't recognise. He hoped it was Becca's landline.

'Is that DS Joseph Russell?' a woman asked. Joe said yes. No one apart from Matt, his mum and Linzi ever called him Joseph. 'It's DS Wendy Clarke in Leighton Buzzard.' Her name didn't ring any bells. 'Your name was flagged up on the system in relation to cases involving missing girls dating back more than twenty years?'

Joe froze. 'Yes,' he replied after a pause.

'Well, the remains of an unidentified child killed historically have come to our attention in this area, and I thought it might be of interest to you.'

Joe sat back in his chair and fought the urge to be sick. The support worker he'd delegated to locating Audrey approached him. She looked concerned at his ghostly white appearance.

'Are you okay, Joe?'

'Yes,' he muttered.

'I've located Audrey Moreau.'

'Can you email me what you've found? I have to be somewhere.'

Without waiting for a reply, he picked up his jacket and bag and hurried out of the building.

CHAPTER 48

It was quicker for Joe to take the tube to Euston station than to get permission to sign out a car and explain why he required it.

He also doubted he'd be fit to drive, as the war between his medication and his migraine was in full swing. It was going to get worse before it got better. While technically he wasn't travelling to Leighton Buzzard on police business, the investigation into Linzi's disappearance was still an open case, albeit a cold one. However, leaving such a high-profile manhunt to deal with a personal matter would have been frowned upon. He gave that little consideration. When it came to finding his sister, nothing was going to prevent him from going.

He swallowed another pill and jumped on a train with seconds to spare before it left the platform and rolled slowly up the track. It was the same route he'd taken on many occasions to Milton Keynes shopping centre, where he'd spent hour upon hour searching for Linzi in a stranger's eyes. He could reach Leighton Buzzard in thirty minutes, and he'd been advised it was a short walk to the police station from there.

Joe found a quiet corner of the train, rested his head against the wall of the disabled toilets, slipped on his sunglasses and closed his eyes.

From the moment he'd received the telephone call, nothing else in the world mattered. Not the promise he'd made to Matt, not Operation

Chamber, not the five murder victims to date nor any potential victims. And to his shame, not even little Evan Williams. All that concerned him was a piece of his past he couldn't reconcile.

DS Wendy Clarke had informed him that a girl's remains had been found in the cellar of an old farmhouse that had lain derelict for two decades. They estimated her as between the ages of six and ten, and she had likely died in the region of twenty to twenty-five years ago. With his eyes shut tight, all Joe could see were patchwork images of the last time he'd seen Linzi alive. She was running across a school playground and into a single-level building ahead. She'd only been in attendance for two days and had already made friends. She hadn't just come out of her shell, she'd burst her way from it, then smashed it into tiny fragments so as never to return. Joe, however, had been more reticent to let down his guard. It had been the right call.

The land on which the former farm stood had been sold to a developer to build warehouses on, and it was being razed to the ground by a demolition team. Only after the roof and walls of the house fell had they unearthed a second cellar which hadn't been on the property's blueprints. Inside were the skeletal remains of a child, and some close-to-disintegrated clothing and shoes. Clarke had offered Joe the opportunity to identify photographs of the clothes by email. He'd insisted on seeing them in person.

The small market town was a twenty-minute drive from where Joe and Linzi's mother had moved them to. Their father had often travelled the Midlands, working as a mechanic specialising in farmyard machinery repairs, so it was possible that even though the family hailed from Nottingham, he might have known someone from the wider farming community who lived in Leighton Buzzard. They might have taken Linzi for him, or disposed of her body.

Joe shuddered when he considered what might have happened to her alone in the darkness of that cellar, or how long her ordeal had lasted. He'd read stories about girls held captive for years, some even forced to have children with their captors before finally escaping. *If* they escaped. Or maybe their father had locked her in there himself out of spite, and simply allowed her to die.

Suddenly, Joe realised that for the first time since Linzi had vanished, he was contemplating her death. Everyone who knew his story had reached that conclusion years earlier. And for a moment, he actually wanted the dead girl to be Linzi, because it might allow him to start moving forward, no longer held back by a foot in the past.

Against the odds, Joe must have drifted off to sleep, because he awoke with a start as the train passengers were advised Leighton Buzzard was their next destination. Within a quarter of an hour, Wendy Clarke was ushering him to a seat by her desk.

'Do you mind if I ask why you're so interested in cases like this?' she asked, sweeping her red hair back and tying it into a tight ponytail. 'The note on file said you wanted to know about any cases where the victim potentially dates back more than twenty years.'

'My sister went missing then,' he replied. She raised her eyebrows in the expectation he'd continue, but he offered nothing else.

'Is there a cause of death?' he asked instead.

As she leafed through several pages inside a file, Joe caught a glimpse of a photograph of a smallish skeleton laid out on a silver metal table. His stomach sank and he averted his eyes, focusing his stare at a noticeboard instead. Clarke appeared to realise what she'd revealed and swiftly tucked the picture away behind another piece of paper.

'You know the routine, it's not official until the inquest opens, but blunt force trauma to her head. Possibly with a mallet or a hammer. She'd been hit twice, breaking her skull.'

That offered Joe a peculiar kind of relief. He hoped that whoever the poor girl was – be it his sister or a complete stranger – her final moments had been quick and her terror only fleeting.

'Can I see her clothes?' Joe asked.

'Of course.'

Clarke led him into another room, where an exhibits officer showed him three clear, sealed plastic bags laid out on a table, with evidence numbers written on stickers. The first contained a pair of small black plimsolls. They were relatively unscathed for being hidden away for so long. They were also the kind his sister had worn. In the second was a pair of dirty white socks and yellow underwear, which he could just about make out the day of the week printed on. It said 'Tuesday', and Linzi had vanished on a Thursday. It offered him a glimmer of hope. The third bag contained a school uniform – a dress that appeared to be navy blue. But Linzi hadn't been wearing a uniform. She'd not been at the new school long enough for their mum to take her shopping.

He steadied himself against the table, unsure if it was relief that was moving the ground beneath his feet or the result of too many migraine tablets. He shook his head at Clarke, and she smiled for the both of them. She passed him a tissue from a box, which he used to dab at his eyes.

Before catching the train back to London, Joe gave a DNA sample and was told the results would be back within the next three days. But he already knew the answer. There would be no match, and Linzi and the girl's cases would remain open.

By the time his train pulled out of Leighton Buzzard station, his head was feeling a little less cloudy and now he could see the gravity of the fool's errand he'd been all too willing to accept. He was ashamed of his own stupidity. Leaving the most high-profile case of his career mid-investigation was the least professional thing he'd ever done and he was sorely disappointed in himself. He could have made do with emailed photographs of the girl's clothing. But once again Joe had put his obsession with finding his sister above everything else. Where Linzi was concerned, his tunnel vision was absolute.

This was the long-awaited wake-up call he needed. He'd already put his marriage at risk, and now he was doing the same with his career. If he didn't make a change now, he would be left with nothing, and that frightened him. Twenty-six years of chasing a ghost was too long.

He checked his phone to see missed text messages from Nikhat and Bryan informing him of what he suspected, that the property where Dominic/Megan had been living was now empty.

Forensics were inching their way around it, but his team leaders were returning to the office. Attached to another text was a photograph of Dominic that had been sent out to every police officer in the force before he'd left for Leighton Buzzard.

As his train approached Euston, the voicemail signal flashed on his screen. He pressed play. It was from Nikhat.

'Joe, mate, not sure where you are right now, but you might want to meet us in Webster's room as soon as you can. A uniform's on his way in. He claims he's arrested a man called Dominic Hammond.'

CHAPTER 49

Joe ran along the police corridors and swiped his access card to gain entrance to the major incident room.

As the doors opened, he noted there were definitely more detectives and support staff than there had been when he left. A temporary partition wall had been removed, so that two incident rooms had become one large one. The humid air smelled of percolated coffee and sandwiches. The overhead fluorescent bulbs seemed to illuminate the room more brightly, and threatened to counteract his migraine medication.

He hurried towards Webster's office, where Bryan was closing the door. Inside, a uniformed officer was taking a seat. 'Sorry I'm late,' said Joe, breathlessly. 'I was following up a lead.'

The officer introduced himself as DC Nigel Morris and Joe recognised his name as the person who'd left a message asking for Becca to call him back, earlier that afternoon. He'd forgotten about it the moment he'd received his own call regarding the girl's body. Morris was a tall, slight man with salt-and-pepper stubble. Joe pegged him as somewhere in his late thirties, and the type of detective who preferred real policing out on the streets, rather than office-bound and climbing the career ladder. Officers like Nigel Morris were the backbone of the force.

'You said in your message that you think you arrested the man we're searching for?' began Webster, leaning forwards and staring him dead in the eyes.

'Yes, it was three years ago, on the evening of June the first,' he began. 'I remember the date because it was my birthday, and I couldn't get anyone to swap shifts with me. Anyway, we were out on patrol around the Shepherd's Bush area when we were called to a disturbance on . . .' He paused, and removed a well-worn notebook from his pocket. ' . . . on Stanlake Road. The woman, Audrey Moreau, was being harassed by her ex. Some kind of domestic. The two of them were outside the front of her flat and it was getting heated. I tried calming him down while my oppo dealt with her. As they went inside, he was getting more and more agitated and telling me how she wasn't letting him see his baby, and he begged me to help, but there was nothing I could do. When his missus finally came out, she had a suitcase with her and threw it in the back of her car. My crewmate followed with a baby in a car seat and helped her strap it in. Then the kid's dad started really losing it, shouting his name – Etienne, if I remember right. He caught me in the stomach with his elbow and then right in the balls, and started grabbing the baby seat and screaming blue murder. My crewmate had no choice but to go in with the CS spray to restrain him. He still was effing and blinding and trying to fight us, so we had to use minimal force until we could cuff him. Then the van we called arrived, and he was taken away. By then, his missus and baby were already gone.'

'So he does have form then?' said Joe.

'Not unless he's been nicked for something else, because he never made it to the station. He had some kind of allergic reaction to the CS; he was complaining of burning to his nose and throat, saying he couldn't breathe. The van took him to St Mary's for treatment, but it was the night of that terrorist attack in Hammersmith where those three ISIS nutters started attacking people in the shopping centre with knives.

The injured were also being taken to St Mary's, and somewhere in the commotion, Hammond disappeared in A & E.'

'So he escaped police custody before he was brought back or processed,' said Nikhat. 'Was a warrant issued for his arrest?'

'Not that I'm aware of,' Morris replied.

Nikhat and Webster looked at each other like they were predicting what a problem this was going to be for the force further down the line.

'My oppo also took notes when talking to Moreau. You might want to have a word with her.'

'And who is she?'

'She's one of you lot in CID now. Becca Vincent.'

All three glared at him.

'Beccs?' Nikhat replied.

'Yeah, she was the one who helped his ex into the car so she could escape.'

Joe felt the colour drain from his face.

CHAPTER 50

Becca briskly walked the fifteen minutes from the tube stop to her house so that she could take care of her poorly daughter.

Making the decision to step away from one job to take on a much more important role was like lifting a weight from her shoulders. Finally, she was ready to be there for her daughter in a way she never had been before. It didn't matter to her if it took days, weeks, months or years to reconnect. If Becca could offer Maisie the focus and determination that she'd given her career, especially with Operation Chamber, half the battle was already won.

Her phone buzzed again. It must have been the sixth time that afternoon. Joe's name and number flashed up, but she held back from answering as she didn't want to disappoint him with news that she'd left the investigation. She would send him a text later in the day, after she had assessed the situation at home, explaining to him the reasons behind her decision. But she wouldn't apologise for it – she was done with apologies. Choosing to be a full-time mother was nothing to be sorry for. All that mattered now was family.

Two more text messages appeared, one from Joe and one from Kirsty Nutkins, the manager of the woman's refuge shelter Becca supported.

An Abigail Johnson has just come to us – says you sent her – thanx, Becca read, and nodded her head slowly in satisfaction. It appeared Abigail had found the strength to leave Nicky Penn. Becca hoped it was one less woman who would end up like Emma.

She ignored Joe's work-related text and turned her phone off. She hoped they'd stay in touch, and not just to talk about work. She could do with a friend like him.

Becca felt her heart swell as she opened the front door, only to be greeted by her deaf neighbour Mrs Patel's television turned up high as she watched her afternoon magazine shows.

'Hi,' Becca called out as she hung her jacket on a wall hook. 'Where is everyone?' Her eyes fell to the three pairs of wellington boots on the doormat. They belonged to the three generations of Vincent women, the wearers as bright and colourful as the plastic and rubber they put on their feet. Between them, they'd survived challenges that would have torn many other families to shreds. This new transition in their dynamic was going to repair the damage Becca had caused.

As Becca picked up the post lying on the hall stand, she read each envelope to check to whom it was addressed. She dropped what looked like junk mail into the bin.

'Mum,' she shouted, wondering where everyone was and why both sets of curtains were drawn. 'Why is it so dark in here?'

As she entered the living room she did a double take.

A small boy, dressed in pair of Spider-Man pyjamas, was sitting on the smaller of their two sofas, staring at her blankly. Seconds passed before she could register it was Evan Williams.

Becca stopped in her tracks, unable to make sense of it. 'What the . . . ?' she muttered, her voice trailing off as she looked around the room. It was only then that she saw her mother and Maisie at the dining table. She looked them up and down; their hands and feet were bound together by tape and rope.

If Becca had moved more quickly, instead of trying to process the scene like a trained detective, she might have heard the figure behind her before he grabbed her by the shoulder and spun her around. Instead, something was squirted into her eyes that burned and blinded her, before she felt two sudden thumps to the side of her head. She didn't get to see her assailant's face before she collapsed to the floor and the room went black.

CHAPTER 51

'Where is Becca now?' asked CS Webster, a note of concern in her usually calm voice. She glanced beyond the walls of her Perspex cube and scoured the manned desks outside, as if suddenly realising she'd not seen her for much of the day. 'She needs to be aware of this.'

'Beccs dropped the dashcam off to forensics, then texted me to say she had to go home – a family emergency,' Nikhat replied.

'Have you spoken to her since?'

'I've tried calling her but she's not answering.'

Webster tapped her bottom teeth with a bitten fingernail. 'Do we have a concrete reason to assume she is at risk from Hammond?'

'She used CS spray on him, then helped his girlfriend and kid to escape – in his warped mind, I think that's enough of a motive to want to hurt Becca,' said Nikhat.

Webster nodded. 'Joe, how did you get on trying to find out more about Audrey Moreau?'

Fuck, thought Joe. One of the support staff had emailed details to him hours earlier, but like the message from Morris asking for someone to call him back, the hunt for Linzi had pushed everything else to the back of his mind, including reading the email. 'Yes, we've found her,

I was just about to open the email before I came in here,' he replied instead, then read through the message on his phone.

He paused for a moment as he let the words in front of him register. 'Oh shit,' he said out loud. 'We need to go now.'

◆ ◆ ◆

The migraine Joe desperately wanted to fight off was threatening to return with a ferocity he'd not felt in years.

His head throbbed with the rhythm of his pulse as the marked police car twisted and turned on its approach into the borough of Islington. The relentless noise of the screaming sirens inches above his head wasn't helping either. Even with the windows shut tight, his hypersensitivity made the sound close to crippling.

Webster sat in the front passenger seat, barking orders into a mobile phone and coordinating other vehicles and crews. Joe saw her free hand clenched into a tight fist, mirroring the steely veneer of her expression. He knew all too well the potential scenarios running through her head, because he was considering them too.

DS Bryan Thompson's phone rang and he answered before the second note of his ringtone played out. His hand shook as he held his phone.

'We'll have two uniforms standing outside Becca's house within five minutes, guv,' he relayed as the caller continued to update him. 'Do you want them to knock when they arrive?'

'No. Get them to radio in and wait until the armed response unit gets there.'

Nikhat drove, the headlights of the car urgently flashing and warning motorists ahead to move to one side. Bryan sat next to Joe in the rear of the vehicle. Joe remained silent, pressing redial and calling Becca's number over and over again in the ever-declining hope that she might answer. But the phone went straight to voicemail each time. It was the same with her mother Helen's number. With each failed call, he became more and more despondent. In a situation he had no control over, the only thing he could manage was his breathing, so he allowed just enough air to enter his lungs before gradually expelling it.

Joe had lost count of the number of times over the years that he'd tried to reassure victims of crime that what had happened to them wasn't their fault. He'd tell them it was the person who'd made a decision to perpetuate the crime who was to blame, not the casualty. He had genuinely believed every word he'd said. Until now.

Because if Dominic Hammond hurt Becca, no one would ever convince him that it wasn't Joe's fault.

'Damn it,' Webster blurted out, bringing him back into the present. 'The dashcam photos have leaked. Online news sources have also named Hammond, and social media is going crazy with it. How far away are we, Nikhat?'

'Eight minutes,' he replied, looking at the arrival time on the satnav.

It would be the longest eight minutes of their lives.

CHAPTER 52

Becca had no idea where she was or why she was lying on the floor.

As her senses slowly returned, all she knew was that she was on her side, her head was resting against a carpeted floor, and noises around her suggested she was not alone. She lifted herself up a little and a searing pain jabbed at her right temple.

Her eyes were raw, like sand had been kicked in her face and then rubbed into each eyeball. She desperately wanted to scratch at them, but when she tried to lift her hands, they barely budged. Something was binding her wrists tightly together. She moved her hands again and there was a rattling, like handcuffs. It was the same with her legs; they'd been tied at the ankles and the restraints dug into her skin each time she attempted to free them.

Immediately, she felt sick with fear. How had this happened? She attempted to calm herself by concentrating on her breathing, to gain a better understanding of her circumstances and surroundings. *Don't panic*, she told herself. *Gauge the situation before reacting*. But it was easier said than done.

After taking in the familiar scent of sandalwood and white musk, she assumed it was coming from the reed diffuser on the mantle of her fireplace. *I must still be at home*, she thought. *I'm in my lounge*. Although the familiar brought her little comfort. As her chest rapidly rose and fell, she attempted to piece together the moments before her blackout. Images gradually began to drip-feed from her memory and into her present. Evan Williams on her sofa, her mum and Maisie sitting side by side, their mouths gagged and Helen's hands and feet tied together . . . and suddenly it hit her like a ton of bricks.

I'm the next name on his list.

This time, her panic was impossible to suppress. Becca wriggled like a snake held down by a forked stick. She tried in vain to manoeuvre herself into an upright position so that she could check on her family's welfare. 'Mum,' she wanted to say, but she'd also inhaled what had been sprayed into her eyes and it made her throat scratchy and sore. 'Maisie?' she croaked. Now she heard a muffled reply but she couldn't make out the words.

A blurred figure appeared before her and she felt a pair of hands grab her underarms, dragging her into an upright sitting position. Then her head was yanked backwards with such force that the vertebrae in her neck made a sound like a whip cracking. Suddenly, her face became wet as a liquid was poured on to it from above. Thinking it was acid like the fireman had been doused in, Becca tried to shake free.

'Stop struggling, it's water,' came a man's voice. It was the first time she'd heard the killer speak. He didn't sound like she'd expected. His voice was normal, almost. Then he forced open her mouth and poured water inside it too. Some went down her throat, the rest she spat out.

She blinked hard and he wiped her eyes with something soft. Slowly, her vision returned.

'Look around. I want you to see what you have done,' he said, his tone measured and containing little emotion. 'I want you to look at the people you cherish above all others and understand the position you have placed them in.'

Maisie's head was buried in her grandmother's chest, a blindfold across her eyes. Becca was sure her daughter was unable to make sense of what was happening but that she knew that it was bad and wanted to hide from it. Becca recognised what each of her daughter's different-sounding cries meant, even when suppressed. The ones coming from her now were the tail end of something that had been close to hysterical. Becca desperately wanted to reach out and hold her daughter tightly and tell her everything was going to be all right.

'Why are you here?' she whispered, her voice still hoarse. 'What have I done to you?' He didn't reply, and instead offered her a thin smile.

Becca looked at her mum again. Tears streamed down Helen's cheeks. Evan's face, however, was blank, like someone had pressed pause on him, only allowing him to blink and breathe. Becca hated to think what the poor child had already been forced to witness.

She turned to face Helen again and opened her mouth, but she didn't know what to say. Instead, she nodded at her, hoping that small gesture would reassure her that Helen had done the right thing in summoning Becca home earlier, no matter how difficult it must have been. Maisie's safety always came first.

Finally, her eyes shifted back to her assailant, who was now standing with his back to her, surveying the chaos he'd created. He turned and crouched, so their faces were inches apart. Becca knew he looked familiar, but in her heightened state she couldn't think where from. His dirty blond tousled hair hung close to his collar and his stubble was thick. She wished she had Joe's powers of recollection for facial features. He smelled stale.

'Please, whatever you think I've done, you're wrong.'

'Take a look at me,' he said. 'Really take me in.' He circled his face with his fingers to emphasise his request.

Becca paused for a moment and remembered that, when she'd arrived home, there'd been no sign of a forced entry, unless he'd broken in through the patio doors. Helen must have allowed him inside – had he been familiar to her? And in that moment, Becca knew him too.

'You were here last week! You're one of Mum's clients.' She shuddered that the most wanted man in Britain had already been inside her home.

In all but Dumitru's murder, it was assumed he'd worn protective clothing so as not to leave evidence. However, in her house, he was dressed casually in a T-shirt and jeans. Did it mean that he wasn't going to kill her, or that he no longer cared what evidence he left behind? A man who no longer cared was much more dangerous than a cautious one.

'It wasn't the first time our paths had crossed, detective,' he said. 'You've also been inside my flat.' Becca frowned and shook her head. 'You probably don't recognise me without the make-up or wig. Then, I was Megan Bingham.'

'Shit,' said Becca, furious with herself for failing to realise something wasn't right with Megan's story.

'But let's go back even further – say, three years ago.'

Becca knew the longer she could engage her captor in conversation, the greater the chance her family stood of getting out of this alive. So she played along and racked her brain. However, she couldn't recall under what circumstances they might have met. 'No, I'm sorry, I don't remember,' she said eventually, shaking her head.

His eyebrows knotted like he was examining her face for micro-expressions. After a short pause, he appeared satisfied she was being truthful.

'Okay,' he said, and rose to his feet. He looked down on her. Becca's eyes were swollen and red, like plum tomatoes. Her hair was wet and matted. She knew she was weak and unable to protect herself or those she loved.

To Becca, he appeared to be making a big deal out of picking up a police-issue rigid baton that he'd left resting on the shelf above the radiator. Becca's pulse quickened as she watched him. Then she and Helen stared each other dead in the eyes.

'Let me refresh your memory,' her assailant continued. 'Three years ago, you were a run-of-the-mill PC when you and a colleague were called to a flat in Shepherd's Bush.' He gave her a moment to catch up with him, but Becca drew a blank.

'Three years is a long time,' she replied.

'Not when you're trapped in my life.'

'What I meant is that in my job, I meet dozens of people every day . . .'

He shook his head and put his finger to his mouth to shush her. 'I don't care what you meant.' Becca fell silent. 'Do you recognise the name Audrey Moreau?'

'Yes,' she replied again. 'A car that was involved in an accident at the weekend was registered to her.'

'But you don't remember her before that?'

'No.'

'Audrey was my fiancée, and three years ago you turned up at her flat because of . . . a misunderstanding.'

Becca cleared her throat. 'What was the misunderstanding about?'

'We were having a disagreement and you jumped to the wrong conclusions and took her side.'

Becca felt chills run through her. Audrey Moreau had worked at Maisie's first nursery, in Finsbury Park. She remembered her because cases of domestic abuse stuck to her like Velcro. 'You were her ex-boyfriend, and you were threatening her,' she said.

His response was fast and physical, and came in the form of a kick to her side, then her lower back.

'Turn round,' he directed to Evan, but the boy remained motionless. 'I said turn round!' he yelled, and this time the frightened little boy obeyed him.

Meanwhile Becca slumped to her side, gasping for breath. In her uniform days on the beat, there had been many scuffles in which she'd been punched in the stomach and winded, but this pain was much deeper than anything she'd felt before. He must have caught her square in the kidneys, and it was how she imagined it felt to be electrocuted. She watched helplessly as the assailant pulled his leg back to boot her again.

'Stop!' came Helen's muffled voice. He turned and went towards her, moving the baton to his left hand and holding it above her head.

'One more word from you and so help me God . . .' he snarled.

An anxious Evan might not have understood what the threats meant, but he knew enough to be frightened of the man's tone. He pushed himself along the sofa, trying to get away from him, his body still facing the opposite direction. The boy's kidnapper moved towards him, lowered the weapon and held the boy's arm firmly. 'I need you to stay where you are,' he ordered, and Evan froze.

Becca regained control of her breath, despite the stabbing pain in her side. With all her strength, she pushed herself back into an upright position, anxious to take the attention away from the innocents and pull it back towards her.

'What's your name?' Becca asked. 'I've just realised I don't know it.'

'You mean you don't remember.'

Becca nodded. It made her head ache.

'Dominic, not that it matters.'

'Tell me what happened that night, Dominic. From your perspective, explain to me what went on.'

'Oh, *now* you want to know!' he replied, folding his arms indignantly. 'Because back then you didn't give a fuck what I had to say! You were too busy sticking your nose in and assuming the worst of me. And you assumed wrongly.'

'I understand that now. So, please tell me what happened. I'm listening.'

Dominic began pacing the lounge, backwards and forwards five steps at a time, like a Russian bear held captive in a cage. He tapped the baton absent-mindedly against his leg. Becca spotted a small circle of white paint on the tip, and recognised it as her own police-issue weapon. She guessed the metal handcuffs digging into her wrists also belonged to her, and probably the CS spray that had hurt her eyes too. If her memory served her correctly, he was using everything on her that she had used on him.

Dominic stopped moving. 'My fiancée and I had a disagreement over our son,' he began. 'Before that, she'd had some sort of breakdown and walked out on me when she was six months pregnant. She left her job, didn't tell me where she was going, and all I had was a telephone number that she never answered. Can you imagine what it was like to be me, knowing that my flesh and blood was somewhere out there? And that it was the woman I loved who wouldn't let me see him?'

'No, I can't imagine it,' Becca replied. She had not seen Audrey again after that night, as just days later, Helen had found her a nursery much closer to home. 'It seems very unfair.' Her answer appeared to satisfy him, and his pacing resumed.

'I searched for Audrey for a year before I finally found her, and by then my son had been born. The first and only time I ever caught a glimpse of him was when you made them leave me.'

'I didn't make them . . .' Becca interjected, but Dominic ignored her.

'All I wanted was to meet him, to look at him, to hold him, to smell him. And you made sure that I couldn't do any of that.'

Becca watched helplessly as his face reddened, like the anger was rising inside him again, and she flinched as he swung the baton hard into the wall above her head, leaving missing chunks of plasterboard. She shut her eyes tightly as flakes of paint fell like confetti. The noise made Maisie squeal, and she tucked her head even closer into Helen's chest.

Becca opened her eyes and nodded slowly, hoping he saw she was sympathetic to his pain. She imagined what it might feel like not to have Maisie in her life. It was unbearable, so she blinked the thought away.

Dominic shot her a glance, a shaft of sunlight creeping through the closed curtains and illuminating his wide eyes. 'Do you remember arresting me?' he asked. 'Do you remember putting me in handcuffs and calling for a van to take me away?'

'Yes,' said Becca truthfully.

She recalled PC Morris, her teammate that night, and how he'd tried to calm Dominic down while Becca followed a petrified Audrey into her flat. Many times throughout her career Becca had seen women like Audrey, women who had been bullied and beaten and who, having found the strength to leave their partners, lived in constant fear of being found by them again. Men like the one in front of her never changed, they only altered their colours to hide in plain sight. She had not wanted to let Audrey become another statistic like her sister; not on her watch. Her shoulders weren't broad enough to carry upon them the guilt of two needless deaths.

Becca had offered to help find her a bed at a women's refuge for the night, but Audrey had plans to escape much further away. Becca remained with her while she hurriedly threw clothes for her and the baby into a suitcase and removed two passports from a drawer. Audrey carried the case while Becca picked up the sleeping child in his car seat.

'Where will you go?' asked Becca.

'Back home to France for a while,' Audrey replied. 'Back to where I can feel safe again.'

Becca helped to secure the child in the passenger seat, and Audrey turned to mouth the words 'thank you' to her before driving away. Becca had allowed herself a moment's satisfaction for a job well done before calling for a backup vehicle to take him to the station.

'That other copper, he would have listened to me if you'd given him the chance,' Dominic continued, bringing her back into the present. 'But you had your own agenda. I could see it in your eyes.'

'He didn't see the texts you sent her, but she showed me them. You called her a bitch and a whore, you warned her that when you found her, you were going to "cut her vagina into pieces" so that no other man would ever want her. Remember telling her how you'd rather kill her and your son than lose them? She was petrified of you.'

'Lies!' Dominic yelled.

'I saw the messages with my own eyes.'

Dominic dropped to his knees and grabbed a handful of Becca's hair, yanking her head to one side. 'Shut the fuck up!' he screamed. 'Shut up! Shut up! Shut up!' Then, as he let go of her, he shoved her head backwards with a sharp jolt so it hit the wall.

Becca heard Maisie scream again, followed by her grandmother trying to comfort her.

'Tell her to be quiet,' growled Dominic.

'It's not her fault,' Becca said, jumping to her daughter's defence. 'She doesn't understand. Neither does Evan. Why don't you let them go? This is about me and you, not them. They're innocent.'

Dominic leaned over and gripped Becca by the cheeks and chin, his fingernails digging deep into the surface of her skin. He moved his mouth so close to her eyes that his breath forced her to keep blinking as he spat out his words.

'My son was innocent too, but because of you, Etienne and his mother are dead. Why should I spare you and your family the same fate?'

CHAPTER 53

Becca's mind raced.

If Dominic's ex-fiancée and son were really dead like he claimed, it was the worst-case scenario for her. It meant that Dominic had nothing left to lose and he was likely going to kill her, perhaps all of them. But what role did he think she had played in their deaths?

Finding herself tied up and held hostage by a serial murderer wasn't something her tutors had prepared her for in police training college. So she had no frame of reference to draw upon. She knew that, for a successful outcome in a hostage scenario, the negotiator must try to offer an element of sympathy and quietly gain some control. But what are you supposed to do when negotiator and victim are one and the same?

As far as Becca was aware, every name on Dominic's list had one thing in common: with the exception of Dumitru, the others had been brutally tortured and murdered. Now she had to find a way to avoid the same fate. Somehow Dominic had to see her as a human being – a mum and a daughter – and not the police officer he believed had allowed his fiancée and child to escape him and then somehow die. The clock was ticking.

Becca watched in silence as her adversary made his way towards the closed curtains and peered through a crack. The front window gave a full view up and along Becca's road, to a T-junction at the far end. Apparently assured there would be no surprises, he paced the living room again, this time picking up framed photographs and ornaments to examine them more closely before dropping them.

When he passed Evan Williams, he ran his fingers through the boy's hair. Evan didn't react. But that tiny fragment of tenderness might be his Achilles heel, thought Becca. Despite bringing a child with him into a violent scenario, he'd turned the boy's head away and blindfolded Maisie. Perhaps somewhere, buried deep inside his dark, dark heart, he had an affection for children.

'There's some orange juice in the fridge if he's thirsty,' Becca offered. 'My little girl can't get enough of it.'

He studied her for signs it was a trick, then went to the kitchen, returning with a plastic tumbler of juice. He offered it to Evan but the boy didn't react. Dominic appeared disappointed. Becca struggled to reconcile the brutality of his killings with his sadness at the child's rejection.

'What happened to your partner and little boy?' Becca asked tentatively. Urging him to recall something that pained him was a risk, but it might help disarm him. 'Did you patch things up before . . .' She didn't want to say the words 'they died'. However, by the look of disbelief spreading across his face, Becca instantly knew she'd made the wrong call. He stormed towards her.

'You don't even know? You don't even remember?' he growled.

'I was never told.'

'Did you try to find out?'

'No, Audrey said she was going back to France.'

'While you were spraying my eyes with pepper spray and knocking me to the ground with this baton, Audrey and Etienne were making their way out of London. They got as far as the North Circular when their car was hit by a van that pushed it into the path of other cars . . .' Dominic's voice trailed off.

'I'm so sorry,' Becca said quietly. This time she managed to brace herself when she saw him raise his leg before he stamped upon her. She heard a rib snap, robbing her of her breath.

'I don't want your apologies,' he said.

'Please stop, for the sake of the children,' she heard Helen beg, her words now audible as the tape peeled from her lips. Then Becca watched helplessly as, without a second thought, Dominic moved in Helen's direction and raised the baton with his right arm. He winced briefly before switching hands and hitting her square on the back of her head. Her eyes rolled back in their sockets until the lids snapped shut.

He turned to take in the bewildered children. Evan was still facing the wall while a sobbing and blindfolded Maisie had followed the direction of her grandmother, squirming until her body was half engulfed by the sofa cushions and her face hidden behind Helen's back.

A terrified Becca made no attempt to lift herself back to a sitting position. She'd been powerless to prevent him hurting her mother, and crucially she couldn't stop him from doing the same thing to the children.

'Please, leave them alone,' Becca said, gasping for air. 'I'm begging you.'

Dominic turned to face her and let his smile settle for a moment. 'And what will you do if I don't?'

Both captor and captive knew the answer was absolutely nothing.

'Quite the pathetic little figure, aren't you, detective – now you don't have your uniform or partner to hide behind.'

'I was doing my job.'

'And I'm doing mine.'

'Your job isn't to hurt children.'

'Neither is yours, but you killed my son.'

'What happened to Audrey or Etienne wasn't my fault. I wasn't driving the car that went into them.'

'You didn't need to be driving it. When you put him in the car, you didn't strap him into his car seat properly. The inquest said that when the vehicle rolled over, the chair came loose and was thrown into the back and landed under Audrey's baggage. Etienne suffocated. If you hadn't stopped me from being with them, none of this would have happened. You took everything I had away from me. All that has happened is your fault.'

Dominic's claims confused Becca. She thought back three years, and recalled it being dark inside Audrey's two-door car as she'd fumbled around for the front passenger seatbelt and clicked it into place. Dominic seemed so convinced it was the truth, but how could she trust a word that came from his mouth?

Think, Becca, think, she told herself. She knew her way around a child seat like the back of her hand – she had secured Maisie into her mum's car plenty of times before she'd done it to Etienne. Surely she wouldn't have made a mistake? She racked her brain and was beginning to question herself, when suddenly she remembered what had happened next.

'It's not my fault!' she fired back, her eyes opening wide. 'As I went to close the door, Audrey unclipped the belt again to remove Etienne's cardigan. It was a red one, one of those chunky knit ones. She told me he'd get too hot in it.'

'You're lying,' he retorted, shaking his head. 'You'll say anything to save yourself, even if it means putting the blame on a woman who can't defend herself.'

'I'm not, honestly,' pleaded Becca. 'In the hurry to get away from you, she must have forgotten to attach it again.'

Dominic began to applaud her. 'Valiant effort, detective, valiant effort. But I don't believe you. Audrey was a good mother, a *perfect* mother. She'd never have put our child at risk.'

'She did it by mistake, and before you could get to her again.'

'You can keep going for as long as you want, but I'll never believe you.'

With no way to prove it, Becca was exasperated. Her plan to humanise herself had failed. Now the only way for her to keep Helen and the children safe was to keep him talking and feed his anger, because if he was getting more pleasure from torturing her than killing her, she was buying them precious time.

'What responsibility do you take for their deaths?' she asked.

'What a stupid question. None. I loved them.'

'No, you were obsessed by them. Obsession and love are two very different things. You're a bully who couldn't get his own way and you scared that poor woman into running.'

Dominic took Becca's baton and brought it down hard several times on her arm. She howled as it stung her skin. She remained lying on her side, her eyes streaming with tears and trying in vain not to stare at the blood trickling from an open wound on the back of her mum's head.

'Why did you kill the others?' she quizzed. 'If I'm to blame for everything, what have the others got to do with it?'

'What you started, they finished.'

'Then why not kill me first?'

'If I began by killing a policewoman, it would've attracted too much attention and manpower too soon. So I started slowly, with two immigrants nobody gave a damn about, then I worked my way up to the paramedic, fireman and nurse. Society seems to take the murder of a police officer even more seriously than any of the other emergency services, yet you save the least amount of lives. With you dead, my work is over. Knowing that you've been to the crime scenes and seen first-hand what I'm capable of makes it even sweeter, because you're more fearful as to what can happen next.'

He was right, thought Becca, but she wouldn't give him the satisfaction of seeing it reflected in her expression.

'What's your endgame? You kill me and then what? You think you can ever go back to any kind of normality? Where do you think you can escape to, because you'll have every police officer in the country looking for you. You'll never be able to rest.'

'That's none of your concern. But what I will tell you is that soon I'll have the public on my side. No matter what your colleagues think of me, the country will understand I was driven to do what I did and that I'm not the monster the papers tell them I am.'

'Are you that deluded?' Rebecca scoffed. 'All the public will understand is that you're a psychopath who likes to abduct little boys.'

Dominic shook his head. 'They'll learn each one of you deserved what came to you.'

'You're kidding yourself.'

'We'll see. Actually, there's no "we", is there? You won't see anything because you're as good as dead.'

It was either fear or the kick to the kidneys that prevented Becca from holding her bladder any longer. The crotch of her jeans felt warm as she wet herself. 'If you're going to kill me, could you at least put the children in a different room,' she added, every muscle in her body trembling. 'Look at them, Dominic. Maisie is beside herself and Evan is non-responsive.'

'Etienne!' he yelled suddenly, and jabbed his index finger at a startled Becca. 'His name is Etienne, and don't try to tell me what is good for my son!'

'But he's not your son, is he?' Becca fired back. 'Your son is dead. You told me that yourself.'

Dominic glared at her, his anger mutating into confusion, like he'd lost himself for a moment. He glared at the boy on the sofa as if to reassure himself that he wasn't the one in the wrong. But Becca was correct, and it temporarily perplexed him.

'You have to give him back to his parents, because he isn't yours,' she continued.

'Don't tell me what to do.'

She used her elbows to push herself up on to both buttocks and looked him in the eye. 'Etienne had a lucky escape from you. You're not fit to be a father, you're not even fit to be a man. Who the hell brings a child to the house of someone they're going to kill? Do you reckon you're teaching people like me, the ones you think wronged you, a lesson by torturing and killing us? Of course you're not! You're just a sick bastard blaming other people for your own actions. Audrey ran away because you were violent and abusive towards her and she didn't want you doing the same to your son. You have your own family's blood on your hands.'

Dominic put his hands on his hips and staged a laugh. 'Oh fuck, Becca. You're about to regret every single word of what you just said when I start cutting out your tongue.'

As he lurched towards her, the phone in his pocket vibrated. He read the text message, then glared at Becca.

She muttered something deliberately quietly. 'What did you say?' he asked. Becca repeated it again but it was still too quiet for him to register. He squatted down and grabbed her face, his hand like a claw, pulling it closer to his. Then she seized her one and only opportunity.

She pulled her head back and then threw it sharply forward, her brow colliding hard with the bridge of Dominic's nose. The shock of the collision made him lose his balance and he fell to his side, clutching his face. Earlier, Becca had noted he was right-handed, yet twice when it came to lifting the baton, his right shoulder appeared weak and he'd switched hands. She lifted her legs and tied-together ankles as high as she could and slammed them down on Dominic's right collarbone. Her theory was right – it was weak. The crack was loud enough for them both to hear, and he yelled. She repeated the action a second time, then manoeuvred herself backwards to slam her heels down on his groin too. He rolled to his side, facing away from Becca. Now she threw the weight of her feet into the side of his head. Then, using all her remaining strength, she pushed her back up against the wall and rose to a standing position.

She had to think fast. The baton lay on the floor inches away from her, but even if she could reach it, it would be no use. She wouldn't have the flexibility with her bound wrists to cause much damage. Instead, she shuffled her way into the hall.

'Maisie!' she yelled, turning her head to her daughter, Dominic now out of view. 'Come here and open the front door.' But Maisie remained with her face hidden between the cushions and her unconscious grandmother's back. 'Maisie,' Becca shouted again. 'Please, sweetie, follow Mummy's voice and help me.' Again, there was no response or movement.

A creeping realisation came to Becca as to why Maisie was staying put. She felt safer by the side of her unconscious grandmother than with her mum. Helen was the person who could calm her down, who put Band-Aids on her cuts and grazes, who read her bedtime stories and whom she turned to for safety when she was afraid. Becca's lack of involvement had made her a mother in name alone.

Tears poured from Becca's eyes as she willed something inside her daughter to overcome her fear and stir. She judged the distance ahead of her – if she could make it those few extra metres to the front door alone, then perhaps she could open it and scream for help.

'Stay where you are, darling,' she shouted. 'I'll come back for you. I promise.'

Suddenly she heard her daughter stir. 'Mummy, don't go,' came Maisie's muffled voice.

Becca stopped in her tracks. A mother wouldn't leave Maisie alone in a room with that man for even a second longer. And her maternal instinct was too strong. 'Okay, sweetie,' she sobbed. 'It'll be all right. I'm not ever going anywhere again, I promise.'

She remained where she was standing, her whole body shaking. Then, from the corner of her eye, Becca saw Dominic roll slowly on to his back, his hands moving towards the floor to push himself up. She knew she had just missed her last chance. So she took a deep breath, and once she heard the dull clicking of a bone returning to its socket, she turned slowly to face the man who wanted to kill her.

Then came the scrape of the police baton being dragged along the wall, and a whooshing sound as it cut through the air.

CHAPTER 54

The red steel battering ram twice collided with the front door handle. At only half a metre in length and weighing just sixteen kilograms, the ram's three tons of impact force made short work of the lock and it folded in on itself.

Once the door fell open, five members of Specialist Firearms Command, clad from head to toe in black and grey and brandishing semi-automatic rifles, burst into the hallway and disappeared out of sight, yelling warnings as they ran.

As instructed by command, Joe, Bryan, Nikhat and Webster remained in a safe zone behind their car, each focusing their attention on Becca's house. Behind them were two more police cars, and the armed unit's van was parked at an angle in front of them all. Two marked vehicles blocked both entrances to the suburban road. One reversed to allow three ambulances and a first responder unit to enter.

From behind blinds, shutters and net curtains, Becca's neighbours craned their necks to gawp at the sudden activity on their doorstep. Some were oblivious to the potential danger and left the safety of their homes for a closer look. They were given short shrift by uniformed PCs, and returned, tails between legs.

For much of the day Joe's face had been locked in an enduring frown, even before the call that had taken him to Leighton Buzzard. It wouldn't ease until he knew Becca and her family were safe. And as each second ticked by, he felt the knot in his stomach expand until it reached the size of a fist. What was taking them so long? He fought the urge to scream 'Come on!' at the top of his voice.

Finally, the police radio clenched in Webster's hand crackled to life. 'Clear,' came a man's voice, and together Bryan and Joe let out long, relieved sighs. But the words that followed made Joe shudder. 'Send in the paramedics. Urgently.' Now he knew for sure that his instinct had been right. Dominic Hammond had targeted Becca.

His and Nikhat's eyes locked in a shared understanding, before they ran hell for leather the hundred metres up the road to Becca's house. Joe reached the broken front door but was forced to wait until a team of paramedics hurried past them and entered. Then he dashed across the hallway and into the lounge and froze, surveying and trying to process the carnage before him.

He struggled to know where to focus his attention first. The heavy curtains were closed and gave the room a dusky, ominous feel. But he could still make out streaks of blood across the walls.

On the sofa was a young girl whom he recognised from Becca's photographs as her daughter. She was blindfolded and crying, and held her hand tightly over her own eyes. She wriggled, trying to escape the paramedic attempting to calm her, check her for injuries and whisk her away from the chaos.

Joe's eyes were drawn further into the room, where another paramedic was crouching and talking to a little boy dressed in pyjamas. To Joe's shock, he recognised him as Evan Williams, then thanked God that he was safe.

Flashing lights outside were visible between a crack in the curtains and caught his attention. Another ambulance pulled up and more medical technicians exited. Joe's head – still dizzy from his migraine – turned from left to right; his eyes catching up a second later. Where was Becca?

Two men and a woman in green uniforms were on their knees, crowded over a body and obscuring the face and torso from view. He noted the injured party's legs; the cut of the material and one remaining shoe suggested it was a woman. Joe approached, trying to recall what colour trousers or footwear Becca had been wearing when he saw her that morning. But in the sensory overload of the room, his memory failed him.

'Five, six, seven, eight,' Joe heard as a paramedic pushed down on her chest before pausing. She was lying flat against the floor, her shirt open, a red bra pulled down exposing her breasts. He corrected himself: it was a white bra, but it was badly bloodstained. His breathing quickened.

He glanced at her wrists; they were facing at awkward angles and clearly broken. However, there was no sign of Becca's tattoo on the left one, with her daughter's name. He followed the crimson trail up her chest and towards her face but he couldn't see her silver locket either. It must be her mother, he realised, part of him relieved and part of him guilty for thinking like that.

When one of the medical team moved to reach into their bag, Joe continued to follow the blood trail up to Helen's throat and chin and then finally her mouth, nose and eyes. Bloody hair was matted across her face, but where it parted and left a gap, there was a visible shoe print on her cheek. The poor woman had taken a hell of a beating, he thought.

'Move please,' another paramedic ordered from behind, and Joe turned to see her carrying equipment to place by Helen's side. He recognised a defibrillator. It made a high-pitched whining noise when it was switched on. Despite not locating Becca, he couldn't take his eyes off

Helen as both paddles were rubbed together before the space around her was cleared and then they connected with her chest. Her back arched and her body jolted with the first electrical shock. The procedure was repeated as the paramedics alternated between breathing air into her lungs and manually trying to restart her heart with the current.

The sudden noise of a stretcher colliding with a door frame caught his attention and he watched it being carried towards another unconscious figure he hadn't seen. It must be Becca, he thought. Blood was covering her face too, although to his untrained eye, her condition didn't appear as serious as Helen's. He moved towards her.

'Is she alive?' asked Joe, his heart palpitating in his throat.

'Low pulse, and barely,' a paramedic replied.

'Can we get some light in here?' a voice yelled, and suddenly the curtains were opened, bathing the room in sun. But to Joe's horror, it wasn't Becca being lifted on to the stretcher before him.

It was Helen.

Amid the gloom, the blood and the confusion, mother and daughter had been barely distinguishable. And it was Becca whom the first set of paramedics were trying to revive.

Joe turned back to her and noticed the light reflecting on a broken silver chain and locket by her side. He squinted at her wrist and could just about see the faint trace of the name 'Maisie' under a film of blood.

Everything Joe had learned in his years as a police officer, he forgot in an instant. He was almost paralysed, his body cold and trembling in the spring heatwave, watching helplessly as they continued trying to resuscitate his friend.

You did this to her, said a voice in the back of his head.

He was no longer aware of time, or how much of it passed before the paramedic holding the defibrillator paddles became the first to shake her head. She glanced at her colleagues, and they in turn nodded their silent agreement.

As they moved to one side, one patted Joe's shoulder as if she understood what he was feeling. But she didn't. The only way that was possible was if Becca's death had been her fault. It wasn't. It was his.

It's because of you she's dead. You are to blame.

He looked around the room. Webster and Nikhat stood shoulder to shoulder, motionless; Bryan held his head in his hands, crying silently.

Joe dropped to his knees and clasped Becca's hand in his, soaking his shirt cuffs and the knees of his chinos in her spilled blood. An equally grief-stricken Nikhat quietly reminded him that forensics were on their way to process the crime scene and he was in danger of compromising the body.

In a matter of minutes, Becca had gone from a detective, friend and colleague, to another victim of a serial killer that needed processing.

CHAPTER 55

Minutes after the text message arrived, DS Becca Vincent was dead.

Dominic stood over her lifeless body and felt waves of elation wash over him, like the afterglow of an orgasm he hadn't wanted to end. While there hadn't been time to make her suffer in the ways he had planned, when it came down to it, the result was the same. She had got the end she deserved. They all had. Now his revenge had reached its climax, he was surprised by how emotional it made him feel, and he began to weep and laugh at the same time. That final blow to her head marked the end of the man she had made him become.

He had wanted to remain in the house for longer, but the text and a flashing blue light that hadn't been switched off quickly enough gave away the arrival of her colleagues. Dominic needed to escape quickly. He grabbed his rucksack and made for the patio doors leading into the courtyard. But what to do with Evan Williams? He turned to face the boy, who was sitting on the sofa, carefully watching his captor. Dominic paused, resigning himself to the fact that no matter how much he might have wanted it, the boy would never truly belong with him. He would never be the Etienne he'd lost. And he had to leave him behind.

Dominic kicked his way through the glass, ran across the courtyard, vaulted the six-foot-high fence and landed in the alleyway. He sprinted along the first passage and then into a second before reaching a main road. He'd abandoned Plan A, to leave through the front door, jump into the stolen car he and Evan had arrived in and then go to the flat where he'd currently left his few belongings. Plan B was to go straight to the lock-up garage where he'd left Audrey's Mercedes. But first he had to ensure he wasn't being followed.

He ran past a parade of shops, looking nobody in the eye but aware of how he stood out with his bloody face and clothes. He had rented out many a property in the area, so he was familiar with the roads and was careful to change direction often. He ran through pocket parks and churchyards, across car parks and dual carriageways – anywhere that would throw off officers later sifting through CCTV cameras as they tried to predict where he was heading next. At his pace and through such differing environments, not even police sniffer dogs would be able to retain a trace of him. The longer he continued to run, the harder his body attempted to shuttle more oxygen to his working muscles.

Frequently, he'd glance over his shoulder or look skywards to reassure himself police helicopters weren't keeping tabs on him from above. As far as he was aware, he was completely alone. Nevertheless, he continued to chop and change routes so as not to be boxed in.

It took him an hour and a half, but finally Dominic arrived at the lock-up garage, completely exhausted and dripping sweat on to the concrete floor. Bending double, he rested his hands on his knees. His throat burned from the acid rising from his stomach, and he spat on the floor before falling into a hacking coughing fit. As he stripped naked to cool down, he hoped his heart would cease trying to beat its way out of his chest soon. He had not run that distance, that fast or for that long since his university days.

Once his breathing was under control, he pulled at a cord to turn on the strip light. Dominic had never felt such thirst before, but his only option was to guzzle from an old bottle of distilled water he kept for the car battery. It tasted stale but at least it refreshed him.

A fiery sensation in the socket of his collarbone re-emerged. Becca's aggressive retaliation had taken him by surprise and he had run out of painkillers. Twice inside a few days it had been dislocated, and twice it had been pushed back into place. His mistake had been not to sedate Becca like the others. He'd wanted her fully conscious, to comprehend everything that he was going to inflict upon her. But her survival instinct had figured nowhere in his plan.

Inside the car, Dominic flipped down the sun visor and examined his fractured nose from all angles in the horizontal mirror. He was struggling to breathe through it, and hadn't had the time to adjust it at Becca's house. So with his thumbs either side of his nostrils, he counted to three and pushed it sharply until it was realigned. Pain ran through the centre of his face and reached his head like a thousand ice cream headaches all at once. As he waited for it to ease, he stared into the dark, hollow circles that housed his soulless eyes and remembered a time when they'd been illuminated by Audrey. It seemed so long ago.

An image of her in France came to mind, from the second summer he'd spent with Audrey and her family at their rented chateau in the Loire Valley. Their days were spent either blissfully relaxed around the swimming pool, or manic and occupied by her nieces' and nephew's constant need for entertainment. But neither he nor Audrey had minded. He was fascinated at how their family maintained such a deep connection with one another. Sometimes he felt like an integral part of their world, on other occasions he was an imposter waiting for someone to yank the rug from under his feet and steal them all away from him. And a few days later, that someone arrived.

Audrey's three-months-pregnant sister Christine had appeared with the children the day after he and Audrey arrived. But her husband Baptiste had been away on business in Los Angeles, and when he turned up five days later, the family dynamic was tipped on its axis. At least, that's how it felt for Dominic.

Baptiste was someone he barely tolerated. Dominic felt inferior to him in every way, from his smart appearance to his education, his breeding and his high-rolling career. Baptiste revelled in his alpha-male status, while Dominic languished much lower down the pecking order. And Dominic hated him for it.

From the moment the taxi dropped him off, Baptiste wasted no time in making his presence felt, ignoring his wife and children and devoting his attention to Audrey instead. It wasn't the first time Dominic had noticed his inappropriate behaviour. Be it Easter holidays, birthdays, Christmas celebrations or the annual summer get-togethers, Baptiste frequently made suggestive comments to Audrey, or offered lingering glances and inappropriate touching.

He'd refill Audrey's wine glass before anyone else's; he encouraged her to smoke when she was drunk; and he took more photographs of her than of his offspring. However, everyone but Dominic appeared oblivious to Baptiste's incessant flirting. Audrey either didn't notice or wasn't bothered. And that wound Dominic up so he was like a coiled spring.

After three days of standing on the sidelines and doing little to stop Audrey's lecherous brother-in-law, it all became too much for Dominic, and he revealed to her how such behaviour made him feel. Her response was to laugh at his accusations and pat his shoulder condescendingly.

'You're being ridiculous,' she replied as she slipped out of her underwear and between the bedsheets. 'He's just a flirty kind of guy.'

'Your whole family speaks fluent English but he insists on talking to you in French in front of me because he knows I struggle to understand.'

'His English isn't as good as ours.'

'He's an international financier. Have you heard him on the phone? He seems to get by on it pretty well outside the family.'

'You sound childish.'

'Earlier tonight you let him put his hand on the small of your back when you went out for a cigarette.'

'Are you spying on me?'

'And when you laugh along with all his terrible jokes you're actively encouraging him to behave like this.'

Audrey sat bolt upright. 'Stop it, Dominic,' she snapped. 'You actually think I would cheat on you with my pregnant sister's husband? I have known Baptiste since I was fourteen years old, and we are family. Last time you accused the nursery's owner of showing me an inappropriate amount of attention at the Christmas party. Then it was the removals man who brought the furniture to our flat. It doesn't matter to me if men find me attractive, because I'm not interested in them. You're enough for me.'

But how long for? Dominic asked himself. He'd travelled this road before with Cally and he would not – *he could not* – allow history to repeat itself. As Audrey turned to face away from him, Dominic had vowed to take control of the situation before it controlled him.

A sudden sneeze brought him back to the present. He picked at the dried, crusty blood and snot glued to the walls of his nostrils, and wiped away more stains from his lips, chin and stubble with cotton wool pads and a bottle of antiseptic. Then he bound his weak shoulder in tape and bandages like he'd seen athletes with sports injuries do.

Dominic went to the rear of the car, opened the boot and reached for the first aid kit Audrey had insisted on keeping inside for emergencies. He'd teased her for always being over-prepared, but now he was grateful for her efforts. Next to it, in a sealed bag, was the dress belonging to her that he'd worn when he was Megan on the tube platform and sent Dumitru falling to his death. It seemed fitting that something of his late fiancée's was with him as he'd dispatched one of the architects of her demise. It was the only item of Audrey's left; that and a silver ring he'd bought her from a market stall on their last trip to France.

Most of his possessions fitted into a mini backpack by his side – his wallet, keys, passport and a ticket. The remainder were at the flat he'd planned to stay at next but which he had abandoned due to its close proximity to Becca's home. He had an appointment hours from now, and didn't want to risk being spotted in an area where there was going to be such a heavy police presence.

Back in the driver's seat, he slipped the keys in the ignition, plugged his phone into an adapter slotted into the cigarette lighter and waited until there was enough charge for it to come to life. Then he scanned the bookmarked online news sites. His story had progressed, and now crystal-clear images of his own face reflecting back at him from all over the Internet took him by surprise. He'd also been named. According to the reports, Dominic Hammond had revealed himself during a road rage attack on a teenage girl whom he'd threatened to kill. In finding Evan Williams and then killing Becca, he'd forgotten all about the girl.

His identification was the lead story on every British news website; he sat atop Facebook feeds and was the number-one trending story on Twitter, with thousands upon thousands of users retweeting his pictures. To his dismay, their hashtags also caught his attention. Days ago, opinion on him had been split between those calling him sick and others fascinated by his psyche. Now hashtags like #scum, #coward, #cop-killer, #violentwomanhater and #paedofilth were being thrown around.

'They don't get it,' he muttered. 'Why don't they get it?' He threw the phone on to the passenger seat and it slipped into the footwell. He clenched his fists and reminded himself to be patient, because tomorrow it would all make sense to them. Then he'd be understood as the grieving widower and dad who'd been failed so badly by those who were supposed to help him. They'd know he'd been pushed to take extreme measures through no fault of his own. He was a victim.

The lack of air circulating around the garage added to his fatigue, and he was struck by an overriding urge to sleep. He turned the cooler on, switched off the light and fumbled his way around until he was spread out across the rear seat.

He would need to rethink the rest of his plan and how he would escape London. But that could wait. Everything could wait, for now.

CHAPTER 56

The briefing that followed Becca's murder was like no other Joe had ever attended. It was a sombre affair, underpinned with shellshock, fury and frustration.

There hadn't been enough room to house all the detectives who were offering up their time and skills, so the doors were left wide open for those standing patiently outside in the corridor to hear.

Webster kept running the pads of her fingertips on one hand over her bitten nails on the other as she spoke and listened. She tried to keep the tone of her voice deliberate, but from her drawn face, it was clear she too had been deeply affected by Becca's death. She and Nikhat took it in turns to delegate lines of inquiry to different departments and teams. Bryan looked beside himself, like he'd lost a family member. Joe recalled that his desk contained framed photographs of his four daughters and assumed that, with Becca being a close family friend, he'd considered her a fifth.

'Early – and I stress these are very early – autopsy reports suggest Becca was attacked with her baton,' Webster said. 'Her head injuries were so severe that even if paramedics had been able to resuscitate her, it was unlikely she'd have led a normal life again.' The room muttered its disgust.

No one verbalised it, but Joe was sure everyone who knew Becca was thinking the same thing – she was better off dead than severely mentally impaired.

'Her mother, Helen, has a bleed on the brain and is being kept in a medically induced coma,' continued Webster. 'She remains in a serious but stable condition. Evan Williams and Becca's daughter, Maisie, are also still in hospital undergoing psychiatric evaluations, although Evan has been reunited with his parents.'

'I don't need to remind anyone that we need to find Dominic Hammond before he attacks again,' Nikhat interjected. 'We have public sympathy on our side – that's eight million pairs of eyes in London alone looking out for him. I want each credible phone call logged and followed up, no matter how long it takes. I want uniforms out there, CCTV scanned from streets, shops and public transport. I want us to throw everything we have at this. For the sake of Beccs and our other colleagues in the emergency services who have lost their lives – William Burgess, Zoe Ellis and Garry Dawson – let's nail that bastard quickly.'

Bryan spoke next, but despite Joe's best efforts he couldn't concentrate on what was being said. Quietly, he slipped out of the room and along the corridor, into the gents' toilets.

He sat in a cubicle with the toilet lid down, his head in his hands, feeling as guilty and useless as when Linzi vanished. He should have known his father would find them, he should have been on the lookout for his car. Maybe then he could have protected her. Now he had Becca's death on his conscience and he didn't know how he was going to live with it.

Outside, the corridor gradually became noisier and Joe assumed the briefing had come to an end. He unlocked the stall door and took a step back when Webster entered the bathroom.

'How are you feeling, Joe?' she asked. It was the first time she'd called him by his Christian name.

'Okay, ma'am,' he replied, but he struggled to convince her.

'You didn't miss much else. There are CCTV sightings of Hammond around the same time as we pulled up outside Becca's house,' she said. 'Looking at a preliminary timeline, as we were waiting for Specialist Firearms Command, he escaped through the rear doors and into an alley we should've had covered.'

'Any idea in which direction he went?'

'Not yet, no. But your VIIDO colleagues have volunteered to start going through the footage to piece it together. We're already getting hundreds of tip-offs from members of the public who think they've spotted him.'

Joe nodded. 'What can I do next?'

'You can go home and get some rest. I've just sent Bryan and Nikhat home too. I need you all at your best tomorrow.'

He didn't have the energy to protest. 'Okay,' he replied, and made his way to the door.

'You have to remember it's Hammond's fault that she's dead and not ours,' she added.

But Joe knew that if he'd returned DC Nigel Morris's call and read the email about Audrey's death sooner, he might have put two and two together and reached Becca's house in time. Her murder was on him.

CHAPTER 57

The uplights attached to the exterior of Joe's apartment building bathed the inside with a milky-white glow.

It was an unwritten rule of his and Matt's that whoever was last to bed had the job of closing the blinds and checking the front door was locked. But by the time Joe arrived home, soon after midnight, the blinds were the last things on his mind. All he needed was to feel the skin of his partner against his own in the sanctuary of their bed. First he slipped off his trousers and shirt, screwed them up and threw them into the kitchen dustbin. They were stained with Becca's blood, and he never wanted to see or wear them again. Then he went back downstairs to examine his reflection in the bathroom mirror; the bruising from his black eyes was fading and his skin looked paler than ever. His stomach was empty but he wasn't hungry. He couldn't remember the last time he'd sat down and eaten a meal that hadn't come from the inside of a wrapper or a vending machine.

Earlier that evening, he'd texted Matt to inform him he'd be late, but offered no reason for it, vaguely blaming work. And he resisted mentioning anything about his unplanned journey to Leighton Buzzard or how the rest of the day had unfolded so catastrophically.

Matt was a light sleeper until he inserted his foam earplugs, then he became oblivious to the world around him. Tonight, Joe was grateful that he didn't stir when he slipped his arm over Matt's chest. He didn't want to talk. He just wanted the comfort of silence.

However, try as he might and as exhausted as he felt, Joe was forced to accept sleep wasn't going to be an option. His head wouldn't cease from spinning as he tossed and turned, and he feared waking up Matt. So he climbed out of bed and made his way upstairs and into the dining area. He sat and slouched across the table, propping his head up with the palm of his hand and letting his hair flop into his eyes. Oscar followed him up, hoping he might be on the receiving end of a late-night walk. As he brushed back and forth against Joe's bare legs, his owner took little notice. He was too preoccupied with London's skyline beyond the window.

Because of its unparalleled view across East London, their flat had been considerably more expensive than others in the same block, especially with the capital's overinflated prices. Sometimes he lost himself in the brick-and-steel horizon, contemplating what Linzi or his estranged mum might have thought about how his life had panned out. He'd have liked them to be proud of how different he was from the man who'd raised him. Perhaps Matt had been right, and moving forward had been the best thing for his mother to have done. If he'd accepted Linzi's fate like she had, perhaps Becca might still be alive.

In the distance, he could make out a tiny red flashing light, way up in the sky. It was affixed to the roof of Canary Wharf's fifty-storey One Canada Square and warned aircraft of its presence. Above the skyscraper, random white streaks of lightning illuminated the building and those around it, followed by booming claps of distant thunder. The rain wouldn't be long to follow, he assumed, grinding to a halt the ragged heatwave that had held the city hostage for more than a fortnight. It couldn't arrive soon enough, he thought.

He picked up Matt's iPad and it flickered to life. He scrolled through the online news feeds. Becca had become the front-page headline in every early edition of the following day's newspapers. His colleague and friend was the perfect story – a hero cop slaughtered by the serial killer she was hunting; an abducted child found in her home alongside her orphaned Down's syndrome daughter. It wrote itself.

Many chose the angle of the fearless single mum who'd sacrificed her own life to save two children and her mother. The broadsheets illustrated their stories with official photographs of Becca supplied to them by the Met's press office. He'd only ever known her to wear suits, so it surprised him to see her in a police constable's uniform. For a moment, he wanted to smile at that, but he choked up instead. She'd had such a bright future ahead of her. And Joe had allowed it to be taken away.

As he continued to read, Oscar lay on the floor against Joe's feet. He reached down to rub the dog's belly and scratch him behind the ears, and wished people were as uncomplicated as pets.

Of all the images of the day, there was one that remained with him more than the others. It wasn't of his battered, bloodied and almost unrecognisable colleague. Nor was it her mother being stretchered into the back of an ambulance or the haunting blankness on Evan Williams's face.

It was of Maisie, and her small hands held tightly over her blindfold, crying and aware that something awful had happened around her, but too frightened to see it. In her six years in this heartless world she had lost two mums, and there was a chance her grandmother might not pull through either. That too would weigh heavily upon his shoulders.

The gentle patter of rain that began to fall against an open window gradually became heavier. A rumble of thunder startled Oscar. He barked twice, then ran down the stairs and to the safety of a sleeping Matt. Joe made his way to the window and stretched his arms outside. He grabbed at the cascade of droplets and the rain felt good against his skin.

Joe looked below him at the cobbled roads that surrounded his building, the way American tourists expected all London's streets to be. Walking tours passed his home daily, usually made up of foreign tourists on Jack the Ripper treks. They made their way to Whitechapel, a stone's throw away from the flat. A hundred and thirty years later, and Jack had still not been identified. Now he was looking for his own serial murderer, but this one had a name and a face.

Joe had worked a double shift and was physically exhausted. As regular as clockwork, every four hours he swallowed more of his migraine tablets to keep staving it off. When this was all over and when Becca's killer had been caught, then he would accept the mother of all headaches without complaint. He'd lock himself in a pitch-black, silent room and let it do its worst. Then he'd reschedule his cancelled appointment with the specialist at the hospital in Old Street, and admit he'd not taken his advice and that he wasn't looking after his health. He would start seeing his counsellor again, and he would be the husband Matt deserved.

Just not now.

Now, he was going to catch Becca's killer.

He went back downstairs, showered in the dark and then fumbled quietly inside drawers for fresh clothes unblemished by death. He took Matt's car keys from the hook by the front door, left him a brief note promising to explain all later and telling him that he loved him, and made his way out of the building and towards the car parked further down the road.

As the rain bounced off his hunched shoulders, he vowed that if it was the last thing he did, he would predict Dominic Hammond's next move and beat him to it.

CHAPTER 58

Dominic didn't give Becca's body a second thought as he stepped over it and made his way towards the window. He glanced between a crack in the curtains to see her street surrounded by armed police. Some knelt down in plain view, others were hidden behind marked cars and vans, and all had him in their sights.

He panicked and went to move, but his body wouldn't allow it. He was frozen in the moment but felt eerily calm, almost resigned and ready for the impending impact as each weapon expelled a hail of bullets in his direction.

Crashing thunder claps and the sound of rain lashing against the garage's corrugated iron roof woke Dominic with a start from his dream. It was the noisy, bucketing rain that had made him think he was under fire. Upon opening his eyes, his pitch-black surroundings meant he couldn't decipher where he was. And for the briefest of moments, he wondered whether it might not have been a dream and if this was death.

He fumbled around for his phone and, turning on the torch app, realised he was still in Audrey's car. His muscles and joints ached as though he'd been hit by a debilitating bout of influenza. His mouth was dry and there was a dull throbbing in his head, nose and shoulder from his brawl with Becca.

His watch read 2.05 a.m. – he'd been asleep for nine hours. But now he needed to move, and to move quickly. Having been identified in the media, it would only be a matter of time before the police discovered the garage rented in John Bingham's name. With a single entrance and exit, he was a sitting duck.

Dominic's clothes were filthy – they were stained with not only his blood, but Becca's and Helen's too. They reeked of his sweat, and needed replacing before he began the final leg of his journey. He slipped them back on and hurried his stiff limbs in the pouring rain towards a large metal Salvation Army clothing bank that he'd run past on his way to the garage. It had been overfilled, and clothes spilled from the hatch. He released a hinge attached to the back, crawled inside and picked out a T-shirt, shirt, suit jacket, jeans and a pair of trainers. He returned to the garage to change into them, then made his way towards a 24-hour petrol station three streets back.

There, he filled his basket with bottles of still water and some male grooming and hygiene products, then hurried out the door before the assistant behind the security screen lifted her head from her mobile phone to notice.

Lightning stabbed at the sky above him as he returned to the garage one last time. He used a disposable razor and the reflective side of a compact disc to shave for the first time since he'd convinced Becca and her colleague he was Megan. Nail scissors from the first aid kit were used to transfer his wavy hair into a short, tight crop, then he slipped on a pair of magnified reading glasses and sprayed his musty-smelling second-hand clothes with deodorant. After cleaning his teeth, he was ready to go.

But when he turned on the car's ignition, nothing happened. He tried it again, then once more before pausing. Finally, he remembered – he had fallen asleep with the air vents open and the cooler turned on. It must have drained the battery. He slammed his fists on the steering wheel, furious, hurting his inflamed collarbone. Taking Audrey's car with him had been part of the plan from the start, and was the reason

291

he had spent so much money rebuilding it. Now, through his own carelessness, he had no choice but to abandon it. He felt like he was letting her down.

Thirty minutes later he was taking shelter under the cover of a kitchen showroom's canopy. Finally, the right vehicle appeared. The second-generation VW Polo was old enough not to have doors that automatically locked when the ignition was switched on, and common enough not to stand out.

With his good arm, Dominic yanked open the door and punched the driver seven times in the head and face, knocking his glasses into the passenger footwell. Then he leaned across the dazed boy to unclip his seatbelt, before dragging him out of the car and dumping him in the empty road. Pulling away, he was pleased to see the petrol tank was three-quarters full. That would be more than enough fuel to help him reach his destination.

The thunder and rain began to ease as he left his old life in London for ever and approached the M20. He turned on the radio and flicked through the dial of stations before settling on one playing late-night love songs. Adele's 'Someone Like You' caught him by surprise. He recalled how Audrey had loved that song, playing the album on repeat while they were holidaying in France. But the night he'd caught her slow-dancing to it on the dimly lit patio with Baptiste was the moment everything changed.

Earlier that week, while playing hide and seek with Baptiste's children, he'd discovered one of them giggling under a bench inside a garage. It was on Dominic's way out that he'd spied a bottle of antifreeze.

According to the limited Internet access his phone offered in the middle of the French countryside, it would take a relatively low dose in Baptiste's wine of choice to bring his holiday to a swift end. For days, Dominic battled with his conscience, until he spotted his adversary in the orangery covertly taking photographs of an unaware Audrey in her swimsuit. Dominic's response was to add the poison to not one but two bottles, just to make sure the job was done properly.

That night – and to Dominic's joy – Baptiste wasted no time in draining his first Shiraz alone. The antifreeze's naturally sweet taste disguised its bitter damage. And because Baptiste was feeling particularly greedy, he quaffed much of the second bottle alone too. A severe stomach ache meant he missed breakfast the next morning as his body attempted to break down the ethylene glycol in his system. Soon after the hallucinations began, Baptiste was stretchered out of the chateau and into the back of an ambulance, his face bereft of the smugness Dominic hated so much.

While the rest of the family took turns in keeping a hospital vigil, Dominic spent the remainder of his holiday occupying the kids, and through them living the childhood he'd never been allowed. He'd also put both wine bottles through two dishwasher cycles before dropping them into the recycling box. When the gendarmerie came to investigate the poisoning, there was no evidence to find. It could have happened in any of the many restaurants Baptiste had visited during his time at the chateau.

Over the following months, Audrey spent her Friday nights travelling straight from the nursery where she worked to the Eurostar terminal at St Pancras. She'd return to Paris to assist her sister and mum with the children while Baptiste remained hospitalised. Although it was impossible to prove, Christine blamed the miscarriage that followed on the stress.

Audrey returned home to Dominic every Sunday night, completely shattered. He held his tongue, despite growing increasingly tired of her choosing her family over him. Eventually, he settled on a way for Audrey to make him her priority again. They would have a baby together.

She had forgotten to pick up a repeat prescription of her contraceptive pill, and that night as he seduced her with alcohol and a delicious home-cooked meal, she initially brushed off his sexual advances. Eventually she succumbed, but insisted he wore a condom – unaware he'd earlier made several pinpricks in the latex. A week later, when she still hadn't found the time to go to the pharmacy, he repeated his tried-and-tested seduction technique. And when, within a month, he was awoken by the sound of Audrey vomiting into the toilet bowl, the blue tick on the pregnancy-testing kit she'd bought confirmed it.

Audrey's Parisian trips grew less frequent, and Dominic watched proudly as her stomach became more pronounced and they planned for the future. The excitable father-to-be booked them into every class available for expectant parents. And, whenever possible, he made sure they were on weekends so that she couldn't travel. She had to rely on text updates regarding Baptiste's wait for a liver donor. On learning they were expecting a son, Dominic couldn't have been happier. And Audrey had decided to name him Etienne after her late grandfather.

But the day Dominic went to work and left his mobile phone at home was his undoing. He returned to find Audrey sitting at their dining room table, her eyes bloodshot and her skin pale. His first concern was that she had lost their baby, and an empty chasm opened up inside him.

'My iPad ran out of battery so I used your phone to get online,' she began. She chose her words carefully, as if they were rehearsed. 'I wanted to type into the search engine "antenatal classes" but the predictive text took over and finished "ant" with "antifreeze". Your history said you'd searched the phrases "how much antifreeze will kill a man" and "antifreeze symptoms".'

She paused to let the silence hang between them. Dominic's heart went from nought to sixty within a beat. It was a foolish mistake not to cover his tracks, and one that he had not repeated since. 'I googled it when Baptiste was taken to hospital and the tests said he'd been poisoned,' he explained.

Audrey's eyes worked their way around her partner's face, searching for signs of deceit. 'Honestly, darling,' he added. 'I know we didn't see eye to eye, but can you honestly see me wanting to hurt him? Or anyone?'

She remained poker-faced, which made him uneasy. 'Baptiste was admitted to hospital on Saturday, August twenty-sixth,' she said. 'And your phone says you looked at this website on Wednesday, August twenty-third.'

Dominic's mind raced through the dwindling options available to him. He could tell the truth and face the consequences, or continue to lie and hope that she chose to believe him. And even though Audrey was neither gullible nor stupid when it came to technology, he opted for the latter, protesting with increasing desperation.

'Remember when we got to France and my phone had problems finding a network?' he reasoned. 'It took, what, three days before I got a signal? It probably put the clock and the dates out of sync.'

'It took a further three days between Baptiste falling ill and the poisoning diagnosis. Why would you suspect antifreeze six days earlier, of all things?' Her arms remained folded, her cold gaze fixed upon his.

They remained like two chess pieces on opposite sides of the board, each waiting for the other's move. Audrey was the first, hurling his phone at him. It clipped his shoulder, then hit the mantelpiece and crashed to the floor. He moved towards her and she caught his cheek with a slap. He responded by grabbing her shoulders and pinning her to the wall.

'You have to believe me,' he begged.

'You are a liar,' she yelled. 'A sick, twisted liar.'

Her words hurt him like no other woman's ever had. 'Please, Audrey.'

'Let go of me or I will scream this fucking building down.'

Dominic reluctantly obliged, and she stormed off to the bedroom. He followed her, watching her drag a suitcase from under the bed and stuff it with clothes.

'You're not going to leave me,' he said.

'Watch me,' she replied defiantly. 'Everything you told me about the evil things your mother did – well, you are no better than her. I am not going to share my house and my child with you. We are going far away.'

'No!' yelled Dominic. 'You can't take my baby.'

'I can and I will.'

Dominic felt a red mist descend upon him. It was the first time in years that he had been unable to control it, and he never had in front of Audrey. He grabbed at her arms, trying to shake sense into her. 'You're not going to be like all the others,' he spat. 'Nobody is ever going to leave me again.' He grabbed her jaw with one hand and pinched her cheeks so tightly that they met inside her mouth. In that moment, he loved her so much that he would rather kill her than allow her to live a life away from his side. But when he saw the same fear in her eyes that Cally had in hers when she'd found him in her halls of residence flat, he let go.

Audrey made good on her promise to scream, only stopping when he shoved her into the wall. She fell into a heap on the floor, landing awkwardly on her wrist with a crack. Only then did he realise how far over the mark he had stepped.

The rest of the night he refused to allow her to go to the hospital's accident and emergency department to get her wrist examined, for fear that once she set foot out the door, she wouldn't return. He used the time to try to convince her that he wasn't responsible for Baptiste's life-changing illness. And as dawn broke, she finally wavered and blamed her pregnancy hormones for her irrational behaviour. Eventually, and convinced that they had reached an understanding, he offered to go to the pharmacy and buy her some painkillers. Only, when he returned just fifteen minutes later, she was gone. The only trace of her was a solitary dress he'd bought for her birthday, hanging on her side of the almost-empty wardrobe, and a silver ring on the chest of drawers.

In the days and weeks that followed, he'd called Audrey's mobile relentlessly, becoming increasingly agitated as to where she and their unborn child were. He left a barrage of voicemails and text messages; sometimes when he was sad and lonely he begged her to return, on other occasions when he lost control of his temper, he threatened her. He didn't know if she was even reading or listening to them.

He asked Pamela, the neighbour downstairs, if she'd seen Audrey leave, and wasn't convinced she was telling the truth when she said no. He turned the entire flat upside down searching for clues, until the police arrived on his doorstep, called by someone concerned he was being burgled.

When he turned up at Audrey's nursery he was informed she was on indefinite sick leave. Then he drove to her parents' Parisian home, only to be told she wasn't there, and he was threatened with violence if he ever returned. Clearly, they'd been warned something serious had occurred between their daughter and him, but not what he'd done to Baptiste, or the police would have already been involved.

Dominic's longing for the love of his life grew all-consuming with each passing week. He'd close his eyes and remember how velvety her pregnant belly had felt when she rubbed oil into her stretch marks. He'd recall how she smelled different, earthier, with another life growing inside her. As the weeks progressed into months, that smell gradually disappeared from the flat.

Two months after Audrey's disappearance, Dominic had yet to set foot back in the engineering company that employed him. After emailing his manager Luke a curt resignation letter, he ignored the barrage of emails threatening legal action for breach of contract. His savings were substantial enough to live off as his need to find Audrey became an obsession.

It wasn't until nine long months after the due date of their boy that a miracle appeared in the post – a letter addressed to Audrey from her bank. An administrative error and data breach meant the envelope was addressed to her, but the top right-hand corner of the letter contained a different one – a new address in West London.

On his arrival at her front door within the hour, he hadn't rehearsed what to say. He decided he would simply throw himself at her mercy instead. Then, when she saw how truly sorry he was, she would allow him inside to meet his son and they could start rebuilding their lives together as a family.

He knocked, and as the door opened and revealed Audrey's face, he thought his legs might give way. He gave her a smile that went unreciprocated.

'*Non!*' she yelled, panicked by his appearance. '*Éloigne-toi de moi.*'

She slammed and locked the door before he could lift his foot over the threshold.

'Audrey, please, I just want to talk,' he began.

'Go away,' she begged. 'Leave us alone.'

Us, he thought. All that separated him from his son was that door and her stubbornness.

'I just want to explain. Back in France I wasn't thinking straight. The thought of losing you to Baptiste became too much to bear, which is why I did what I did. You have to forgive me.'

'I have called the police,' Audrey yelled.

His body tensed when he heard the sound of a baby's cries inside – he was so tantalisingly close to seeing his boy. Dominic rushed towards a window at the side of the property, and through the frosted glass he could just about make out a sliver of light he assumed to be coming from the door of her flat. He rapped on the door again, and when Audrey didn't reply, he banged the palms of his hands against it, then his fists. He could feel the toughened glass begin to wobble in the wooden frame. His last resort would be to smash it.

Eventually the front door opened and his words temporarily left him as he shrank back to the quiet little boy who feared his mother's ire.

'How did you find me?' Audrey demanded.

'All that matters is that I'm here,' he replied. 'What I did – I know it was wrong, but I did it for us.'

'Don't lie to yourself,' she replied, her eyes flitting around the street behind him. 'You did it because of your own insecurities. You did it because, deep inside, you are a bad, broken man.'

'I'm not, I promise you. I just want to see our baby. I've already missed out on so much. It's not fair.'

'You are jealous and manipulative and I don't want you anywhere near him.'

'I've changed, I promise you,' he pleaded. 'Just let me prove it to you.'

'No.'

'You have to!' he snapped, and slammed the palms of his hands on the door over and over again.

Suddenly two uniformed police officers, a man and a woman, appeared from behind him. He felt relief; all he had to do was persuade them his motives were well intentioned and they would talk Audrey round for him.

'Step back from the door,' the female officer began.

'I'm glad you're here,' he said. 'I need you to make my fiancée let me see our son.'

'He's not my fiancé and he's harassing me and my baby,' Audrey replied.

'Sir, I asked you to take a step back. I won't ask again,' the female PC reiterated, more sternly.

'I'm not going to hurt her; I'm not going to hurt either of them.'

'He's been aggressive to me in the past,' said Audrey. 'He fractured my wrist and sent me threatening messages. I can show you. I have them saved on my phone.'

'No, they were sent in anger,' he protested. 'I sent good messages too, telling her how much I love her . . .'

By the look of contempt on the female officer's face, Dominic knew whose side she'd chosen. He turned to her male partner. 'I'm just trying to see my kid,' he said. 'You can see that, right?'

'Do as she asks please, mate,' he replied in a less confrontational manner.

Dominic watched helplessly as the female officer followed Audrey into the flat, where they remained. *A14117*, read the identification embroidered in white lettering on the dark epaulettes of her uniform.

He made a mental note of it, as he would make a complaint about her later. He paced up and down, and twice approached the doorway only to be blocked by the male officer. 'It's better if you stay here,' the PC said. 'I'm telling you for your own good, okay?'

Dominic reluctantly nodded until, to his dismay, Audrey appeared again, carrying a suitcase. She wouldn't even look him in the eye as she made her way to the side of the road and towards her old Mercedes. The female PC followed, with Etienne in a car seat. Dominic was mesmerised by the sight of his son under the street lights – a mop of blond curls, two closed eyes and a red woollen cardigan. The child, who had the potential to erase everything bad that had ever happened in his life, every terrible decision he had made and everyone who had ever rejected him, was being snatched away from him again.

Enough was enough. They couldn't be kept apart any longer. With all his strength, he caught the male PC off guard and elbowed him in the stomach, before shoving him to the ground. Then he took his opportunity and ran towards Audrey.

'No!' he yelled, and reached to try to grab the car seat. 'He's mine, let me have him!' The female PC turned and tried to shield the baby from him, which only served to increase his rage. He grabbed her shoulder, spinning her around, banging the baby seat into his leg. The knock woke Etienne up and his face curled as he began to cry.

'Give him to me!' Dominic shouted as the male officer appeared behind him and grabbed hold of Dominic's arm to twist it behind his back. But Dominic was too quick and gave him a sharp elbow to the groin, incapacitating him. This time, Dominic managed to attach one hand to the car seat, pulling it towards him.

'Get off!' screamed Audrey, dropping her suitcase. 'You're scaring him!'

'He's *mine*,' Dominic repeated over the noise of Etienne's wailing, and he yanked the car seat harder, pulling it out of one of the female

PC's hands. *Just one more jerk will do it*, he thought, *just one more jerk and I'll have my son.*

He didn't see what was in the female PC's hand as she lifted it to head height; only the molecules of spray being discharged from it. And, by then, it was too late to shield his eyes from the bitter sting. Blinded, he let go of the car seat to protect his face with his hands. Then he felt a blow to his stomach from a foreign object, then two more to the backs of his legs, forcing him to drop to his knees.

Dominic couldn't see anything, but he heard the car doors open and the sound of luggage being thrown inside.

'I'll strap him in,' he heard the female PC say as her colleague handcuffed him.

'No, please no,' Dominic pleaded. 'I'm begging you.' But in his heart of hearts, he knew the battle was lost. Etienne had been taken from him a second time.

He sobbed at the sound of the engine turning over, and as the car pulled away at speed, another vehicle arrived and he was pulled to his feet and thrown into the back of a police van.

For weeks afterwards, Dominic frequented the area around Audrey's flat, awaiting her return. She'd only taken one suitcase with her, and that wasn't enough to hold all the worldly belongings of a grown woman and a baby. Finally, he witnessed a neighbour leaving the building, and he grabbed his chance to enter.

'You don't live here,' barked the man, considerably taller and broader than Dominic. He blocked the doorway with a muscular arm.

'I'm a friend of Audrey Moreau's,' he replied. The man looked him up and down. Three small teardrops had been inked on his cheek, under his right eye. 'I was passing, so I thought I'd see if she was in.'

'Nobody told you? Sorry, mate, but she died.'

He glared at the stranger, unsure he'd heard correctly. Why would he say something so preposterous?

'Died?' he repeated.

'Yeah, a few weeks back.' His arm relaxed. 'Her and her nipper. Car accident. Spoke to her parents last week as they were clearing her place out. Sorry.'

'You're sure it was Audrey?'

'Yeah, the French girl. What was her kid called . . . Etienne, yeah, that was it.'

The man looked at Dominic apologetically and closed the door behind him, leaving Dominic to process the news alone. He steadied himself against the wall as the last remaining fragments of the world he longed for crumbled to dust.

Weeks later, Dominic was sitting inside the West London Coroner's Court in Fulham, silently listening to the whole sorry story of his partner and son's deaths, and those who had failed them. And when he learned through a private investigator of the two Romanians' roles, he was physically sick.

It took a complete breakdown before Dominic admitted himself to a psychiatric hospital for help. But there was little any expert or any medication could do to stop him from reliving the last moments of being with Audrey and Etienne, over and over again. Gradually, Dominic recognised what his doctors couldn't – there was one thing he could do for himself and the people who'd been stolen from him. And that was to punish the six people who were to blame.

And here he was, mission accomplished, his vow fulfilled, with just one thing left to do. Everything he had worked so hard for, all the sacrifices he had made and every single drop of blood on his hands had been worth it. For the first time in more than three years, he felt satisfied.

A motorway road sign caught his eye. *Dover – 35 miles*, it read, and the corners of his mouth inched upwards.

'I'm coming home,' he said.

CHAPTER 59

Joe returned to the major incident room of Operation Chamber four hours after he left.

A clock on the wall approached 4 a.m., but despite the early hour, the murder inquiry was still bustling with activity. He automatically made for Becca's desk, but had second thoughts. He stared at the paperwork spread across it and recalled her telling him how her colleagues avoided using it because of the mess. Now, and despite the crowded room, it was being left alone out of respect for their fallen colleague. He chose a desk in the corner of the office instead.

It was closer to CS Webster's Perspex cube, and he took a moment to watch as she spoke into a mobile phone and typed on a keyboard. Since he'd seen her earlier, an extra button on her blouse had been unfastened, and her usually tight, neat bun was unclipped. Her hair rested unevenly on her shoulders, as if she had run frustrated fingers through it many, many times. He doubted she had been home in days.

Joe paid seventy pence for a machine to fill a polystyrene cup with something resembling tea, and he swallowed another migraine tablet.

'I thought she'd sent you home,' came Nikhat's voice from behind him.

'Likewise,' Joe replied, turning his head and pinching his eyes, which stung more than he could ever remember.

'Are you busy? I've had a copy of Audrey Moreau's inquest notes biked over to me. Could you go through them and summarise? I know it's not strictly "super-recogniser" stuff but . . .'

' . . . it's all hands on deck, of course.'

Nikhat passed him an A4 brown envelope, and, armed with a note-book, a yellow highlighter pen and a biro, Joe began to carefully read through each page, line by line.

After turning the final page, he approached two uniformed detectives to assist him with some background research. Almost two hours later, he sat back in his chair, his muscles tense and his head spinning. All the pieces had just slipped into place.

◆ ◆ ◆

The first cool breeze in a fortnight made its way through an open window behind Webster, rattling the plastic beads chaining the vertical blinds together. The storm Joe had hoped might wash his guilt away had only taken the humidity of the heatwave with it. Outside, he noted the darkness beginning to give way to the pinks and oranges of the early morning sunrise. It was a new day for everyone but Becca.

'This is what we know about Dominic Hammond so far,' began Webster. 'He has no form, no outstanding warrants, no county court judgements and no next of kin. His last known address dates back two and a half years, no money has gone in or out of his bank account and he is not on the electoral register. After the death of Audrey and his son, he sought psychiatric help and admitted himself to St Theresa's Hospital in Walthamstow, where he remained for a month, and then spent the following two months as an outpatient before he dropped off the grid. His colleagues at the letting agency where he worked tell us he goes by the name John Bingham and not Hammond. DS Russell, can you update us on what you've found?'

A dozen pairs of eyes fixed on Joe. Three of the detectives inside Webster's room he didn't recognise, one he recalled having met seven years earlier on a half-day training course, and another he'd seen once before at an investigation when he'd just graduated. Meanwhile, Nikhat and a still-distraught Bryan flanked him.

Not entirely comfortable being the centre of attention, Joe took several deep breaths and cleared his throat before briefing them on why Becca and PC Morris had arrested Hammond and how he'd given officers the slip at the hospital where he was being treated for an allergic reaction to CS spray.

'I'm convinced that Hammond blames Becca for everything that followed. If it wasn't for her, he would have got to his family and they'd still be alive.'

'Why did he spare her colleague?' asked Nikhat.

'I can only assume it was because Becca helped Audrey and her son into the car, sprayed him and used the baton to subdue him. Meanwhile, Audrey's car was travelling on the M4 when a white van clipped it and sent it spinning into the path of six other vehicles. It was hit many times and flipped over on to its roof. The van driver fled from the scene on foot, and I believe it was the first victim, Stefan Dumitru. He was captured on CCTV later at Gunnersbury underground, catching the tube towards his home in Mile End. I think Darius Cheban was his passenger. We know they'd been inside the vehicle at some point, because their prints were found all over it and on empty bottles of vodka inside the van. They were arrested two days later, but had an alibi for their whereabouts from other members of the Romanian community. Our colleagues who were investigating couldn't get enough evidence to convince the CPS they had a case, so they were never charged.

'Now, we move on to the inquest into Audrey and Etienne's deaths. It reveals a catalogue of errors that followed the crash itself. The murdered firefighter, Garry Dawson, was in the first rig that attended the scene and was responsible for checking inside each vehicle to prioritise who needed help first. He admitted later that he only saw Audrey, unconscious in the front seat. But the brunt of the impact had dislodged Etienne's car seat, which hadn't been secured properly, and thrown it into the rear and under luggage so his body couldn't be seen. It wasn't until his mother had been cut from the car forty minutes later that the boy was discovered, suffocated. The coroner reported he might have survived if he'd been found earlier.

'Over in Turnham Green, the ambulance service's computer system went into meltdown following the high number of calls about the terror attack in Hammersmith the same night. Many of their ambulances and first responder vehicles were diverted there. But paramedic William Burgess and his rapid response vehicle were supposed to be first at the scene of Audrey's accident. Because control's computers were unable to send directions to his TerraFix, he relied on his phone and a road map instead. However, he became disorientated and ended up in a cul-de-sac in a disused industrial estate.

'I believe that Hammond blamed all four of these men – and Becca – for the deaths of his estranged family. His revenge was to push Dumitru under the tube train where he'd alighted the night of the accident, and he waterboarded Cheban using the same type of alcohol found in their van. Burgess had his eyes removed and his fingers shredded as his punishment for getting lost, and Dawson's body was mutilated by the equipment he'd have used to free Etienne from the car if he'd spotted him.'

Joe paused to get the measure of the room. To his relief, his colleagues were looking at him intently rather than shaking their heads.

'Where did the nurse come into it?' someone asked.

'Zoe Ellis's phone records, texts and calls reveal she was in a relationship with someone for at least four months. The number doesn't correspond with Hammond's work phone, but that doesn't mean he doesn't have an unregistered one. Her friends and colleagues never met the man she was seeing, and despite her being an active social media user, he appears nowhere on her accounts. She kept their relationship very, very private. She trusted him, so when he lured her into the hospital storeroom with the promise of sex, it was likely she agreed. Her death looked worse than it probably was, if that makes sense, because the initial post-mortem report reveals she died from a massive overdose of morphine, before many of the syringes were injected into her. The others died prolonged deaths and he tortured them, but not her. He had feelings for her.'

'How had she wronged him?' asked Webster.

'Audrey Moreau didn't die, like her son, at the scene of the accident. She was unconscious when she was admitted to the hospital's trauma centre with severe head injuries. Then she began to wake up and, in her confused and distressed state, became combative. A trauma doctor wanted to induce unconsciousness, and used the drug Propofol so that a tube could be inserted down her throat to help with her breathing. Later, nurse Zoe Ellis, sleep-deprived and coming to the end of an active double shift in which victims of the terror attack were also being admitted, checked on Audrey and noted she was showing signs of coming round again. In the chaos, she picked up the wrong notes, and because she's a qualified nurse prescriber, she was allowed to administer drugs. She gave Audrey a dose of morphine that, while not a large quantity, when mixed with an anaesthetic, proved fatal.'

Joe put his notes down on the table. 'I haven't had the time to discover whether Ellis, Dawson or Burgess faced disciplinary procedures, but regardless of whether they did or didn't, whatever punishment they may have been given was not enough to satisfy Hammond. I think he brooded on it for a very long time. People can become obsessed by hate, even when it's directed towards the wrong people. They can keep their loathing bottled up inside for years and years, until eventually it consumes them. I think that's what happened with Hammond.

Each of the six deaths, including Becca's, were born out of his need for revenge. Each murder is about him getting his own back on the people he believes killed his family.'

'Is there anyone else mentioned in the inquest who he might be targeting?'

'None that I can see.'

Heads turned as the door opened and a uniformed female PC entered. 'Ma'am,' she directed at Webster, 'the suspect's work-issue mobile phone has been briefly switched on again. We've triangulated his number and he recently passed a tower, heading south on the M20.'

'Shit, he's left London,' said Nikhat. 'Where does that road lead?'

'Dover, I think,' Joe replied.

'Why? What's his link to there?'

As a super-recogniser, in his spare time Joe didn't just examine recent photographs of idents, he'd put historic ones to memory too. A name, a face and a location suddenly collided.

'John Bingham,' he said eagerly. 'That's the name of Lord Lucan, the earl who murdered his children's nanny, then vanished without trace in the 1970s. Perhaps using his name, Hammond's telling us what he's going to do next? Everyone thinks Lucan left the country at a cross-Channel port. I think that's what Hammond is doing. He's done his work here – now he's going to Dover to catch a ferry and escape to France.'

CHAPTER 60

'What's the mass risk? Do you believe he's armed?'

Area Commander Andrew Beech asked his questions with urgency. As her senior in the chain of command, CS Webster had been answering to him throughout the investigation. He was a man hovering somewhere in his fifties, with a thick head of red hair and piercing hazel eyes. His position as Gold Commander meant he was in charge of the manhunt's resources.

'We don't know what the mass risk is,' said Joe. 'We can only go on what we know about him. His kills have all been meticulously researched and executed. It's my view that he's capable of anything right now.'

'Why France?'

'It's where Audrey Moreau's parents live. Perhaps he has unfinished business with them too?'

'Is he likely to try to hurt anyone boarding the ferry, or while on it?'

'We can't be sure.'

Beech rubbed his chin. 'He could get flagged by border control or passport officials before boarding and become detained that way.'

'That would be the best-case scenario. But if Hammond can murder six people including a police officer without getting caught, I don't doubt he's managed to procure a false passport from somewhere.'

'Is it feasible to stop the ferry from leaving until we've searched it?' asked Nikhat.

'If we had intelligence that it was a certainty he was on board, then yes, it would be possible,' said Webster. 'But we just can't be sure. Plus an evacuation would be too chaotic. The ferry operator tells us it's full to capacity every day this week. A cheap-break offer in a newspaper means it's going to be busy down there.'

'You mentioned earlier that forty-nine boats a day leave from that port. How do we even know which one he'll be on?' asked Beech.

'The journeys are by booking only, and as he's set off early, I reckon he's got whatever name he's using down for the first trip of the day,' Joe replied. 'It's for passengers travelling by foot. He won't want to hang around in Dover longer than necessary and risk getting caught.'

Beech eventually agreed to deploy a dozen officers from the team to Dover, and contacted colleagues at Kent Police and the local Port of Dover Police to inform them of the operation. Kent Police also sent eight members from its armed response unit as backup to board the boat, plus plain-clothed officers on dry land to try to capture Hammond before he made his way on to the ferry.

En route to the coast in a convoy of police vehicles, Joe was relieved to receive word that Dominic's phone had been switched on again and that triangulation had pinpointed it in the vicinity of the port. His theory was looking increasingly likely to be correct.

With the first ferry to Calais leaving at 8.25 a.m., the race was on.

◆ ◆ ◆

The team arrived with only minutes to spare, and they briefed their Dover colleagues as they raced to board it. Passenger logs offered no clues as to the name that Hammond had booked his place under. With so much space to cover and so many holidaymakers, they split up and spread out. The armed police examined the toilets, lifeboats, inside and under vehicles in the lower deck, staff quarters, the freight drivers' lounge and even the children's play areas.

Joe rooted his feet to the rubber-clad decking moments after the ferry left the port. He looked straight ahead, his nose drawing in deep salty breaths and his mouth exhaling them from behind gritted teeth. It had been four years since he had last travelled by water. A two-week honeymoon to Australia had found him and Matt journeying to the Great Barrier Reef. However, soon after setting sail the nausea had begun, and for much of the choppy journey, Joe had been on his hands and knees on the catamaran's stern, helplessly spewing the previous evening's barbecue ribs over the side. He had vowed there and then never to go anywhere by boat again.

Today, the choice had been taken out of his hands. The ferry was a hundred times the size of the offending catamaran and it should have rendered him less sensitive to the rolling waves. But his overly acute internal-balance-sensing system was once again winning out. He kept staring at the fixed, steady horizon to ease himself of his seasickness. He could just about make out the Calais coastline as the boat chugged through the crests and troughs of the waves, a lasting reminder of the previous night's storm. Above, a sky of dark, ominous clouds and more rain loomed.

Other detectives assigned to Operation Chamber were spread out thinly across the boat. With two thousand passengers on board, there were six decks and six hundred vehicles for Dominic Hammond to hide himself in. If he was there, the twenty officers deployed to locate and arrest him had their work cut out for them.

Meanwhile, and with the urge to vomit slowly passing, Joe made his way into the largest of the eateries, a self-service restaurant packed with benches and tables. He blanked out the clatter of cutlery, the shrillness of excited school parties and the insipid sound of panpipe music emitted by tinny speakers. He stood facing away from the horizon, his fists clenched, concentrating on each and every face in that room in turn.

Joe was acutely aware that if he'd gotten it wrong and Hammond wasn't on board, he'd feel like an incompetent idiot after so many resources had been deployed based on his intelligence. And if it turned out at a later date that Hammond had been on that ferry and had remained unrecognised, his reputation and that of the VIIDO was on the line. Any progress he'd made in showing sceptical colleagues the importance of super-recognisers would be for nothing. The only positive outcome was for Dominic Hammond to be on board and for Joe to be the one to find him.

He focused hard and let his brain do what it did best. It processed, disassembled and refined each face, searching for recognition. For three, maybe four faces, force of habit caught him searching for Linzi. He shook his head to get rid of her; the dead would not get in the way of the living again.

Occasionally, he spotted one of his colleagues from London or Kent and they'd give each other a shake of the head. And each time, Joe felt that little bit more beleaguered. He glanced at his watch – a third of the ninety-minute crossing was now almost complete. Panic came hand in hand with the renewed queasiness. He needed a change of location.

He made his way through the restaurant and took a seat in the corner of a heavily populated snack café. When that proved fruitless, he chose the forward deck, where he took another moment to centre himself by glancing at the horizon. The French coastline was growing in size with every passing metre. Meanwhile, both the sky and his mood were growing darker by the minute.

By the time Joe reached the rear of the ferry, he was running out of places to scan faces. They were due to dock within forty minutes, and if Hammond was aboard and the French authorities didn't catch him when he disembarked, he might never surface again.

He looked on as a group of Australian backpackers in brightly coloured waterproof clothing bade farewell to the English leg of their trip with selfies against the backdrop of the island behind them. When they parted, they took shelter from the drizzle and exposed a partial side profile of a man watching England shrink in the distance. Joe stopped in his tracks.

Standing alone, the man was leaning against the white metal railings. He wore silver-framed glasses, ill-fitting mismatched clothing, and his hair was much shorter than the dashboard-camera footage of the man Joe was searching for. The stranger scratched his head, turned slightly and yawned. Joe's photographic memory took in the man's nasal bone, which appeared swollen and slightly angular. He examined the depth of his eye sockets and the droop of his brows, the anatomical variation of his cheekbones, the width of his lips, the dimple of his chin. Finally, he spotted the tear in his earlobe. All of this, he calculated in no more than two seconds.

It was then Joe knew for certain that he had recognised Dominic Hammond.

CHAPTER 61

The serial killer who had brutally beaten Becca to death was standing in front of him. Joe couldn't breathe – his throat felt constricted and his heart and brain were in competition to see which one could race the fastest. He needed help.

Pulling his phone slowly from his pocket, he dialled Nikhat. It rang twice before the empty battery symbol appeared and the screen went black.

'Fuck,' he muttered.

He turned his head, hoping to spot one of his colleagues close by, but with one officer for every hundred passengers, it might take time. And he couldn't risk leaving Hammond alone to disappear again.

Joe moved closer, so that just five metres separated them. He removed his handcuffs from his stab-proof vest pocket, cleared his throat and took a deep breath. 'Dominic Hammond,' he began, the wind carrying the name forwards.

The man ahead turned, and a smile slowly crept across his face. Hammond gave no indication that he was surprised to have been located nor if he planned to fight his way out of the corner he was backed into. Joe remained on high alert for the latter.

'You found me then, Detective Sergeant Russell . . . Nice to see you again.'

'You need to come with me, Dominic.'

'No, I'm afraid I don't.'

'There's nowhere for you to go.' Joe looked around to emphasise the point, and Hammond laughed.

'You think?' He nodded towards the choppy waters below.

Joe took a step closer. Hammond responded by moving his hands to grasp the railings behind him more firmly. Joe calculated that – at chest height – it wouldn't take much effort for Hammond to swing his legs over them and drop into the deep. He stopped.

'You won't survive it.'

'Who says I want to?'

Small droplets of water splashed on to Joe's brow. The drizzle was developing into a heavier rain. The ferry hit a swell and dipped, causing bile to rise up from his stomach and into his throat. He swallowed it back down and it didn't go unnoticed.

'Struggling to find your sea legs, Joseph?' Hammond asked. Joe didn't like hearing him use his full name.

'It's over,' he responded. 'You won't get to France without us arresting you. And even if by some miracle you did, our French counterparts are waiting for you on the other side.'

'You make a lot of assumptions.'

'As you're on a ferry and France is our only destination, they're more like certainties.'

'Then, please, tell me – as you appear to be the expert on my travel plans – why am I going there?'

'To target Audrey's family or to disappear. It's my job to bring you back and to stop you doing either. You've caused enough people enough pain.'

'Pain is relative. What I inflicted upon the names on my list was physical and fleeting. What they did to me, to my family? That runs so much deeper and lasts a lot longer. But I doubt that you have much idea how it feels to be really hurt by anyone or anything, do you?'

Joe immediately thought of Linzi and his father. 'Now who's the one making assumptions?'

'Come on then, Joseph, try to convince me you have any idea what it feels like to be me.'

Joe knew from his police training that when trying to talk someone around to your way of thinking, finding common ground is crucial. He briefly considered revealing his own circumstances in the hope Hammond might believe he wasn't alone. But something held him back.

'This is about you, not me,' he said.

'I thought as much. You really don't have a clue.'

The rain dripped from Joe's forehead to his cheeks and he brushed back his wet hair. He blinked hard, unsure if it was the Channel's salty spray or something else blurring his vision. Around them, nearby passengers made their way under cover, leaving the two men alone.

'I'll tell you who knows what hurt feels like,' said Joe. 'The little girl whose mum you beat to death in front of her. No matter what you might think Becca had done to you, her daughter didn't deserve to see any of that.'

'She saw nothing. She was blindfolded and buried herself behind her grandmother's back. And don't give me that "what you might *think* Becca did to you" bullshit. I know full well what your colleague did. I was there. You were not.'

'The night Audrey and Etienne died, you were being abusive and threatening. It was Becca's job to protect them from you. What else was she supposed to do?'

Hearing the names of his loved ones coming from his enemy's mouth appeared to sting Hammond. He threw his wet glasses to the ground. 'Audrey was taking my son away from me *again*, so of course I was angry – any decent parent would be. Should I have just stood there and waved them off? Don't be so naïve.'

'Try to see it from a police officer's perspective. Becca saw a scared mum trying to protect her child from a man who had a history of violence towards her.'

'You didn't see the way your friend looked at me,' he spat. 'Like I was dog shit on the sole of her shoes. She wouldn't listen to a word I had to say. She was deliberately aggressive and she had no reason to be.'

'You had fractured Audrey's wrist in a fight once before. Becca told her colleague that night she'd seen abusive texts you'd sent to her – hundreds of them.'

Hammond shook his head. 'No, it was just bruising.'

'She showed Becca a photograph of her wrist in plaster.'

'Then it was an accident. I don't remember . . . she must have come at me, maybe I pushed her and she fell. She can't blame that on me.'

The ferry dipped again and Joe lost his footing. He slipped forwards and Hammond responded by turning his body like he was ready to jump overboard. Joe held his hands up in front of him, indicating he wasn't coming any closer.

'What blame do you take in any of this, Dominic?' Joe asked. 'Surely you can't believe you're completely innocent? And why did Audrey want to leave you in the first place? If you're as wronged as you make out you are, she'd have had no reason to run away not once, but twice. If you'd left them alone that night, she and Etienne would probably still be alive right now.'

'Stop using their names!' Hammond yelled. He glared at Joe like it was the first time he'd ever contemplated that he might have had a role to play in their deaths. Then his eyes turned as dark as the skies above them. Joe clenched his fists, hoping Hammond might launch at him. He would take his chances against the rage of a psychopath if it meant Hammond let go of his grip on the railings.

'You don't know what the fuck you're talking about!' Hammond continued, taking one hand off them and jabbing his index finger at Joe. 'None of this was my fault! Stefan Dumitru, Darius Cheban, William Burgess, Garry Dawson, Zoe Ellis and Becca Vincent. Every one of them was responsible for killing my family, not me. If your friend had strapped Etienne in his seat properly, he would still be alive.'

'If you hadn't gone to her house to terrorise her, Audrey and Etienne would never have left their flat.'

'Don't try to lay the blame at my feet.'

'How about Zoe Ellis's baby. Who killed that?'

'What are you talking about? She didn't have a baby.'

'She was three months pregnant when you murdered her.'

Hammond's eyes widened. 'You're lying,' he said.

'Not according to the results of the post-mortem. She was almost twelve weeks gone. The first trimester, isn't that what they call it?'

The boat pitched, but Hammond didn't budge. Joe wondered if he was trying to recall a sign he might have missed that his girlfriend was carrying his child.

'That's two children you've sent to their graves now, isn't it?' Joe added.

Hammond didn't move, and continued glaring at Joe as if he hoped his enemy was about to admit he was lying. And Joe knew the revelation had wrong-footed him.

'You know, Dominic, throughout all the effort we put into finding you, a tiny part of me began to give you a grudging respect. I can't remember the last time I read about someone getting away with so many killings in such a short space of time. They must have taken meticulous research and planning. I assumed you must have such a powerful reason for doing what you were doing. But I was wrong, wasn't I? You weren't avenging their deaths like the hero you think you are. You were finding other people to blame so you don't have to look at yourself.'

As the heavens opened with a torrent of rainfall, it was difficult for Joe to tell if it was rain or tears cascading down the killer's cheeks.

'It must be so easy for you to stand there and judge me when you have no idea what my life has been like,' Hammond fumed.

'And vice versa, Dominic. You've made all kinds of assumptions about me and the people you killed so that it fits in with your narrative. Like you, I've had shit times, and I will continue to have shit times. But I don't blame everyone else for them. If you're so convinced your actions are the right ones, you'll come with me and everything you say will go down on record so the world knows your truth.'

Hammond sneered. 'Look at you, pretty boy,' he said. 'What could possibly be so wrong with your life?'

Joe paused to weigh up the pros and cons of what he was about to say next. 'I'm thirty-three years old, and by the time I reach forty, I'll be almost blind,' he replied.

Hammond cocked his head to one side like he didn't believe him.

'I've built my career on my photographic memory and never forgetting a face, but within seven years I'll have virtually no eyesight left,' Joe continued. 'It's called macular degeneration. Sometimes I'll lose my vision for a few minutes at a time or I'll get shadowy central vision, distorted fuzzy vision, migraines, dry eyes . . . and it's fucking my eyesight up.'

Joe recalled the shock of his diagnosis when, after extensive testing, specialists at London's Moorfields Eye Hospital had informed him of the damage to his macula, a small area in the centre of his retina. It was the part he needed for sharp central vision and it allowed him to see objects straight ahead. His case was rare in one so young. It was also incurable.

The more pressure he put on himself to do his job and find his sister, the more damage he was causing. He was already getting blank spots in his central vision, and although he wouldn't go completely blind, eventually he would be unable to write, drive a car or recognise a face. The diagnosis also brought with it a time limit on finding Linzi, so it became a full-time obsession, eventually leading to a breakdown.

'Boo. Fucking. Hoo,' Hammond replied. 'At least you'll still have your life. Do you know what Audrey and Etienne's lives were worth? Two paragraphs in the *Evening Standard*.'

'You can't measure a person's worth by the column inches in a newspaper! The crash happened the same night as the Hammersmith terror attacks, so of course they were going to make the headlines.'

'What about the inquest months later? That was a whitewash. The coroner didn't have the balls to admit that four people who were supposed to save lives failed at their jobs. Your friend didn't even get a mention. They should've all been sacked and sent to rot in prison. Instead, do you know what punishment each of them got? A slap on the wrist from their employers. When I contacted the papers, online media, bloggers and TV channels to get them to report on it, none of them gave a damn. As far as the world is concerned, Audrey and Etienne never existed.'

'But they did to you, to their family, to Audrey's friends too.'

'It's not enough! Everybody needs to know what I lost and why those six deserved to die. Even in death they need to be held accountable. You think if all I did was go around stabbing them to death the media would have given me as much coverage as it has? It takes theatrics to get attention; it takes originality to feed the public's hunger. Each death had to be different, each one had to say something in the manner in which I killed them. You think I enjoyed doing this?'

A flashback of Becca's battered, bloodied body came into Joe's head. The torture and sadism was as unnecessary as that inflicted on her predecessors. 'Yes, I think you did,' he said. 'You've blamed everything you've done on Becca's actions. She's become an excuse to make this your life, to let it define you. It's your legacy, and killing innocent people is all anyone will ever remember you for.'

Hammond shook his head. 'It's because of my love for Audrey and Etienne that the public will remember my name. And they'll understand what I've done is for them.'

'How will they ever know that? If you jump overboard, no one will ever hear your side of the story.'

'They will, because you're going to tell them.'

Hammond slipped his hand inside his trouser pocket and threw a mobile phone towards Joe. 'It's my burner. On it you'll find videos I recorded of my story in my own words. When this is used in evidence, everyone will know that I was a good man and I could have been a good father. There will be a public inquiry as to why it took so long to find me, and then all the people on my list will be included and have their names dragged through the mud. Finally, my family will get the justice they deserve.'

'Why not just turn yourself in and have your day in court?'

'Because I have somewhere else to be.' Hammond turned his head towards the water again. 'Audrey's family wouldn't tell me where or when their funeral was. I found out weeks afterwards, then I begged them for their ashes. But they'd already scattered them, between the two countries she loved, England and France. Down there, under the foam and the waves, is where I'm going to see them again.'

'So this is where it all ends?'

'You sound surprised. What's the most widely regarded theory as to what happened to Lord Lucan after he fled the murder scene? That he jumped overboard on a ferry from Newhaven to Dieppe and drowned.'

Joe was desperate to keep Hammond alive; he had to make him face justice for what he'd done. And to do that, he'd need to play for time and keep him talking.

'How have you kept one step ahead of us?' Joe asked.

'How do you think?'

'Someone on the inside was tipping you off, weren't they? You had time to dress as Megan before we came to your flat, you left the house opposite the fireman's shortly before we found it and you escaped Becca's home moments before we arrived.'

Hammond gave a wry smile.

'Who was it?' Joe continued.

'Look around you, detective. When everyone comes running, they'll be the last one to reach us.' He looked beyond Joe. 'And talking of running . . .'

Suddenly, he gripped the railings again and turned his body.

'No, wait!' shouted a panicked Joe.

'Over here!' a voice behind him yelled, and he turned to see Nikhat and an armed officer followed by a handful of others hurrying across the deck in the lashing rain. Joe turned and lurched towards Hammond, grabbing at any limb or piece of clothing that he could to stop him.

It was too late. Hammond was already halfway over the railings before he and Joe made eye contact. Then, within a heartbeat, he fell out of sight.

CHAPTER 62

The drop from railings to water lasted longer than he'd estimated.

The last clear image Dominic registered was the detective sergeant's face above, watching helplessly as his mark hit the water before plummeting below the surface.

A moment before impact, Dominic's body twisted and he landed on his side – his ribs, neck and thigh taking the brunt of it and robbing him of his breath. Each of his senses was simultaneously assaulted as he was dragged down, as though he'd been clamped in the jaws of a shark. The pitch-blackness disorientated him, and every part of his skin burned with the impact and the cold.

The pressure of water filled his ears until the deafening thrash of the propellers and engines burst his eardrums. The riptides they created tossed and turned him like a washing machine. From left to right, up and down, backwards and forwards, the water's swell neither dragged him any further towards the blades nor set him free. It toyed with him, trapping him in limbo, and it terrified him. He screamed, and water filled his lungs and hurt like a fire was burning him from the inside out.

It wasn't supposed to be happening like this. Many nights, when sleep was impossible, Dominic had imagined how it might be when he threw himself off the ferry's stern. He'd picture that moment between dropping and impact, when he was mid-air and weightless and how much calmness it would bring him. Then he'd picture the moment he reached the water and how the current would draw him toward the propellers and, within a second, it would all be over. He'd imagined Audrey and Etienne waiting for him on the other side, his family reunited.

But, to his dismay, what was happening to him now bore no resemblance to his imagination, and Dominic knew he had made a monstrous mistake. He wanted his death to be immediate, not like this. He thrashed his battered legs and stretched out his arms to grasp all that he could not see. With his remaining strength, he fought against the violent ebb and flow, desperately trying to swim to the surface. But he had no idea in which direction the surface was. The power of the water rendered all his attempts futile.

The thumping vibrations of the engines became heavier and heavier and the freezing temperature mercilessly pricked his skin like needles. His eyes were robbed of their sight – then, without warning, he felt himself being dragged further and further under water, deeper and deeper, before suddenly his legs were as light as a feather. Then his arm went the same way and he no longer felt it brushing against his side. Dominic quickly realised the blades were slicing him; hacking him into pieces, limb by limb.

He recalled the suffering that he'd doled out to the six names on his list, one by one. Now he was experiencing the pain of each of them – only, to him, it was happening all at once.

CHAPTER 63

Joe pushed past his Operation Chamber colleagues and the officers from Kent's armed response unit as they raced towards the ferry's stern. He vomited across the deck at the storm's rising swell.

After locking himself inside a toilet on the lower deck, he retched many more times until there was nothing left in his stomach. Wiping his mouth with toilet paper, he replayed Hammond's final moments in his head, frame by frame, knowing there was nothing he could have done to prevent his suicide. There had been too much physical distance between them.

Joe briefly considered the potential sequence of events if he'd managed an arrest. Hammond would have faced a trial, and his reasoning behind each murder would have played out in a public court of law. The reputation of the emergency services personnel involved, who had likely made errors that contributed to the deaths of Audrey and Etienne Moreau, would be in tatters. The number of lives they'd saved throughout their careers before Audrey and Etienne's accident wouldn't have mattered – they would only be remembered for the mother and son they had failed. Some people might even develop a level of understanding for what Hammond did. The very thought of it made Joe shiver. It wasn't fair.

Now, with his certain death, Hammond's legacy was instead contained on a burner mobile phone in Joe's hand. Nervously, he switched it on and began to look through it – it contained six video clips, each lasting approximately fifteen minutes, and in which Hammond looked directly at the camera lens and explained his reason behind each killing. Joe didn't have time to listen to each one, so he skipped through to get the gist of them.

By the time he'd finished, he was never surer of anything in his life – he would not give Hammond a voice after his death. Each sanctimonious, accusatory and pious clip could not see the light of day. He couldn't risk allowing any support for Hammond. He slipped the phone back into his pocket, and as the ferry's horns sounded, he began his unsteady return to his colleagues. For a man who'd spent his career following the letter of the law, it was the first time he had ever broken it – and while it made him uneasy, it was the right thing to do.

Joe's written statement made no mention of the phone. Instead, he detailed how he'd attempted to talk Hammond out of his suicide threat. He also failed to mention much of their conversation, cherry-picking moments that enhanced Hammond's madness. However, he was sure to bring up Hammond's admission that he'd had inside help, and without delay, it was reported to the internal investigations unit.

By the time he left the office and reached the flat that evening, Joe wanted to put the blur of the past two days behind him. But he owed Matt an explanation for his absence, and found his partner waiting for him in the lounge. In the first hour of their heart-to-heart, he offered a horrified Matt abridged highlights of what had happened to Becca and of later, on board the ferry. He kept to himself the trip to Leighton Buzzard and hiding Hammond's phone. Their conversation ended when Joe could no longer keep his eyes open and Matt helped him to bed.

In the early hours, Joe suddenly awoke from a light sleep recalling Hammond's words. 'Look around you, detective. When everyone comes running, they'll be the last one to reach us,' he'd said of his mole in the force. Hammond had lied to himself about the level of violence he'd shown Audrey and how everyone else had been to blame for her death apart from him – was this another one of his mistruths? Joe thought back to the moment he'd returned to the stern from the ferry's toilets, and recalled the last member of Operation Chamber to arrive.

A chill ran through him as he leaped out of bed, ran up the staircase and into the lounge. He blamed fatigue on why he'd not thought to look earlier, as he fished Hammond's phone from his jeans. Turning it on, he played each of the videos in their entirety. But there was no mention of Hammond's insider. He checked the call register – there were only two numbers Hammond had dialled. The first went to the voicemail of Zoe Ellis. The second rang four times before it was picked up. Joe immediately recognised the voice.

CHAPTER 64

The air was cooler than it had been in days, as Joe parked Matt's car by the side of the road. Lights from the all-night café illuminated the eerily quiet road.

He took a moment to prepare himself for what lay ahead. Joe knew what he should have done – turned the phone over to his superiors as evidence once he realised, other than the videos, the incendiary evidence it contained. But it was too late for that now. He recalled with clarity the horror in his colleague's voice when he'd answered the call from a number belonging to a dead man.

'It's Joe Russell,' Joe had said without emotion. 'Meet me in the café opposite the ambulance station in Turnham Green where Burgess was snatched. One hour from now.'

DS Bryan Thompson was already there by the time Joe arrived and took a seat.

'How did you get hold of Dominic's phone?' Bryan began. He chewed nervously on the insides of his cheeks.

'He must have slipped it in my coat pocket,' Joe lied. 'So you're not denying you know him?'

'Is there any point?' Bryan asked. Joe had interviewed enough suspects in his time to recognise a broken man. 'Who else knows?'

'No one – yet.'

'Why?'

'Why? Because I need you to tell me I've got this hopelessly wrong and that there's a perfectly rational reason why you've been calling and texting a serial killer.'

Bryan ran his fingers through his thinning hair, then stretched out his hands and placed them on the table in front of him. 'Dom and I were friends,' he replied.

Joe shook his head and began to open his mouth. He had so many questions, but he didn't know where to start. 'How?' he eventually asked.

'We met in the mid-nineties,' Bryan said quietly. 'He was standing at a urinal in a public toilet in Soho; it was a popular cruising ground for closeted gay men and rent boys at the time. He was a skinny kid back then . . . looked like he needed a good meal inside him . . . so I guessed he was turning tricks because he needed the money. He was trying to catch my eye, playing with himself. I knew his type, I'd arrested plenty of Dominics before. Then, suddenly he recognised me as a police officer; he told me later I'd done a talk at his school once about drugs. He almost broke his neck trying to run out of there, but I caught him. He was terrified I was going to nick him, but I wasn't on duty or in the toilets to arrest male prostitutes or cottagers.'

'Then why were you there?'

Bryan looked at Joe like he was hoping for him to come to his own conclusions rather than admit it out loud.

'You were cruising too?' Joe asked, and Bryan nodded. 'Fuck! What happened?'

'We came to a mutual arrangement. We'd meet, things would . . . happen . . . there'd be a financial transaction and he'd be discreet about it. In return, I introduced him to other like-minded men I knew . . . we both got what we wanted out of it.'

'What kind of "like-minded men"?'

'People who . . . liked their companions on the younger end of the scale.'

'How old was Hammond?'

'Fifteen. Almost.'

'Jesus Christ, Bryan, you were part of a paedophile ring?' Bryan couldn't look Joe in the eye. 'How long did this go on for?'

'Two, maybe three years. Then Dom started going to the gym and building himself up and he didn't appeal to the same market any more. The boy was different from the others like him, he had ambition. He found a new crowd who paid for his way through university, but we stayed in touch. And after his mum drank herself to death, the only constant he had in his life was me. I became a sort of parental figure.'

'Don't kid yourself,' Joe chastised. 'Parental figures don't pay to have sex with vulnerable young men.'

'I suppose not,' Bryan offered redundantly.

A waitress recognised Joe from his last visit and gave him a smile as she brought over a fresh pot of tea. Food and drink were the last things on his mind.

'Is it true, what they're saying on the telly?' she asked. 'You got that serial killer?'

'We believe so, yes,' Joe replied, willing her to go away.

'I told you he looked normal, didn't I? It's always the ones you least expect who surprise you the most.'

Joe glared at Bryan. 'It certainly is.' He waited until she was out of earshot before he continued his questioning.

'How did your "arrangement" develop into this huge fucking mess?'

'We lost touch for more than a decade, then out of the blue, he suddenly appeared a couple of years back. He wanted to meet but I didn't want to see him; that part of my life was over, I was happy with Yvonne and the kids. But he sent me a video he'd secretly recorded of us and that he'd kept for years. It was grainy, but you could hear my voice telling him what I wanted to do to him. He sent me pictures that he'd taken and old text messages. He told me he needed my help with some names, addresses and telephone numbers. I thought that when I gave them to him, that would be it, but then he said something big was going to happen, and whether I liked it or not, I was a part of it; that I had to get myself involved in the investigation and tell him what was going on as it happened.'

'Or?'

'Or he'd tell my wife and girls about him and me.' Bryan clutched his empty mug, like he was afraid to let go. His hands trembled. 'It would have torn my family apart. He said he'd report me for historic rape too, as he was underage back then. I'd lose my job, my family, my pension . . . everything.'

'So what did you do?'

'Everything he asked of me. I told him what leads we were investigating, which ones we were following up, how close we were to finding him, when to leave each place he was watching us from . . .'

'Did you know from the start that he was going to kill people?'

'No!'

'Then surely after the Romanians were murdered, you should have come forward.'

'It was too late, I was in too deep by then. He promised me, after they were dead, that would be it, but then he killed again. And again, and again and again. I didn't know what to do, Joe. I was trapped.'

'What about Beccs? She was your friend. She looked up to you. She told me that when she started in CID, you took her under your wing.'

'I know, I know.' His words were constricted as his throat tightened. 'But can't you see I had no choice?'

'We all have choices,' Joe replied. 'And, believe me, I've made some bad ones. But this, Bryan? You're an accessory to multiple murders. How can you live with yourself?'

'I can't,' he replied. 'I can't. I've not slept since this all started, I'm sick all the time; what I do try to eat, I can't keep down, so I bring it back up . . . I don't know what to do.'

They held each other's gaze as Joe considered what he'd learned. He knew that by turning Bryan in, he'd have to admit Hammond gave him a phone that was still in his possession. Meanwhile, Bryan wiped his eyes and stretched his hands across the table again. He sat up straight and offered Joe an apologetic half-smile.

'So what happens now?'

'I think you know that I have to do the right thing by Beccs . . . by all of them.'

Bryan let out a long breath. 'I understand. Do you mind if I use the toilet before we leave?'

Joe hesitated as he got his bearings. The café was one of a row of semi-detached shops. At one side of the room was an emergency exit sign leading to the rear of the property, on the other were the toilets. There was no escape route for Bryan, so Joe gave his approval and watched his broken colleague make his way over.

How could a good man make such bad decisions? he asked himself, then reflected on some of the bad choices he himself had made. He'd placed finding his sister before both Matt and Becca, and as a result, he had lost one and was barely clinging on to the other.

Joe picked up his tea for one last sip, then placed it back on the table next to the cutlery the waitress had left. Suddenly, he realised the knife and fork on Bryan's side were no longer there. The penny dropped.

His metal chair fell to the floor with a loud clatter as he scrambled to reach the toilet door. Opening it, he glared at the only cubicle inside. Only just visible in the gap between door and floor was a motionless foot pointed at an awkward angle.

'No, no, no . . .' he yelled, and banged on the door with his fists, calling out Bryan's name. Behind him, he heard confused voices and footsteps approaching. He took a step backwards and lifted his leg.

Within two kicks, the cubicle door had buckled from its hinges and come crashing down on a body slumped on the toilet. Joe threw the door behind him, then took in Bryan's almost-lifeless eyes. Blood oozed from three separate gashes to his neck. His hand still held the serrated knife he'd taken from the table.

Joe tried to stem the flow with his hand, but he knew it was too late. And within less than a minute, he watched as a second person died before his very eyes that day.

EPILOGUE
FOUR MONTHS LATER

The thumping bassline of a reggae song Joe didn't recognise travelled through his body, making it vibrate. It came from a sound system with six large speakers secured together by rope and tied to the back of a moving flatbed lorry. A DJ manning two turntables had the crowds dancing as the vehicle slowly followed the parade, surrounded by half a dozen women in colourful leotards and large blue and purple feathers emerging from elaborate headdresses.

Joe waited for a second float to pass, this one packed with children of all skin tones, dressed in animal costumes and dancing along to a song from *The Lion King*. They waved to him, and he waved back as he crossed the road and made his way through the crowds and towards Ladbroke Grove tube station. It had been closed to incoming trains, to divert revellers into less heavily populated areas.

Throughout the bank holiday weekend, almost two million revellers visited or participated in the Notting Hill Carnival, the biggest of its kind in Europe – and second only to Rio in the rest of the world. It was one of the reasons Joe loved London; he couldn't think of any other annual event in the capital that offered the same level of eagerness to celebrate ethnic diversity.

Joe and his fellow super-recognisers were volunteering their assistance as some of the nine thousand police officers scheduled to be on duty across the two-day event. When the super-recognisers stationed themselves inside music or sporting venues, there could be hundreds or thousands of new faces to add to their memory banks. But the carnival was in a different league when it came to the sheer volume of people. Joe had already made six arrests based on recognising suspects from the centralised forensic image database. Between them, the team had arrested thirteen in all.

He strolled against the flow of the carnival crowd, taking in partygoers' appearances one at a time. The concentration of bodies made the air humid and heavy, permeated by a mixture of spicy foods and the odour of cannabis. In the past, Joe had jumped at the chance to work the carnival and to also use the opportunity to search for his sister. But this year was different. Each time he thought about Linzi, he was reminded of how badly he had let Becca down. His sister and his colleague were now forever intrinsically linked.

After Dominic and Bryan's deaths, Joe had taken six weeks off work as sick leave to get his head together and make sense of it all. He'd also used the time to try to get his and Matt's relationship back on track. They'd wandered around museums and galleries together, taken day trips outside the capital and enjoyed the tourist traps that Londoners rarely took the time to experience.

But Joe's conscience wouldn't allow him to relax. Keeping things from Matt had made it impossible to maintain a normal routine. Since working on Operation Chamber, too much inside him had changed. And as the person who knew him best, Matt recognised something was still troubling Joe. Eventually, he'd coaxed the truth from him.

In the frankest conversation they'd ever had, Joe had sat with Matt on a bench on Hampstead Heath, overlooking old woodlands, ponds and London's skyline, as he gradually unravelled like a spool of thread. He left nothing out: from his ill-fated trip to Leighton Buzzard, to how he had failed Becca. He revealed why he had kept Hammond's phone and then handed it over to his colleagues following Bryan's suicide, but minus the memory card that held the videos.

When his confession was complete, he could barely look his partner in the eye. They sat in silence as Matt took Joe's hand in his. 'When it comes to Becca, nothing I can say is going to make a difference,' Matt said eventually. 'That's something you're going to have to live with. But you have to remember, you didn't kill her, Dominic Hammond did. You might have been able to prevent it, you might not have. You'll never know. But we need to find you a coping mechanism, and you need to go back to counselling as a priority. As for the phone, I'd have done the same thing. You prevented the victim's families from having their loved ones' names dragged through the mud. The law doesn't always take into account morals, and sometimes in doing the wrong thing we're also doing the right thing.'

'I'm supposed to uphold it, not break it. That makes me as guilty as the people I go after.'

'No, it doesn't. You made a judgement call and you can't take it back.'

'I went on record saying I only found the phone in my jacket just before I called Bryan, and that Hammond must have slipped it in there, not that he gave it to me. What if they sack me for not handing it over straight away? Part of me thinks I should beat them to the punch and resign.'

'If you get reprimanded once the internal investigation's over, we'll have to deal with it. But no, you shouldn't give up your career voluntarily. You're a good man, Joe – that's why I love you. And I know that you can go on and do much more good in this world as a detective, while your vision still allows it, than you could if you were a civilian. Don't become another one of Hammond's victims.'

Joe had nodded and clenched Matt's hand more tightly. After all he'd subjected him to in their time together, now was the time to start putting him first.

During his time away from work, Joe had attended Becca's funeral at Islington Crematorium. It had been a formal, sober affair, with a sea of uniforms filling each pew and the aisle and with a heavy media presence outside. He'd watched as her father and mother sat together at the front; Helen was still visibly injured and wore a bandage across the side of her head. But by all accounts, she was slowly recuperating, at least physically. She held on to her estranged husband David's arm as if she feared that by letting go, she would collapse to the floor. Maisie was temporarily in his care as Helen recuperated. But he had chosen to keep his granddaughter away from the funeral while he attended. At the wake afterwards, Joe considered approaching Becca's parents to offer his condolences, but decided against it. He had still not come to terms with how culpable he felt about their daughter's death.

Now back with the VIIDO team, he'd promised Matt he'd ease the pressure on his eyesight too. That meant less time 'snapping' in front of his computer, and more screen breaks and nutritious meals, all of which his specialists had suggested might slow down his macular degeneration. It wouldn't prevent the inevitable, but it might give him more time.

Joe had known that he had a duty to inform his superiors of his medical condition as soon as it had been diagnosed two years earlier. Instead, he'd chosen to remain in denial. It was time to start facing the truth and stop hiding from it. So he vowed that, after the carnival weekend, he would offer full disclosure.

With his shift coming to an end, he had almost reached Ladbroke Grove station. The crowds were beginning to thin out, and a rumble in his stomach took him by surprise. He realised he hadn't eaten all day. The waft of cooked meats and Caribbean spices caught his attention, and he looked at a mobile food truck with a queue of half a dozen people. He checked his wallet for cash and made his way towards it.

Suddenly, a face caught his attention. It was the way her crystal-clear blue eyes mirrored his that first made him do a double take. But she wasn't in his line of sight long enough to absorb any other part of her face. Without thinking, he followed the stranger. She walked towards another food truck and remained with her back to him. Her hair was the colour of Joe's, and hung dead straight to her shoulders. She turned a little, and he noted her skin was pale too, like his.

Every time Joe tried to take in the woman's face, she moved out of sight. Despite everything that had happened with Becca's death and the promise he'd made to Matt and to himself, he still desperately wanted to approach her. But as he moved his feet forward, he stopped. Then he took a step back.

He had been here before, so very, very often. The anticipation, the desperation, the longing, the excitement, followed by the disappointment and the crippling days of sadness. How many more times could he chase the past before he admitted defeat? How many more lives would he fail to save before he learned his lesson?

Joe stared at the woman's back one last time, just as her head turned in his direction. Then he closed his eyes before he could take her in.

No more, he thought. *No more am I going to put the dead above the living.*

It gave him an unexpected sense of relief. Only weeks ago, nothing could have held him back from following her, until he knew for certain that it wasn't Linzi. But now, he knew without getting any closer that it wasn't. It was never going to be Linzi. Linzi was dead. And while that wasn't ever going to be an easy truth to accept, it was something he was coming to terms with.

Joe turned his head, opened his eyes and walked a handful of footsteps before he heard the words.

'Joseph?' a woman's voice called. 'Joseph? Is that you?'

He stopped in his tracks, and thought his legs might crumble beneath him.

ACKNOWLEDGMENTS

I can't quite believe that I'm writing a list of acknowledgements for my fifth book.

I'd like to thank my partner-in-crime and sounding board John Russell for all his support and helpful suggestions with this story. As always, you've been incredible. And, of course, a big thank you to my mum, Pamela Marrs, who is still the most voracious reader I know.

Thanks to my dog, Oscar, who has now made his way into this fifth tale, only just beating Tracy Fenton, Queen of Facebook's THE Book Club (TBC). Both she and the club's eight thousand members have from the very beginning been – and continue to be – nothing short of brilliant. Thanks also to the members of two new book clubs I've gotten to know and chat to over the last twelve months, including Bee Jones from Lost in a Good Book and Wendy Clarke from The Fiction Café Book Club – I am very grateful for your support.

There have been many people who have helped me to get the factual elements of this book correct. So, in no particular order, thank you to Samantha Laing and Mandy Wray for the medical advice; Dee Finch and Emma Lee for walking me around a ferry; and to Edy Watkins for his invaluable tube train advice. The following people also get my gratitude: the immensely talented and inspirational Louise Beech, Nick Doherty, Jo Edwards, Andrew Webber, Julia Langton, Karen Lee

Roberts, Kath Middleton, Jim Ryan, Darren O'Sullivan and Danielle Graph.

My gratitude also goes to the Thomas & Mercer team, and especially fiction editor Jack Butler and editor Ian Pindar for their enthusiasm surrounding *Her Last Move*. Thanks also to Gemma Wain for her eagle eye. It was my most challenging story to date and you all helped to transform it into something I am really proud of.

Thanks to the Met's super-recognisers, who inspired this story. The work they carry out is ground-breaking and not as widely recognised as it should be. If you want to find out more about them, I urge you to read the following magazine features:

www.theguardian.com/uk-news/2016/nov/05/metropolitan-police-super-recognisers

www.newyorker.com/magazine/2016/08/22/londons-super-recognizer-police-force

www.newstatesman.com/politics/uk/2016/08/super-recognisers-scotland-yard.

Whether you're new to my books or have been with me from the start, a huge thank you for choosing to purchase this. You'll never appreciate just how much it means to a writer that you have invested your time and your money in their story.

Finally, this book is dedicated to every member of the emergency services worldwide – including my late dad, DS Charlie Marrs – who risk their lives to save ours when we are at our most vulnerable.

ABOUT THE AUTHOR

Photo © 2018 Robert Gershinson

John Marrs is an author and former freelance journalist based in London and Northamptonshire. He spent the past twenty-five years interviewing celebrities from the worlds of television, film and music for numerous national newspapers and magazines. *Her Last Move* is his fifth novel. Follow him on Twitter @johnmarrs1, on Instagram @johnmarrs. author, on his website www.johnmarrsauthor.com and on Facebook at www.facebook.com/johnmarrsauthor.